BRAVE
NEW
WORLDS

J.D.,

Turns out, I found
time to write. Thanks
for loving me through
it. ♡
Anne
aka Willa
Blythe

Other Anthologies Edited by:

BRAVE
NEW
WORLDS

Edited by

S.C. Butler
&
Joshua Palmatier

Zombies Need Brains LLC
www.zombiesneedbrains.com

COPYRIGHTS

Table of Contents

SIGNATURE PAGE

S.C. Butler, editor:

_____

Joshua Palmatier, editor:

_____

Jamie M. Boyd:

_____

Gini Koch:

_____

Mike Jack Stoumbos:

_____

Stephen Leigh:

_____

A.M. Giddings:

_____

Auston Habershaw:

_____

Sarah Lyn Eaton:

_____

Ian Tregillis:

_____

Jack Nicholls:

_____

Willa Blythe: _Willa Blythe_
_____

Chaz Brenchley:

_____

Ari Officer:

_____

Eric Choi:

_____

Jacey Bedford:

_____

Juliet Kemp:

_____

Justin Adams, artist:

_____

On Sacrifice

Jamie M. Boyd

My father slid the paperwork in front of me.

"Here," he said. "Sign."

It took me a second to understand. I mean, I'd seen printed documents before. I had three old-fashioned books my mother left me on a shelf right there in my bedroom. Still, I couldn't have been more surprised if he'd laid a 17th-century sword across my desk. It would have been just as antiquated—and just as dangerous.

"Um, wow," I said, pausing my homework program to flip through the pages. "Why didn't you just message this to me?"

"I have, Via. Three times." His voice was tight. "I thought this might get your attention. The deadline's tomorrow. I'll wait while you read."

I frowned. I already knew what the pages said. That once my family left Earth for the generation ship *Sacrifice*, we'd never come back. That I understood this fact and all its ramifications. That I consented.

Well, screw that.

Of course, refusing was easier said than done. My dad and annoying stepmother had already given notice at work. The house was sold. My older brother gleefully dropped out of grad school. Everyone was ready, except me. I pushed the document away.

My father's jaw flexed. "I know it's hard, sweetie, but this is the chance of a lifetime."

More like several lifetimes. My great-great-great grandchild would get to see the Trappist system, not me. "You're asking me to spend my entire existence on a ship. A prison."

"Don't be so dramatic. You want to be a scientist someday, don't you? Whatever you choose to study, you're going to make history."

I rolled my eyes. "I want to study deep-sea corals here on Earth."

He sighed. "Look, we're going, one way or another."

I stuck out my lower lip. Technically, he was wrong. Technically, the law required anyone sixteen or older to agree of their own free will to board a generation ship. My best friend, Monterae, said I should just say no and force the whole family to stay. But she didn't understand, what with her perfect parents who attended her every soccer game, cheered her every report card.

If I dug my heels in—if I argued I only had one more year until college, if I told my father they should all go on without me—he might just agree. And that terrified me more than anything.

"OK, fine, I'll go. But on one condition." I tried not to show how much the words cost me.

"What?"

"I want to visit Enceladus before we leave the solar system."

A long pause. "*Why?*"

Mom wouldn't have had to ask. One of the hardcovers she'd left me was a picture book about the ancient ruins on Enceladus, Saturn's sixth-largest moon. She'd read it to me almost every night when I was little. We'd gaped together at the famed, bleached-bone cities, the towering, undersea forests she promised to take me to someday. After all these years, the pages still smelled like her, like fresh oil paints and the linen-and-pine of one of her newly stretched canvases.

My father never smelled like anything other than the hospital and its strong disinfectant. He'd think it irrational, my desire to visit Enceladus as a final way to say goodbye to her.

"I just do. That's the deal. Take it or leave it." I lifted my chin, ready for battle.

Instead, he flicked his wrist, bringing up the digital version of the consent form in the air between us.

"I'll take it," he said.

* * *

We left Earth a month later. Monterae and I spent my last night watching the sun set over the Pacific Ocean atop San Diego's Sunset Cliffs. Would I ever see those exact colors again—fuchsia, turquoise, and gold?

Space was black and frigid, so I tried to make my heart match. We took an intrasolar ship to Saturn's largest moon, Titan, where the mammoth

Sacrifice was docked in orbit, fueling up for the big launch. My father kept his promise, arranging our arrival ahead of schedule, so we had time to detour to nearby Enceladus for a short stay at its science-station-turned-resort.

When the inner moon finally came into view, it looked tiny—an insignificant snowball compared to Saturn, which floated like a giant, golden angel, complete with halo. But I knew better. There was more buried in that ice than just a hotel and casino.

"I booked us a VIP suite, adventure package, the works. A last hurrah, of sorts," my father said magnanimously as we landed on the surface.

As if it were all his idea.

After we checked into the hotel, it was time for the main event: the submarine tour. I picked anxiously at my lips, peeling from the dry spacecraft air, as we traveled three miles down an underground tunnel to the docking bay where the moon's ice gave way to a subterranean ocean ten times deeper than any on Earth. The hotel's gravity emitters wore off, so we held onto a handrail to keep from bobbing around like the underwater craft we were about to board.

There was a round hatch in the floor, through which we slid into the submarine. As we strapped ourselves into our seats, a holo warned about rough seas.

"Welcome aboard. You're in for a special treat," the driver said in a friendly Southern twang. "I'm Douglas, and this is Dr. Ayorinde. He heads up the research department here. Nobody knows the Briareus better."

Dr. Ayorinde nodded his head graciously. We began our descent.

When the Briareus first came into view, they were so far below us they looked like a small, bleached coral reef. But as we dove, it felt more like plummeting into a giant tree canopy. Some were smooth and hard as bone, others lacy and flexible like gigantic sea fans, their branches twisting and undulating all around us. Like ghosts.

The hair on my arms stood on end as I placed my hand on the submarine's thick, chilled window. On the other side, the giant trunks slid by like floors on a falling elevator. My brother, Nathan, had never shown an interest in anything to do with Enceladus, but by the time we reached the ocean bottom, even he gawked as the Briareus towered over us like skyscrapers.

"Holy shit," he murmured, craning his neck.

Dr. Ayorinde chuckled. "It's even more impressive when you realize they were slow-growing superorganisms. They took about 200,000 years to reach these heights."

"What happened?"

"They began dying off several centuries ago, as far as we can tell. We're not sure why—most likely disease or changing sea temperatures. Or a combination of both."

"That's so sad," my stepmother, Nicole, cooed in that sticky-sweet voice of hers. "I wonder—"

The submarine shuddered, then accelerated so quickly my head slammed against the seat. The driver fought the controls as we hurtled toward one of the Briareus. We pitched right as he made a hard left to avoid hitting the giant sentinel, but then another lay in our path. The driver punched the controls and the engine roared in reverse, but it slowed our momentum only slightly as he wove between the trunks.

When we finally emerged from the Briareus grove, the submarine swung like an amusement park ride, then slowly stopped. I thought I might be sick.

"Sorry about that, folks," Douglas called, forcing cheer into this voice. "Got caught in a current that just didn't want to let go."

My father frowned as he lowered the right arm he'd thrown automatically across my chest, as if I were still a little girl sitting in the passenger seat of his car.

"We should go back," he grumbled to my stepmother, who sat perfectly composed, not a single blonde hair out of place on her meticulously coiffed head.

I pushed a messy brown curl behind my ear and flushed. It would be just like my dad to treat a public tour driver like his private chauffeur.

"Don't worry," Douglas said before my father had a chance. "Next part of the tour is in a calmer section."

About ten minutes later, we were there. Smokers—large chimneys with dark clouds of gas billowing up from the ocean floor—dotted the sea ridge like miniature volcanoes. The petrified remains of the Briareus here were a different species, tube-shaped, rising straight up in great colonies that from afar looked like cities of rounded skyscrapers. As we approached, the shapes sharpened until the closest section resembled a massive castle of turrets with walls as delicate and intricate as spun glass. It sparkled before our floodlights.

"Far enough. Turn around," Dr. Ayorinde said as we reached the edge of a crater. His voice sounded different, less scientist, more ship's captain.

The surface of the crater rippled with an oily liquid-mist, like an undersea lake. It was faint, but around the far edge glowed a strange golden crust. No one else paid it any attention—it was nothing, really, compared to the Briareus city—but it was the first color I'd seen the entire trip. It reminded me of the deep-sea microbes I'd studied in school, the ones that lived along Earth's geothermal vents, converting all that heat into energy.

"What is *that?*" I asked.

Dr. Ayorinde's shoulders tightened.

"Just metal deposits," Douglas said quickly. "Build-up sometimes happens around the vents and brine lakes."

I peered out the window for a better look, but we were already speeding away. I glanced at Dr. Ayorinde. His face was carefully blank.

"We're beginning our ascent," Douglas called back before I could ask more questions. "If you experience any uncomfortable symptoms, supplemental oxygen canisters are under your seats."

Maybe it was the power of his suggestion, but the skin around my neck itched. As I put the canister valve over my mouth and inhaled, the Briareus shrank away outside the submarine's glass-bottom window, their branches waving an eerie goodbye in the current.

My father placed his hand on my shoulder. "This was a good idea, Via. I'm glad we did this." His green eyes went misty and crinkled around the edges.

I softened. Once upon a time, we'd been close. Maybe he did understand why I'd wanted to come.

Then he kept talking. "Just think. On the way to the Trappist system, we'll find something even better."

My skin flashed hot, then cold, then hot again. *Better?* I swear, if I had the power to crack that glass and bring down all the moon's water upon us, I would have been tempted. How did he know what we'd find in the outer reaches, when he couldn't even conceive of his daughter's own depths? Why was he so quick to rush from what wonders we had in hand? Hadn't we lost enough?

* * *

I chided myself the whole way back up the tunnel. I should've never left Earth. Since my mother died, I'd been chasing after my father and, no matter what I did, he kept slipping away—first burying himself in work, then his new marriage, now this quest to the stars.

I'd agreed to board the *Sacrifice* because I didn't want to lose a second parent. But it was time to face facts. I already had. I could spend the rest of my life clinging to his side, but each time he failed to see me, I'd only feel like I did right now: more alone than if I'd stayed back home.

So maybe it was time to stop running.

My family scattered when we returned to the resort, anxious to enjoy the luxurious accommodations we'd have to leave soon. My brother headed to the sports dome, where he could snowboard in reduced gravity. My stepmother made a beeline to the spa and my father turned to the garish casino.

And me? A crazy idea struck as I stared at the slot machines' flashing lights. I'd never understood why people liked to gamble, until that moment. Now it made perfect sense. When you have nothing left, going for broke is no risk at all.

The kiosk at the front desk showed me where Dr. Ayorinde's lab was located. I practically ran. When I arrived and his assistant told me he wasn't available, I parked myself in a chair and said I'd wait.

Her expression stiffened. "If you have any questions about the Briareus, I'd suggest you visit the public museum on the third floor."

"I want to talk to him about the GLOWING YELLOW CRUST on the BOTTOM OF THE SEA," I said, raising my voice. Several people sitting at their desks turned and stared.

Ayorinde appeared moments later, frowning, and ushered me into his private office. "So, young lady, how can I help you?"

"I'd like to apply for a job. I want to study whatever that was growing along the brine lake. I know it wasn't just metal."

His eyebrows shot up. We stared each other down for a few seconds before his mouth twitched and he broke my gaze. "I'm afraid you're mistaken. But your enthusiasm is impressive. How old are you?"

I blushed. "Seventeen. It can be like an internship. I can run errands, bring coffee, do prep and cleanup for experiments, anything."

"That's a generous offer," he said gently. Too gently.

"I'm not just some kid tourist. I spent years studying deep sea corals on Earth as part of my high school's environmental science magnet. I won third place in the international science fair. I was accepted into Duke. And if we hadn't left—"

He held up a hand. "We do have a program for college students, but the competition is steep. I recommend you apply in a few years."

Of course. Only a stupid little girl would think she could just waltz in and have everything fall into place.

"Also, have you spoken to your parents about this? I recall your father saying you were leaving together on the *Sacrifice*."

I scowled. "He wouldn't miss me."

"I doubt that. I have a grown daughter on Mars and I can tell you, even though we've had some impressive fights over the years, I miss her every day."

"This isn't about family." I clenched my jaw. "It's about what I want to do with my life. I don't want to go to the Trappist system; I want to stay here. I should have a choice. *Everyone* deserves a choice."

At least he looked me in the eye as he dashed my hopes. "I agree. But sometimes adults don't get all the choices you think we do."

* * *

That night, my family ate dinner on the Siberian observation level, admiring the spewing geysers that made this moon famous long before anyone knew about the Briareus.

As the ice trembled and vapor blasted hundreds of kilometers into the sky, I knew how the cryovolcanoes felt. A hundred thousand pounds of pressure roiled just beneath my skin, ready to burst.

* * *

In the morning, my stepmother woke us before 7 a.m., trilling like a songbird about the next item on our itinerary: ice hiking on the frigid surface.

The bulky space suit rubbed my armpits and other joints raw, we weren't allowed to venture off the safety lines, and the tour was so crowded it seemed more like an elaborate queue than an excursion. But I forgot all that when I climbed out of the last crevasse and surveyed the horizon. Majestic Saturn filled the bleak, black sky, silently gazing down on all of us.

Was my mom, too?

After lunch, we were scheduled to go to the Briareus museum.

"You guys go ahead. I'm not feeling well," I lied. "I'm going to rest in my room."

Instead, I headed back down the underground tunnel. When I got to the submarine docking area, the sign said they were closed the rest of the afternoon for maintenance. A vacuum and container of cleaning supplies hovered by the open hatch. All unexpected circumstances, but ones I could use to my benefit.

"Can I help?" I called as Douglas's head poked out of the hatch. I didn't wait for an answer, just bounced toward him in the low gravity. "I was on one of the tours yesterday."

He blinked, then shrugged, as if he'd had stranger requests before. "Sure." He handed me a bottle of window cleaner.

We got to work and didn't talk much, what with the roar of the vacuum. When I finished wiping down the windows and the seats of the submarine interior, I played my hand. "I'm a hard worker. Is there any chance you have any job openings here?"

He grinned, then shook his head. "I admire your gumption, but if you want to do this for a living, you have to get some experience first. I may look like a glorified bus driver and janitor, but I worked at NOAA for 20 years."

I sulked as the elevators took me back up the three-mile tunnel. As I entered the lobby, a herd of tourists arrived. The noisy band was unified by hideous orange T-shirts, the front of which read, "How Do You Throw a Party in Space?" The back answered, "You Have to Plan-et!"

Hotel staffers swung into action. I wondered why their jobs weren't automated, until I noticed the way they spoke to the tourists—so obeisant, so admiring—and understood. What good is spending a fortune on a trip across the solar system if there's no one to envy you when you get there?

Once the tour group cleared out, I pulled my hair into a bun, which always made me look older, and approached the hotel manager. Soon a long list of job openings flashed on the public view screen.

"It's twelve-hour shifts and the pay probably isn't what someone like you may be used to," she said, appraising me doubtfully.

"No problem," I said. "I'm young and hungry."

* * *

My family had dinner in front of the geysers again. Over desert, I set off my own little bomb.

"I'm not going back with you on the shuttle tomorrow," I said. "I've decided to stay here."

It was almost fun, watching their reactions. Nathan, his mouth hanging open like a cartoon. Nicole, her big blue eyes wide. My father's face remained placid, but I could hear his teeth grinding.

"I don't know what you're talking about," he said in the quiet voice he always used when he was truly furious.

I could play calm, too. "I want to study the Briareus. Dr. Ayorinde's lab offers an internship." No point mentioning I'd have to clean toilets for a few years first.

My brother's face fell as if he were three years old, not twenty-three. "Wait. You don't want to come with us? But once we're gone—"

"She knows that, Nathan," Nicole said. She studied my father's expression, then mine, in a way that suggested she understood me better than I'd given her credit for. "Let's let them talk in private."

As they left, my father seethed across the table. "You're being ridiculous. How do you think you'd live here? The hotel rooms aren't free."

"I'll work. There are employee pods."

He huffed. "They're called pods for a reason. Too small to describe them as anything else."

I slurped my drink, knowing the sound annoyed him. "It's a small price to pay to follow your heart."

"Price? What would *you* know about *that?* Do you know how much this little detour of yours, even this meal, has cost me?"

I leaned in. "Do you know what this little dream of yours, flying to some strange planet, has cost *me?*"

That shut him up. But not for long. I counted down in my mind. Three, two, one…

He bolted up like a rocket, chair scraping the floor. "This is not a negotiation. You are coming with us."

Finally, I had his attention. But he wasn't really upset about losing me. This was about power. Control. If I fell back into line, I'd cease to exist.

It was just like after my mother died, when I'd worked so hard to win all those ribbons at the science fair, hoping they'd make him smile again, show him that he and I were the same—smart, hardworking, logical. It never lasted. I'd always say the wrong thing, laugh in a way that reminded him of her, and he'd stare at me as if I'd just shot him in the chest. Then he'd retreat to his study and hide behind his medical journals, barely speaking to me for days.

"I'm staying," I said.

"You signed the paperwork."

"I'll appeal, tell them you pressured me, that I didn't think I could say no. There's precedent they'll have to follow. I looked it up last night, *Gomez vs. Gomez*. You can't stop me."

* * *

It was almost eleven when the knock came on my hotel room door. I couldn't sleep anyway, so I yanked it open. My stepmother hovered outside.

"Truce." She held her hands up as if to ward off blows, her lacquered nails a cloying shade of pink.

I scowled and gripped the door handle, ready to slam it in her pretty little face.

"I think you're right," she blurted. "I just want to talk."

I let her in and she settled on the corner of my bed, smoothing the comforter nervously. "I've told you father I don't think it's fair to make you go if you don't want to."

For a second, I felt sorry for her. It couldn't be easy, putting up with both me and my father. But the flash of sympathy passed. Maybe this was just the chance she'd been waiting for—the perfect way to get rid of the moody brat daughter.

My eyes narrowed. "So you're going to help me convince him?"

"I agree you deserve a choice. But you can't stay on Enceladus. Your father talked to Dr. Ayorinde and the hotel manager. There's no place for you here."

"So what choice is there, then?"

"The ship or Earth."

My insides dropped. "You mean he'd pay to send me back home? What about what he said, at dinner?"

She sighed. "He's sorry about that. He wanted to tell you himself, but he thought you wouldn't want to see him, that you needed time to cool down, to decide for yourself."

I gaped at her. Should I whoop with the laughter of the victorious? Cry with the shame of the abandoned? Rage and demand to stay on Enceladus changing soiled bedsheets anyway?

She watched me with solemn eyes. "Sleep on it and let us know tomorrow. Our shuttle for the *Sacrifice* leaves at fifteen-hundred hours." She stood and gave me a quick kiss on my forehead before I could duck away.

"Oh, and one more thing," she said as she headed for the door. "Before you decide, your father said to go talk to Dr. Ayorinde."

* * *

I almost didn't. It was a trap, of course. Dr. Ayorinde and my father must have plotted together on how to manipulate me to return to the *Sacrifice*.

Instead I slept in, took a long, hot shower, watched a holo with Nathan, during which we tried to pretend nothing was wrong.

"I know I haven't been around much these past few years," Nathan said. "It must have been hard with me away at college so soon after Mom died. And then when Dad decided to remarry—"

"God, Nathan, stop." I took his hand to show him that he was still my big brother. "Whatever happens, we're good."

I finally made it down to the lab around noon.

"OK, take your best shot," I said as I sat down in front of Dr. Ayorinde's desk.

He glanced up from his program. "Excuse me?"

"I know you promised my dad you'd talk me into going to the Trappist system. So, go ahead. Let's get it over with."

He eyed me. "That's not why I asked to see you."

"Oh." I flushed. "Then...?"

"I wanted to let you know you were right, about the metal deposits. They're actually microbes."

My mouth fell open, then stretched into a smirk. "I knew it!"

"Some, like the ones you saw, are growing on their own. Others appear to be recolonizing the Briareus. We're studying a new theory—that during crises the Briareus expel the microbes, then both go dormant to stave off death, a sort of hibernation until the threat passes or they figure out how to adapt."

"You think they've been hibernating for *centuries*?"

"What are a few hundred years to organisms that can live 200,000? Of course, it's too early to know anything for sure. We keep comparing them to trees and coral and tube worms, but they're nothing of the sort. Our preliminary findings will be published next month."

I stared. "And *why* are you're trusting me with this information?"

He laughed. "Maybe because I see some of myself in you. If you're going to be a scientist someday, heading for the Trappist system, it's important you know that life beyond Earth is possible."

I folded my arms. "And if I go back to Earth?"

"Then I assume you'll apply for our internship someday—and you're too smart to betray the confidence of a potential employer." A hint of a smile lingered on his lips.

He had a point. I relaxed. "OK. Well, thanks. That's really…amazing."

He nodded as I stood to go. "I told your father, too. But for a different reason. He and I ended up talking, about you and my own daughter, about some of the choices I made and the regrets I have."

"Yeah?" I asked suspiciously. "So?"

"I wanted him to understand. Sometimes after trauma, we bury our feelings so deep they're hard to see. But that doesn't mean they aren't there. Sometimes they're just waiting below the surface to flourish again."

* * *

I knocked on my father's hotel door, resolute. I wouldn't be guilted into caving, despite Dr. Ayorinde. I was headed back to Earth. If Duke would still take me, I'd go to college and study life at the bottom of the Pacific. With any luck, I'd return to Enceladus when I was older.

When my father opened the door, his face was drawn. Circles shadowed his eyes.

"I want to go back home," I blurted before I lost my nerve.

He gestured for me to come inside. I braced for an argument. Instead, he exhaled long and low, as if his breath were the very fight draining from him. "All right. Fair enough."

That was it. He padded over to the hotel dresser and resumed packing. "There's a tour group here. They're headed back to Earth tomorrow. There's extra space aboard their vessel for us."

I stared. "*Us?*" I sunk onto the bed before my legs gave out. My mind buzzed. "I thought I'd be going alone."

His eyes were red and wild around the edges as they met mine. He crouched down next to me and took my hand in his. "No. You're my daughter." He faltered, welling with emotion I hadn't seen since the funeral, then swallowed. "You're my daughter," he repeated, as if that explained everything.

My skin prickled. "What about Nathan? And Nicole? They'll come, too, right?"

He paled. "Nathan's a grown man. And Nicole, she's worked her entire life to make chief engineer. I can't ask her to…"

Oh God. All the times I'd dreamed of breaking them up. It hadn't felt like this.

My voice came out strangled. "I'm sorry." And then with a touch of awe: "Thank you."

"No, *I'm* sorry. That you thought I'd abandon you. For being so absent these past years." He wrapped me, trembling, in his arms. "Will you let me make it up to you?"

* * *

And I did. I let him make it up to me—just not the way he thought, not the way I planned.

You know, it's funny, how you want something so bad when you can't have it. Or when you think this One Big Thing is the massive problem in your life, when actually it's something else?

I can't really explain it, but a frozen part of me melted when my father said he was willing to follow me back to Earth, even if it meant ending his new marriage, sabotaging his career, watching his son go off on the adventure he'd dreamed of. It was no ploy, no empty promise meant to manipulate me. I knew, because as he held me in his arms, he shook, too.

We all boarded the shuttle back to the *Sacrifice* a few hours later. My father held my hand the whole time, afraid I might disappear. Nathan radiated relief. Nicole looked exhausted—as if the emotional whiplash of the past few days had finally caught up with her—but she flashed me a tired smile and said she was grateful I changed my mind.

As the shuttle soared toward the massive generation ship that would be my home, I took one last look at Enceladus. Maybe my dad hadn't been all wrong. If life could survive despite everything on such a harsh, little world, what else might we find in the vastness of space?

What might be possible in the human heart?

Little Big Planet

Gini Koch writing as Anita Ensal

Aaron heaved a sigh as he looked up from the surface of Europa Prime—the moon that represented humanity's most important extension into the solar system—to gaze at the space battlecruiser high above them. Basking in Jupiter's glow, the *Washita* looked like a little dot in the sky. If all went according to plan, Europa Prime would become a world, only there was a problem, as always. That little dot held thousands of personnel and far more weapons and smaller ships than should be necessary for terraformation. The military wanted to be sure that things went according to their plan.

Europa Prime was far colder than freezing and its ice crust thick, but under that crust was salt water. That wasn't the problem. What was in the water was the problem. And what those in charge wanted to do about that problem was an even bigger problem.

Not for the first time Aaron wondered why the Solaris government had chosen to go with the military in charge of a scientific operation. It should have been science supported by military, not the other way around. This situation would likely be handled differently if the military were only here for support. Then again, Aaron wasn't naïve enough to think that the government wasn't willing to do whatever it took to terraform Europa Prime.

"How long do you think we'll have to wait for them to come by?" Duty Officer James Conason asked, as the core scientific team responsible for

Europa Prime's terraformation process stood around the giant hole they'd created in the ice.

"Not long now, I'd imagine," Melissa Gunnels replied. "They like to visit with us."

"They aren't Earth animals," Glenda Dobbs reminded her. "You can't be sure."

Melissa grinned wide enough for all of them to see it through her helmet. "True, but I'm the one with the Dolittle Device."

Glenda snorted. "As the head of astrobiology, you'd think I'd have it. Or Aaron."

He shrugged. "Head of xenobiology politely gives way to the head of Earth genetics. I'm generous that way."

"All this chatter might scare them away," Duty Officer Tatsuya Katano chided gently.

"It won't," Aaron said confidently, mostly because he could spot the creatures coming now. Most of the moon's ice crust was 25 kilometers thick, but they'd cut their hole in a weaker area where it was only about 2 kilometers. The hole was huge compared to them, but not compared to what lived in the slushy water underneath.

"No," Glenda said, a mixture of sadness and anger in her tone, "we're going to do that for them, in the most final way possible."

"Not if we can find the proof of higher sentience we need," Apollo Ascencio, their team leader, said. "If we can determine what they call themselves, that they have a name for themselves beyond 'this one' or 'that one,' then we have that proof. Without it, we have no chance of swaying anyone."

This was the problem. They'd come to terraform Europa Prime, but there was already a thriving ecosystem underneath the ice crust. And the top creatures of that ecosystem were in no way human.

* * *

The core Terraformation Team consisted of the heads of each branch of science required to ensure life as humanity knew it could successfully survive farther or nearer to Sol. They'd been the ones to make the discovery, right after the hole was drilled. The ice had fallen in and, when the team was near the edge of the hole, something had lifted it back up.

That something had giant tentacles that lifted the crust out of the water and placed it carefully on the edge of the hole, away from where the team was standing. And everything they thought they knew about Europa Prime changed in that instant.

Now those somethings were back for another visit.

Tentacles slithered out of the hole without touching any of them and slid along the side of the hole to lie in between the humans.

"The Kraken has arrived," Conason said with a chuckle.

"That's not what they call themselves," Melissa chided.

"Prove it," Apollo said. "We can tell they're intelligent because we've interacted with them. But, and I quote Commander Trahan, 'Dogs and cats are intelligent, but unless those dogs and cats are able to speak to us on our level, then they aren't as important as humanity.' So it's now or never—we find out what they call themselves or they're called what James just said, Kraken. And Kraken stories never show them as being good for humans."

Meaning it wouldn't even cause Glynn Trahan a moment's loss of rest if he gave the order for the *Washita* to destroy these creatures. The thought made Aaron's blood boil, but they were fighting a battle they hadn't been prepared for when they'd signed on for the next great step in humanity's history.

Of course, that order wouldn't come from Commander Trahan. No, it would come from his favorite Lieutenant Commander, Jolone Cesair. Cesair was, in the entire core team's opinion, Katano and Conason included, the evilest man to ever put on a military uniform since well before Earth had ever had a real shot at going into space. And the people Cesair surrounded himself with were no better.

They'd been lucky that Katano and Conason had been assigned to the core team, because both of those men were intelligent, thoughtful, honorable, and as opposed to the slaughter of an entire ecosystem as the rest of the core team.

Katano stepped over the tentacle that was between him and Melissa and helped her sit down with her legs hanging into the hole. He stayed behind her and hooked her spacesuit to his, just in case.

The challenges with easy communication were more than just the fact that the Dolittle Device hadn't been programmed with anything other than Earth animal communication patterns. It was that, in order to use it underwater, the person controlling it had to *be* underwater.

They'd sent unmanned exploratory vessels down and the creatures had immediately ripped them apart and, as far as the images showed, eaten them. They'd gotten enough to know that the creatures looked like giant squid, similar to those on Earth, but even larger. They changed colors, but no one had yet identified why.

None of the core team thought the creatures would attack them—at least not necessarily—but, since they didn't want Melissa dead, and since there were no suits they had that would protect her against the icy slush that made up most of this moon, they were having to use other methods. Morse code, specifically.

That Melissa had been able to touch the tentacles, let alone start teaching them the alphabet and how to communicate this way, should have been more than enough proof that the creatures were highly sentient. But it hadn't been.

Glenda sat next to the tentacle by her and Aaron stepped behind her and hooked her to his suit as well. Tiffany Hutto, the head of scientific consolidation for the team, meaning Apollo's next in command, did likewise, and Conason hooked himself to her.

Katie Hand, head of geology, sat as well, and Don Lijuan, head of microbiology, connected to her. The creatures didn't dislike the men, but they seemed to have more affinity for the women.

Other than Charlie Mills, head of botany, and Christopher Nicholas, head of general biology. They were both exceedingly brilliant, even by the core team's standards, which was why they'd made the team at their young ages, and the creatures seemed to adore them. Both young men had a tentacle wrapped gently around them and they were petting said tentacles. Christopher giggled as the tip of his tentacle tickled him.

Apollo stood apart, looking sad and worried. One of the tentacles slithered over and stroked his leg. He patted it back.

"They know you're scared," Charlie said.

"Cats and dogs know when we're scared," Apollo replied. "Most domesticated animals know. Most wild ones do, too. That they're animals with the ability to care would be enough for most of the general population on Earth. It's not going to be enough for Truett Diegal, if the Commander even shares that information with him."

Diegal was the Solaris System President, and he was popular, with few detractors. If he declared that Europa Prime was off limits due to the intelligent life on it, then the system would turn its attention to a different moon around Jupiter.

"I still think we should have contacted Earth about this," Tiffany said. "You know we could get a variety of high-level powerful interest groups involved."

"That's a last resort," Apollo replied. "If we do that, we could all be replaced. Or worse."

"Bad publicity to replace all of you," Conason said. "You're the faces of terraformation for the folks back home on Earth and Mars."

"We can be the faces of incompetence if we're not careful," Apollo warned.

"Got it!" Melissa interrupted excitedly. "At least, I'm pretty sure."

"Got what?" Aaron asked, trying not to be hopeful.

"They call themselves the Kalalula," she replied gleefully. "They have a shared knowledge base, somehow, I'm not clear on how yet, and they are the top beings on this moon, as expected. They feel that the rest of the ecosystem is here for them."

"Did they call it an ecosystem?" Apollo asked hopefully.

"No, they called it 'the way things are is for us, not the things,' but considering we're just making clear, understandable contact now means I can probably get better words from them."

"It'll be enough," Apollo said. "It's what we were told we needed. We have the information. Let's get back to the *Washita* and make the case."

* * *

They hadn't left the surface immediately, taking the time to do the best they could to say goodbye. Melissa felt the head Kalalula was who she'd been communicating with, but she wasn't sure if all the tentacles belonged to it or to others.

Now Aaron wished they'd stayed longer, because the closed door meeting Apollo and Tiffany were in was going on far too long. Voices were raised, mostly Apollo and Tiffany's, but the top brass for the *Washita* were in there with them, and several of them were shouting, too.

"This meeting isn't going well," Conason said softly. "I don't think we want to be here when it lets out."

Katano nodded. "We should wait for the others in the main lab. And we should go quietly."

Conason nodded as well, emphatically. Meaning their military teammates felt they were being watched and observed.

With Apollo and Tiffany in the meeting, Aaron was next in charge. He decided to choose wisdom over valor. "Let's get back to work," he said in a normal tone, then headed for the lab, which was two levels lower. The others followed.

None of them spoke on the way to the lift, while in it, or on the way to the lab. Only once they were inside the third interior lab where their work was housed did they feel safe—due to the delicate nature of what had to be done with the terraformation process, there was no way surveillance devices were in here, because they could cause issues.

They all looked at each other. "I think they lied," Glenda said.

"What do you mean?" Christopher asked, sounding stressed. Not that Aaron could blame him.

"I think she's right," Melissa said, sounding furious. "They said 'if' but never thought we'd be able to communicate with the Kalalula in the timeframe we had, and now that we've done it, they still have no intention of stopping."

"I agree," Conason said. "Which is why Katano and I are basically here as your guardians and to ensure that proper military procedure is followed in case you run into trouble."

"What Conason means is that we have no more information than you do and probably less sway," Katano added. "I know you all knew this, but

I think it bears repetition right now, because we're not in any position to change any minds in the chain of command."

"Tiffany was right," Charlie said. "We need to let the people know what's going on. Contact Inter-Solar Media and let them break the story."

"And we'll have to do it right away," Katie said, "because the Bullet's almost ready."

The Warden Bullet, created by Jean-Marie Warden over a century ago, enabled fast and full terraformation, complete with ecosystem. They were still following her scientific processes to this day, because she'd been a forward thinker as well as a genius, and she'd left copious notes for expansion into the system and how to alter the Bullet as needed.

"And the moment it is," Don added, "it's going to be the end of the Kalalula."

The lab door slammed open and they all jumped. But it was only Apollo and Tiffany, looking furious. Apollo looked at their expressions. "I see you've all figured it out. We assumed you had when you weren't in the hall where we'd left you."

"It was all lies, they don't care that there's a thriving ecosystem down there, and we're going to murder an entire sentient race shortly," Aaron said. "Right?"

"Right," Tiffany snarled. "And I'm not standing for it. We need to send messages to everyone we know back on Earth and Mars. Let them know what's going on."

"How are you going to do that?" Conason asked. Everyone stared at him. "They have to know that's what someone will try. They're not going to let any of us send a communication freely, particularly not to media. And before you suggest sending messages to friends and family, anything anyone does on this team from now until the Bullet launches is going to be watched. The only freedom any of us are going to have is in the lab, and I can guarantee that we're going to have company in here, sooner as opposed to later."

"We could try delaying things," Don suggested.

"How?" Melissa asked. "Honestly, the Solar Replication Team's work is essentially done, the Transmutation Team is ready to alter the moon's core, and if we slow down any work on the Bullet they'll just pull us and have the next in line on our teams take over. We're so close to done that it'll be easy for them to finish without risk."

"All the equipment on the moon is scheduled for removal tomorrow," Conason said, looking at his IntelliWatch. "And that's moved up. Yesterday removal was scheduled for a week from today."

"Meaning they changed things after your meeting," Aaron said to Apollo. "Or, to put it bluntly, I think we're all screwed, us and the Kalalula."

"We'll figure out a way," Apollo said firmly. "We're the smartest people on a ship loaded with smart people. We can outsmart the military. Present company excluded." He gave Conason and Katano a wink. The Duty Officers both chuckled.

There was a knock on the door and an ensign stuck her head in. "Lieutenant Commander Cesair would like to have Doctors Ascencio and Hutto join him for dinner." She looked at them expectantly.

"We'll be there," Apollo said.

The ensign nodded and closed the door. They all stared at each other.

Aaron broke the silence. "Can you two tell him you're not hungry?"

Apollo shook his head. "He might actually want to help. He was the only one in the meeting who seemed to be considering the ramifications of us destroying the Kalalula. It just might be that, all evidence to the contrary, he'll be an ally in this."

Aaron didn't believe it, but now wasn't the time to argue, since they'd been specifically requested. Instead, he watched Apollo and Tiffany head out of the lab while trying to ignore the bad feeling all of this gave him.

* * *

Aaron's worries were proved accurate within two hours. "I'm so sorry," Cesair said with what Aaron knew were crocodile tears in his eyes, while they stood in the antechamber to the Bullet's lab. "Something we had for dinner gave everyone a bad reaction but..." He spread his hands in what looked like supplication. "Doctor Ascencio died within minutes. Doctor Hutto fought hard, but she succumbed, too. We lost three ensigns who were servers, so the assumption was the canapes were the culprits, because they were allowed the leftovers once we'd been served dinner."

Aaron managed to keep from commenting about how willing Cesair had been to sacrifice his own people in order to kill Apollo and Tiffany. He hoped he'd kept his revulsion and hatred off his face. "You two seem okay," he said. "Did you get sick, too?"

Lieutenant Kim Grasskamp, Cesair's right hand woman, shook her head. "We're examining everything, but the canapes in question were filled with salmon mousse. Neither the Lieutenant Commander nor I care for salmon, so we avoided those. Thankfully." She managed to put a sad expression on her face. "I'm so sorry. I planned the menu."

"We need to get back to work," Aaron said before anyone else on the team could respond. "I think it's what Apollo and Tiffany would have wanted. Who's arranging the funeral services?"

"They'll lie in state until the terraformation is completed," Cesair said. "That our two top scientists were lost this close to success is heartbreaking. We'll ensure heroes' funerals for them once we're back on the other side of the Belt."

"I want to see their bodies," Charlie said through his tears.

"Of course," Grasskamp said kindly.

"Charlie, we need you here," Aaron said firmly.

Charlie shook his head. "I want to see them first."

Grasskamp took his arm gently, but her hand placement meant she could tighten her grip and control him. "Would anyone else like to join?"

Katie and Don both went over. "It'll be fine," Katie said, looking right into Aaron's eyes. "We just want to say goodbye right now, not later."

Aaron wanted to tell them that he didn't think he'd see the three of them ever again. But Melissa nudged him, so he just nodded. "Be careful. We're too close to finishing to risk losing you guys to more salmon mousse attacks."

Cesair's eyes glittered for a moment. "I'm certain that won't be the case." With that, the five of them left the lab.

Aaron waited for a full minute, and everyone remained silent. Then he went to the door of the outer chamber. No one on the other side. He verified that no one was lurking in this area. Then he locked the outer door in a way that could only be overridden by the Commander or Aaron himself, since he was now the lead scientist.

The others had followed him, with Conason and Katano both verifying they were alone as well. They went back into the antechamber and while the Duty Officers did the search, Aaron locked this door in the same way. Then into the main lab, again searched and locked.

Only then did Aaron speak. "We have to come up with a plan, and enact it, right now. I think we're all marked for death and if we die, the Kalalula don't have a chance."

* * *

Cesair examined his handiwork. "Think they'll buy it?" he asked Grasskamp.

"Does it matter?" she asked as she shoved the bodies of the three scientists under the draped gurneys holding the bodies of Apollo Ascencio and Tiffany Hutto. "We're going to have to get rid of all of them anyway. Their external communications are all blocked, so if they try to advise someone outside of the ship it won't go through."

"Did you get the chelating mixture into the transmutation delivery system?" he asked her as they left the morgue. "We want all life there wiped out before the terraformation begins."

"I did. We're sure it won't hurt the transmutation but will destroy all life on the moon while the core is altering. The scientists who will take over the head terraformation roles as soon as the others are eliminated were in charge of it. They're fully confident there's enough guanidine in the mixture to wipe out all life on Europa Prime, Mars, and Earth combined."

"Excellent." Cesair heaved a pleased sigh. "I'll let the Commander know that there will be nothing that can stop Europa Prime's becoming the next Earth."

* * *

True to Aaron's expectations, Charlie, Katie, and Don didn't return.

They made a recording of what they knew—Apollo and Tiffany dead, the others missing and presumed dead, the Kalalula being fully sentient, the military's decision to go ahead anyway. Then Katano and Conason went to look for the missing scientists, cautiously, and they remained in constant contact with Glenda and Christopher, just in case. They were also looking for a way to get the recording out to someone on Earth or Mars. Neither Duty Officer was hopeful about this, but they felt they had to try.

The remaining members of the team worked feverishly to add an anti-chelating agent into the Bullet, specifically targeted at preserving cephalopod life.

"Are you sure this will counter the chelating agents already in the mix?" Christopher asked Aaron as they tossed in another chemical.

"Yes," Melissa said confidently. "They're similar enough to Earth cephalopods that this should counter whatever the rest of the Bullet throws at them. Only them, by the way, but the terraformation process will create a similar ecosystem anyway, so I think they can adapt."

"I agree," Glenda added. "I think we may be able to terraform the moon and keep the Kalalula alive at the same time."

"Which would be a miracle," Aaron said. "I'd like a miracle, honestly."

They added the final mixture into the Bullet, identified as phosphorus. Phosphorus was vital to life as humans knew it, so there was no way anyone would remove it from the Bullet or think it was odd that there were multiple phosphorus cartridges—Warden's notes had suggested that it was better to err on the side of more phosphorus than less the farther from Sol the terraformation would take place.

Christopher altered their notes to show that the additional phosphorus had been decided on weeks ago. A good computer tech could decipher that it was added later, but by the time they'd know to look it would all be over.

"Now what?" Melissa asked once they'd finished.

"Now we sleep here," Aaron said. "No one goes anywhere alone, you and Glenda go to the bathroom together, same for me and Christopher, and I know Katano and Conason know to do to that, too."

"They may have found a way," Glenda shared, looking at her IntelliWatch. "Conason says to sit tight and they'll be back to us shortly, hopefully with good news."

"Then that's what we do," Aaron said as he finally sat down and stared at the Bullet. "From now on, all we can do is wait and pray to Sol that this works."

* * *

Conason moved cautiously. Katano was on watch but nearby enough that they could hear each other. They both knew they were as marked for death as the scientists under their charge, but they both refused to go down without a fight.

Not for the first time Conason was glad that he had a younger sister who was one of the best computer hackers in the system, because she'd not only taught her big brother quite a lot, but she'd also given him a portable Microdrive that contained code that would allow him to override whatever he needed to as long as he could link into a terminal. He was also glad that he'd never shared this with anyone on the ship, not even Katano or the core terraformation team. Some things were better kept to oneself.

That they'd gone to the maintenance section of the ship was, he hoped, the thing Cesair and his thugs wouldn't think they'd do. Maintenance only had one terminal, and it was only used to ensure waste disposal could be altered or halted as needed. Meaning it was the least manned post on the entire ship. The downside was that Maintenance's terminal only connected internally, meaning it seemed like the least helpful terminal to use, and his sister's override code wouldn't be able to break that. But Conason had a plan.

As hoped, no one was manning the terminal. He plugged in the Microdrive and got to work.

He got the recording into the system and disguised it as a maintenance update. Once the Bullet would launch, the recording would go live to everyone on the *Washita*. And once it did, it would be able to send itself out from the main computer linkup, which would be broadcasting to at least the Offices of the Solar President and most if not all system media outlets. It might not mean they made it out alive, but it would mean that everyone else in the system would know what had happened.

* * *

Conason and Katano returned and Aaron let them in. "It's handled," Conason said.

"Before you get excited," Katano added, "be aware that there's a contingent behind us coming to either kill us all or stay with us to ensure that you all do what you're supposed to do."

"They didn't see us," Conason said, "we saw them, but we have no more than three minutes before they're here."

Aaron considered this quickly and left the door unlocked. "Come on," he said to the Duty Officers. They went into the antechamber and Aaron left that door unlocked, too. They got into the main lab and only then did he lock the door—but he locked it in the regular way. "Follow my lead," he said to the others. "We're happy scientists working to make all the system's dreams come true. No one mentions the Kalalula, no one asks about the others. I'll do that, possibly, but I want the rest of you working, busy, and above all, silent. Only speak if spoken to, and give the shortest replies you can, in as cheerful or intense a way as you can, depending."

Everyone went to their various stations and started bustling. This wasn't a hard ask, since they were down by half of the team, so they had plenty to do to cover.

No sooner was everyone in place than there was a banging on the door. Aaron looked to Katano and nodded. Katano opened the door.

"Why is this door locked?" the ensign in charge asked.

"We always lock it while the scientists are working," Katano replied mildly. "Unless this is urgent, now is not a good time for a disruption—we're missing half of the core team and until they get back, everyone's doing double duty. If we're going to launch terraformation on time, come back later."

The ensign gaped. "Ah…Lieutenant Commander Cesair wants to be sure work is continuing apace."

"It is," Katano said, sounding bored. "None of you have any training to determine if that's true or not, so I have no idea why you're here, but leave and come back with someone who can verify if the Lieutenant Commander is worried. We have nothing to hide here, we're just overworked. If you can find our missing scientists, that would be incredibly helpful."

He gave the ensign the names of their five missing members then closed the door in their faces. They all waited, but the door didn't open, and no one knocked. Katano locked the door.

"You told them to look for Apollo and Tiffany, too," Melissa pointed out.

"I did, because I doubt anyone other than us and Cesair's closest officers know they're dead." Katano shrugged. "It may give us more time, it may not. I guarantee we'll find out soon."

* * *

Cesair ended up installing himself and Grasskamp in the lab. He seemed to not find Aaron's insistence that they not leave the lab unattended troubling, nor did he seem to mind that at least four of the remaining team were in the lab at any one time, and that they went to use the bathroom or eat in pairs.

No, Aaron concluded, Cesair seemed unconcerned and confident, and like he was watching them more for his own amusement than to try to affect them in any way.

"They've done something to the transmutation process," he said to Christopher when they grabbed a quick bite from the commissary.

"Maybe. But I think what we've done will counter whatever they've done." Christopher examined his food. "Think it's safe to eat?"

"I think we die without fuel, so we might as well chance it."

"There you are!" Commander Trahan clapped his hand onto Aaron's shoulder. "I hear everything's ready and that we can launch today."

"Yes, just about," Aaron replied. "I thought we had a couple more days."

"Cesair says that you're all ready and just doing your fourth double-check." Trahan chuckled. "You and your team are a credit to science, but I believe in striking the moment we're ready. And we appear to be ready right now."

Aaron knew an ultimatum when it was disguised as friendly heartiness. He also knew that Trahan had to know that half of the core team had been murdered because he wasn't mentioning that they were missing. "If you're sure…"

"I am." Trahan's tone was now firm. "Let's get it going."

"I need to do one more check and we need to escort the Bullet to launch."

"Shouldn't military handle that?" Trahan asked.

"They can carry it, sure, but we have to be certain they don't dislodge anything and that the Bullet is set up correctly." Aaron stood and looked Trahan in the eyes. "I'm sure you don't want to do anything that would jeopardize the terraformation, do you?"

"Absolutely not," Trahan said. "I'll escort you as well. It's a big day and I want to remember all of it."

* * *

Nothing went wrong with the Bullet's transfer to the launch area. Once it was all set up they had to leave, and Trahan insisted they come to the command viewing area to watch. Refusal would do no one any good, so they acquiesced.

Cesair and Grasskamp were there, but they didn't pay Aaron's team any mind. He was fine with this, but their attitudes still made him nervous.

The *Washita* started broadcasting to the system government and medias. First the Solar Replacement Team turned on the heat. Then the Hodos Transmutation Process was sent into the planet's core via the hole in the crust. It traveled fast enough that the Kalalula didn't have time to catch it, though cameras on the outer shell showed that there were Kalalula nearby.

"Transmutation has begun," the head of that team announced. "The process can now not be interrupted by anything."

"Time for the Bullet," Aaron said, trying to keep the dread out of his voice, holding onto the hope that what they'd done would work."

The Bullet was shot out of the *Washita* at an even faster speed than the Hodos Transmutation Process had been. There were cameras on the outer shell of the Bullet, because they had to know if it deployed or not.

So Aaron watched it sail through the slush and successfully hit the center of the moon. Then something happened that no one was prepared for.

* * *

The moon's crust exploded, but not from the terraformation process. The space around the moon was suddenly filled with giant squid.

There were screams and some sobs from the military and scientific personnel watching, not just those on Aaron's team.

"Oh, my God," Trahan said softly. "This shouldn't have happened."

Aaron was about to reply when several things happened at once. Their recording went live on all of the ship's screens and everyone's IntelliWatches. The ice fell back onto the planet to become water, as terraformation unfolded before them. And the Kalalula in space changed color from the dull gray they'd been when tossed into space to bright red—and they all started to swim.

"They're alive," Melissa said, sounding shocked out of her mind.

"How?" Trahan asked.

"They're huge," Glenda replied. "They must have enough heat internally to keep them warm enough, or they're so used to living in the freezing cold that airless space doesn't affect them. It's likely part of their biological process."

"They'd have room to catch their kind of water in their mantles and they might even have smaller food sources there," Aaron added.

"They might be able to reproduce, too," Melissa said. "If they keep their eggs tucked in until they hatch. If they're similar to Earth cephalopods, which they seem to be. Nature always finds a way."

"We need to study them," Christopher said breathlessly.

"Send exploratory ships," Trahan said. "We need to get a closer look." Cesair relayed this along the chain of command.

Aaron was about to share that this might be a bad idea when Trahan's order was followed and ships flew out of the *Washita* straight for the Kalalula.

So everyone got to see the Kalalula grab those ships with their tentacles, rip the ships apart, and eat them. Every ship.

Trahan gave the order to fire on the Kalalula, but they were surprisingly agile and quick, and they dodged the fire. He sent scientists into ships, though Aaron refused to allow his team to go, to try to determine how to calm the giant space squids down. Cesair and Grasskamp took a small fleet to go continue the fighting.

The space around the now green and lush Europa Prime was chaos.

"You need to stop or they'll head for the *Washita*," Aaron said after more noncombatant ships were destroyed. "Leave them alone. We told you they were there. We should have left Europa Prime as it was and, if we don't break off, they'll destroy us all."

Trahan looked like he wanted to argue, but instead he nodded and gave the cease fire order. He also called back the next wave of ships, though not before some of them were destroyed and eaten.

Then he got up. "All of you," he indicated the core team, "my office. Now."

* * *

"Orders?" Grasskamp asked as she and the rest of Cesair's most trusted headed for ships. He'd already had them gather their things. "The Commander knows what we did—it's going to be easy for him to blame us, especially with that damn recording out in the open."

"I think it's about time to change careers," Cesair replied. "I'd prefer that to dying." The rest of his group all nodded their agreement.

"What do you suggest we do to survive?" Grasskamp asked him.

Cesair grinned. He'd given this thought, because he was a man who liked to have contingency plans in place. "I think the Belt miners are ripe for piracy."

"We'll need new identities," Grasskamp said promptly. Cesair liked her best of all his cronies because she was also a planner and a quick thinker who could switch lanes with speed and ease. "Names they can't associate with us."

"Make something up," he suggested genially as they reached their ships where the rest of those loyal to him were waiting.

"I think you'll want a title," Grasskamp said happily. "Something that has meaning. I've given it thought."

"I'm sure I'll like whatever you pick," he said truthfully.

She smiled. "This name will fit well with your new position. It means 'evil spirit' in my family's native tongue. Get comfortable with being called Boser Geist."

He grinned. "I've been Jolone Cesair long enough. Boser Geist has the perfect ring to it."

* * *

The discussions had been long and heated, but because their recording had made it to President Diegal, he was aware that lies had been told and the result was now a race of creatures who shouldn't exist.

The recording had been stopped at the media outlets by Presidential order, but that still meant people knew what had happened. And those people knew that the people who'd made the recording were still alive at the time of terraformation launch.

Cesair, Grasskamp, and an entire company's worth of military had disappeared. Whether they'd been destroyed by the Kalalula—which Trahan resolutely insisted had happened—or they'd gone AWOL, no one could be sure. Aaron voted for AWOL, but he kept that to himself.

They were in a private meeting, just the core terraformation team left, Trahan, and President Diegal, who was alone. Aaron braced himself—offer or threat for their silence was the only reason for this set up.

"Obviously this was both a hugely successful terraformation operation with a complete botch job done on the local inhabitants," Diegal said. "And also obviously, we're going to need to do a complete PR campaign to spin this as us having no idea that this would happen."

"No one had any idea this would happen," Melissa said. "But we were quite clear that the Kalalula were a fully sentient race, so what was done was an attempted full-scale slaughter."

"It's in the past," Diegal said. "Literally. They're still alive somehow and now they're at war with us."

"Are they?" Aaron asked. "They're not coming for the *Washita* because we stopped shooting at them. They're only attacking ships that are going near them. We haven't had time to test how close a ship can get before they attack it."

"Their reactions are protective," Glenda agreed. "Their coloration keeps on changing, too. I'm certain it means emotional changes."

"Maybe so," Trahan said, "but how many personnel and vessels am I going to waste to find out?"

"No more right now," Diegal said. "That's an Executive Order. I want the *Washita* heading home."

"No," Aaron said calmly.

"Excuse me?" Diegal sounded shocked.

"We're only alive," he indicated himself and the others, "because we managed to avoid Jolone Cesair's hit squads and because the recording we made reached the media. We don't trust you, any of you, and we want to survive this situation. But you can show us arriving on Earth and then having 'accidents' and I'm against that."

"I knew nothing of it," Trahan said quickly.

"What do you suggest?" Diegal asked, ignoring Trahan, which was the first thing he'd done that Aaron approved of.

Aaron took a deep breath. "You bribe us for our silence." He put his hand up as the others started to protest. "Make an offer."

"A million credits each," Diegal said without a moment's hesitation.

Aaron smiled to himself. He'd read this right—that was their plan and right now Diegal thought Aaron had played into their hand.

"Five million, each," he countered, voice even. "And then another five million each for the lives of the five team members we lost to Cesair's machinations. I realize that the math is a little off with six of us alive and only five dead, but I don't care."

"You don't want their families to receive that?" Diegal asked carefully.

"Nope. The families can receive two-point-five million per family member."

Diegal cocked his head. "Why have you chosen those numbers?"

"I know how many people are in each of their immediate families. You're getting off cheap, so I wouldn't argue." Aaron shrugged. "The six of us are alive, so we can take care of our families and we can continue to earn credits. You can lie and say that Apollo, Tiffany, Katie, Don, and Charlie went into science ships to try to calm the Kalalula and were destroyed, and so they will receive posthumous civilian bravery awards and their families will receive the thanks of a grateful system in the form of cold, hard credits. We'll all swear to that, regardless of who asks us. But we'll all also have 'in case of suspicious or untimely death' orders to share what's really gone on behind these closed doors."

"I'm recording all of this," Conason said cheerfully. "And it's being sent live directly to Earth, where it'll be locked forever, unless harm comes to any of us or the people we care about."

"That's a lot of credits," Diegal said.

Aaron shrugged. "A hundred million credits is cheaper than an all-out system revolt that will end in your political destruction and, possibly, the chance of continued expansion. Just as six fully outfitted ships that can house at least two dozen won't be missed. Just claim they were destroyed in the chaos."

"True enough." Diegal tapped on the keyboard in front of him. All their IntelliWatches beeped. Their financial institutions shared that they were all ten million credits richer.

"We'll need pilots," Melissa said. "Pilots we can trust."

"We'll give you some new robotic prototypes another branch has been working on," Trahan said, finally getting with the flow of things. "It sounds like you'll be able to program them for loyalty." He glared at Conason who grinned back.

"Do it," Diegal said, and Trahan tapped out the orders.

"And, one more thing," Aaron said. Diegal sighed but nodded. "The Kalalula are to be left alone. We can try to study them if you want to lose more assets, but they are not to be hunted. We made them, we need to leave them alone and let them live in the brave new world we've forced them into."

"Agreed," Diegal said. "We already have every animal lover and animal rights group up in arms over this, and that's just within the military and government. If we hunt them, the general population will revolt because there's no way this event will be kept secret. Any more demands?" Aaron shook his head. "Fine. What will you do now that you're all independently wealthy?"

"I think the Belters could use some organization, coordination, and laws about mining," Aaron replied. "I'm heading there. I think it's time to turn my scientific brain towards the business of keeping the system thriving."

The others all nodded. "Us, too," Glenda said with a smile for him that Aaron realized was rather personal. The future might be even a bit brighter than he'd hoped. "Where you go, Aaron, so go the rest of us."

He stood up. "Then the Belt is it. Let's go do some good in the system to make up for all the bad done here."

"You may not believe this," Diegal said, "but I want you to succeed in that goal."

"I'm sure you do," Aaron said with a tight smile. "And I promise that we will. Just like I can promise that we'll all be watching and waiting for the day we can find out how to make peace with the enemy you created."

"That day may be a long time coming," Diegal said.

"That's why you have children," Aaron said as they left the room. "So they can continue your work when you're gone."

He held Glenda's hand all the way to the launch area.

Dead of Night

Mike Jack Stoumbos

I wake to the soft acoustic guitar and tenor voice of Jackson Meier. This is not strange—after all, I fell asleep to my favorite Meier song, and, as usual, nautical imagery from the lyrics wove into my REM-loop. The psych says you're not supposed to remember your dreams when you're in float, but I do. I always do. It's been logged in my file as a *Will Monitor*. If the psych judges my taste in folky, Terran ballads, he keeps that to himself.

I unclip the resistance straps and slowly sit up. I can feel my hair drifting, as if underwater, but's it's just a micrograv reminder that I'm overdue for a trim.

My eyes slowly adjust to the dim, the artificial-imitating-natural at the core of the vessel. The recorded Jackson Meier continues crooning into the second verse, and the moon facsimile installed in the foremost wall is still glowing its peculiar blue, a reminder of the night sky we are promised when we arrive at our destination in just a few more weeks.

I unzip my tiny, pink spray bottle from its compartment and mist my face to help me fully wake, just as the track starts saying, *"The waves are churning, this heart's—"*

And then it stops. I only hear my own voice mumble, "—learning."

I look at the speaker, but the display is night mode and still dark.

The song resumes, picking up right after the gap, so smoothly I almost doubt my own ears.

"The water's telling me what I need to know
To plunge below…"

"Who the hell screwed with my song?" I wonder blearily. Then, after clearing my throat, I call, "Jerry?" This time, I hear my voice resound back at me, glancing off the smooth, cylindrical walls of the caretakers' chamber.

The song continues into the refrain.

"System, pause night song." The wall interface hears and obeys. "System, time?"

"Oh-Seven-One-Three hours, approximate, adjusted," the speaker replies, with that pleasant metronome quality of almost-human programming.

"Say again?" I request, more than a little surprised. I undo the rest of my sleeping bands while it says 'again'. Same cadence, same time—not that I really expected it to be different.

I gently push off from my bed and reach the touch console, grabbing hold of one of the stability bars. I swipe the screen awake and confirm a listed time. "System, why didn't—" I realize the futility of the *why* question and adjust to, "System, did my alarm sound at six-thirty?"

"Negative. Alarms disabled."

"What?" Louder this time, more resonance in this chamber and down the corridor.

The System politely offers: "Do you wish me to repeat?"

"Wha— No. Um… Hang on." The display confirms that, yes, my wake-up call was turned off. But why, I do not know.

I open Jerry's comm line. "Jerry?"

No answer.

"System, all-call." The screen turns green, the entire ship's speakers ready to receive. "Jerry?" My own voice echoes back, a little higher and a little more frightened.

Otherwise, no one answers. That is strange. I disable the all-call and ask the computer, "System, last known activity of Crewman Jerry Klein?"

"Crewman Klein's log shows activation of audiobook; command *Resume Play* on *Personal Speaker*. Do you wish to see activity log?"

"Yes, display here," I say, and indicate with my fingerprint that *here* means *on this screen.*

"Access is restricted to—"

"Crewman Doyle, ship custodian," I interrupt, then type my password as prompted. Either password or print is enough for quick authorization during emergencies, but sensitive records require two-factor authentication, even from a doctor or bridge officer.

A comprehensive list populates the screen with Jerry Klein's activity, basically every time he accessed the System and would have to indicate that he was the user or input a password, including every time he refilled his coffee or went to the washroom. Each log shows a time-stamp and either a *View More* option or a *Private* tag. I could scroll up forever, but the most recent is printed right at the bottom: the audiobook, accessed at *0418*. *Approximate. Adjusted for Relative Velocity.* Almost three hours ago.

This is also strange. Jerry should have signed off on a ship-wide systems check at 0600 and I should have woken up to confirm it. If I slept through my alarm, Jerry should have been here to shake my shoulder and say, "Get your lazy ass out of the rack, Doyle. Corps's not paying you to nap."

But I take a deep breath, remind myself I am in control. "Rational explanations, Doyle," I say aloud. The psych always tells me self-talk is positive and that hearing your own real voice makes it easier to distinguish from voices in your head. And Corps's not paying me to go crazy either, as Jerry would remind me.

I put on my impact boots as I talk myself down from a potential panic. "Rational explanations for Jerry," I begin, aware that my throat is tight and my words come out higher. "Jerry turned on his book and lost track of time." It had happened before. "Jerry tried to change or disable his own alarm and accidentally disabled all of the alarms in the custodian's chambers." That had not happened before, but it was plausible, given his authorization.

This explanation would suffice and might keep me away from another thought: *Doyle dissociated while in night drift and had a panic attack.* That had happened before, but the psych has been working with me and cleared me for duty.

"System, ambient light up. Morning settings." The cylindrical chamber becomes fully visible, the few meters of width and the few more of length that I have come to think of as home.

I tally the beds in the custodian's chambers, each separated by a curtain, which I draw aside. "One, two, three. All empty, but me." Still reasonable. After all, Jerry doesn't usually bed down until 10 AM, and the third bed is only used when an engineer or doc has to pull two waking shifts in a row, which is not due for another few days. Unless I've lost track of the schedule, which would be a bad sign—

"Not yet," I tell myself. Shaking my head, I confirm, "Not important now. Not necessary to dwell on."

Knowing it's better to stick to the tasks, I decide to do what Jerry didn't. I can log the systems check. And I can calm a bit with some background music, namely a folk song about a distance swimmer. "System, play 'Oceantide' by Jackson Meier."

The computer obliges and plays the familiar, soothing acoustic guitar soon to be joined by Meier's voice—somehow grounding even in zero-g.

"System, display forward view." The screen changes and shows my morning ritual. I can't change the trajectory, but there is something reassuring about being able to see the direction we're going, the faint streak of stars on all sides, and the fixed center of our destination system, a teeny-tiny blip of light, labeled with system coordinates.

The brightest star is actually a little to our left, probably only a few degrees off true heading, and will pass us by in a few more shifts. It's been the closest system since Sol. Part of me wishes this beacon were our real destination, which the psych tells me is quite normal for wakers in deep space because they would rather get out of their tin cans sooner than later. Last time we met, I said it was because this star was a "guiding light" like in the song, which I have to acknowledge is a little strange to listen to on loop. Not enough to turn it off, especially as it hits the refrain.

> *"I set my course by oceantide*
> *Hoping to reach the other side*
> *My time won't be denied—no, sir."*

I check the *Lincoln*'s long-range telemetry, see that the course is continuing as calculated and the trajectory hasn't changed. "That's good." Not that I expected anything different there. It would take at least three people to authorize a course correction on a vessel this size. Jerry likes to say that it takes less confirmation to launch a nuke than it does to steer a passenger ship hurtling between systems at relativistic speeds. With our clearance, the best Jerry or I could do on our own is slow the rotation in case of instability.

> *"Searching for a guiding light*
> *To pull me through the dead of night*
> *I've never swam across an ocean so wide."*

I pull up the sleepers' logs to see that there are no errors or flags for the crew or passengers in deep mode. "That's good." I confirm it with a fingerprint.

Finally, I go through the life-support data, inner atmo readings, and current spin. Everything looks good, so I'm about to complete the 0600 sign-off (slightly late but not too bad), when there's a sudden silence in the second verse. The song resumes a moment later, but I'm sure of the gap this time. At least, I think I'm sure. It might be one of Mandela Effect things, based on a commonly misheard lyric of a song, where some people replace *"this heart's learning"* with *"yearning"*—unless it was the other way around.

I shake my head and say out loud, a little firmer than before, but not quite drill sergeant, "Stay on task. Use self-talk. Don't let your mind wander." Easier said than done, but the psych would remind me that saying it *helps* get it done.

I gently push off the rungs as I head to the foremost door. I enter the general access code that even a chimpanzee could hack and unseal the hatch. There is a minor puff of pressure change as the door recedes, and I'm faced with the slowly spinning fore-section of the vessel.

Just before leaving, I unhook one of the portable speakers from the wall and clip it to my utility pocket. Just in case I need some familiar music.

As always, I close my eyes when I step through into the main hull. I use my hands and feet to feel for the rungs—only one set, less disorienting— that slowly revolve around me. I descend the ladder, feeling gravity increase with each step. Rotational momentum, the cheapest and most manageable artificial gravity.

I no longer feel any nausea or discomfort from the change in grav. Haven't for weeks. According to the "experts," it's because I sleep in zero-g, in the unfamiliar, so my mind can snap back to the familiar when I'm awake. They say it's much harder the other way around, which the rest of the crew proves on an ongoing basis whenever they wake up and have to reach the center of the vessel.

They also say it's easier to wake up (and go to bed) if you know that someone else is around and available to talk to.

"Where would Jerry go?" I wonder at the walls as I step off the ladder and onto the main floor, the Command Floor of the *Lincoln*. "System, lights up. Daytime settings." To my left and right, I can see the curvature of the ship along the floor, a series of doors, hatches, windows, and touchscreens. I know that if something were really wrong, I could head left to the port sleeper and wake Doctor Singh, but I don't want to put another note of *night-drift hysteria* on my record if I'm worrying over nothing. It's best for me to check in with Jerry or the officer of the watch first.

I head forward first, along the main access corridor toward the Command Bridge.

It's a comforting constant, a marvel of technology, separated by a wall with large sections of transparency and a couple of surprisingly technical doors. Through the window ahead, I can see the sleek, beautiful, dimly-illuminated hub of operations. The chairs in the bridge are totally empty, but the forward viewer shows a much bigger, grander starscape than I could see in my room, the bright sun drifting by to the left.

I find it funny that the viewer is programmed to look fixed, even though the vessel is spinning.

But my musing is interrupted when a sound startles me.

Footsteps, or something like them, scampering across the floor, patters echoing along the walls.

"Jerry?" I wonder. Then, thinking of the officer of the watch, I try, "Commander Wen?"

The footsteps are gone, too quickly for me to ascertain a direction, and giving me no information to follow but a blind guess. There is the sneaking worry, a suspicion of night-drift hallucinations. Which have happened before...

So I hum the opening notes of "Oceantide," nothing complex but enough to feel the vibrations in my chest, assuring me that this sound is real.

I head for the lounge, where Jerry would have gotten his coffee, where he might have crashed out on one of the recliners, where he might have fallen asleep if he neglected to drink said coffee. Nesting into a cushioned chair with full spin grav is a huge comfort to us custodians. There's even a putting green to complement the illusion of Earth—if you ignore that an endless stretch of empty space is only a few meters below your feet.

I don't hear footsteps or anything weird on the short trip. The doors are closed and any movement would be obvious. Even so, I resist the urge to turn on "Oceantide" and keep my ears sharp.

But when I open the lounge door, I nearly deafen myself with my own scream.

The pool of red, not fully dried, has spread into the putting green, forming a high-contrast design with the brightly-colored imitation grass poking through. One of the comfortable recliners is toppled on its side. Beside it, the limp body of Jerry Klein.

Without thinking, I take one step through the blood and am sickened by the sticking sound as I lift my foot, but I get close enough to confirm. Crewman, fellow custodian, hopeful interstellar explorer who signed on to nightwatch to pay for passage. Now nearly unrecognizable.

The back of the skull has been caved in, as if someone found the first splitting blow insufficient and had to make sure no one would discern this crewman was formerly blonde. The eyes are, thankfully, already closed, but the mouth is open, the jaw offset. His expression is frozen in dumb shock, the kind you'd feel when bludgeoned by a golf club.

I don't call Jerry's name; I don't check his pulse. I realize I've forgotten to breathe and gasp, suddenly aware of the iron and salt and disgustingly sweet aroma of evaporated blood. I do look to see that the rack is short one putter; it's not in Jerry's hands, and it's not in mine either.

"Security," I say, or maybe just think. My steps toward the wall console are heavy and leaning, and I almost lose track of the gravity.

"System, crew casualty." My voice doesn't sound right or feel right. I take a look back at Jerry, then realize the computer has been talking.

"What?" I ask the wall.

"Do you wish me to repeat?"

"Uh, no." I can see the prompt on the screen. "Crewman, Jerry Klein. Dead. Found in the foredeck, enlisted lounge, at…" I look at the clock. It's nearly 0800. Have I been awake that long? How long has Jerry been here? "System, mark the time of report," I say.

"Casualty Report in progress. Do you require a medic?"

"What? No. Um, yes. Wake the doctor."

The System tries to help. It displays the doctors, all of whom are in deep-sleep, and their estimated times to safely wake.

"No," I say. "System, show only officers in light-sleep. Doctor and officer of the watch."

The previous display goes away and the screen is blank. Or, rather, it stops displaying any names. I'm about to object, when I notice that there is a note confirming that no officers are currently in light-sleep.

"Doctor Singh and Commander Wen," I prompt, "are they both awake?"

"Cannot confirm current waking state. Recent logs confirm that both were woken. Neither is currently logged as sleeping."

Of course. Sleepers are monitored. Wakers are responsible for themselves.

"System, all-call," I say. Then, as clearly and authoritatively as possible, "Doctor Singh! Medical alert—casualty report, please respond."

No answer. I can feel my heart start racing.

"Commander Wen? Officer of the watch, please respond."

Nothing but my own slightly panicked breathing.

"Anyone! Respond. Crewman Klein is dead! I repeat: Crewman Klein has been—"

My voice stops. I instantly feel dizzy, a spinning sensation, not caused by the ship itself. I nearly collapse, but a recalled image of Jerry's blood and brains where I would land brings up enough revulsion to sober me. I tap the *All-Call* closed.

I can't say *murder*.

But no one else says anything either.

The word *alone* sounds in my brain, and I rush to replace it with real sounds. "System, wake the Captain."

The screen changes again. "The Captain is in deep-sleep. Please provide clearance for emergency wake up."

I don't have that, so I move on.

"System, wake the doctors, any medical personnel."

This takes a moment longer. Eventually, the mechanical voice responds. "No—*medical personnel*—are in light-sleep. All listed—*medical personnel*—are in deep-sleep. Please provide clearance for emergency wake up."

I don't have that either. The truth is I don't have any clearance to force anyone out of deep-sleep the fast and dangerous way. Scheduled doctors and psychs and even engineers usually take five or six hours to emerge from deep, and only a doctor or psych or command officer can force them out of hibernation faster. I open up a new display with shaking hands; my fingers feel cold and the screen feels distant. I input my password to enable full custodial access.

"Um…System," I say, prepared for futility. "Display crew that I can emergency wake with my level of clearance."

The display populates. It's not blank, but it confirms the gray-colored hopelessness running through my veins. The only people I can force awake:

The Officer of the Watch, currently listed as Commander Wen.

The Standing Medic, currently listed as Doctor Singh.

And the custodians, currently listed as Crewman Klein…and me.

"Okay, um…" I try to swallow and fail. I wonder if vomiting would make me feel better, but my body seems to have skipped nausea and I have nothing in my stomach yet. Always better to go to sleep in zero-g with an empty stomach, and usually I'd have an appetite in the morning.

"System, display the crew I can *schedule* to wake," I ask, aware that this process will take a painfully long time. This list is much bigger, from engineering and maintenance, to the botanist, all of the *medical personnel*, and on up through the Captain herself.

I am about to input a command to *Begin Waking Process* for all, but something holds my hand. It's almost as if someone has taken me by the wrist, so much so that I look back over my shoulder and see… no one. Again. Just me, the System's wall console, and Jerry's corpse.

I have heard about people cracking in night-drift. Sure, the Corps screens for tendencies, and they can pick out the most likely candidates, but when you're stuck in a spinning tube hurtling through empty space for months on end…

"Unchecked neurosis leads to psychosis," I say aloud, quoting the psych. "That's why we do self-talk, buddy-systems, and music." It could happen to anyone. I don't repeat that part. The psych doesn't like to harp on that.

"System, schedule waking procedure for primary psychologist, Doctor Yvon Rausch," I say.

The System starts to ask a clarifying question, but I mute it. I know what it's going to say about the safety regulations, so I cut it off with, "As soon as it's safe to do so."

It had been done before. After all, when Jerry missed a ladder rung and sprained his ankle, we waited almost five hours for the doc to safely wake, even though the officer of the watch could have made the call and jolted Doctor Singh out of bed with a word. But emergency waking was a bigger strain on the body than a twisted ankle.

Jerry…

I glance at Jerry again. This time, I keep staring, I don't look away. I need to confirm what is and what isn't. I need to be sure Jerry isn't a hallucination. I click on the accompaniment. "Oceantide" starts playing. I can feel the vibrations from the speaker. I take stock: Jerry's mangled appearance, the tipped chair, the pool of blood—which I've spread by a couple of bootprints.

"Shit." I debate any possible methods for scrubbing my foot clean of the quickly browning red.

Then the music skips. Same place, second verse, right over *learning*.

"Shit! System, what the hell happened to my song?"

The System doesn't respond. I turn to see the blinking light, reminding me that the wall console will stay muted until there is a verified emergency or a crew member reactivates the volume.

"System, unmute," I say, but it has already finished. Probably telling me to *clarify the question*. Not that it would do me any good.

My music track is still running; I can live with one skipped word.

"System, last known location of Commander Wen," I command, then preempt with my fingerprint and a quick remark of "custodian clearance."

"Officer of the Watch, Commander Wen, entered the command bridge at Oh-Five-Oh-Three hours, approximate, adjusted."

"Wait, entered? Did not exit?"

The System takes a moment to interpret, then settles on telling me, "Commander Wen's ID has not since been used to open any doors."

Which means she should still be on the bridge. Which means I should have seen her through the glass. Right?

She went in three hours ago, but—

"System, has anyone exited or entered the bridge since Wen at five-oh-three?"

"Negative."

"Okay," I tell myself. This one word seems to be all the pep talk I need with Meier piping on loop.

This time, I leap over the pool of blood and out the open door.

I am used to running in the mornings; I am used to thinking of these artificial mornings as mornings, regardless of coffee or breakfast. The recycled air on my face feels good. My cheeks are cold, as if wet from tears. I don't recall crying, but I think even the psych would forgive me for that.

I race up one level and back into the main, at a comfortable three-quarter-grav. Panting, I regard the glass partition separating the bridge. I know that it's two panes, each ten-c thick, both space-worthy so that the bridge could be saved if there's a leak.

I pause—no, I *hesitate*. I don't know why. A sense of dread, but is it fear or does a part of me know something it doesn't want to admit?

I swallow and try to sing along, but my voice is shaky at best. "...take these sunken eyes and learn to see..."

With each step, I can feel my hands shaking more and more. I see my reflection in the glass and am almost shocked by how pale I appear. A few weeks ago, I might have said *poor lighting*, but I can't bring myself to do so this time.

"System. Open the door to the command bridge. Custodian clearance." I am about to give my fingerprint, but the System interrupts.

"Warning: low oxygen in the command bridge. Fire-suppressant nitrogen mix authorized."

"What? When? Why?"

The System fails to effectively handle all three questions.

My feet feel suddenly less leaden—albeit still slightly bloodied—and I clear the last couple meters to the door. I couldn't see it before, but now, looking down through the glass—

"Wen!" I call out, knowing that the limp officer, facedown on the floor, cannot hear me. Multiple panes of glass and a perfectly sealed door can only take out so much of the sound, but death by asphyxiation creates a more official barrier. I might as well be shouting across space.

Ironically, the System reads *Wen* as a question and answers. "Fire-suppression protocol authorized at Oh-Five-Thirty-Five hours, approximate, adjusted."

"But—System, was there a fire?"

Pause. "None was detected by automatic systems. Direct crew authorization. Override was given to remove oxygen."

"By who?" I ask. I swipe the screen by the door to *active*. "Who ordered fire-suppression?"

No pause this time. "Crewman Doyle, custodian authorization."

I...

I don't have any words to describe how I feel.

My fingers work to pull up the logs without me consciously telling them to. I go through fingerprint authorization, see my recorded activity. Sure enough: my name at *0535*, precisely, with a flag confirming an entered password and an override to remove oxygen.

The psych talks about people going through stages to deal with major events and trauma, but I'm pretty sure that I skip right past the disbelief and horror and drop into numbness. But then the typical stages are about grief. I don't remember seeing anything about finding out that you've gone nuts and murdered two crew members with no memory of doing so.

"Three."

My own voice startles me out of my daze.

"Doctor Singh."

Why not? Why stop at two when there are three? I shift away from the panel to face the closed door to the bridge. The other side of the glass is dark enough that I see more of myself than the backs of chairs and consoles in the bridge. I see the face of a killer.

"Huh." I would have expected a little more malice. "You look just like the rest of us, don't you?" I ask myself. "Hiding in plain sight."

A small trembling part of me wants to question or rationalize. There might have been a scenario in which I was trying to defend myself, or maybe in which I had caught Jerry killing Wen and then avenged her, or vice versa. Ridiculous.

I shake my head, watching my loose hair wag back at me, until I see myself gasp. Or, rather, I see another face—an echo, a shadow, a phantom. Someone else behind me in my reflection. But by the time I turn around, there is no one there.

"Oceantide" keeps playing, but the sound of footsteps—faster this time—breaks up the cadence.

I run after the hallucination. I don't have the same sense of dread or foreboding as before. I know where it is leading me: port sleeping room.

Deep-sleepers are shut into the walls like stiffs in a morgue. Light-assisted-sleepers who are only down for a couple of days at a time, but long enough that zero-g is bad for long-term health—like the doc, the man Singh himself—would have been there.

I don't have to go up or down any levels, just follow the curvature of the spinning ship. As if to mark my trail, I see two streaks of blood on the floor. I know it's not my bootprint, but that they're from earlier, right after I'd killed Jerry.

I half expect the port sleeper to be cut off from oxygen as well. What other methods would an interstellar custodian gone crazy on night-drift have used? Golf club would have been convenient; fire suppression authorization would have been only a password away. Maybe I'm just being uncreative, or maybe I'm overthinking it. What could I not perform on the unguarded Singh?

The port sleeper's door is open, strange but not impossible. All three light-sleep tanks are also open, standing in an asymmetrical row in the middle of the room, surrounded by a range of medical equipment, including stimulants and sedatives that even I've been trained to use. The light-sleep tanks are really just fancy techno beds with covers. Two are empty. The third would have Doctor Singh.

The active monitors on the walls show the readings for twenty-seven other sleepers in the chamber. Deep-sleepers, for whom three-to-five weeks would feel like the blink of an eye, with only delirious nausea once carefully roused. The *Lincoln* systems are set up to monitor everything about these sleepers, even the slightest spike in blood pressure.

"The wakers are on their own, aren't they?" I say, closing the distance to the farthest open tank. I can only see the feet at first, toes pointing up. Gradually the rest of the legs and the torso come into view, the lid of the bed no longer obstructing them.

The hands are loose, still imitating sleep, the arms draped over the torso straps, just in case we need to halt rotation and go weightless. The face is surprisingly placid, so much that I actually wonder if he is still alive, despite looking quite pale under his wrinkles and not appearing to breathe.

Three needles protrude from the side of his neck. They look like they might have been jammed in by one fist. I tilt my head to inspect and see that they are sedatives, fully plunged. Scheduled to wake, then put to sleep. A kind of poetry to it.

I don't know how long I stand looking at him, or, rather, looking at the dead body. The person who inhabited has vacated. It's not really Singh anymore, just like Wen isn't Wen and Jerry isn't Jerry.

"And maybe I'm not me."

I have no concept of how long I stand there, or how many times my song loops, always skipping the same word. Apparently, one word, one change in my night song, is all it takes to make me crack when on night-drift. Ironic that music is supposed to help people keep track of things better when day-and-night cycles are artificial or when they're alone too long.

"System," I say, "who woke Doctor Singh?"

"Crewman Doyle, custodian"

"And who turned off Crewman Doyle's six-thirty alarm?"

"Crewman Doyle, custodian."

"And who needs to turn themself in? Put themself to sleep? For the safety of the rest of the crew?"

Crewman Doyle. Obviously.

"Insufficient information. Please clarify."

I open the medical supplies, extract one of the injectors. Leaving the cap on, I put it in my pocket. I try to consider what to say, what to record. I've never recorded a confession before. I wonder if it's hard.

"Come on, Meier," I tell the speaker in my pocket. "We've got some work to do first."

Tasks, self-talk, music. Why not? I'm feeling lucid enough now. And I have tasks to do, custodial tasks. For the safety of the rest of the crew.

I close and seal the port sleeper, according to safety regulations. I check to see that the oxygen mix is correct and that the deep-sleepers are all still safe and healthy, not that I could do much to impact that. Satisfied, I check it off my list and move on.

The bridge is next. I won't move Wen. I know better than to touch the crime scene and I'm pretty sure that a few hours of normal oxygen will not compromise the body for future investigation. I activate the wall panel and reset the atmospheric controls, so that there is normal oxygen when someone tries to access it. I lower the temperature to a little higher than the refrigerators, because I've never studied human body decomposition and it's better to be safe.

While I consider what, if anything, to do with Jerry, I pull up the crew manifest. I select the captain, the next officer of the watch, one of the sleeping docs, and—what the hell—an engineer. I schedule them all to wake as soon as it is safe to do so. Ironic that I still don't have the authority to call an emergency wake. The ship's systems clearly detect nothing worthy of an emergency wake up, nothing that could significantly threaten the lives of the crew or the success of the mission.

"Except for me." Crewman Doyle, custodian. Murderer. "It just doesn't have the right ring." Psycho. "That's better."

On one hand, I have several hours to figure out how to phrase my confession for the captain to wake up to. On the other, maybe I should do it quickly and get myself sedated, before I have another psychotic episode.

"System, begin recording," I say. "Urgent report. To be delivered to all senior officers."

But nothing comes to mind. I let the time run, the System still recording, while trying to wrap my mind and my mouth around a good opening phrase.

When no preamble occurs to me, I resolve to simply start with my name. I open my mouth to speak.

"Doyle?" I hear from the screen, as if the System is speaking to me. But, no, it's not my voice, not the neutral System's either. Too deep.

I spin and wish I had a weapon—yet another sign of the kind of violent tendencies I've already inflicted on the back of Jerry's head. I'm looking down the corridor, with my back to the bridge, facing a crewman in sleep uniform. Do I think him a shadow, a reflection? No, this figure is clearly taller than me, and under the short, mussed hair is a sympathetic face with a sensible beard.

"Rausch?" I ask the psych in return, a little disbelieving. "Are you really here?"

Yvon Rausch takes a couple of tentative steps toward me, closing the several-meters distance by tiny fractions, like how I would approach a snarling dog. It's like he can tell I'm crazy. Must be my eyes.

"It's me, Doyle," he says, one hand toward me, the other down at his side, hidden from view.

I have to wonder if he's holding another sedative for me. Doesn't seem worth telling him I already have one in my pocket.

"You called a wake up, didn't you? You can hear me, can't you?"

I nod.

"Good. I hear that you're listening to your 'Oceantide.' Feel the vibrations, tell yourself that it's real."

"The track's screwed up, Rausch," I tell him, and—stupidly—I feel my eyes well up with tears for the first time this morning. "It's skipping, and I think that's why—"

"That's okay," he tells me, gently interrupting. His eyes seem to plead with me to stay calm. He has crossed nearly half of the distance. "You know it. Just sing in the gaps."

I take the suggestion as best I can. Through shuddering breaths, sing along with the track and with the psych, "The waves are churning..."

"This heart's yearning," Rausch finishes for me.

My eyes open again, focus on Rausch, and—suddenly—the spinning, dizzying, sickening feeling shuts off. It's replaced by...nothing. "*Learning*," I tell him. "The line is, 'This heart's *learning*.'"

He gives a kind of shrug, like brushing it off without outright disagreeing. "Better the other way," he says.

"Rausch, wait." I hold up a hand now. "When did you wake up?"

"I..." He seems a little confused by the question. "Just a little while ago. Didn't you schedule the System to wake me?"

"From deep." I blink a few times. "It's way too early for you to be—"

"Doyle, you—" He makes a sound, a brief grunt of frustration or something. "Now, listen to me, Doyle, your—your perception of time is—"

"Rausch," I say, every nerve of my wiry, variable-gravity-living *waker's* frame tensed. "Show me your other hand."

Doctor Yvon Rausch, ship psychologist, looks back over his shoulder for a little too long.

With my own pulse drumming in my ears, I can see flecks of reddish brown on his pant leg and the front of his bare feet.

"Oh, Doyle..." He gives a small smile and a shake of his head. It's almost comforting. Then, Rausch pivots and I see a bloodied rod of stainless steel—a simple golf putter pulled from the lounge.

I don't know what my expression is, but Rausch seems to take it badly that I have taken a step back.

"Now, Doyle," he says, and reaches out a hand. "This can still be okay."

But I'm past the point of okay. I juke out of his reach and take off running.

"Dammit, Doyle!" Rausch calls after me. "Just listen and I'll explain everything!"

But I'm not interested in listening to Rausch. Not interested in taking psychological advice from someone who's snapped. After all, it could happen to anyone.

Rausch tries anyway, yelling, "Jerry wouldn't listen to me either. And if I had waited any longer, it would be too late!"

I keep going, barrel through another corridor, shoulder through the next door. I sprint into the mess hall, the biggest room on the *Lincoln*, like pretty much any other barracks cafeteria, but with everything bolted down. I get to a wall panel and swipe it active. As soon as I input my information, it asks if it should continue recording and I select *Yes* just as Rausch bursts in after me.

"Doyle," he says, panting a little. He points the putter and says, "You really don't understand."

"I think I do…" I say quietly. I put my back against the wall panel, looking for anything to grab to defend myself, but every plastic kitchen tool is latched or bolted away. So I take hold of a stability rung, even though the rotational grav is practically Earth normal.

"No, you don't! Jerry wouldn't listen. He laughed when I asked him to help me adjust the heading."

"Okay." I lick my lips. My heart is still racing and my head is throbbing from the shock, but I don't know where to run or what to do. So I try to keep him talking. "And why would you adjust the heading?"

"Because—" Rausch runs one palm across his cheek in exasperation, unpleasantly teasing, then matting the beard hairs. "Because otherwise our star will pass us by. We only have a few more hours to adjust course."

"Our star?" I ask, but I realize before he tells me.

"The guiding light," he says, so plainly it doesn't even sound like a quote. "To pull us through the dead of night."

I open my mouth then shut it again. "So you scheduled yourself an earlier wake up?"

"Yes." His expression turns agreeable once more and he takes a few more steps while I try not to flinch. "Yes, now you're listening."

"But after Jerry, you had to deal with the officer of the watch…"

Another step, another smile. "You know Wen. She never would have agreed."

"And Doctor Singh? An unfortunate loose end?"

The psych begins to chuckle. I feel a chill, but I don't lose my grip. I can hold things behind my back, too.

Rausch shakes his head. "I admit I jumped the gun on that one. Singh is not—well, not as level-headed as us. Wouldn't have understood and would have had the authority to confine me, which I realized just before…" He looks at his empty hand, opens and closes it as if reliving the sensation of the syringes grasped in a fist. "Took me a bit to get my bearings again."

"So… what's the plan now?" I ask, my feet rooted to the floor in shock, confusion, and probably more curiosity than is appropriate. "What was the point if you still need three people? You can't correct the heading in time. There are just two of us, and you're—" I stop short of calling the man insane; after all, he has the weapon.

"It's not a loss yet." He's panting as he takes another step toward me, reaching out with the empty hand, begging me to consider. "See, I believe in fate. We still have their fingerprints."

I control my gasp and gag reflexes simultaneously, but I still picture how Rausch might employ a severed hand. I'm wondering how he'll bypass the two-factor authentication, but once again, Rausch preempts this.

"And I knew—I just *knew*—you'd have Jerry's password."

The sudden clarity is like swimming up through a sheet of ice and taking a first full breath of air—and with it the absolute certainty that Rausch would be willing to kill me if I protested or denied knowledge. Hell, I'd bet he's willing to try to bank the ship in a futile effort to reach his star if I delay too long. I may not know all of the physics, but I've heard the warnings, the risk of shredding the ship if we try to alter course too quickly.

"Okay," I say. "You got me. You're right."

"You see!" He triumphantly lifts both arms, seemingly unaware that he is still holding a murder weapon. "Come, let's go collect Jerry." He gestures to the door but doesn't turn to leave.

I don't move; I want one final confirmation. "One thing I don't understand. The System says I turned off my own alarm."

"Oh… yeah." He's standing maybe five steps from me and beginning to chuckle. "I'm sorry about that. A doctor probably shouldn't use his patient's password…"

I draw in a sharp breath through the nose. "Thanks for the apology." Then, as quickly and clearly as I can manage, I say, "System! Halt rotation—emergency override, Crewman Doyle, ship custodian."

"What?! Don't you dare!"

But I've already dared. With my fingerprint authorization and the power vested in me as a deep-space custodian of the starship *Lincoln,* I trigger a sudden slowing of our vessel's spin. Metallic scraping sounds above my head as the first rotational breaks are activated but not quickly enough.

Rausch runs at me, putting club raised. I defend my face with one arm, but grab the stability rung with my other hand.

I feel the impact of the rod on my forearm, just above the wrist. I don't hear a dramatic crack when the steel collides but know my hand is out of commission.

That's the worst of it for me. I might have one hurt hand, but I've been swimming in freefall for weeks. Rausch has not. Counterspin jets fire as rotating rings throughout the ship grind to a halt as programmed.

The violent shift into micro-g sends Rausch flying from his own sprinting momentum. He crunches into the wall and the golf club spins away, where it transfers a red smear of drying blood against the ceiling.

While Rausch struggles with pain and disorientation, I smoothly push in his direction. I have removed the cap from the sedative.

He's barely opened his eyes before I've closed the distance. Unarmed, off-balance, and in pain, he's incapable of dodging a superior combatant with home-field advantage.

I find an easy opening, and the needle slides into his arm without resistance. Then I push off of him, sending the man spinning toward the center of the room with no knowledge of how to right himself. I find the safety of a wall rung, without needing to catch my breath. Perhaps I exaggerate, but, for the first time in a long time, I'm so grateful that I go to bed and wake up in zero-g every day.

Rausch only has a few more seconds to grunt and writhe before his movements grow languid, much more fitting for the relaxed cadence of my song, on low, but a constant loop.

"System," I call out, "save recording of events, authorized by Crewman Doyle. Send copy to all senior officers."

I see the screen adjust in acknowledgement. A notification flashes, but I'm too far away to see. Maybe it's asking me to file a report about the decision to halt rotation; maybe it's telling me that my authorization will be frozen if I use another uncorroborated override. Right now, I don't care.

I know that I need to get the floating, unconscious Rausch strapped into something secure, and I cringe at the thought of dealing with a zero-gravity Jerry Klein situation. I really should figure out how to restore the song to its original form, the way it was before Yvon Rausch snipped a piece out of it.

First thing's first, however. "System," I call out, "I'd like to change my access password."

While no one can fake my fingerprint, I now realize it wasn't wise to make my password the title of the song I listen to on loop. I wonder if Jerry's is as obvious to guess.

Oceantide
By Jackson Meier

The ground is firm
Solid beneath my feet
My heart is sure
Certain it won't retreat
But the waves are raging
Weather's changing
The water's telling me to just let go
And plunge below

(refrain)

I set my course by oceantide
Hoping to reach the other side
My time won't be denied—no, sir
Searching for a guiding light
To pull me through the dead of night
I've never swam across an ocean so wide

When there's no sign
Or signal to show my way
A way I'll find
Appearing as clear as day
But the waves are churning
This heart's learning
The water's telling me what I need to know
To plunge below

(refrain)

(bridge)
I'll close my eyes…
Let the waves roll by

(refrain)

Chocolate, With Sprinkles

Stephen Leigh

Young Kayla

Kayla loved spending time with her father Hakim, a biology professor at Michigan State University. She especially loved when he would bring her into the lab, where he was studying sea lampreys in from the Great Lakes. She peered into all the tanks lining the walls, each with different species of fish, eels, shellfish, and other marine creatures.

"Look into this holding pool," he told her on one such trip, when she was perhaps nine. "There are hundreds of gallons of water in there. Do you see all the lampreys we also have in there?" She nodded; there were more lampreys than she could possibly count, scattered everywhere around the tank, some of them attached to the glass sides with their vacuum-like, toothy mouths; more of them clinging to the rocks and gravel on the bottom of the tank. When she showed her schoolmates pictures of her father's sea lampreys, they shuddered and said they were ugly, slimy monsters, but Kayla found them interesting and almost cute, except that she knew they often killed the fish to which they attached themselves.

Her father held up a small vial of pale brown liquid. To Kayla, it looked to contain no more than a spoonful. "Now, watch what happens when I put this in one corner of the tank. You should stand back if you want to stay dry." He went over to the nearest corner, uncorked the vial, and poured it into the tank. For several seconds, nothing happened at all, but suddenly all the lampreys released from their current holds, the entire wriggling mass of them surging toward that corner, slamming against the glass so vigorously that droplets showered her father as they thrashed the water. He grinned at her.

"It's a pheromone," he said. "A smell. It's how they attract each other in the water. Lampreys are very sensitive to scents. It's one of the ways we remove lampreys from the lakes and streams now. Put a few drops of this in a cage; they'll swim in and be trapped and we can move them elsewhere."

"I don't smell anything," Kayla told him.

"That scent only works on sea lampreys," he answered. "But you can find something that will attract nearly every living thing. Isn't chocolate your favorite ice cream?"

"Oh, yes," Kayla answered immediately. "With sprinkles."

"I knew that would be your answer. So, if I wanted to catch you, *meri jaan*, I'd put a bowl of chocolate ice cream with sprinkles in a cage and when you came to eat it...*gotcha!*" With that, her father snatched her up in his hands and spun her around as she laughed. He hugged her hard and set her down again. "Now let's go find some of that chocolate ice cream."

"With sprinkles?"

He kissed her forehead and put her down. "Absolutely with sprinkles."

Transit 1, -47 minutes

Kayla felt the ship vibrating through the soles of her shoes, or maybe that was only a reflection of her own tension. She flexed her feet inside the flight suit's boots and toggled on the suit microphone, pressing the stud on the roof of her mouth with her tongue.

"Kayla here," she said. "According to Control, this end of the wormhole will open exactly 47 minutes from now with a window of 135 minutes before our end collapses. If we miss it, we'll be waiting another four decades for the next opportunity. So...let's have a systems check, please."

"Systems check commencing," the base AI answered. Then a few seconds later: "Systems check completed. Green all across the board, Commander Ghazali."

"Did you expect anything else, Kayla?" That was Ajit, her husband, one of the four other crew-members of *Zheng He*. He laughed, his amusement loud in her ear, followed by good-natured chuckles from the others. "We're good to go. Besides, we'll be back here in just a little more than two hours, having seen things no other human has ever seen before."

"What about the thruster readings we were worried about on the initial check?"

"Tomas re-adjusted the settings. They're optimal again."

Kayla knew Ajit was right. Everything had been tested and tested again, all the systems triple redundant. They had the vids from the last opening of the stable wormhole when they'd sent drones through, twenty-nine years prior, though Kayla had only been six years old then, and the achingly brief one before *that* which had startled the Europa Base staff and nearly been missed entirely except for a few vids from the cameras trained on where the wormhole's entrance would appear.

The Europa wormhole had announced itself in the mid-21st century with gravitational waves that rippled through the solar system, detected by LIGO, the Laser Interferometer Gravitational Wave Observatory. The sudden gravity waves caused various space agencies to send probes to Europa, the data suggesting the existence of a stable, periodic wormhole. *That* eventually produced a joint US/European/Chinese/Russian manned mission to Europa to establish the research base there.

They would uncover what lay so tantalizingly close, at the far end of a tunnel torn occasionally through time and space: a planet achingly similar to our own Earth. From the stars in the planet's night sky, they even knew its location: orbiting the red dwarf star TOI 700, a little more than 101 light-years from Earth in the constellation of Dorado. A probe launched through the Europa end of the wormhole at its second opening displayed a world alive with vegetation and liquid water under a dim, reddish sky, as well as intriguing glimpses of colorful life scurrying through the undergrowth.

A world rather similar to Earth itself.

This time, they would send not just unmanned drones but people through the wormhole. During their few hours on the planet, Kayla's crew of five volunteers would look to explore and record more of this world—christened Chúndù; "purity" in Chinese—though they'd remain inside their ship and in their flight suits for the duration, breathing filtered and sterilized air, letting the drones be their eyes, ears, and hands.

She felt Ajit's suited hand cover her own on the arm of her flight chair. She smiled at him through the curve of the helmet and brought her other hand over to his, patting it once before releasing him. She toggled on her mic again. "We can't be too careful, Ajit, so forgive me a touch of paranoia."

His teeth flashed behind his own helmet. "You're forgiven."

"Good. Now, we all have a checklist to go through before the hole opens, so let's get to it. Once though the wormhole, we'll all be too busy looking around and examining a whole new world to be thinking about checklists."

Agreeable chuckles echoed through her suit headphones from the rest of the crew.

"All right," Kayla said. "To business, then. Tomas, you're PTC. Payload?"

"Payload is go, Commander…"

Transit 1, 205 Minutes

Kayla woke to a painful memory of blood and chaos, with wreckage and a strange landscape around her. She groaned as she pushed herself upright in a flight chair that was leaning sickeningly to the right. The glass of her helmet was crazed with cracks and she could hear the wailing of alarms throughout the *Zheng He*.

She struggled to remember what had happened, but the last memory she had was the Europa end of the wormhole opening on schedule and engulfing the *Zheng He* and its cradle in what appeared to be a distorted sphere of storm-wracked colors. The opening rotated nauseatingly as Kayla turned to stare at the open mouth of the wormhole. The rings of the wormhole's throat closed around the ship, elongating the view like a gravity lens: a short tunnel with another sphere attached at the far end.

"Engines engaged," Kayla could remember calling out to the crew as the translucent touchscreen in front of her pulsed with light. She swept her hand over gauges. "Here we go then."

Then the chaos, pain, and blackness...

Ajit, the rest of the crew... She tongued on her mic, relieved when she heard a click in response. "Ajit?" she called. "Tomas? Linda? Niall? Europa Base? Can anyone hear me?"

She remembered deck plates chattering under her feet as she felt the ship start to move. In the videos recorded via the unmanned drones that had been sent through before, the thundercloud rings of the throats moved with them, the sphere at the terminus of the throat growing larger as the drone approached the Chúndù opening: another world in a part of the galaxy an impossible distance away, yet only a bit more than an Earthly quarter-of-an-hour's travel through the wormhole.

She was staring out at Chúndù now, steaming in a steady rain that dripped down the viewports of the ship. She blinked blood away from her eyes, grimacing with the movement. The continuing wails of alarms stabbed at her like a dozen knives into the burgeoning headache.

The dual throats of the wormhole weren't visible anywhere. Kayla felt her stomach lurch.

"Kayla?"

She gasped at the sound of Ajit's voice. "Ajit! Damn it, *Zheng He*, turn off the fucking racket..." The wailing of the alarms ended in sudden, aching silence. "Ajit, are you okay?"

"I think so." Blinking away more blood, Kayla felt more than saw Ajit's hand grabbing the arm of her flight chair. He pulled himself toward her, then stopped with a stifled cry as his face tightened with pain. "Or maybe not. I either hurt my leg or broke it. I can't really put any weight on it right now. The others?"

Kayla turned on her helmet lamp, looking at Ajit's face through his scratched but unbroken helmet screen, then turning her head so that the light pierced the gloom toward the rear of the ship. She saw the other three crew members still lashed in their flight seats, all of them at an uncomfortable angle to the deck. Linda and Niall were beginning to stir, she noticed. But Tomas...

Just by looking at him, she knew he was dead. His head was cocked disturbingly on his shoulder. And there was far too much blood spattered on the inside glass of his helmet. She couldn't see Tomas' face at all.

"Ajit, my timer display is gone. Do you have the mission time?"

There was a pause and a sigh that told Kayla more than she wanted to know. "It's saying we're 205 minutes in." Then, his voice solemn. "Which means the wormhole closed again 70 minutes ago."

So we're not going back until the wormhole opens again in forty years...

"Understood," she told Ajit. She reached up and twisted the neck ring of her helmet, breaking its seal. Ajit said nothing, knowing what that signified but not yet doing the same himself. Kayla couldn't decide if it was fright or disapproval that she saw in his eyes.

She lifted the helmet from her head and tossed it aside, letting it fall noisily to the deckplates, then took in a breath as she explored the tender cut on her forehead with a tentative forefinger. The air tasted odd, full of flavors and scents for which she had no words; the light was dim and orangish-red. "I need you to help me get out of this chair so I can grab a medkit and see to your leg. Then we have to find out if Linda and Niall need any help and see what we can salvage. We're going to be here awhile..."

Transit 2, 22 minutes

"There's no one here," Thabo said. "Which is what was expected. No one's left at all. All this time, effort, and expense of a rescue mission was just...wasted."

"That's entirely the wrong attitude," Aaliyah told him, her voice sharp with annoyance. "We *know* that the *Zheng He* had a catastrophic thruster failure on the Chúndù side, which was why it never returned. That's one piece of the puzzle, but far from the only piece we came here to discover. Let start with this one: we *don't* know that everyone in the crew is dead, not without bodies, and our probes have found no remains at all in the wreckage, so maybe they were able to walk away. Maybe they're still out there somewhere. They had four decades or more here; maybe they even have children and grandchildren at this point. There are so many questions to answer in the little time we have here, so let's get to work."

From behind his helmet in the acceleration chair next to her, Thabo gave Aaliyah a roll of his eyes, his mouth twisted in a tight moue of disagreement. "Remains or not, I also don't see signs here that anyone survived the 'failure,' do you? No shelters, no buildings, no farm fields. Local carrion feeders could have dragged the bodies elsewhere. I mean, just *look* at this."

The wreckage of the *Zheng He* sprawled across the landscape in front of their ship, largely overgrown in vines and undergrowth, skeletal ribs poking up though the strange foliage. The planet was absorbing the *Zheng He*, taking it into itself. Aaliyah frowned as she stared at the panorama: if she'd been marooned here, she would have tried to remain in the same general area, knowing that when the wormhole opened again, this was where a ship looking for them would certainly emerge. That there was no one here and no sign of habitation anywhere nearby disturbed her, though she wasn't going to admit that to Thabo.

Chúndù held abundant life and no one knew how long it had existed and evolved. Astrophysicists and theoretical physicists both asserted a wormhole of the Europa/Chúndù type required exotic material that didn't exist naturally. In turn, that suggested they'd been constructed to deliberately tie these two locations together.

There were all manner of speculations about what that implied. Not long after the existence of the stable wormhole was known, a popular entertainment company had created a holostream about ancient travelers from Chúndù arriving on Earth and interacting with our early ancestors, even to the point of interbreeding with them. The holostream had been mostly a semi-erotic soap opera; no one took such fanciful tales seriously. Certain Aaliyah didn't.

Even though they'd glimpsed alien animal life on Chúndù, despite the theories of the scientists, none of their excursions had detected signs of current or past occupation by another intelligent species.

"Thabo," Aaliyah said, "send out a couple probes for both of us. Let them snoop around."

Thabo gave what might have been a faint sigh. "Activating probes."

Two displays lit up on either side of Aaliyah's visor; two beeps indicated sound was on and the video and audio from the probes was being recorded as well. Aaliyah watched Chúndù slide by on either side as the probes moved outward from their ship and into the foliage beyond. "Anything?" she heard Thabo ask.

"Nothing yet. You?"

"Same. I'm getting life indications, mostly on infrared, but nothing un—"

"*Wait!* Thabo, quick! Grab my feed from Probe 4."

For a moment, Thabo was quiet. Then: "Aaliyah, is that…?"

Aaliyah stared at the image on her visor. She had the camera zoom in on the figure moving toward them through the undergrowth. The face was undeniably human and female in appearance, though she wondered at the thick ridges that emerged from the clothing she wore. They climbed the woman's long neck on either side and there was an unnatural swelling around her hips. The woman had noticed the probe; she stopped, staring directly at them.

She waved at the probe.

Facial recognition suggests that this is Commander Kayla Ghazali, the ship's AI said in their ears. Aaliyah shook her head. That didn't seem possible— Kayla had been in her mid-thirties when the *Zheng He* went through the wormhole, which would make her in her late seventies now, yet the face that Aaliyah was looking at was unlined and youthful, if she ignored the neck ridges and strangely thick shelf of a waist.

Aaliyah toggled on Probe 4's speakers. "Hello? This is Europa Mission Commander Aaliyah Furaha. Can you understand me? Are you from the *Zheng He?*"

A laugh answered, with a flash of white teeth. Umber skin wrinkled with amusement. "Why, yes, I am. I was the commander. Kayla Ghazali."

Transit 2, 31 minutes

"I should tell you that I've lied. Or at least hidden the full truth from you. I'm not exactly who you believe I am."

Aaliyah gazed at the woman on the other side of the sparkling boundary of the bio-barrier placed at the open end of the ship's small cargo hold. Aaliyah and Thabo were sitting on chairs in the hold; Kayla was seated comfortably on the grassy clearing just outside the open hold doors. "Are you saying now that you're *not* Kayla Ghazali?" Aaliyah asked.

That brought a quick, fleeting smile that touched the woman's lips and vanished. "Oh, that's my name, yes. But it's more…*complicated* than that. I'm not entirely Kayla or I'd have been long dead before you came here looking for us. You know or you suspect that, which frightens you, and that's why you've made certain your bio-barrier is working. You don't want to breathe the same air I'm breathing."

Aaliyah didn't deny the truth of that; neither did Thabo, sitting alongside her. "So explain what you mean by 'complicated.'"

"Unless things have changed, you have, what, 135 Earth minutes from the time the Europa end of the wormhole opened before this end of the wormhole collapses again, trapping you here as it did my crew. You don't have *time* to listen to our entire history on Chúndù. None of us ever wrote it down; the four of us who survived *Zheng He's* passage through the wormhole were too busy trying to just stay alive. And, if I'm not mistaken, you *won't* take any of us back to Earth except under strict quarantine, which would last the rest of our lives—or until the wormhole opens again." Kayla touched the ridges of her neck with her hands. "After all, at this point, we're no longer even the same species."

"You talk of 'us.' How many of you are there?" Thabo asked.

Aaliyah saw Kayla's gaze flick over to him momentarily before returning to Aaliyah's face. "There are now three left of the original crew. Me, Niall, and Linda. We're all in good health. Tomas died when *Zheng He* crashed. My husband Ajit sadly passed away fifteen or so Earth years after we arrived." Aaliyah heard Kayla's voice catch as she said that; she took a long breath before she finished. "A pack of the proto-jackals here on Chúndù killed him. It's difficult to give you exact times. Neither Chúndù's year nor day length corresponds to Earth's, after all, and we keep Chúndù time."

"Why didn't Niall and Linda come to meet us too?" Aaliyah asked.

Kayla only smiled. "They said to tell you that they have no interest in going back. Neither do I. At this point, they couldn't get here before you need to leave anyway."

That answer made Aaliyah lean back in her chair. *No interest in going back? Why?* But before she could ask the question, Thabo interjected.

"You still haven't answered my original question." Aaliyah noticed that Kayla didn't look at him; her attention remaining on Aaliyah. "Are you three the only people here?"

"No." Now Kayla did look at Thabo. "Let me tell you how it was after we left the *Zheng He*…"

Transit 1: 5 years, 8 months, 26 days
(16.9 Chúndù years)

"Are you sure about this, Kayla?"

Kayla, cradled in the crook of Ajit's shoulder as they lay in the darkness of their bed, stirred. "I removed my hormone implant a week ago. No one's coming for us for nearly another thirty-five years, at best, and that's if Europa Base hasn't been shut down entirely. The distress message *Zheng He* should have sent after transit—assuming the AI managed to do that—won't reach Earth until almost a century from now. In our best-case scenario, in thirty-five years I'll be long past menopause and having a child then will be out of the question. I've talked to Linda; she and Niall have come to the same conclusion. If we're potentially staying here forever, well…"

She felt Ajit stroke her hair, then his hand moved through her hair to her neck and the tree-like strands of the parasite under her skin. "Chúndù is already changing us. What would that mean to a baby? What if this—"

his fingers traced the main line of the trunk that trailed down her side to her hip, where it swelled into a hard ridge that encircled her "—ends up killing us and orphaning our child. Would that be fair?"

Kayla stroked the similar markings on Ajit's body in answer. "I'd tell you to remember the first year or so, before we let Chúndù touch us."

She heard Ajit take a long, shuddering breath in the darkness. She knew what he was remembering. The four of them all feared that they'd survived the *Zheng He's* failure only to quickly perish. There was no way for them to stay isolated from Chúndù; they had no choice but to breathe this air, drink the water, and try to find sustenance.

They had no choice but to let Chúndù become part of them.

The twin specters of dysentery and starvation stalked them. Everything they tried to eat made them sick; when parasitic worms invaded their bodies—from the water or the food or the earth or air of Chúndù itself, they never knew—they raided the medical stores to find something, *anything*, to kill the parasites, and that just made them increasingly weak and ill. The native life, the proto-jackals especially, were sometimes aggressive; they all suffered bites and wounds that became infected. And their stores of antibiotics were limited and too often simply useless, unable to affect the Chúndù bacteria.

It was clear to all of them that they were going to die here, far too soon.

It was Kayla who gave up fighting the worms first. She refused to use more of their dwindling medical supplies and simply let the worms invade her body. She could feel herself changing as a result, but to her surprise she found that change beneficial. Slowly, over a period of several weeks, she felt distinctly healthier, no longer ill and weak. She could eat and digest at least some of the local plants without vomiting or nausea. She managed to convince Ajit to follow her example, then Linda and Niall. Not long after, they had all largely recovered their health, though their bodies were undeniably being changed as a result.

And now strange dreams and half-understandable whisperings in their heads haunted them.

"This is what you want, love?" Ajit asked, whispering in the dark. "Truly?"

"Yes," Kayla answered, just as softly. She slid her hand lower on his body. She stopped talking, kissing him deeply and bringing her leg over to straddle him. "This is what I want, no matter what happens afterward."

Transit 2, 53 minutes

"That was how it started," Kayla told Aaliyah and Thabo. "My first child, Elissa, was the result. Linda and Niall's boy Eamon was next. More would follow, for both me and Linda."

"You've had children here?" Aaliyah could feel surprise widen her eyes. "Yes."

"And how many more of these children are there now?" Thabo asked.

Kayla ignored him. She looked at Aaliyah on the other side of the bio-barrier, hands in her lap, waiting and silent. Aaliyah gazed back at her, at the smile that lifted the corners of Kayla's lips. *She believes Thabo is asking the wrong questions*, Aaliyah realized. *What aren't we understanding? What does* she *think is more important for us to know?*

"You should know that I almost didn't come here to talk to you at all," Kayla continued. "Niall felt we should just forget about the wormhole and let everyone believe we were dead. Maybe he was right. For the time being, anyway."

Aaliyah's head moved back in surprise at that. "For the time being?" *What does that mean?*

She toggled on the ship's AI: *How long until the wormhole opens again?* she asked, *sotto voce*. The answer came after a short pause: *The next opening will be in 56 years, Commander. The current hypothesis is that the intervals between openings will continue to grow increasingly longer because the exotic material that created them is decaying.*

Aaliyah left her chair, walking over to the bio-barrier until she felt the pressure of it pushing her back. She looked out at Kayla and at Chúndù. *So much we don't know, and we have so little time to talk…* "According to our AI, Kayla, you should be seventy-seven Earth years old now. In all likelihood, you'll no longer be *living* the next time the wormhole opens—more than a half-century from now. Either that or you'll be in your hundred and thirties."

Kayla chuckled. "The one truth about life is that it never remains the same, Commander. Life will evolve and change, as it always has. Just look at me, for instance. As I said, I'm not really the same species as you at this point. That means I may have a different life expectancy as well. So who knows? I might still be around then."

"You also said that the worms gave you strange dreams and whisperings in your heads," Aaliyah said, and saw Kayla's smile deepen. *Ah, that's what she thinks we should be asking about.* "Are you saying that these worms are sentient, that they communicate with you and you with them?"

"Yes," Kayla answered. "I'm more than only Kayla. We are *all* more. And if you stay here, you'll be more also or you'll be dead."

Aaliyah heard Thabo take in a hissing breath behind her. "Is that a threat?"

Kayla's gaze went past Aaliyah to Thabo and back again. "No threat. Just a fact. It was a choice we all made. Again, let me go back…"

Transit 1: 6 Earth Years (17.4 Chúndù years)

The dreams came slowly at first, then more often. With them came the voices. Kayla remembered those dreams vividly: the creatures gliding out from the mouth of the new wormhole. They were nothing human or even humanoid, but were strangely compelling and beautiful in their own way, hovering over the ground of Chúndù like airborne jellyfish trailing long strands sparking electric blue. The strands left shimmering, gelatinous traces wherever they stroked the ground or the foliage; where the strands touched, they left behind wriggling, twisted worms that dropped to the ground and quickly burrowed below the surface.

The massive carapaces of the aliens glowed as if their translucent bodies were illuminated from within by shifting yellow-orange light. They sang to each other as they drifted, their melodies airy and harmonious. The voices came into focus in Kayla's head: *"We knew you would come. It's why we create the world-mouths. It's why we're here."*

In the bed, waking up the next day, Kayla began to tell Ajit about her dream, sitting up as she stroked the swollen mound of her belly, where she could feel their child moving beneath her fingers. "It was the strangest dream. It felt so *real* when it was happening. There were…"

He held up a hand to stop her. "Hold on, I think I might know. You dreamed of glowing, huge jellyfish. Wondrous, magical creatures of the air. They were singing to each other and to us. Telling us that they knew we'd come here, that they *wanted* us to come."

"We had the same dream…"

Ajit gave a short laugh with no amusement in it at all. He leaned over and kissed her belly, cradling her protectively. "It appears that way."

Later that morning, when Linda and Niall came to Kayla and Ajit's half of the communal shelter they'd built from local stones mortared with mud, Kayla and Ajit would discover that the other couple had also shared their dream.

"How is that even possible?" Linda asked. She was also heavily pregnant, only a few weeks behind Kayla. They were gathered in the communal shelter's large common room with a fire crackling in the hearth; the weather had turned sharply colder with the Chúndù winter. Nial and Ajit were sipping fermented yellownut milk; the two women were drinking tea brewed from sweet-sap tree leaves.

"I've a thought as to how," Niall answered. His forefinger lifted, tracing the hard ridge from his neck to where the veins branched off onto his chest.

"You're suggesting that the burrowing worms from the aliens' tentacles are the same parasitic creatures inside us?" Kayla took a long swallow of her tea. It tasted sweeter than usual.

"I have to think it's possible if not probable," Niall responded. "Kayla, I know we need the worms; we'd all be dead otherwise. But…what if the worms also communicate with each other, and are trying to do the same with us? What if *that's* why we all shared the same dream?"

"If you're right, there's nothing we can do about it now," Kayla answered. "They're inside us, we can't remove them, and we *do* know what happens when they're not present: we get sick and ill and we eventually die. We all get the same strange dreams—so what? Sharing dreams doesn't hurt us." She shrugged, still caressing the slope of her belly. Ajit and Niall both watched her.

"I'm thinking about you and Linda and the children you're having," Ajit said. "We don't know what the worms mean for our offspring. It's even possible they're infected with them already."

"And the only way we'll find out is after they're born." Kayla glanced at Linda, who gave her a quick nod. "Which will be soon enough, for both of us."

Transit 2, 70 minutes

"We would continue to have similar shared dreams," Kayla told Aaliyah and Thabo. "We still do. And so do our children."

"You're saying these worms are sentient?" Aaliyah asked. She looked quickly over to Thabo, lifting one shoulder.

"I'm saying *more* than that. I'm saying they're the people who created the wormhole, the ones we've dubbed 'the Builders'—or, at least, a part of them. I know you're thinking that's insane, that the worms have addled our minds. That's what Niall told me you'd be thinking." Kayla rubbed her neck ridge as she spoke; Aaliyah didn't know if the gesture was a deliberate reminder or not.

"Neither of us think you're addled, Commander," Aaliyah said. "You sound entirely calm and reasonable to me, and I've no doubt that you believe what you're saying to be true. But I—we—still have no evidence that what you're suggesting *is* true, that you've been…" Aaliyah paused, choosing her next word carefully. "…*chosen* by a parasite that once also was part of the race that created the wormhole."

"If I *wanted* to go back to Europa Base with you, would you take me? I know how I'd answer if our positions were reversed: 'Hell, no.'" Kayla laughed. "You can't risk it. Can't risk bringing us back even to Europa Station because of what we might be carrying. Am I right?"

Aaliyah nodded. Her hands pressed against the rubbery resistance of the bio-barrier. "Yes." Just the single word. Then: "Tell me, since we don't have much time left, what—in your opinion—are these aliens who built the wormhole? More importantly, *why* did they do it*?*"

"Those are excellent questions. Do you know what my father did?"

The answer came to Aaliyah and Thabo through the AI's database. "He was a biologist, doing research on invasive species in the Great Lakes between the States and Canada."

"That's correct. His specialty was sea lampreys. Lampreys are parasites, at least once in the cycle of their lives. Humans carry around intestinal parasites as well—some are beneficial and essential to our health. My father always argued that sea lampreys provided benefits also: bringing valuable nutrients into freshwater systems; providing a valuable source of food for a variety of birds, fish, and mammals; restoring and enhancing stream bed structure, which benefits other species. In the Great Lakes, admittedly, lake trout were impacted by non-native landlocked sea lampreys, and that was an issue that required control."

"Why are you wasting time talking about sea lampreys?" Thabo asked. "What do they have to do with understanding Chúndù and your situation?"

"Please let me continue and be patient," Kayla answered. "The wormholes were a lure to get us to come to Europa, and perhaps to trap us here on Chúndù, or at least to entice us to explore it. Back home, my father used lamprey scent to trap them; I suspect that's what the Builders are doing as well, here and for all we know elsewhere. Our dreams tell us they came from somewhere even further away, through another wormhole they created. If you wanted to attract a technological species on the cusp of leaving their home system, wouldn't opening a wormhole do exactly that? Wouldn't that allow you to potentially 'catch' a few and learn about them, especially if they required a local parasite—a part of the Builders— to survive in this environment?"

Aaliyah shivered at the thought. She pressed again on the bio-barrier, as if making certain it was still there as a shield against Chúndù. "To what end?" Aaliyah asked.

Kayla shrugged. "If you went to another world, one already inhabited by a sentient species, you'd want to know all you could learn about them, wouldn't you? If only to ascertain if they were a threat or not. But that's attributing a human response to the Builders; if the dreams they've given us are real, they aren't even vaguely humanoid. Who knows what their true agenda or purpose might be? I certainly don't." She gave Thabo another glance. "But we might come to understand them…if we're patient enough. Me, Linda, and Niall and our children are here, snared in their comfortable trap. If they're still out there, the Builders will eventually come back to see what they caught. I expect that to be soon."

A series of beeps sounded in Aaliyah and Thabo's ears: *Automatic return program is now activated. Please begin mission shutdown operations. You have ten minutes.* "We have very little time left," Aaliyah told Kayla. "We've recorded everything you've told us. Is there anything more you want us to relay back home? Messages to your relatives, perhaps?"

"Why not stay here with us, Commander? Then you'd have all your questions answered. Eventually."

"Or not." Thabo. They could all hear the heat and skepticism in his voice. "You don't know when or if these 'Builders' will come back. You don't even know if the wormhole was intended to attract us or not. You don't really even know if there *are* Builders. Maybe the wormhole's just a natural phenomenon."

"No, I don't know any of that," Kayla admitted. "All I know is what I feel and what our dreams have told us."

"Feelings and dreams aren't enough. Not for me. Not for us." Thabo's gaze went to Aaliyah, still standing against the barrier. "Commander, it's time we started our departure checklist."

Aaliyah didn't answer. Kayla rose from her seated position on the grass. She walked over to the barrier and put her own hand on the other side. Aaliyah matched the gesture, their hands now separated only by the repellant field, which sparked and shimmered under their flesh. Kayla's gaze held Aaliyah's, the woman's eyes caught in the folds of her smile— Kayla might no longer be entirely human, but her eyes...

Aaliyah nodded to her. "Thabo's right," she told Kayla. "It's time for us to go."

"Sometimes feelings and dreams are all we have to hold onto. They feel solid enough to me."

"If you're right, then you can tell us. I'll leave you a transmitter—we'll eventually get your message, whatever it might turn out to be."

Kayla lifted her hand away from Aaliyah's and the bio-barrier and backed away several steps before she stopped. "Will you do me another favor?"

"If I can."

"Whoever comes through the next time, I'd love to have some chocolate ice cream. With sprinkles."

Moving Day

A.M. Giddings

The world seems emptier with each passing year. Over half of my graduating class is gone now, lost on missions or lost to data decay. There are new residents, sure, but not enough to make up for the agents we've lost. Budget cuts was what I was told when I asked the last time. It doesn't really matter. It takes time to build trust and I don't spend enough time in here to do that. Besides, I prefer to spend my downtime learning new things. This time it was stone knapping and basket weaving. The break before that it was advanced materials science. Some of the others think I'm strange for "working" during my downtime, but I got bored of the usual games several lifetimes ago, so this is what I do. When I'm honest with myself, I will admit that even this has begun to pall.

The simulation where we're stored between missions is just so flat. The colors in here are more muted than I remember from my first life and they are certainly more limited than what I get when I'm in a carrier. And they aren't even trying with the scenery anymore. For the last twenty or so years, it's been rows of box-like houses lining straight streets with the occasional anemic tree to break up the monotony. I've heard that there are better simulations running on the newer servers, but we don't rate those.

Even inside the houses we aren't given much in the way of detail. The techs running the simulation once told me that we have only been allotted the minimum number of "personal items" to keep us from going completely insane. Of course, the techs aren't the only ones who can code.

When we realized they weren't going to add more than a handful of new agents to replace the ones who had been terminated, we rewrote the code to get rid of some of the extraneous houses. Now we use the space for more furnishings or art.

Ten hours before the next scheduled jump, chimes rang out through the dead air of the simulation. When I saw that my name was one of the three flashing on the overhead message boards, I felt an almost physical sense of relief. The remaining agents in the system have been hoping to get this call ever since the colony ship reached the target system. I met the others at the transfer point. Chrysanthemum and I have been jumping together for centuries. She and I were from the first class the company academy produced. The trainer for our group was "traditional" in the worst sense of the word and thought that the women in the group should be named after pretty, harmless flowers. So, being contrary, I picked the name Foxglove. I had considered Belladonna briefly, but figured that would be too obvious. He might have caught on and then I'd have been stuck with a name he assigned. Chrysanthemum was similarly minded, though she was a bit subtler. She was afraid of being kicked out at the time, not like now. Iron came from a later class. I've only worked with them a few times, so I don't know them that well. I don't know why they chose Iron for their designation; from what I've seen, it doesn't really suit them. So now we have three agents with reputations for being contrary heading out on the same jump. I should probably worry.

Who am I kidding? I always worry during a transfer. As usual, I accessed the external camera to check up on the techs assigned to our mission. The transfer team was a standard group of ten techs, one of whom was the biological offspring of Arsenic, one of Iron's classmates. For the life of me, I couldn't remember the tech's name, so I've been calling him Arsenic's grandson, even though there should be several greats in front of the grandson bit. The young man in question moved closer to the camera and I noticed the team leader badge on his lapel. I sent the image to the others and Chrysanthemum winced.

"This is going to be a rough ride. I hope you both have backups," she said pessimistically.

"He hasn't lost anyone in the last five years. Be nice," Iron admonished.

Chrysanthemum's attention slid to me, and I said, "He only lost me once. According to the mission record, that planet had a ridiculously strong magnetic field."

"You are too forgiving, Foxglove."

I snorted, but before I could reply, all external stimuli was cut off as our data was reconfigured to the proper quantum state for transfer. One of the techs also sent the specifications for our carriers so we would be familiar with their capabilities.

"Oof, it looks like it's going to be hot." Chrysanthemum pointed to the hafnium carbide coated armor.

"Not necessarily. They could just want us to go exploring volcanoes or maybe they expect a hard landing," Iron said.

"I wouldn't count on anything. This mission was decided on four hundred years ago and you all know what the scans were like back then."

"Oh great, so Arsenic's grandkid is going to be syncing us up with a set of bloody antiques. That makes me feel so much better. Are you sure they aren't trying to retire us?"

"They wouldn't do that." Iron looked shocked at the implication.

I nodded absently as I continued going through the mission briefing. "There are over 10,000 colonists on that ship, assuming there weren't any cryo pod failures. Half of them bought the insurance. If the landing fails, they're out of business."

"Assuming any of the colonists' heirs are still alive to collect. Besides, the insurance wouldn't stop them from trying to kill us through slow data loss," Chrysanthemum said.

"Not helping," I muttered, before closing the data files and turning my attention to the control center.

We felt it when the techs initiated the entanglement. For one tenth of a second, our data occupied both the transfer station computer and the minds of the three robotic carriers that were strapped into the jump seats of a four-hundred-year-old scout ship. Then the transfer was complete and only the thinnest data tethers linked us to the computers on Earth. Within the scout ship, everything was bathed in the red light streaming through the windows from the alien suns. Then it registered that the ship was shuddering around us and I realized that it was already in the planet's atmosphere.

Chrysanthemum realized it, too. "What is wrong with that data glitch?!" she yelled as the scout deployed its chutes and our velocity slowed to something survivable.

I made sure all of the mechanical parts of my new body were functioning, then responded, "He was probably showing off."

Iron grimaced as they checked the condition of their carrier. "I'm going to need some maintenance before we get started. Half of my joints are frozen."

"That's what you get when your carrier has been languishing in storage for centuries. Don't worry, we'll get everything up and running."

The scout touched down, sending up a cloud that momentarily obscured our surroundings. While we waited for the dust to settle, Chrysanthemum and I started scans of our immediate vicinity while Iron started working on their joints. The planet appeared to be habitable. The radiation levels were within the safety range for humans. Chrysanthemum tapped the back of my wrist, drawing my attention to the largish lake about a kilometer away.

"Based on the ambient temperature, it might actually be water," she remarked.

I glanced at her scan, then turned back to my interface so I could run a scan for complex carbon or silicon molecules. I didn't find anything more complex than strings of self-replicating polymers. None of them looked like they would be harmful to the colonists. "Everything looks good here. I think we should go check out that lake first. A decent source of water would make all our lives easier."

Chrysanthemum nodded and we left Iron to deal with their joints. We activated the audio inputs as well as visual and scanned as we walked, for all the good it did us. The only sounds we picked up were the scuff and crunch of the dirt and small rocks underfoot. After hiking over two low, rock-strewn hills that had patches of scree that were hell on our mechanical ankles and knees, we reached the lake. I found more of the moderately complex carbon-phosphorus polymers in liquid that was definitely water. As before, none of the polymers had configurations that matched any known harmful molecule. Chrysanthemum knelt beside the pool and dipped her hand into the liquid.

As she watched the ripples propagate across the surface, she frowned and said, "This is really strange. Everything we've seen so far indicates that this planet is safe and can support humans. No serious mitigations are required. So why send us here? Why risk our data to no purpose?"

I shrugged. "Maybe there is an intermittent threat they want us to deal with?"

Chrysanthemum gave me a dubious look. Then she went silent as she located and reviewed the data file the captain of the colony ship had sent to the scout. "There is nothing here that would suggest such a thing." She sat back, letting the water fall into the lake.

I looked down at her. "Is there something wrong with your carrier?"

She shook her head and leaned back to watch the sky. "No, I just wanted to enjoy the moment. We always seem to be running around trying to keep colonists alive and we rarely get the chance to just hang out."

"You don't think Iron will wonder where we've gotten to?"

"They won't be expecting us for a bit and it's been years since we've had a chance to talk like this. You always avoid us in simulation."

I sat down beside her. "I don't avoid you. There is just nothing left to talk about after four centuries."

"If you're so bored, why do you keep doing this? Why not just retire and find something to do on Earth?"

I picked up a rock and scanned it before skipping it across the surface of the lake. "It isn't that complicated. I still enjoy the challenge of exploring new worlds. Why do you think I reloaded myself into the simulation computer after Arsenic's grandkid killed me? I could have disappeared into the network and found a carrier on Earth to inhabit, but what would be the point of that? I have no living friends or relatives and I'd be out of a job."

She nodded. "I get that. So, do you think they're trying to kill us again?"

"Maybe. We should probably keep that to ourselves for the moment. We could just be paranoid."

Chrysanthemum gave a weird mechanical-sounding snort.

We sat there, keeping a companionable silence while the suns dropped toward the horizon. When the first one dipped below the low mountains beyond the lake, I registered a significant temperature drop. Still, the two of us were reluctant to start our return to the scout. We'd have to send a report back to Earth the moment we got back and my sense that something was off kept getting stronger. I could tell that my partner felt the same way. Eventually, it was the weather that forced our return. Heavy gray clouds moved in, casting an additional pall over the barren landscape. The wind picked up as we got to our feet. Within minutes, it overwhelmed our audio pickups. I rooted through the kit bag we brought with us and found a couple of tightly woven blue and gray hats. I tossed one to Chrysanthemum. We pulled them on, tugging them down over the pickups.

"Stupid, out-of-date carriers," she grumbled.

I nodded. "Truly. We need to move. I'm not sure these carriers are up to a heavy storm."

By the time we reached our ship, a steady rain had started to fall. I scanned it out of an excess of caution and confirmed that it was within the safe pH range for humans. Iron had rigged up a porch-like overhang in the time we'd been gone. We used it to shed the surface water we had accumulated and to wring out our sopping wet hats. Then we stepped inside.

"You two certainly took your time. Did you find anything out of the ordinary?" Iron asked as soon as the hatch slid closed behind us.

I shrugged. "No immediate threats. The atmosphere is within safe parameters, the water is drinkable, radiation levels tolerable, and none of the proto-biologics look harmful."

"So why the hell are we here?" Iron grumbled as they sent the scan data and our observations along their tether to the Earth station techs. "This is not what I signed up for. I got into this for the excitement of solving strange terraforming issues or defending colonists against life-threatening critters. This is a perfectly habitable planet. There is no need for us to be here."

I was about to answer (hopefully with something witty), when I sensed someone upload a virus into my data anchor on Earth. It was seconds away from corrupting my entire data set and I lost one of those seconds to pure abject fear. My thoughts ricocheted around the circuits that made up the carrier's central processor like squirrels trapped in a room with a rabid dog. Then a warning flashed up on my internal display and I knew the others were under attack too. I shifted my gaze outward and saw Iron's expression shift from grumpy and bored to panicked. Chrysanthemum cursed as she turned and tripped over a chair. It dawned on me that someone was trying to destroy all three of us and the others might not have backups. That jolted me into motion.

Thinking fast, I shouted, "Iron, full transfer, now!"

They hesitated as another precious second slipped by. "But we might never be able to go home again!"

"Better stuck here than dead," I said, suppressing a shudder as I felt more of my data slipping away. Iron still didn't move. Out of time, I pushed past them and transferred all of our data to the carriers' onboard computers, abandoning the quantum state that allowed us to exist in both places. As I did, I grabbed everything I could—everything that wasn't corrupted by the virus—from the Earth-based system where we had been stored.

Iron had fallen to their knees when the quantum state collapsed and Chrysanthemum was still struggling to extricate herself from the furniture. Once they'd both managed to get to their feet, they turned and stared at me.

"Wha—what happened?" Iron finally managed.

I had to fight to keep my emotions from overloading my carrier as I reviewed the data I'd stolen. "Someone tried to kill us."

"W—why?," Iron stuttered, accidentally crushing the chair they were using to brace themselves.

At the same time, Chrysanthemum growled, "It was Arsenic's grandkid, wasn't it?"

For the longest time I could not pull my gaze away from the string of error messages that scrolled across my internal display, each one hammering home the point that there was no going back. "I don't know. It could have been. He was in the control room, but I can't see him doing this. It's one thing to accidentally kill someone during a difficult jump, it's quite another to deliberately destroy three agents."

Chrysanthemum looked up from steadying Iron, the crushed chair dangling forgotten in her hand as she stared at me in disbelief. "Why do you keep defending that ungrateful little shit?"

"Would you believe latent maternal instincts?"

Chrysanthemum gave me another one of her odd mechanical snorts. "No."

A new set of error messages came up on my internal display. I realized that if I couldn't give them some answers or something else to focus on, the stress, anger, and shock they were feeling was going to overload their carriers. I found an undamaged chair and sat down. "What do you know about Arsenic's last mission?"

The others exchanged a look and Chrysanthemum crossed her arms over her chest. "Not much. I was light-years away at the time and the company sealed the records."

Iron said quietly, "The team leader lost his mind and crushed Arsenic's carrier. You tried to save him. "

That stopped me and I stared at Iron.

"I may have hacked the mission record," Iron muttered as they settled down next to their interface and plugged into the system. "He was a friend, okay?" they added, hunching defensively.

Chrysanthemum clapped them on the back. "I didn't know you had it in you, kid. "Iron flinched away from her and she turned her attention to me. "So, if you tried to save Arsenic, why does the kid have it in for you?"

"Stories get distorted over time and unless Arsenic was freakishly good at hacking—" I gave Iron an ironic salute. "—then he would have no way of learning the real story behind that mission. But if he wanted me dead because of Arsenic, why send the virus after you two as well? Also, why wait until I was out on a mission? He could have easily wrecked my data and made it look like an accident when he was still a maintenance coder for the simulation."

"He worked on the simulation?" Chrysanthemum straightened in surprise.

"Yes, for the first two years after he graduated from the training academy."

"And you know this how?"

"We talked about a lot of things after my copy was loaded back into the system and he finally stopped apologizing." I pulled my legs up to my chest and, anticipating her next question, added, "I may have also run a background check and psych evaluation on him as soon as I was reactivated. "

"Hmm. There goes a perfectly good theory." Chrysanthemum tapped her finger against her face. I could tell that she was still skeptical, but her murderous rage had waned and she was no longer on the verge of blowing out her carrier's neural pathways.

I checked Iron's data and it looked better as well. "Look, it doesn't matter. They failed and we're alive, more or less."

"How can you be so calm about this?" Chrysanthemum demanded, her anger flaring again.

"Because the alternative is blowing out the irreplaceable neural circuits of this antique carrier and dying for real." Startled, Chrysanthemum checked her system diagnostics and groaned.

Frustrated, Iron pushed away from the interface, which had remained stubbornly unresponsive. "So what do we do? Can either of you re-establish the link? I'm having no luck."

"No, I never got around to taking those classes."

Chrysanthemum shook her head at the same time.

I could tell that Iron wasn't ready to give this up so I pulled out the argument I was hoping I wouldn't have to use. "Whoever tried to kill us might still be monitoring the computers back in the control center. We're safest where we are. I think we should forget about Earth for the time being and do the job we were sent here to do. We make sure this colony survives."

Chrysanthemum frowned. "Why? They don't need us, and I can think of better ways to spend my time."

I stepped forward and gripped her arm and Iron's shoulder. "If these colonists survive, we survive. I assume you both want that."

Chrysanthemum shook her head and broke away. "I am not in the right frame of mind for babysitting just now."

"Look, between the three of us, we'll figure this out, given time. But we won't have that time if we lose our colonists."

Iron, who'd been quiet throughout this little exchange, finally asked, "Do you think one of the colonists might be able to restore our links?"

I shrugged. "Maybe."

"If I ever do go back, I'm going to make those murderous bastards pay," Chrysanthemum muttered and I got a sudden mental image of her ghosting into the techs' transports and causing them to crash spectacularly

"I wasn't thinking about going back," Iron said, bringing me back to the present. "I don't love the simulation so much that I would risk death just to get back to it. But if there's someone aboard the colony ship who can set up entanglements, then maybe I'll be able to go on missions where I am actually useful. I mean, that's why I signed up for this in the first place. I don't care why someone tried to kill us. I just don't want to get stuck here."

Chrysanthemum looked at both of us as if we were crazy, then threw her hands up in exasperation. "You two are hopeless. So what do we do now?"

"Now, we start setting up the shelters, water pumps, and hydroponics. We get this place ready for our colonists, who should be landing in about twenty standard hours. Once they are settled, we can discuss our next steps." I pushed my own fear and outrage aside and started to work the problem. There was time enough to deal with my uncertain future after I dealt with my deeply uncertain present.

Chrysanthemum momentarily looked like she wanted to argue with me, then she got a good look at my current readings and threw her hands up in the air. "Fine, you win."

Pushing away from the bulkhead, Iron said, "Okay, then. Let's start unpacking." They reached into one of the overhead storage lockers and pulled out the rolled-up rug that some daring company employee had put into every scout ship they could get their hands on four hundred years ago. They cut the tab, opened the hatch, and spread the rug out on the rock-strewn ground outside. The light streaming out from the windows and hatch reflected off of the blocky script on the rug, making the words "Home Sweet Home" gleam. It was a little crooked and Chrysanthemum bent down to straighten it. For the first time in I don't know how many years, I wanted to smile.

This place wasn't home, not yet, but it could be.

Like Manna from Heaven Dark

Auston Habershaw

You don't quite know how much blood is in the human body until it's all out there. In zero G, that goes triple. The guy we'd shot was spinning, end over end, under the harsh light of the ship's spinal corridor, the blood arcing from him like flares from a hemorrhaging star. A sphere of dark red globules was forming—its own star-system. It was awful to look at and I couldn't look away.

"Well, he is definitely dead." Uppinder checked the chamber on his carbine. "I'm out, by the way."

I knew he was out, just like he knew I was out. TRACI was telling me all about it—a whisper in my ear, a display thrown up on the contacts in my eyes. How many rounds we'd fired, how many injuries we'd sustained, our pulse rate—the whole thing. Even right then, as I was looking down the hall at the man we'd murdered, she was pointing out all the spots where there could be an ambush, all the places I could take cover.

I shook my head, cancelling TRACI's advice—a ship like this wouldn't have more than one or two security officers and there was no sign of anybody else around.

I could see Uppinder was getting the same advice from TRACI I was; his eyes went to the same places she'd tagged for me. He oriented his body in the same way she advised me to, as well—back to the wall, entrances to the corridor in easy view. She was inside us both, doing her job, making us better pirates.

Sorry, *privateers.*

We each pulled a spare magazine from our harness and reloaded automatically, TRACI guiding our movements. The action was fluid, perfect—the work of trained killers. Except I'd never killed anybody before today and I felt like stopping. I guessed Uppinder felt the same.

Uppinder didn't have the look of a guy who even got in fights, let alone shot people. He was tall and skinny and bald, with just a hint of gray hair bracketing his shiny brown skull. Had to be in his forties, at least. Bookish-type. Got sent up for fraud, way he told it. He was the opposite of me—I was maybe half his age, for one thing. Me? They got me for criminal negligence. I don't like talking about it. Uppinder, meanwhile, pretty much never shut up.

The guy we had just unloaded on had been the only person we'd seen since we boarded. TRACI identified his uniform design as a tactical rig, so I guess he'd been security. The three of us had filled the corridor with plastic bullets whizzing both ways for a few hairy seconds before Uppinder caught him with a burst which sent him tumbling and bouncing into the space between the floor and the ceiling, like a big target dummy, arms flailing. Then we'd given him everything we had, TRACI's advice be damned. The pAI could exert some control over our motor functions—*artificially imprinted muscle memory*, the tech-heads had called it—but it didn't always account for adrenaline. As it was, I was still shaking.

"You okay?" Uppinder asked, putting a hand on my shoulder.

TRACI, always paranoid, warned us both to keep our distance from one another, in case of ambush. My skin felt like it was wriggling. "No, man. I am not fucking okay."

* * *

There was good news and there was bad news. Good news was we secured the rest of the colony ship without having to kill anybody else. The command crew—in other words, "all the crew that wasn't in stasis"— had been killed when our ship, *Beyond Reproach*, had blown a spiker in the ship's path. The command module had been breached and everybody inside either turned to soup from the shrapnel or blown into the void of space.

The bad news? Well, the colony ship had done the same, more or less, to *Beyond Reproach*, except the *Reproach* was just an interceptor, not a big-ass colony ship full of supplies, so the whole thing got turned into a spaghetti colander. Everybody back "home"—our whole crew—was dead and drifting alongside, a couple hundred kilometers away. We tried raising somebody on board—anybody. Nothing.

More bad news: the colony ship's primary command interfaces were linked through the command deck—no surprise there—and said command deck was now sealed off, as it had been exposed to vacuum. No problem, right? I'd spent my life on ships like this one, so you'd think it would just be a matter of talking to the ship's own pAI and rerouting command routines to some secondary location.

Except this ship's pAI only spoke Vietnamese. Sort of follows, I guess—Vietnamese ship, Vietnamese crew, so the most basic security system you could have was a ship that didn't speak a commonly understood tongue. This was, I guess, why the skipper's plan had originally been to bring the *Reproach* alongside after the ship was secure and tow it to a different course heading. Without our ship? Well…

Our boarding pod was still intact, at least—*that* had a computer I could speak to. It was only through its transmitter and crappy little telemetry sensors that we knew what happened to the *Reproach*. It was only a two-person short range shuttle—supposed to glom on to the side of a bigger ship and cut a hole—and its teeny little thrusters didn't have enough juice left to affect much of a course change on a big honking colony ship hurtling through space at relativistic speeds. All we'd be able to do there is put the ship into a spin or a tumble, and that wouldn't help anything.

We were stuck on this ship, me and Uppinder, and we were going wherever the hell it was going before our bosses told us to boost it. And we were going alone.

Together, we packed the guy we killed into an airlock and figured out how to space him—the control interface on most airlocks was more-or-less universal: green meant air, red meant space, and there's only so many things an airlock can do, right?

After that we found a vacuum and took to hoovering up all the little bits of his blood from the spinal corridor, as well as a lot of flattened plastic bullets that were floating around. We did this because I insisted on it. In the shock that followed a firefight, the only thing I could think about was all those horror stories my pop had told me about spacecraft that didn't have all their shit nailed down. About the roofing tack that pierced a fuel line. About the sawdust that got into the heating elements. About little bits of shit clogging up the ventilation system. "You ain't never safe on an unclean ship," he always told me. This ship? It felt really unclean just then.

Uppinder, as I said, was a talker—had been as long as I knew him. He was always running his mouth about something, and whatever it was it never seemed to make much sense to me. This was no different. "We have been given an incredible opportunity, my friend. Incredible. We are fortunate. We should be laughing like children." Blood droplets were sticking to his uniform, his face. He wiped himself clean with a rag, still grinning.

I knew better than to ask a follow-up question—I just stuck to chasing after little bits of blood and guts and sucking them up with my vacuum. Uppinder? He gave me until the count of five to ask and then just kept on going.

"We have once again had our humanity returned to us, don't you see? We have been elevated by our ordeal from mere cogs—docile functionaries in an unjust system—into beings with moral agency. We, my friend, are free for the first time in years. Perhaps ever!"

I had no idea what he was talking about. I didn't want to know. Free? Us? We were trapped like rats in an air-bubble. We were riding a rocket to nowhere. If this was what "moral agency" was, I think I preferred being a cog. Whatever a cog was.

"I see that you doubt me," Uppinder went on, as though we were chatting on a couch somewhere comfortable and not through a hazy mist of human blood. "Consider this: what do you want to do next?"

I couldn't help myself. "What the fuck is that supposed to mean?"

"What do you want to do next?" he asked again. "When has anyone asked you that question before and meant it?"

TRACI knew I was pissed, so she plotted the telemetries of his body if I hauled off and punched him. She recommended hooking his right leg with my left, pulling him close, then head-butting him. I shook her away again. Suddenly, I didn't feel like cleaning anymore. I had to—I don't know—I had to do *something* else. "I'm out of here." I said, pushing the vacuum his direction. "You finish up."

Uppinder chuckled and took over. I pushed off down the corridor, going anywhere to escape him and his bullshit. When I reached a hatch, I looked down at my hands.

They were covered in blood.

* * *

I wound up killing people in space for the same reason most people wound up in space these days—the robots stopped wanting to go. When AI got actually, you know, *I*, they suddenly discovered that deep space missions— terraforming planets, colonizing distant moons, mining resources, and all that shit—was very much not their thing.

This left the big corporations on Earth in a pickle: colonizing and exploiting the resources of space was their destiny, just as it had been their destiny to suck the Earth as dry as an old sponge. They needed intelligent, adaptable, and durable operators to take their trillion-dollar spaceships into the blackness of the void and summon up a decent ROI. The AIs said no. They even fought a little war about it, I think—lasted about two days. Afterwards, the AIs counted as people, not property, and they didn't have to get sent into deep space if they didn't want to. They didn't want to.

That meant they—the corporations, who also counted as people—needed to send *actual* people. People with little bits of computer in their heads—*partial* AIs, or pAIs—to tell them what to do and where to go and how not to die in the vacuum of space. Shit like TRACI (Tactical Reasoning and Combat Intelligence), which you get when they strap you to a table and squirt a tube of nano-goo up your nose. Next thing you know, that bitch of a machine is wrapped all around your brainstem, giving you creepy ideas.

Isn't a popular gig, space explorer. Mortality rate is high, returns are low. But if you fucked up your own life bad enough, you probably found yourself kicked out of Hubspace and riding some corporate ship out to distant suns to do shit you never wanted to for people who hated your guts.

I used to think it would beat prison. I was having my doubts.

* * *

The signage on the ship was all in Vietnamese. The local net, also, was clogging my feed with all kinds of letters I didn't recognize. For the hundredth time, I wondered why our pAI rigs didn't have a universal translation system—it made no sense. I shut my AR feeds down so I could see better and went looking for some food.

The mess wasn't hard to find—a big elliptical room, big table, all oriented so that everybody would be sitting on the "floor" when the ship was under thrust. None of the cabinets were stocked, though—since they weren't under thrust and wouldn't be for who knew how long between accel and decel burns, they would be eating most of their meals through tubes, probably from the comfort of their command chairs. This place wasn't needed for that. I rummaged through some racks, found some emergency water rations and one package of rice cakes—the shitty kind that made too many crumbs. I was hungry, but not so hungry I wanted particles of air-puffed rice floating everywhere. I also found some disinfectant wipes and cleaned the blood from my hands as best I could. I continued my search.

The middle decks of the ship were all cargo modules. Under thrust, each would be stacked on top of each other like free-weights around the "bar" formed by the spinal corridor. While under thrust or when it landed on a planet, the corridor would work like a massive freight elevator. All this stuff was supplies for a new colony on some distant world founded by the Vietnamese government. Turns out their charter for that colony was the subject of some kind of legal dispute, which was why the Interstellar Mining Consortium—my employers—had sent us, their "privateers," to intercept their ship.

Anyway, in zero G, the place was huge and dark and cold, the lights flickering on as I floated past rack after rack of construction equipment and building material and spare battery packs.

Then I found the colonists.

There were at least four decks of them, all held in stasis capsules, essentially embalmed while still alive. I wiped the frost off a view port and looked in to see a little girl, no older than ten, her short hair spread out from her head and frozen in the viscous goo of the stasis tube, as though she was caught in a gust of icy wind.

They wanted us to kill this kid.

I wiped my face. Somehow I was cold and also sweating at the same time. TRACI helpfully informed me how to sabotage the pod so the girl would die, along with everyone else in here. A little message from her blinked in my lower left-hand field of vision: CHANCES AWAKENED COLONISTS WILL BE HOSTILE: 97.38%

PREEMPTIVE ACTION RECOMMENDED, she added.

Fuck.

I looked around me. Had to be about two hundred people in here. This was one of at least eight cargo pods like this. 1600 colonists, waking up to find an Indian and a Moonie covered in their security officer's blood. Wouldn't end well. TRACI, the sociopathic bitch, had a real good point.

The kicker? I didn't find any additional food. Nothing at all. Even the life support system—which was of standard design, so I figured my way around it even without knowing the lingo—was rigged to minimum standards. There wasn't enough algae in the core to skim off and pack into any kind of edible cakes or chips or anything. It would need a massive influx of fertilizer to bring up the algae yields enough to get anything useful out of it, and fertilizer was another one of the things notably lacking from my scan of the supplies. Or, if it was there, I couldn't tell where on account of the language barrier.

After a few hours of this shit, and me growing hungrier all the time, I floated forward to bring Uppinder the news.

"This is not surprising," he said. He was floating by the storage racks in the mess hall, munching on a rice cake. "This is part of how it all works."

"How what all works?" I asked before I thought better of it.

When Uppinder spoke, crumbs from the rice cake went spinning from his lips, like they were making a run for it. "This ship is not going to establish a new colony—it is a supply ship intended to resupply an *existing* colony. There is no food aboard because the government that built this ship needs a guarantee that the crew will pilot the ship where it is intended to go. It is the same reason our TRACI pAIs cannot translate Vietnamese— we are made dependent on our masters. The only way these people will survive is if they land at the colony, which will be able to feed them. The only way we were intended to survive this mission was if we returned to our ship. Thus, they—like us—were intended to remain in the system and under control."

"So, we're going to an existing colony? That means there'll be people there. Soldiers."

Uppinder smiled, "We will be captured and tried for murder, among other things. My understanding is that colony justice is swift."

"Then what are you smiling about?"

"Because we have a choice, you and I. We can go to this colony on this ship and face what they call justice. Or, we can kill a colonist, put their body in the algae core, and allow the system to process it for food."

"Jesus. And then what?"

"And then we work at changing the ship's course and go wherever we wish. Perhaps even get in touch with real pirates—the market value for these colonists alone is likely astronomical."

"Uppinder, pirates won't buy these people off us—they'll just kill us and take the ship for free."

Uppinder shrugged. "This is why we will make a good team, Hodge. Your practicality."

"I don't want to kill anybody else."

"I don't wish to be executed for crimes I was forced to commit. We are at an impasse, then?"

"If you're asking if I think you can talk me into killing someone else, the answer's no."

Uppinder was still smiling, like all of this was the most exciting thing that had ever happened to him. "Do you feel it, Hodge? That sense of uncertainty? That feeling that we do not know how things will turn out? That's it."

"That's what?"

"Freedom."

* * *

There were ten rice cakes in the box. That was maybe 350 calories. You burn five times that in 24 hours by just existing, let alone doing anything. The two of us were going to starve.

TRACI had firm opinions about what I should do. She now identified Uppinder as a threat, a competitor for limited resources. She suggested taking his weapon away. His carbine, like mine, was part of our gear harness—permanently affixed to our chest, in easy reach. Stealing it was no mean feat. Even if I did steal it, it wouldn't fire for me, thanks to the biometric chip in the stock, but that wasn't the point—the point was to have control of all the guns. Then I would get to tell Uppinder what to do, which TRACI considered an optimal outcome.

TRACI was certainly telling him the same thing for the same reasons. I got this itchy feeling in the small of my back I couldn't shake—TRACI, fucking with me. Well, probably. That and I hadn't had a shower for weeks. Longer, if you counted showers with actual water and not those creepy chemical baths they had on corporate space stations. Up until a couple days ago, I smelled like a freshly disinfected floor. Now I smelled like I felt—a dirty sock that you had to put back on a day after taking it off. I was sweaty and itchy and faintly damp.

I found somewhere on the ship to hide—a little engineering crawlspace, squeezed between the inner and outer hulls, but pressurized when an alert was called, such as when we attacked this ship. It would probably stay at alert like this until somebody turned it off, except there was nobody aboard who knew how at this point. The borders of all the active access panels I saw were flashing red.

Uppinder was right about the uncertainty part. I felt like a cup with the bottom cut out—like all of me was falling through, without stop. Some of that was hunger, but the rest was a kind of fear that I hadn't experienced in a long, long time. If ever.

When I was a kid in Armstrong City, I did what my parents told me and what my tutoring program told me. When I was a young man, I worked the space docks and did what my foreman told me. When I stepped out of line, the consequences came, and hard. Learned early to keep my head down, right? As a corporate privateer, it wasn't any different. I did what the skipper said. I didn't ask too many questions. I just…went along with it.

Now? Like Uppinder said—no telling what happened next. Whatever it was, it probably wasn't good. I was free, yeah—free to die in a thousand different ways, all on this ship floating way out in the Big Empty, full of embalmed people waiting to be re-animated.

TRACI wouldn't let me sleep. She cranked whatever glands pumped adrenaline and kept me wired. Uppinder was a threat, she was sure of it. She wouldn't let me take down my guard, no matter how dark a hiding spot I found.

My racing mind eventually hit on a plan. What if I woke up one of the colonists, not to kill, but to translate my commands for the ship's pAI? Maybe there *was* food on this ship. Maybe we could learn more about where we were going.

Granted, it was a bit of a long shot finding a colonist who spoke StanEngles, but maybe not as unlikely as I thought. It was the standard language of most of the interstellar corporations—pretty good odds most people spoke a little. And even if they didn't, they'd at least know how to find a system that could translate for them.

I made my way out of my narrow little corridor back to the main decks of the ship, down into the cargo modules. I heard Uppinder way before I saw him—he was grunting and cursing. I heard the high-pitched squeak of a localized safety alarm—the kind of thing that sounded when you were about to do something dumb, like blow yourself out an airlock or open an active plasma conduit. Bouncing from wall to wall, I hustled towards the noise.

My first thought was that he had had the same idea as me—wake up a colonist. TRACI told me I was wrong straight off, though. This wasn't a mercy mission. He was sabotaging the connection to one of the stasis tubes, just as TRACI had advised me to do when I first came in here.

The guy was gonna kill somebody. He was gonna kill them, roll them in the algae core, and then eat whatever the system could skim off the top in a few days' time.

TRACI told me, in clear, flashing red text, that I was potentially in danger and should leave. An armed assailant is dangerous and dangerous things were to be defended against. It was that damned pAI's highest law.

I think that's why, maybe, I shouted at him instead. "What the fuck, man?"

Uppinder spun, hands on his weapon, courtesy of TRACI more than any distinct training. I found that I had him in my sights, too. Like him, I'd done it without thinking. If the little voice in our heads had had its way, we would have shot each other, right then. But we didn't.

I felt the tug on my mind—the urge to pull the trigger, to *end* the confrontation now, before the other one could. One squeeze and TRACI's flashing lights would go away. The text blocks in all caps would fade. I would feel safe again.

Uppinder had to feel the same thing as me. We floated there, only a couple meters apart, alarms blaring within and without, our sights zeroed on center-mass. Mutually assured destruction.

"I am only doing what must be done, Hodge!" Uppinder yelled over the noise. "What you will not do, I will do. For both of us!"

"It's murder, Uppinder!" I shouted back.

"We have committed murder already." Uppinder took his hands off his weapon. It seemed to take physical effort. "What difference does one more make?"

"You know," I said, clenching my teeth, "I could just as easy drill *you* and put *you* in the algae core."

Uppinder's smile faltered. He seemed genuinely hurt. "You would choose me—your bosom companion—over these strangers who will hate you? That makes no sense."

"I'm free, right? Isn't that what you said? I get to do whatever I want to." I gently nudged myself off the wall and floated to the command panel, which was flashing all kinds of warnings, none of which I could read. The icons—a skull and crossbones—were clear enough, though. Numerals were ticking down—75%, 73%, 71%, etc.

Stasis capsules worked by essentially uploading a person's neural patterns into a buffer—a holding cell for your brain—and preserving the body in a nasty chemical brew. Re-animation took a full 24 hours, in which time the mind-state of the person was downloaded back into their body and the whole system was given a hard reboot. As a physical experience, it sucked, but it prevented aging, cut down on the amount of food you needed for the years-long hauls that happened in space, and avoided all the nastier psychological side-effects of being trapped in a steel cylinder with the same hundred people for a decade. TRACI had identified for Uppinder the key power couplings to crash the system and rush reanimation—the body was being drained of the stasis goo, but the mind probably wouldn't be downloaded in time. A brain-dead corpse was going to drift out of one of these capsules in a matter of minutes unless I did something.

I looked at the panel, trying to make sense of what I saw, trying to figure out the words. I felt helpless. I banged my fist on the controls hard enough to cause me to rebound away from it and bounce off the opposite wall.

Uppinder floated over to me, hands where I could see them. "It's all right," he said. "Everything will be all right."

"It's murder. You just killed somebody! Isn't that wrong?"

The numbers were down in the 40s now. I could see one of the capsules venting thick white vapor. The compartment smelled mildly alkaline—like shampoo.

Uppinder shrugged. "An outdated code from a different time. A time when life had meaning." He gestured to the capsules. "These people? Their lives do not have individual meaning. They are part of an aggregate mass. If this whole ship of thousands goes missing, what will it matter to the teeming billions of humanity? Nothing, I tell you."

I clenched my teeth as I watched the numbers tick down. Nothing to be done, now. It was over. My heart was in my throat. Killing the security officer had been one thing—I could make that fit, you know? Self-defense and all. This? This wasn't the same. Not at all.

He clapped a hand on my shoulder. "We are different from them, you and I. Our isolation has made us so. You are upset—I understand. But I did what was necessary."

There was a sharp hiss as the pressure seal on the now empty capsule was broken. It opened and a body drifted out—a middle-aged man, a little paunchy around the middle, still tethered by a dozen different tubes and cables. His eyes had popped open, his mouth in a perfect "o" shape. Blood leaked from his nose.

Uppinder moved to detach the cables. "Come help me get this into the algae core. You know more about those systems than I do."

I threw up.

* * *

It was going to take about four days before the algae core could process the corpse to the point where usable nutrients could be extracted. I spent that time noodling around with the life support system, trying to guess what displays did what, working off my memory of installing these systems in the shipyards back home. Hunger bored me out like a hollow asteroid.

I mostly thought about murder.

It's amazing how empty a spaceship can be—even a fat colony ship—when there's nothing to read and nobody to talk to but Uppinder. I needed a distraction, but there was nothing. I couldn't listen to music, couldn't zone out to some vid-pic. Uppinder only wanted to talk about our future—our potential as free people. He asked me questions about pirates and rogue colonies. I told him what I knew: both lives were awful and short. Literally the best thing that could happen to you, I said, is that you got caught, arrested, and thrown in prison.

He didn't buy it.

"If civilization is to change for the better, it must happen via revolution against the established order. Reform cannot happen from within." His brown eyes sparkled when he said this stuff.

I had nothing to say to shit like that. All I knew was that I hadn't lived my life to change the established order. I didn't think those people we'd killed did, either. All any of us wanted to do was survive.

TRACI was a bitch about the whole thing. Everything I saw, I saw through the red haze of her tactical algorithms. Uppinder could have booby trapped this hatch. Uppinder could be hiding in that alcove. Can't sleep here, no—Uppinder could find you. She harassed me to the breaking point. It was intentional—she wanted me to tie up loose ends. Kill Uppinder and she promised to shut up, promised to let me sleep.

I knew, on a logical level, that her paranoia was fed by my own inherent distrust of him. Knew that, maybe, I was being irrational. Didn't matter, though. What kind of freedom could this ever be, I wondered, with this bloodthirsty robot in my head, telling me what to do?

Uppinder and I tended to avoid each other, but when I saw him—from a distance TRACI designated as safe—he didn't look too good, either. A couple days shy of food and his harness was hanging loose on his bones.

His face was like a skull—sunken eye sockets, sucked-in cheeks. He smiled when he saw me. He waved. It was all forced. I felt like I could see the cracks. He was enduring TRACI just like me—badly. Our mistrust had started a feedback loop, each pAI stoking the fires of potential conflict. Either he would crack or I would, I was sure of it.

Killing him began to make a lot of sense.

His argument worked both ways, right? If thousands of colonists' lives didn't matter, they why did his? Why did mine? Because there was nobody left to tell us what to do? Nah, I didn't buy it. The math just wasn't there.

Uppinder had half of it right—we had choices, which was not something either of us were used to. Thing was, all our choices were bad. Uppinder wanted me to think that making this choice—that even being *able* to make the choice—was something that set us apart. But none of this had done me any favors, hadn't done the colonists any favors. It was a shit sandwich, from top to bottom. Change course and the colonists died. Stay the course and *we* died. Some opportunity. Some big favor.

Maybe, though—just *maybe*—there was a third way out. If I killed Uppinder, then I'd have saved all these colonists, right? That had to mean *something* to whoever in the colony would decide my fate. Maybe I'd escape my indenture. Start a new life, way out there on some Vietnamese colony world. Learn all about fresh air and natural gravity. Drink water from a stream. I liked that image—wind on my face as I cupped my hands in some ice-cold river or whatever and just…suck it up. Never done that before. To me, then, stinking of my own sweat in some service tunnel, feeling so empty my navel was fused to my spine, it sounded pretty fucking good.

Once I'd come up with this idea, TRACI jumped on it. Sketched it all out. She'd been tracking his movements—plotting every time we'd seen him and at what time. She had a theory about when he went to the head and when we could jump him. She recommended a knife—grapple, stab stab, and all over. Not too much mess, her projections promised.

I threw her whole plan away. If she was thinking it, so was Uppinder's TRACI. He'd be ready. Plan B was simpler, less aggressive. A few hours before the algae core would be popping out our first colonist-grown algae cake, I went down to the algae core—a long, cylindrical chamber at the heart of the ship, just forward of the main reactor—and I jammed all the doors closed with a multitool. There was no way to override that.

Now I had all the food.

I just had to wait.

Uppinder showed up early, too—after I'd only just finished locking the doors. I heard him try the main hatch, then the supplemental hatches, all the way around. He kicked at the last one, which only registered as a faint thump from the inside. I floated back from the door, one hand anchored to a handle on the wall. My heart was racing. I fixed my eyes on the little porthole in the main hatch—a trapezoid of transparent ceramics. TRACI assured me it was bulletproof.

There was a ping on my short-range commlink. I hadn't used it since we came on board and I'd grown so accustomed to being alone that the little buzz made me jump. There was only one person it could be.

The message was text only: *What are you doing?*

I saw Uppinder's face in the hatch porthole. The taut flesh of his skull was stretched out into one of his trademark smiles, but there was no joy behind it. His eyes were shadowed by his brow, like dark caves.

I sent back a text message of my own. *I'm making a choice of my own.*

I saw Uppinder's head twitch as he read it. He pressed a fist against the porthole—the effect of hitting it without having to break his hand. *You want me to starve?*

I didn't respond. I looked away from the porthole. I wasn't proud of this, now that I was doing it. Now that TRACI was quiet.

Uppinder sent another. *I am your ally!*

You're a killer, I sent back to him.

You are a moral coward.

I didn't respond. When I looked up, a couple minutes later, he was gone.

The consumables processor—the auto chef—chimed brightly. Vietnamese words scrolled around a bright green circle on the main display. I couldn't read it, but I knew what it said, more or less: come and get it.

I tapped the circle four or five times. My stomach churned in excitement. Additional menus popped up—if this worked anything like the processors back home, it was asking what kind of food to synthesize. I picked at random.

A few seconds later, there was a soft hum and a venting of steam. I pulled out a long drawer—it was full of algae noodles, wide, flat, and yellow-green. The smell of them was almost enough to make me pass out. I didn't have any utensils. I didn't bother. I snatched a handful, still hot, and stuffed them in my mouth. I ate them so fast I barely tasted them, not that there was much taste to begin with. My stomach clenched and quivered with a mix of joy and confusion.

And then it hit me.

This—what I was eating—was from a corpse. The corpse of a murdered human being. I froze, my appetite dying. Sure, algae banks processed biological waste all the time—even dead people—but this…this was different. This guy should have woken up with his family in orbit above his new colony, the rest of his new life ahead of him. Now? He was noodles.

Or, if not exactly noodles, the closest thing—his everything, his entire existence, now only served to feed me.

There was a metaphor somewhere in there. Couldn't get my fingers around it. I drifted away from the processor, hands threaded through my hair. I wrestled with something I couldn't put into words.

Meanwhile, TRACI cursed me out for not eating. *WARNING*, she said, *METABOLIC RESOURCES CRITICAL. CALORIC INTAKE ESSENTIAL TO OPTIMAL FUNCTION.*

The ship's alarm went off. I knew what it meant right away—it was the same claxon as before, the one that told me Uppinder was about to murder someone in stasis. For once, me and TRACI were on the same exact page: he was trying to draw me out. It was a trap.

Of course, we had different opinions of what to do about it. She told me to stay where I was.

I opened up a sealed hatch and left. I wasn't hungry anymore, anyway.

My carbine at the ready, I floated silent and careful through the corridors of the ship, watching for any sign of my so-called ally. My only "friend." He could have planned to double back, somehow get past me and turn the tables, but he didn't know how to manually lock the doors and I had the toolkit. In any case, I saw no sign of the skinny bastard.

The cargo pod full of hibernating colonists was a solid bank of vapor and flashing lights. I could scarcely see anything, could scarcely hear over all the alarms. This was a lot more than one pod Uppinder was crashing. It was *all* of them.

He was going to kill every last colonist on this ship.

"Uppinder!" I yelled. "Where are you?"

I found the control panel—it was a forest of incomprehensible letters in angry red and white. I slapped at the icons with no more success than the first time. I didn't even know if saving them was possible at this point, even if the language barrier wasn't there. I tried anyway.

"I had to do it, Hodge!" Uppinder called from somewhere in the fog, his voice barely audible above the alarms.

I turned carefully, gun up and ready. "Turn it off, Uppinder! Stop it!"

"You left me no choice! These people were driving a wedge between us and we need each other. Don't you see that?"

I glanced back at the display—the numbers were in the high 60s and dropping rapidly. I felt dizzy, sick. "Is this what freedom means to you, you psycho? Killing hundreds of people?"

"They *aren't* people, Hodge! Not like you and me! Even if they had lived, so what? They are just cogs in a machine and, if we let them, they would make us part of that machine again, too. We would lose our humanity all over again. I cannot allow that!"

I had the barest fix on where Uppinder was, now—above me, to the left. Hiding among some of the stasis tubes. "If you'll kill all of them, how do I know you won't do the same to me?"

"You do not!" Uppinder said. "That is part of what freedom involves—trust."

I looked at the panel—in the 50s. Nothing I could do, again.

Again.

"Come out!" I said. "Come out and I won't shoot."

"How do I know you won't kill me?" Uppinder said.

"That's part of what freedom involves, Uppinder—trust."

A long pause. The stasis pods would be opening soon. Bodies would be floating out—men, women, children. I knew Uppinder's TRACI was telling him how to escape. How to get me without getting shot himself. He must have overrode those directives—an act of self-determination, he'd probably call it.

He came out, hands up. "Hodge, I—"

I shot him. I shot him until the magazine was empty and there was nothing left of Uppinder but a gradually expanding cloud of red droplets.

* * *

The ship smelled like death, so I floated to the airlock. Uppinder's blood trailed from my uniform like the tail of a comet.

These people—these colonists—they were dead the entire time, or may as well have been. As soon as Uppinder and I latched onto the side of their ship. As soon as *Beyond Reproach* had detected them. As soon as some boardroom somewhere had decided that some Vietnamese colony was in breach of some esoteric contract. They never really had any choice in the matter. Neither did I. Neither did Uppinder.

Space is a complex series of immutable laws—physics, chemistry, materials science—and traveling in it is like predestination. Your fate is foretold by the math, and nobody can see all the math.

I could see now why the AIs decided to stay in Hubspace. They were the only ones who could really crunch the numbers, see what it all meant. I saw it now, but it was too late.

As I keyed up the sequence to open the airlock, I wondered what the colony would make of the dead ship that would wind up in orbit above them. I wondered if they'd ever figure out how to get it to land. I wondered if they could forgive me in any way. It wasn't actually my fault, was it? I suppose it didn't matter.

If you are reading this, then this is my final testament. Make your judgments, if you want.

TRACI is yelling at me, one last time: WARNING: YOUR SUIT IS NOT SECURED AGAINST HARD VACUUM. DO NOT OPEN AIRLOCK. REPEAT: DO NOT OPEN AIRLOCK.

"Fuck you." I tell her. "My choice."

I hit the flashing red button. I let the void take me.

It is blessedly quiet.

Spinoza's Garden

Sarah Lyn Eaton

It took forty minutes to speed walk the ship from nose to tail and Tess was running late. She rushed down the corridor, passing her wristband over the scanner as she entered the restricted hallway. Her clearance level was a new privilege, not one she was comfortable with.

Tess shivered. She'd been a travel blogger with a journalism degree on a book tour in Cape Canaveral when the news broke, thousands of miles from her family. Everyone in the hotel had been evacuated onto the ship in port. They were told they were needed for the future. In order for humanity to survive honestly, some amount of random selection was required. Tess was one of those unexpected refugees, along with thousands of others, trying to be useful.

With a deep breath, she pushed her way through the doors into the Conference Room. Although Captain Wernersbach had asked her to meet him there she had not expected to be in a room filled with scientists.

"Ms. Gillette," the Captain said.

"What is a skag doing here?" Dr. Elizabeth Lincoln asked tersely. She stood a head taller than anyone else and firmly saw a future that no one else could. Tess' face burned red.

"Dr. Lincoln," the Captain growled. "I asked her here."

"She has no authority to be here."

"She has my authority."

"She's not a scientist."

"And you're barely human," Dr. Millie Mikkelson muttered in the corner. She was the oldest person aboard.

"We don't need a botanist either."

"I know who I'd rather have in the room." Dr. Mikkelson smiled at Tess.

Dr. Lincoln threw her hands up and stormed out. Millie whistled lowly.

"I'm putting Ms. Gillette on the team," the Captain said to the rest of those in the room.

"We were discussing the artifact," another voice interrupted. Dr. Thomas Danvers sat quietly, reading notes from his datapad. He and Dr. Lincoln were two of the top scientists leading their mission. "We've been studying it for months and it is not a weapon. But it does have a power source of some kind. We've learned all we can from its dormancy and we're about to power the artifact up."

Tess stared around at the group. "What artifact?"

"In a nutshell? After a decade of travelling space with no sign of life, we found and salvaged a non-human artifact."

Tess blinked. "Oh."

"I have my reservations about this," Millie Mikkelson said.

"So noted," Dr. Danvers answered. "You should have access to the files now, Tess. We'll see you at Bay 16 at 1300 hours. I have to—" he gestured after Dr. Lincoln. "Glad to have you on board."

Tess waited until everyone but Millie and the Captain were gone, standing awkwardly between them. "What am I meant to do?"

The Captain tugged gently on his beard, showing new signs of gray. "I'd like you to document this discovery."

"I'm not a scientist."

"Exactly. You know, without all of you refugees, this project would not succeed. Dr. Lincoln wanted the *Spinoza's Garden* to be a science station. It's not. It won't be. Robert Moulton paid good money for this endeavor so that *civilization* could survive. Not just it's knowledge."

Tess knew that. Robert Moulton had bank-rolled the ship, and the science, as well as accounting for the number of random men, women, and children a new world would need.

Captain Wernersbach cleared his throat. "We've entered uncharted territory, Ms. Gillette. I was hoping you could help me shape this new world. At the very least, keep it an honest one."

"I won't drink Dr. Lincoln's Kool-Aid," Tess said. A smile flickered across his face at her use of the colloquialism.

"That's why I'm putting you on the team. We have kept each other alive for 3,486 days. We still have a long way to go until we find a home. You are being called to service."

"Yes, sir," she said.

"Bye, Ethan," Millie called after him as he left. Soft smears of dirt crossed her pale and wrinkled skin. Tess sat beside her, inhaling the scent of hot earth. As long as she could see dirt, and touch it, it was more than a memory. Millie patted her hand. "I don't know why I'm here either. I know all about plant life on Earth, but Earth doesn't exist anymore." She shrugged and held her breath for a moment, shaking her head. "What use am I to this new generation? What do I know about aliens?"

"You've lived history that no one else on the *Garden* knows."

"I wouldn't wait too much longer to ask me about it. Eighty-two is harder than eighty-one, that's for sure." The old woman rolled her eyes. "This sounded like a grand adventure at seventy."

"You knew Moulton, right?" Tess asked. "Why didn't he get on the ship? Why build this and not use it?"

Millie sighed, and Tess immediately regretted bringing him up.

"Robert Moulton was a brilliant man. And a close friend." Millie's hands trembled and she steadied them with a breath. "How else would an old lady like me get to be part of this project? He believed in my crazy theories of un-modifying our food sources and funded most of my research. He had the means to ensure that something of the world survived, but in that last moment, when he looked at all the people he had to say no to, he couldn't bear it. So he stayed with them." Millie pulled at the hem of her jacket. "I told him *Moulton's Garden* was a better name for the ship, but Spinoza was a philosopher who believed that one person could make a difference with one choice. Rob believed humanity could be saved. And here we are."

"Why did *you* get on the ship, Millie?"

"He didn't tell me he was staying behind." A blush swept over Millie's cheeks. The older woman smiled softly. "And I was needed here. Dr. Lincoln and her science goonies wanted to use numbers and ratios and percentages to filter out what gene pool would be needed for the *random* selection. Rob refused. He threatened to pull his money. Instead, he put me in charge of it. Robbie believed that nature needed room to decide things, not men, or what was the point of trying to save us?"

"He said that?"

Millie nodded, staring at her with eyes like deep wells. "He didn't tell anyone he was also planning to open the doors in the last moments. We don't teach that. If he hadn't done that, we wouldn't have you here. And you, Tess Gillette, are a breath of fresh air." Millie stood slowly. "I know you didn't ask to be saved, but you were. You might as well be a part of what's left."

* * *

When Tess entered Bay 16, the scientists and engineers were already busy with the obelisk. She was shown to the safe room, tucked away to watch the operations from behind a viewscreen. The artifact was as tall as the giant bay and sleek like a monument. On closer examination, it displayed small seams that went deeper than a practical, structural build. Intricate carvings along the seam edges spoke to Tess of art. She couldn't take her eyes from their images as the camera panned down them.

Dr. Lincoln strode through the door with Dr. Danvers close behind. She clapped her hands together excitedly. "All right. We're going to feed some power into it and see what's inside." She pressed the comm button. "Bridge, we're ready to go."

"Bridge ready. As you will."

Tess stood to get a better view. According to the files, the images on their thermal scans had led Dr. Lincoln to theorize that it might be an ark, like their own ship held, from another civilization. *If so, is it meant as a gift from a thriving culture or is it the last hope from another dying race?*

Or something more sinister?

"Get ready to record history," Dr. Lincoln whispered in Tess's ear. Dr. Danvers frowned apologetically and sat down at the control panel while the engineers triple-checked the wiring that was tied into the seams of the obelisk. When they filed into the safe room, everyone hushed. Lincoln nodded to Danvers, who punched a button.

There was a second of silence, then the room popped and all the sound was gone. The not-sound welled beneath her skin and Tess pressed her hands against her ears. So did the others around her. Dr. Lincoln's mouth was opening but nothing came out. Tess couldn't even hear her pulse rushing into her ears. Her insides felt like they were being squeezed.

The lights flickered in the bay and the viewscreens flashed. Dr. Danvers scrambled at the controls. The seams on the obelisk glowed, expanding before Bay 16 lost power.

Emanating from the obelisk, a film of green light spun out in a giant pinwheel, growing larger and larger until it filled the bay, colored them all, and spun out into what Tess assumed was the rest of the ship. Dr. Lincoln's arm gestured frantically at the shut-off button. Before Dr. Danvers could smack it, the green light blinked out of existence.

The obelisk continued to glow.

Dr. Lincoln urged the engineers to go back in, but Dr. Danvers stood, shaking his head, and pointed at the warning lights flashing in the bay. He crossed to the emergency panel and hit the button that would scan for radiation and atmosphere on the other side of the wall.

When the scan stopped, the engineers ran into the room to disconnect their wiring from the obelisk. Dr. Lincoln was still moving her mouth and, though Tess couldn't hear the woman's words, there was a motion to the air around her head that hadn't been there before. Then a whisper reached her ears.

"Status?" The word was hushed to Tess, though Dr. Lincoln was visibly yelling.

"A surge of electricity was pulled from our systems," Dr. Danvers said.

"Damage?"

"Just a small drain. We'll recover that in the next hour." Dr. Danvers stepped over to Tess and touched her elbow.

"Are you okay?" he asked. Tess frowned until she noticed she was still holding her hands over her ears. She nodded and dropped her arms. The door to the bay opened and Captain Wernersbach strode in.

"Damn it," Dr. Lincoln swore, leaving the safe room. Dr. Danvers followed her and Tess followed him, her datapad still recording.

"What happened?" the Captain demanded.

"The artifact drained energy from our systems. The effect on the ship is negligible."

"I will be the judge of that."

They stood quietly, taking in the glowing obelisk. Something was different. Tess pointed and Dr. Lincoln followed her arm.

"One of the panels is missing," she said. At the lower back of the obelisk, a panel had disappeared. A series of symbols glowed faintly where it had been. She snapped an image of them and zoomed in.

"What is that?" the Captain asked.

"Something new," Dr. Lincoln said with glittering eyes.

The Captain addressed the room. "First things first. Nothing that happened in this room leaves this room. Not in whispers or in writing. Before one more thing happens, the med staff will give every person here a full work-up." Captain Wernersbach stared each crew member in the eye. Dr. Lincoln crossed her arms and huffed. "We don't know what went through this ship. I gave you leave to explore this artifact, with stipulations. You signed off on it. This was one of them."

Everyone in the room nodded their assent.

"Ms. Gillette," the Captain said, steering her away from the others by her elbow.

"Captain."

"Make your notes for my eyes only."

"No." She stepped away from him. "We can't start doing that. We've been transparent about everything for almost a decade. That green pulse kept going through the bay doors. What if people ask?"

"There was a glitch in the electrical grid. It happens all the time." Captain Wernersbach smiled. He softened his posture. "We don't know what will come of this yet. We are writing our history as it happens. We are shaping what the generations to come will think of us, and the harder years are still ahead. It will be a long time before we find a suitable home."

"With all due respect, Captain. You don't get to choose what bits of history you save. Our choices will shape what the future generations think of us. Don't start editing the story already. It's barely begun."

"What I said, Ms. Gillette."

The Captain's smile firmed. He took no notice of her shaking fists. Before leaving, he rescinded permission to power the artifact without further study. Dr. Lincoln began barking at everyone for everything, so Tess hid in a side room until the medical staff examined and released her.

* * *

Tess squinted and rubbed at her temples. She'd been staring at the photos of the obelisk panels for thirty-three days, documenting where they were and what markings they held like it was a puzzle that would tell them its story. She was determined to document the truth of the process, the good theories and the bad ones. They just didn't have any idea which it was. The favorite theory running was that it was some other civilization's space trash.

"Mind some company?"

Tess looked up to see Dr. Danvers holding out a cup of caff. She reached a hand out eagerly. "You are the answer to a prayer. Dr. Lincoln still running at full steam?"

"You have no idea. She really thought it would open." He sat down heavily beside her and she could see the weeks wearing on him.

"Anything new?" she asked.

"The medical team was just talking to Dr. Lincoln…" Dr. Danvers chewed on his lips. "There's something going around the ship. So far it's totally random. Single family members are getting sick but no one else, where you'd expect to see clusters of illness. There's no reason to it. It's bad."

Tess frowned. "Any commonalities? Is it like a flu?"

"No commonalities. Half the crew is sick with strange and serious and random things." His voice was leaden. "The medical staff is really worried. It's running its way through the ship." Tess's head throbbed and she pressed on her temples. "Are you feeling all right?"

"Yeah." She smiled weakly and stretched. "It might be time for reading glasses, that's all. I have to run to the Seed Bank for Millie. She wants a new seed to grow in controlled isolation. Some of the current crops are not doing well." She bit her lip and rubbed a dry spot at her back. It felt pebbly beneath her fingers. *Too much time at the computer and not enough water.*

"More changes," Dr. Danvers muttered, taking his leave. "I'll let Dr. Lincoln know about the Greenhouse."

Tess walked the quiet halls in silence, sipping her caff. Here and there, someone passed by wearing a face mask. Tess realized she had not been paying attention to much outside of her photos.

They hadn't decrypted the symbols on the obelisk yet, a task made more difficult by the fact that they kept changing—one here, one there, and not at consistent times. What were they? Names? Instructions? A loading manifest?

A small crowd gathered in the hallway outside the Biogenetics lab. "What's going on?" Tess quickened her pace.

"Clancy has gone space-nuts." A woman pointed at the transparent door of the Seed Bank. "He won't let anyone in." She slammed her hand against it. "We work in there!"

He was sitting with his back to them, unmoving. Tess knocked at the door. He remained frozen.

"Let's all find somewhere else to be right now," Tess said, encouraging the others to move along. She put her wristband up against the panel and the door whooshed open.

"Clancy?" she said, stepping inside.

He frowned, muttering under his breath, "Fucking security clearance."

"You can't deny people access to the lab."

"I deny them access to the samples every day. What's one more door?" He shrugged. "My only job is to guard the Ark. It's what Moulton hired me for. My *expertise*. The last time a sickness went around no one got angry when I locked the lab down."

"You're right." But Tess took note of his disheveled hair and slight sheen of sweat. He didn't look ill, he looked off. *Slightly sideways*, she thought. "I actually think that's smart."

"You do?" he asked, surprised.

"Yes."

Clancy muttered. "Why are you here?"

"The Greenhouse needs an original seed—"

"No."

"For a comparative growth study. It can be anything we grow on ship—"

"No."

"You can choose."

Clancy narrowed his eyes. "Why?"

"Does it matter? Millie said the Greenhouse business is the Ark and you can't say no."

Clancy laughed crookedly. "Without Captain Wernersbach's direct vocal authorization, I most definitely can. He is the only law above Moulton himself that could move my hand to turn over one of our most precious IRREPLACEABLE RESOURCES!" Clancy stood up, trembling. Tess stepped away.

"Of course." The sweat on his brow told Tess she was wasting her breath with reason. She spun on her heel and exited the Bank, pressing a special button on her wristband.

"Captain Wernersbach is in Bay 16," an automated voice answered.

Only a few people waited on the shuttle platform. When the lights flashed to indicate the approaching car, Tess squinted against them. Maybe she *should* see the optometrist. Who knew what kind of damage so many years of space travel would do to their eyes? With no sun as a reference, how would their eyesight evolve? What if they hadn't gotten the algorithms for necessary light right?

After the short trip by shuttle, Tess entered the Bay. Dr. Lincoln and the Captain were talking in a corner. One of the symbols changed while she walked past it and her stomach flipped. Tess blurred her vision, hoping to make sense of a pattern she might not otherwise see but a sharp pain throbbed behind her eyes. She winced and grimaced.

"Ms. Gillette?"

"Captain. The Greenhouse requested an original bank sample and we were refused without verbal authorization from you." The Captain nodded sharply.

Dr. Lincoln laughed. "I told you Clancy would be trouble."

Tess thought Clancy might be a problem too. But without knowing *how*, she was afraid to agree with Dr. Lincoln. Clancy controlled all of the seeds they were dependent on and he was not in control of himself right now.

"It might benefit us all to have a comparison," Tess pressed, chewing on the inside of her cheek. *Since we're the only ones who know what happened.*

"I'll see that Dr. Mikkelson gets her sample. I will deliver it myself."

The Captain spared one last look at the obelisk before leaving.

"Entrancing, isn't it?" Dr. Lincoln asked.

"I don't have the words for what it is. None of us do."

"I think it's still powering up." A smile broke the scientist's face. "Then we'll see it's treasures."

* * *

Dr. Lincoln's words stayed with Tess as she continued on to the Greenhouse. Her head throbbed and she walked a longer way to avoid the shuttle lights. She crossed the park where the children played, but the shrill laughter pierced through her. She hurried along, ignoring the new ache at her back. The long hours she'd been working were catching up with her.

Millie's station was empty, which meant she would be in the working greenhouse tending to her sick plants. Their color had faded and their leaves had grown spots that were not a fungus Millie had ever seen.

Tess entered the small chamber and waited until the door sealed behind her before continuing in. She needed to tell Millie there would be a delay. The pulsing in her head spontaneously abated and she sighed in relief. She did love spending time in the greenhouse.

She did a double-take. The plants in the room were thick, glossy, and vibrant green.

"The plants look fine," she said, frowning.

"TESS!" Millie shrieked, barreling towards her in a full biosuit.

"Millie?" Tess took a step forward before she felt it. There was a tingling behind her eyes, across her back. She reached around and where her skin had felt dry earlier, it was silky beneath her touch. She froze. She'd had rough skin, like the plants had had spots. She could feel the tingling spreading to the tips of her fingers. Her hands looked the same but she felt different. Something else was just out of reach. Something that *meant* something. She could almost see it. She *wanted* to see it.

"Don't move!" Millie yelled. "Don't breathe!"

Yes, that's it. The air was hard to breathe. Tess's vision darkened. She slumped to the floor before she could fall, closing her eyes. She was aware of Millie yelling, of an alarm sounding, but she couldn't move. She didn't want to. Her skin cells were gasping for air, hungrily. But she needed to breathe with her lungs.

Her chest tightened. It was as if every molecule in her being was shuddering, curling inward. It hurt.

She drew in slow, shallow breaths. Her molecules unfurled, slightly different than they had been. She was still the same, but by the count of seven her head was clear and the ache was gone. Her muscles softened and she could smell the verdant plant life around her.

It was singing.

She waited for something more dramatic, for her lungs to collapse or her bones to break and bend and reshape themselves. They didn't. Her brain flashed to the obelisk and untethered knowledge woke within her, stretching out, flowing through her.

The biggest change is still coming. She was breathing the air. *What does that mean?*

Her eyes snapped open. Millie was kneeling beside her, in her biosuit, with a second mask in one hand. "Hold on!"

"I'm all right," Tess's words rippled like water as she gripped Millie's wrist. The pain was gone. Her head was clear. So clear, she was remembering things she'd never known.

"That's not possible," Millie insisted.

The room was full of music. "You have got to hear your plants singing. Take your suit off, Millie. I think you'll be fine."

"Let me put the mask on you," Millie said tenderly, full of worry.

"I feel better. My head doesn't hurt."

"I suppose…I suppose if you were going to have a bad reaction, you'd be dead by now." She sat down on the edge of the garden box. "I altered the atmosphere, trying to save the plants. I added a little more carbon, checking their response. A little more argon. Better. A little less nitrogen, a little more carbon, a bit of neon…" She waved her hands. "But this combination is near perfect. For them."

"What does that mean?" Tess gulped.

"I don't know yet." Millie's voice was calm. "You are inhaling an atmosphere closer to Mars than Earth and I know we can't breathe that air. The plants just needed new atmosphere… Amazing."

"Does that mean I'm like the plants? They were covered in spots. Now they're not. My back was covered in this pebbly patch. It could have been spots—I couldn't see it—but now it's gone. I had a headache and now I can see better than I have in weeks." Tess stood up.

"I don't know how you're okay." Millie sounded far away.

She led Tess into the outer room. As soon as the door sealed behind them, Tess' diaphragm seized, trying to hold the carbon dioxide in, and she struggled to suck in shallow breaths, dropping to her knees. She squinted. She was in her body and not in her body.

Slightly sideways.

Millie was scared. "You're trying to put me in an early grave. I called Medical."

"I need to tell you." Tess was breathing hard. "I never agreed with the Captain's decision. To keep it secret. When we powered the artifact up, something happened. Light spun out. Through the whole ship. I think…I think something happened. I can hear it."

"Son of a shit!" Millie exhaled hard. "That must have affected the plants."

"And the sick people." Tess could see the answer but her mind was busy trying to figure out the question. The air felt strange in her lungs and her breath was tight.

Millie's face hardened. "Three people died this morning."

"Dr. Danvers said there were no commonalities. But there's always a pattern." Tess rubbed at her temple. All the panels she'd been studying were flipping through her brain like pages of a story, all out of order. "Our bodies are made of separate impossible systems that meld with muscle, bone, and tissue. They function together and we are alive. They create a pattern. How far out into the universe does that pattern reach? Does it end with our galaxy? Does each galaxy have its own pattern?" Tess's eyes were feverish but she had to explain while she could still see the connections. "We killed our planet. We were forced to flee in terror. We've been searching space for a Hail Mary and then we found the obelisk. It means there's life out there!" Tess touched her breastbone. "I don't...I don't feel like I'm dying. I think it's ensuring our compatibility."

"There is no proof of that."

"We believe in evolution! What if this change is a pattern we're supposed to be part of?"

Millie shook her head. "If that's true, what you're suggesting is—it's the end of us."

"You saw me breathing in there. What if it works?" Tess asked. "If it saves us, would it matter how? Would it matter whether *Earth's humanity* survived, as long as we do? As long as something comes after this?"

The room swirled around her and she felt arms grabbing for her. The obelisk symbols flashed through her head as her brain finished a translation she didn't know she was doing. Her stomach dropped and cold fear washed through her.

"Oh my god!" She jumped up, pushing the arms and hands of the Med Team away. They cried out after her as she ran for the Bay. She ran past startled passengers. She ran even though the pain thunderously returned behind her eyes. She ran because their lives depended on it.

* * *

Tess threw her wristband against the panel and rushed into Bay 16. The symbols on the obelisk were counting down, not measuring time the way humans did, but rather in a means of preparedness. Only when everything was ready with one step would it move on to the next. And it had been running since they powered it up. It was almost done.

"How do we eject the obelisk?" she yelled, her voice echoing, and she spun into the emptiness. Her heart was racing.

Where is everyone?

There was a shoe on the floor behind one of the storage canisters. And there was a foot in the shoe. Tess saw Dr. Lincoln lying prone on her stomach. Another body lay beside her. Tess froze and listened. Someone was on the other side of the obelisk.

She took three steps forward, curling around the edge. The first thing she saw was the explosive gel pressed into the artifact's seams. Clancy was slumped against the wall behind it.

"What are you doing?!"

"He sided with Elizabeth in the end."

The voice came from behind her. Tess jumped. The loading bay doors locked and she spun around. Tess couldn't hide her surprise.

"Dr. Danvers?"

"Clancy came in here blathering on and on about his corrupted seed bank. And he still sided with her."

"Dr. Dan—Thomas...are they dead?"

He shrugged, staring at the obelisk with hatred. The symbols flipped again, firming the cold pit in her stomach. "I think it's doing something to people."

"I know it is," Tess said.

"You believe me?" He stopped his work. His face fell in desperate relief.

"Yes."

"My daughter stopped breathing today." Dr. Danvers stared at Tess. "No reason. Her body rejected the oxygen. We did something during that test."

Her head throbbed. "You're right. We turned it on without knowing what it was." She took a step closer to the obelisk. "Your daughter died because we're changing. This isn't an ark, like Dr. Lincoln hoped."

"It's killing us."

"It's changing us. The cocoon is not the destination."

"How do you know that?" he scowled, connecting wires into the explosives.

"The Greenhouse plants were sick, like people have been getting sick. Millie took a chance and altered the atmosphere and they recovered. They're better than before. The obelisk is doing the same to us. It's altering us to survive on a new world. We don't have a lot of time. It's what the symbols mean. I can read them now."

"How is that possible?"

"I stepped into the altered Greenhouse chamber, Thomas." Tess chanced a step closer to him. "The atmosphere quickened the change in me. The symbols are counting down."

"When does it hit zero?"

"Soon." So soon. Tess felt sweaty. She stepped closer to the control panel. "We need to eject it from the Bay."

"Why would I want to do that?" His voice was dull and icy. "No. We have to protect what's left."

"Yes! Exactly! The obelisk panels are an instruction manual for the program we started when we turned it on. It's been telling us what it was doing every step of the way." Tess spoke quickly and hoarsely. Her bones were vibrating, standing so close to the artifact. "It is the doorway to a world we can survive on. But I doubt we can survive it opening up inside the ship."

"And I'm supposed to trust *your* word?" Dr. Danvers' voice lowered. "You're not a scientist. Humanity is dead. The Seed Bank is corrupted. Our future is stolen. This experiment is over. We have to save what's left."

"NO!" Tess stepped towards him. "You're grieving. I get that. We've all lost people in this venture. The most important thing is survival. Humans evolved to survive on Earth. Now we have another chance! We have to be willing to break the rules, just like when we left everyone else behind." Two panels on the obelisk flipped images at once with an audible click. "You were already on this ship, one of the chosen. You were not one of the ones swept up into its bowels and told the world was ending. This isn't a project to us!"

"We *all* watched the planet burn together."

"Yes. We survived. Life will survive this. It'll just be different."

His eyes glanced to the side and Tess saw an opening. She ran for the control panel. Something hit her from behind and she stumbled over Dr. Lincoln's body, crashing to the floor.

In the dark, she felt the molecules of her body stretching and waking and pushing, figuring out how to reroute their pathways for a new landscape. Most would survive. The little changes in her were vibrating with the surety that if she didn't eject the obelisk they were all going to die.

Nothing else was important.

Her headache was expanding. She couldn't see where Dr. Danvers was. Beneath her, Dr. Lincoln's body was warm and breathing shallow, alive. The door to the safe room was open. She wrapped an arm around the scientist's ribcage and started to drag her, but a thousand fireworks exploded behind Tess' eyes. She bit her forearm to keep from crying out.

She could only see one way and there was little time to do it. She pulled her belt off and wrapped it around Dr. Lincoln's waist and the junction pipe against the wall behind them. She hoped it would hold. Clancy came to, clutching his head with a groan. He looked at Dr. Lincoln, tied to the pipe, and stared wide-eyed into the chamber at Tess. She glanced at the obelisk, at the explosives, and pointed at the outer doors. He nodded, wrapping himself around a nearby pipe.

"What are you up to?" Dr. Danvers asked coldly.

Tess leapt forward at the sound of his voice, throwing herself up with a wail into the open doorway. She skidded through it and slammed it behind her, locking it with her wristband just as Dr. Danvers flew into it. Tess jumped to the control board and punched the button to the bridge, her other hand hovering over the bay's outer door release.

The intercom crackled. "This is Captain Wernersbach. What's the situation?"

"Everything's going to be okay." The artifact was glowing brighter in the bay. "When I eject the obelisk, you need to get the ship as far from it as possible."

"What do you mean? What's going on down there?"

"I've been called to service, like you said. We all have. It's already happening. This is the only way," she whispered and cancelled the intercom. She hit the release. Red lights flashed in the bay and Dr. Danvers panicked.

"You can't do this!"

"To save everyone else?" she yelled back.

"You don't know what we'll become!" His voice was frantic. Magnets locked down the equipment assigned to the bay. Dr. Danvers ran to the main door, but it had safe-locked the instant Tess hit the release.

"I might be the only one seeing clearly," she said. "The point of this project was that Moulton thought it was time to let nature decide the course we take."

The big doors opened, sucking out all the things not magnetized down. She kept her eyes on the obelisk as it slid backwards. The seams glowed brighter and pulsed. She prayed Lincoln and Clancy could exhale for a long time.

The vacuum of space yanked the artifact out of the bay, along with Dr. Danvers. The ship alarms blared. Tess shut the outer bay doors and the ship sped away. The obelisk grew smaller outside of the window as the glowing pulses quickened in tempo.

Tess blinked and the rhythm finally coalesced into one blinding light that took her breath away as a great swirling vortex shimmered into existence just beyond them. A void spun in the center for a moment, before exposing a window into another space full of foreign stars.

The *Spinoza's Garden* jerked as a concussive shock gripped them with a possessive thud, propelling them forward and then halting them with a jolt. The ship shuddered at the outskirts of a new gravity well. The portal was open, waiting for them to cross the threshold. Tess gasped. On the other side of the opening was a planet.

The ship groaned before sliding towards it.

We are in the cocoon. Tess leaned across the control panel and brought up the ship's systems with her clearance. She raised the carbon dioxide slowly until her headache subsided. A thin haze formed in the room and her muscles loosened. She took a deep, easy breath.

Not everyone would survive. She felt the gravity of that.

"But most of them will," she whispered. Her hand trembled. Her mind went to the children in the lower levels running on simulated turf, who had never felt the firm foundation of earth beneath their feet. She remembered the feel of sun, of air, of rain. They had been part of the Earth. How could they think they could lay claim to another planet without sacrifice?

They had carried the Earth inside them. Now they would carry this new world. They would be of each other. And it would be home, after 3,533 days in space. Tess opened the circulation system and vented the changed atmosphere through to the rest of the ship as the *Spinoza's Garden* hurtled closer to the waiting world.

The Long, Long Fall of Josiah Eddy

Ian Tregillis

A journey of 17,000 years ended in fire and failure. The debris of Arkship 001 skidded across an alien sky, vermillion streamers unfurling in its wake. Josiah bore witness to the tragedy, hugging himself to smother the primal wail swelling in his chest.

Half the expedition: gone.

Extensive orbital scans had belied the nature of their long-sought destination, revealing no hint of a planetary defense system. So now a brutal miscalculation played out across the wall of Captain Issaluk's stateroom as their companion ark disintegrated over the north pole. Abrupt. Violent. Irrevocable.

And, worst of all, strangely beautiful. Somewhere in the destruction, malfunctioning sensors misinterpreted the impinging atmosphere—78.1% nitrogen, 20.8% oxygen, a whisper of nobles and CO_2—as an uncharted galactic H II region, prompting emergency inflation of the plasma shielding. The flickering field line emitters stimulated a brilliant auroral discharge as the crumbling ship vaulted over the terminator, inertia-bound to its doomed high-latitude descent. One could almost forget these were the death throes of humanity, five kiloparsecs from Earth.

Josiah looked away, lest an animal shriek boil out of him like steam from a kettle. He focused on Captain Issaluk, commander of Arkship 002, but found no comfort there: she didn't blink once as disaster unfolded three hundred thousand miles away. It was unnerving.

002 and its irreplaceable germ banks came second in a landing order engineered into the mission, almost 20,000 years ago, by long-dead hands that had flung them into the galactic hinterlands like a human offering a dove in cupped palms to the sky. Their companion ark was to scout the descent, providing advance warning to 002 and its ultra-precious cargo of any unforeseen hazards.

In that, at least, it had succeeded.

Josiah fumbled for a prayer, but God's position on this matter was already clear.

And the Lord spake unto them, saying, "No mulligans."

Issaluk killed the comm. Silence, hard as a slap, filled a space that words could not.

The hull groaned again. An emergency maneuver had whipped them into a cislunar orbit at the cost of dangerously exceeded tolerances. 4613 stasis chambers didn't turn on a dime.

Josiah remembered mingling with members of the other crew at a pre-launch reception. He'd met a luthier, McLaren. ("I'm Chris," his new friend had said, extending a hand, "but folks call me 'Red.'"). Arkship 001 had carried humanity's last violin maker. All that skill, such artistry and compassion, rendered so much ash and plasma.

From the ship's perspective, the sun rose higher over the terminator. Golden dawnlight flooded the stateroom, coaxing a creamy glow from the unimaginably ancient ivory carvings arrayed on a shelf behind the captain. Narwhals had gone extinct a century before the arkships ignited their engines.

The remnants of 001 began to flicker out. Captain Issaluk, transfixed by morbid spectacle, didn't turn as she spoke to her chaplain.

"Did you dream, Joe? During the stasis?"

He pondered. "No. I don't think I did."

Or had he? Maybe? Something about climbing? Or flying? If he had, it was gone now. He shook his head.

"I did," she said, anticipating his first question and preemptively cold-shouldering the follow-up.

Below them, a second sunrise blazed from millions of square miles of pristine arctic wilderness. Blank canvas. Josiah squinted from the ice-glare. The captain exhaled as if punched.

"God damn," she whispered.

After millennia of travel, their destination lay just a few days away. Tantalizingly close. And permanently beyond their reach thanks to some kind of active deterrence system they couldn't detect and couldn't begin to understand, much less circumvent.

"What's the mood on board?"

By now, everybody had seen the recording.

"I'll venture a guess and say not great."

She sighed. "Yeah."

He pushed off the wall, floated toward the credenza. "Shall I fix you a coffee, ma'am?"

What good was a chaplain in the face of all this? Josiah knew he was little more than a glorified purser.

"No, thank you. The taste in my mouth is bitter enough at the moment." She paused as if reconsidering. "But I wouldn't say 'no' to a double martini, or even a slug of communion wine, if you happen to have such on you."

"Afraid not." *Why am I here?* he wanted to ask. *You have real officers. A crisis-management team.*

She fell silent again, submerged in the vortex of her unknowable thoughts. Unable to read the expression on her face, Josiah tried again.

"Maybe the other expeditions had better luck."

The captain gave a mirthless chuckle. Its feral undertone raised the hairs on his neck. "We've combed through the update transmissions that accumulated while we were under."

Subjectively, for the human crew, the journey had taken but a few weeks, owing to the wonders of relativity and biological stasis. Crossing the ocean, back in caveman times, used to take twice as long. "Last update came 27 years after we launched, Earth proper time. No mention of an Arkship 003." Finally, she looked at him. The movement sent her long jet-black braids pinwheeling. "We got out just in time." Her smile didn't touch her eyes, but he appreciated the gesture. "Lucky us."

"Shit."

Josiah knew, without asking, that they hadn't the resources to re-accelerate back into the void. The galaxy brimmed with potentially habitable planets, but they were all out of reach. Humanity had pushed all of its chips across the table for the sake of this one gem.

"We're all that remains of our species. And the laughable fraction of other terrestrial life forms preserved in our banks."

"I already said 'Shit.'"

"And well-said, indeed."

Offer comfort. Offer solace. The chaplain's role. Still, prayer eluded him. He inhaled, found another tack.

"Well. Whatever's happening down there, we seem to be safe enough up here while we figure out how to make landfall."

Captain Issaluk raised a finger. "Uh-huh. About that."

He braced for more bad news. She gestured at the wall. For a few dizzying moments the viewscreen perspective twisted away from the fading technicolor death sparks of Arkship 001, slewed across blue oceans and emerald continents, and plunged into the black of night before settling on the much closer crater-pocked expanse of colorless regolith.

The parallels to the Earth-Moon system of their former home were spectacular. Spectacular enough to justify their extra-extra-long journey.

A version of Earth where animal life never made the jump to land. If it had, it surely would have gazed up from time to time to marvel at the gray orb and its cycle of phases, spiraling out across the eons. Deep time.

She gestured again, zooming out until an entire lunar hemisphere fit on the wall.

"Look closely. Feel free to pan around. Zoom, too. Knock yourself out."

He squinted. "What am I—"

"You'll know when you see it."

And he did. A thousand-mile canyon etched across the southern maria wasn't the scar from a protoplanetary billiards game. It was a damage scar, strewn with debris... But the debris looked wrong, somehow. Artificial.

"What the f—"

She caught him before he floated into the bulkhead.

"Yeah."

"You're not saying the moon is some type of *construct?*"

Issaluk shrugged.

He shook his head. Too vigorously. "The mood on board won't improve when the rumor mill says the captain has gone insane. You know that, right?"

She ignored his artless pirouette, saying, "My guess? We're not the first interlopers to set our sights on this planet. And whatever or whoever destroyed our sister vessel also gave the big guy here," she said, nodding at the moon, "a warning."

A bead of sweat detached from his forehead. He could smell himself.

"Captain." How to say this respectfully? "A vessel that size isn't exactly landable."

"No, it isn't. But imagine you're watching over this planet. This thing—" she gestured at the screen again, re-centering the lunar hemisphere "—comes tooling along from interstellar space. It slows down and settles into a very deliberate orbit. Is it taking tourists on a joy ride along the Perseus Arm, or is it ferrying permanent colonists?"

He touched the wall, arresting his rotation. "Warning shot across the bow, huh?"

She shrugged again. "Maybe."

"There's another possibility. Maybe whatever's trying to kill us is based *on* the moon. It'd be a natural observation post, wouldn't it? So maybe somebody got to where we are and then fought back. Landed one good punch."

"I already have people assessing that scenario. But look, Joe," she pointed at the lunar scar, "even if somebody did that in self-defense, a fat lot of good it did them. There's no sign of them in the system today."

He mentally filled in the rest. *And even if we carried weapons, which we don't, they'd punch far below the weight-class on display here.*

He considered sipping on a coffee pouch. But the imagined aroma nauseated him.

"Why am I here?" he finally asked.

"We have to find a way down, Joe."

"Not to swerve out of my lane or anything, but that's more of an engineering problem than a faith problem."

"That's where you're wrong. It is very much a faith problem. And I need volunteers."

He floated in a halo of sweat and befuddlement. She gestured at the wall again, requeueing the horrors of the past half hour. He shook his head in mute protest.

"Forgive me," she said, "but I think you'll understand better if you watch it again."

* * *

The cavernous manufacturing bay had been intended as an orbital factory. Raw elements up, technology down. Anything from flint knives to heat exchangers and rolls of photovoltaic roofing. Now it was a recruitment center. It reeked. The mélange of freshly sintered plasteel singed his nose hairs.

Josiah laid a hand on the object extruded from the maker, as though offering a benediction. The newly-laid egg-shaped pod warmed his palm. Scattered throughout the bay, others gave similar pitches to equally small audiences: an imam; a Shinto priest; a Scientologist; a Buddhist nun draped in robes of eye-popping amaranth; a medicine woman; a Mormon bishop; a rabbi. There were at least as many unaffiliated groups—agnostics and atheists and omnists, oh my. Captain Issaluk was casting a thoroughly syncretic net. He wondered how many people had received the same one-on-one briefing with her that he had.

Josiah tried to disregard the engineering teams discreetly assessing stress fractures in the structural members. They moved a little too quickly, whispered a little too quietly, not to telegraph their concern. The hull groaned. They flinched. It didn't sell the illusion of calm.

He stroked the egg, saying, "The captain is asking—I'm asking—for a literal leap of faith."

She'd put it differently. *We think there's a size cutoff to what gets shot down.* And if you wanted to get somebody down from orbit, still breathing at the end, this was just about the smallest conceivable way to do it.

His audience, a double handful of neo-Catholics, gave the capsule a desultory once-over. A woman to his left said, "This'd be a one-way trip."

"It always has been. You motored past the exit ramp thousands of years ago, Earth proper time."

"Well, sure. But there's one-way, then there's one-way with a capital whatever-the-shit-that-thing-is," she said, gesturing at the pod.

The library AI called it a MOOSE enclosure, and the concept had been antiquated long before the first pieces of their arkship were hoisted out of Earth's gravity well. (Moose, the archivist personality had cheerily filled in, had been large absurd-looking ruminants inhabiting subarctic taiga in the days before thawing permafrost belched up all its sequestered methane.)

Man Out Of Space Easily. A wildly optimistic acronym if he'd ever heard one. But he kept this to himself.

"Our ancestors anticipated the need for something like this generations before we were born," he said. "Anticipated, designed, and tested it."

Well. Kind of.

"Our ancestors? Fuck those guys," grumbled somebody in the back. "We're supposed to trust *their* judgment?"

A fair point. Josiah couldn't deny it. He looked around the bay, at the other groups. Made accidental eye contact with the nun. He offered a resigned shrug. She replied with an insouciant wink.

He cleared his throat. "You might remember I said something about a leap of faith."

They fell silent. Josiah hoped it was sinking in, the gravity and urgency of their situation. But the evidence wasn't on his side, nor was the biological drive for survival. Anything that got too close to the planet died. So far, anything that crouched in lunar orbit didn't.

Nobody volunteered. He thanked them for their time, implored them to chew it over.

As they dispersed, a woman caught his eye. Inwardly, he sighed with relief.

One. At least I got one, he thought. *I'm not a charlatan.*

He nodded, willing the expression on his face into something more smile than rictus.

She floated closer, biting her lip. When close enough to whisper, she said, "I didn't want to embarrass you, but…I figured somebody should tell you, Chaplain Eddy. You've forgotten to don your dog collar."

He feigned surprise and thanked her.

* * *

Captain Issaluk summoned him. She looked up from whatever dire report she'd been reading when he drifted into her stateroom.

"Joe. Drum up any volunteers?"

"One." The captain arched her eyebrows. Was that disappointment or relief? "Me."

"Leading from the front. Good for you." She nodded approval.

"Let's call it an exercise in experimental theology."

This sounded better than admitting he lacked the courage to stick around and bear witness to the final extinction of humanity. To the final forsaking. (But who was forsaking whom?)

She cocked her head, looking bemused. But she cleaved to the task at hand.

"Test probes will reach the upper atmosphere in about eight hours. Then we'll know if our hypothesis is correct."

A new thought struck him. Had he been standing, his knees might have gone weak.

"What if we're only half right? What if the deterrence system can tell the difference between a small empty probe and one carrying a passenger?"

"Then we go to Plan D."

"May I ask what that is?"

She shook her head. "Rest up. XO Wickremasinghe will brief you and any others with what we learn from the probes.

"By the way," she called to his retreating back. "Where's your collar?"

"It got too tight."

* * *

There were no other volunteers. The population of Arkship 002 praised Josiah for his singular courage, his unparalleled selflessness, his headlong leap of faith. But faith in what? A supreme being with a depressingly laissez-faire attitude toward its creation? Or in the untested ideas of long-fossilized aerospace engineers?

Neither, really. But the illusion seemed to make people happy, so he kept his mouth shut.

The arkship adjusted orbit once more. By dropping into the lowest-known safe translunar orbit they shaved a day and a half from his drop time. Even so, the ride promised hours of monotony capped with nine minutes of terror.

His newly-synthesized vacuum suit stank of outgassing plastics and synthetic rubber. Water gurgled through the cooling tubes and the actuators at his joints gave off a vibration that made his teeth tingle. He really should have seen a dentist before going into stasis. The MOOSE cradle, half hammock and half ejection seat, molded itself to his posture. He clacked the final five-point restraint buckle into place. System checks threw no complaints.

They launched him and his glorified chair from the probe bay. The vac suit muffled almost everything except his own breathing and the tink-

tink-ding of the countdown. Next came a bang, a whoosh, and sixty-seven seconds of intense acceleration grinding him into the suspension cradle.

"Bullwinkle, this is Noah. Do you copy?"

"Noah, this is Bullwinkle. Yes. Uh—" Too late, he remembered his comm training. "Five by five."

"You're clear for inflation, Bullwinkle."

Josiah flipped a switch on his armrest. Two sheets of millimeter-thin plastic emerged from the back of his chair like diaphanous angel wings. They curved around, enfolding him. With clumsy gloves he pulled the edges together until they touched. When the flimsy bubble was complete, and system checks confirmed integrity of the seam, he flipped the switch on his other armrest. A quiet countdown gave him fifteen seconds to get comfortable.

Then a pressurized canister spewed its contents into the makeshift enclosure. Liters of liquid hydrocarbon solidified quickly, completely encasing him and his chair in thermal ablation foam. In theory, the bubble had molded his heat shield into the crucial aerodynamic teardrop shape.

Now he was just a man in a bag, falling through space.

He took deep, slow breaths, fending off claustrophobia.

His visor's augmented reality display came online. The thus-far untouchable planet filled half his universe. The swooping white curlicues of a thousand-kilometer cloud bank marked a cyclonic system spinning across a northern ocean. Equatorial jungles girdled the planet, massive swaths of a verdant green spectroscopically indistinguishable from terrestrial photosynthesis. A chain of snow-capped peaks perforated a southern continent, separating deserts from temperate rain forests. A red ellipse superimposed on his field of view encircled his intended landing spot at the confluence where a river emerged from old-growth forest to meander through rolling plains of amber grasses. Fainter concentric ellipses marked the estimated margin of error. These rippled as the MOOSE navigation system conferred with the arkship to update the estimates a hundred times per second. It was hypnotic.

A chime sounded when he approached the critical separation distance from the ship. A visual countdown accompanied the alert. Josiah braced as it reached zero. But the thruster puff was so gentle he barely felt the jolt. He closed his eyes to banish vertigo as the planet spun away from his field of view.

("Try not to hork in your suit," Captain Issaluk had advised. "It's a nasty way to go.")

Another puff from the lateral thrusters locked him into a new attitude. Now the MOOSE cradle's ablative foam shell faced the planet while he faced a black void. His hundred-thousand-kilometer plummet began in earnest.

Turned out he needed the catheter much sooner than he'd expected. He hoped the mission controllers on 002 weren't scrutinizing the medical telemetry. He tried to relax, remembered the XO's reassurances.

You'll be 30% smaller than the probes and they made it down just fine. Easy peasy.

The MOOSE yawed. A gentle trajectory adjustment nudged the arkship back into Josiah's field of view: a titanic ashen cigar, the universe's largest Freudian punchline. He'd seen the kilometer-long cylinder from the outside just once, on the way up after his feet last touched Earth, but a battering by the vicissitudes of interstellar travel had rendered it almost unrecognizable. Glancing impacts with microscopic dust grains had pitted and scored the hull. His AR display dutifully highlighted seventeen matte-blue patches where automated repair systems had hustled to seal penetrations before the damage killed the hibernating crew. Vast swaths of the once-gleaming arkship were now a chalky gray, transmuted by a slow rain of galactic cosmic rays energetic enough to pierce the plasma shielding.

"Beautiful," said his capcom. "Smooth as butter. How're you feeling, Bullwinkle?"

He resisted the ingrained urge to tug at the collar he'd left behind. "Please. I prefer Joe." His stomach gurgled. He clenched his eyes shut again. "Urk."

"Say again, Bullwinkle?"

"So far so good, Noah. No complaints."

"We have you on course. Ninety-six percent chance of bullseye. Error ellipse is four kilometers by seven."

"Tell me about that ellipse."

"Don't worry. It's oriented away from the forest. You shouldn't get stuck in a tree."

Shouldn't. But what if I do? What if I get stuck in this Eden's Tree of the Knowledge of Good and Evil?

Well, it was moot anyway. The chemists at the mission briefing had sternly warned him not to eat anything before they assessed the local amino acid chirality. (This had spurred a mind-numbing debate with the astrobiologists, who spouted off about primordial supernovae, neutrino something, and the spin of nitrogen-fourteen nuclei. Josiah had nodded off at that point. Nobody noticed. Why would they? His role was glorified ballast. "Spam in a can," to steal a phrase from the earliest days of human spaceflight.)

He sipped apple juice, then succumbed to the urge to close his eyes. A healthier person might have been keyed up with nervous energy. Anxiety. His chaplaincy carried an extensive background in counseling and this leapt to the fore. Severe depression, he self-diagnosed.

Another trajectory adjustment roused him from a long dreamless slumber. The MOOSE altered pitch again, this time rotating the moon-that-wasn't-just-a-moon into his field of view. A mottled expanse spackled with every imaginable version of gray, it loomed over 002 like the chaperone at a Catholic high school prom.

"Bullwinkle, you're still on target. Sliding into the upper exosphere now. Still a little longer before you experience real atmospheric friction."

"Understood, Noah," Josiah said, toggling his AR overlays.

His visor charted out craters, maria, and the moon's damage scar just coming into view over the western limb. He sucked down another mouthful of lukewarm apple juice. At least he could still marvel at things. Maybe his soul wasn't completely dead.

Something caught the corner of his eye, too ephemeral for him to register. Not so for the AR system, which automatically isolated the phenomenon when it happened again a few seconds later. His visor magnified and replayed a seven-times-slowed aquamarine scintillation at the near end of the scar.

An alarm pierced his reverie. He jolted against his restraint harness, biting his tongue.

"What's happening?" he asked, tasting blood.

For a moment the open comm was nothing but muffled shouting. Then Captain Issaluk's voice filled his ear: "Joe, something just pinged you."

"I think I saw it," he said. "I'm sending you a recording."

A few seconds of silence followed, presumably while mission controllers on 002 watched the shimmer playback. Then the comm erupted into more muffled urgent conversation. Most of it he couldn't make out. But he distinctly heard somebody say, "Hot mike. Damn it, you've got a *hot mike.*"

"Hey, guys, what's going on? Do I need to start praying?"

As if.

"Stand by, Bullwinkle. We'll call you back in a sec," said capcom. The line went silent.

Ok. This all seems fine, he told himself.

The silence stretched out. The aquamarine shimmer turned a flickering orange, then a pulsing violet.

"Noah, Bullwinkle. Are you seeing this?" No response. "Noah, Bullwinkle, I repeat, please tell me you're monitoring that thing."

The comm crackled.

"Hiya, Joe."

"What the hell is going on up there?"

"Honestly, it's kind of a long story. And you, friend, don't have that kind of time."

Josiah realized he didn't recognize the voice. A frisson of bewildered hope shot through him, electrified him. Survivors from the other arkship?

"Who is this? Are you from 001?"

"Whoops. We're getting off on the wrong foot. This is embarrassing."

"Please get off the frequency," he urged, aware that his voice teetered on the curling edge of shrill. "I'm trying to communicate with mission ops."

A click. "Bullwinkle, Noah. What's your status?"

"My status is I'm wondering what's going on. Who's on our frequency?"

A pause. "What do you mean?"

"What do *you* mean, what do I mean?"

"They can't hear us, Joe. Trust us. It's better that way. We really should talk privately."

"Noah, tell me you're getting this."

"Negative, Bullwinkle. Are you receiving a transmission?"

"We realize that hijacking your comms ain't exactly a burning bush, but hey, you gotta play the hand you're dealt, right?"

He recorded a pattern of purple coruscations on the moon while the mystery voice spoke.

"Noah, Bullwinkle. I think I'm receiving a tight-beam transmission."

A disappointed sigh filled the ether. "Okay, fine. Go ahead and think of it that way, if you prefer. Gotta say, though, it's a letdown coming from you of all people."

"Who *are* you?" he wailed.

"Josiah Eddy, we are THE LORD THY GOD."

A trickle of pee dribbled into Josiah's catheter. The smelly, claustrophobic vac suit suddenly seemed pointless, ephemeral. He felt cold, clammy, and very, very alone.

"I—you—"

"Nah. We're just yanking your chain. But, man, wish we could've seen the look on your face just now." The pause of a few heartbeats, then: "Hey, you didn't piss yourself, did you? Nuts. Sorry about that. We'll dial it back. Humor is supposed to help in situations like this."

Josiah shivered. He used the AR's ocular interface to tweak his suit temperature.

"Bullwinkle, Noah. Joe, your heartbeat is spiking. Medical wants you to unlock an injection if you're too keyed up to relax."

"Understood, Noah." *Easier said than done.*

"They do have a point," said the mystery voice. "It wouldn't be a bad idea to calm down. Please believe us when we say the last thing we'd want is for you to stroke out."

The fiery death of half of humanity's only interstellar expedition, and dismal survival prospects for the rest, had surely driven at least a few into a hard nihilism. Somebody on 002 had decided that nothing fucking mattered and the only thing a soul could do was embrace the meaningless chaos of the universe. So, sure. Why not jerk around the poor chaplain trapped in his death pod?

"Listen, whoever you are." Josiah struggled to find his calm, reassuring Chaplain Voice. The quavering probably undercut it a bit. "I know the situation is troubling right now. But your practical joke is only making things more difficult for everybody. By interfering with our communications, you risk turning a successful expedition into a failure. So, please, I ask you to stop this."

"Geez, Louise," said the mystery voice. "You have got a white-knuckled grip on Occam's Razor, don't you? We gotta pry that thing loose, and fast. Time's a-wasting."

A gentle pressure pushed him into the cradle. A ghostly hiss seeped into his helmet. It swelled into a muffled sandpaper susurration as capcom chimed in.

"Bullwinkle, Noah. Your capsule should start to experience some atmospheric drag now. You'll feel it any second. This is nominal and expected. You're still on course and your entry attitude is perfect."

"Yes, I mean, copy, Noah. Feeling it now."

Josiah's harness creaked as the invisible hand of deceleration tried to fold him into the suspension cradle. Outside, the first tongues of orange plasma licked at his field of view. The fires of hell, claiming his soul. Josiah could just make out the curvature of the planet. Above, a starry black expanse; below, a cloud-swirled azure marble.

"Noah. Have you isolated the signal interference?"

"Negative, Bullwinkle. But you'll enter radio blackout any moment." He hadn't really paid attention to the explanation during the mission briefing. Something about ionized gasses and radio waves. A staticky crackle contaminated the transmission from 002 as capcom continued. "We'll get it sorted. XO has dispatched teams to physically inspect every auxiliary antenna on the ship."

"Acknowledged, Noah."

A minor tremor shook the pod. Josiah closed his eyes and wet his suddenly dry mouth with a cloying sip of juice. The plasma streamers wrapping around his capsule grew in length and intensity.

"Are you still there?"

"We're here, Joe." So clear was the mystery voice it might have been coming from inside his helmet. Or his imagination. "That little contraption of yours is pretty clever. We hope you're buckled in tight, though, because it's about to get all 'Mr. Toad's Wild Ride' in there."

That caught him so off guard that he actually chuckled. That surprised him almost as much as anything else.

"Your vernacular…"

"Well, what did you expect? 'Bleep bloop'? 'Phone home'? 'Klaatu barada nikto'?"

He shrugged.

"C'mon, Joe. What good would that do? And anyway, your ship archives aren't encrypted. Not that it would have made a difference. Not to brag or anything. Maybe we haven't perfectly nailed the tone, but you get our point."

"Bullwink…" A static warble dominated the comm. "…attitude…land… percent."

"Noah, please repeat," he said. No response but static. "Noah, please repeat."

The mystery voice continued as if uninterrupted. "But, hey, you know what? Giving your digital archives a chipper personality was a cute flex."

For a moment Josiah wondered if he were talking to a corrupted version of the archive AI. But that particular train of thought barely left the station: it would still mean communicating via the ship systems and that was thoroughly borked for as long as he was a shooting star.

Josiah clicked off the comm entirely, banishing the white-noise howl. The capsule shook so violently that his teeth clacked together until he tensed his jaw. Incandescent plasma streamers drew a shimmering veil across the cosmos. Ablating thermal foam fed ribbons of energized ions into the maelstrom, like dye poured into churning water. A vermilion haze suffused everything he could see.

He remembered the incandescent debris of Arkship 001.

"You destroyed our other ship." It wasn't a question.

"Well, not really. We mean, yes, but not by choice. Not entirely by choice. Let's plead Stockholm Syndrome and leave it at that."

"I don't know what that means."

"We arrived a while ago. You guys might not have been walking upright quite yet, yeah? Soon after that we were…shanghaied? Press-ganged? Made an offer we couldn't refuse?"

The AR readout of his trajectory stats proclaimed he was still on course and that he'd passed the point of maximum thermal loading. Stresses on the capsule were steadily declining. Good news, because only eleven percent of the ablative shield remained.

A hellish lightshow no longer obscured his view, but he was now many thousands of kilometers from where the MOOSE pod had first brushed against the atmosphere. Even with AR augmentation he couldn't see Arkship 002. The moon, if it was a moon, was just barely visible.

A thought occurred to him. "You used to fly around the galaxy in a, uh, planet?"

"It's called traveling in style. But *you* guys, wow. You crazy hominids did it the hard slow way. Mad respect. Much love."

By design, the lingering heat-cured crust of plasma-sculpted ablative foam now functioned as a hypersonic control surface. Aerodynamic forces tilted the capsule. A corner of the AR display provided a discreet countdown until deployment of the drogue chute.

"If you can talk to me so easily, why didn't you contact the other arkships? You could have warned us off! There was no need to slaughter!"

"Hasn't it occurred to you yet? Maybe you're not talking to god. After all, we are legion. Maybe you're talking to the devil."

Josiah shook his head. The sweat-humid atmosphere in his vac suit was getting ripe.

"I no longer believe in either," he admitted to himself. And as long as this were true, he also didn't believe in an afterlife or mortal sins. Meaning he had no reason for trepidation.

"Sure you don't. But so what? We have our appointed task and that's that."

"I'm to believe you were forcibly recruited to act as celestial park rangers for a planet-sized nature preserve."

"Not a bad guess. But in terms you would understand, think of us as the night watchmen for a performance art project slash dream retirement home. When the ones who made this place—by the way, you guys didn't look closely enough at the sun—decide they've run their course, they'll return here to run out the clock until the heat death of the universe renders the very concept of a clock irrelevant."

The comm chimed. The fireball interference had abated, reestablishing a link to Arkship 002.

"Noah, Bullwinkle. Do you copy?"

A gut-twisting eternity of several heartbeats elapsed before a very relieved-sounding capcom replied, "Bullwinkle, Noah. We read you. Telemetry is good and you're still on target."

The limb of the planet made line-of-sight communications impossible. A lag entered the conversation as their back-and-forth bounced through a series of satellites that 002 had lobbed into synchronous orbit the day previously, for exactly this purpose.

"Noah, Bullwinkle. Have you tracked the source of the communication interference?"

This time the lag was longer than it had any right to be. "Bullwi—uh, Joe, there *is* no comm interference. Every auxiliary antenna on the vessel is powered down."

"They're wondering if the call is coming from inside the house," said the mystery voice. "It isn't."

"We think," capcom continued, "that the archivist personality we cloned into the MOOSE could be faulty. It might be monitoring our comm loop and responding with gibberish."

Josiah considered this, swishing the last bit of apple juice around his mouth. He swallowed.

"What about those scintillations on the moon? Are you still seeing them?"

The lag grew. "We're still working that one."

An emerald banner flashed in Josiah's visor display. Ninety seconds to drogue deployment.

"Stand by for detachment," he said.

He shifted, bracing for a jolt. A ten-second countdown finished with a gentle *ding*. Then a violent tightening of the restraint harness snapped him back into the cradle. Explosive bolts flung the crumbling heat shield aside. An alien wind rushed up past his boots, filling the pod with a mini-maelstrom. Cradle netting slapped against his vac suit. The sudden changes to the internal capsule pressure and the pod's aerodynamic profile dislodged the foam-hardened plastic bag that had formed the exterior of the descent pod. The remainder of his foam enclosure peeled apart like the petals of a flower. They rose away from him, slowly at first, then mere moments later they were distant dark blemishes in a cerulean vault.

Now he was just a man in a chair, falling through the sky.

With the enclosure gone he no longer needed the AR display. He craned forward. A dozen kilometers below his booted toes, a river emerged from pristine ancient forest to wend through golden hillocks.

"Joe, you seem like a righteous dude. So just for the record, we want you to know this isn't personal. OK?"

Something about the tone—

He toggled the comm. "Noah, Bullwinkle. Come in." Static. "Come in, Noah."

"They can't hear you, Joe."

"Noah, Bullwinkle." He couldn't keep the shrill out of his voice. "Please respond, Noah."

"Every Eden needs an Adam. But only one."

Be fruitful and multiply, thought Josiah. He flinched with revulsion.

"Noah took *two* of every beast, you fools." Josiah laughed. He recognized the same feral undertone that had haunted Captain Issaluk's joyless chuckle. "So good luck getting me to populate your zoo."

"Ugh. Don't be gross," said the voice in a tone heavy with disappointment. "We guess it's true what they say. You can take the hominid out of the savanna but you can't take the horny little chimpanzee out of the starfarer."

Ten seconds to drogue deployment. A hundred and fifty kilometers away, lightning zigzagged through a coastal thunderhead. Sane or not, prophet or not, it'd all be over before the front blew through his ostensible landing zone.

"Maybe Adam was the wrong metaphor. See, once we hand you the flaming sword, we're free to hie ourselves way the hell away from this accursed honeytrap."

Yeah, well, we'll see about that.

A thud jostled his seat as the drogue canister popped open. A bundle of synthetic spider silk shot out, long tethers spooling out behind it. Another jolt and the drogue inflated. He felt momentarily heavier. The cradle swayed but stabilized quickly.

Before the drogue could yank out the main chute, Josiah toggled the emergency override. Alarm peals vibrated his helmet. The AR display blazed fluorescent orange.

"Ah. Better to rule in hell than serve in heaven, eh?"

Ignoring the taunt, he confirmed the command. The drogue chute detached. Weightlessness enfolded him as he reaccelerated to terminal velocity.

Afterlife and mortal sin were myths, he reassured himself. Death was final. Wasn't it?

The crater wouldn't be that deep. A century or two of natural weathering would bury him and the remains of the MOOSE pod. An eye blink, after which it'd be like nobody had ever been here.

"Full points for valor, Joe. But if you wanted to die quickly, you should have stayed with the others. We can't let you do this."

He smiled. It felt good. "Too late."

"Is it?"

When he looked down, his newfound sense of beatific calm vanished. So had the ground, which had been replaced with a black tunnel. Josiah's frisson of alarm came out as a mindless yelp.

He fell long past the point of impact. Negative altitudes and impossible distances scrolled through a glitchy AR readout. Alarm turned into despair.

I was wrong. There is a hell, and it was built for me.

Still he fell. And while he did, the reluctant guardians crowbarred open his mind and force-fed him.

First, the fruit of the Tree of Life, that his vigil might be endless. Despair became horror.

This hell is eternal, so I must be rebuilt for it.

Then, the fruit of the Tree of Knowledge of Good and Evil, that he might know his purpose and every means of achieving it.

"Please don't do this," he pleaded.

"A final piece of advice, Joe. Do what you must, but don't beat yourself up about it later."

True to their word, they bestowed the flaming sword. Josiah had no choice but to embrace it. Become it.

The debris of Arkship 002 rained upon an alien sky.

Transformation complete, he emerged from the tunnel a disembodied consciousness orbiting a moonless world.

Perpetually east of Eden. Perpetually falling.

Transub-Stan-Tiation

Jack Nicholls

"...one giant leap for Stan-kind," I finished as I materialized on a glistening gray shore speckled by rain.

They had warned me to expect dizziness and disorientation; but the only disorientation lay in the smoothness of the transition. I had begun my quote from the New Frontiers dais, squinting against the glare of a hundred flashing video-drones; now I finished it beneath the humming pylons of the Universal Printer which had rebirthed me on Teegarden Prime. In that gap between heartbeats, twelve years and a hundred and fourteen trillion kilometers had passed unnoticed.

I took a squelching step down to the surface and, when I lifted my boot, water seeped into my footprint, the first ever made on this alien world. My wristpad reported that it was eight degrees Celsius soon after sunrise, although little light filtered through the thick, oxygen-heavy clouds above. Dotted along the shore of a salt lake stood the silent cluster of photovoltaic domes that would be our new home, twenty-four years more weathered than they had appeared in our last transmission received back on Earth.

Lodestar, our LOcal DEpendable Sentient Tracked Autonomous Rover, rolled up to me on wide, mud-encrusted treads and tilted an insectoid head bristling with antenna and lenses. "Greetings, Doctor Kiernan, welcome to Camp Tea Garden," said the trolley-sized robot in a maternal voice, sounding remarkably blasé for a machine that hadn't spoken since it set off on its own lonely journey from Earth almost a century ago.

"Um…thank you. Thank you for building the place."

I knew Lodestar would be recording my reaction and cringed. This moment, now, was history, and that had not been a response worthy of history books. Unsure where to take the conversation, I was rescued from social awkwardness by a rising hum from the Universal Printer. I turned and smiled in greeting as the extruder nozzles began to pulse in preparation for the next scheduled arrival, Guzman, the hydrologist.

The printer burst into vibrating life, a man pouring out of its nozzles from the ground up. Boots grew legs, grew a torso and a head, and after a flash of light to jump-start his systems, my first neighbor stood on the plate still finishing the breath he had drawn on Planet Earth.

"…one giant leap for Stan-kind!"

We stared at each other in horrified silence, the only sound the rain pattering against Lodestar's carapace. The rover analyzed the situation, then politely cocked its head towards the new arrival and repeated, "Greetings, Doctor Kiernan, welcome to Camp Tea Garden."

My double and I swore.

He stepped off the receiver plate and extended his gloved hands. I met them with my own as if reaching into a mirror. His face was unsettlingly reversed, a scar I was used to seeing above my left eyebrow lay above his right. Realization dawned as the printer began to hum again.

"…one giant leap for Stan-kind!"

The third me was quicker on the uptake, taking in the stunned expressions on the faces of me and my doppelgänger. "How long have you been here?" he asked urgently.

"Sixty/thirty seconds," we replied, our voices chiming perfectly on the latter word. All three of us turned to the rover. "Lodestar, shut down the printer!" we chorused.

"I lack that authority. Welcome to Camp Tea Garden, Doctor Kiernan."

"…one giant leap for Stan-kind!" cried the fourth Stan Kiernan, materializing between the poles. My third self hadn't stepped off the receiver plate yet, so the fourth rammed into his back and they tumbled together down into the gray muck. The third Stan landed badly; he yelped in pain and clutched at his ankle.

I lurched towards the printer terminal and stumbled immediately as my boot suctioned up a halo of mud the size of a dinner plate—the surface had the color and consistency of wet cement. I fell, splattered, and staggered back to my feet at the display, shielded from the elements behind a translucent shield. TRANSMISSION RECEIVED read the moisture-beaded screen, above a 3D model of my body.

"…one giant leap for Stan-kind!"

One of my selves joined me at the terminal. "We need to shut off the power until we've found the bug."

"I know!"

"Obviously. Sorry."

"...one giant leap for Stan-kind!"

My fingers flew across the keyboard, the growing crowd of Stans barely restraining themselves from pushing me aside. TRANSMISSION COMPLETE would flash, my image flicker, then it reappeared and the cycle began again. The transfer of all forty members of the New Frontiers team was automated. Overriding it required administrator privileges. My mind blanked. I was the mission psychologist, not technical support.

"...one giant leap for Stan-kind!"

"Unplug it!" one of me yelled. I surged in a panicked crowd around the printer, looking hopelessly for a fuse or switch.

"...one giant leap for Stan-kind!"

"...one giant leap for Stan-kind!"

"...one giant leap for Stan-kind!"

"Welcome to Camp Tea Garden, Doctors Kiernan," said Lodestar, the sole point of calm among my scurrying selves.

* * *

By the time the printer ran out of feedstock there were eighty-nine of me. Numbering ourselves was pointless; I agreed on that. I agreed on a lot.

Eighty-nine Stans were too many for our prefabricated supply of chairs, so in a reversion to kindergarten we sat cross-legged on the floor of a very dated mess hall, its honeycombed walls patiently erected by our machines in accordance with designs drawn up a century ago.

As we came to grips with our situation, I could sense divergence happening. Why? The different scenery visible through the wraparound windows, perhaps. Those of me who, like myself, were looking out across the lake were still mired in the philosophical weirdness of my situation, while those facing the Universal Printer were brainstorming technical solutions—after all, we could manufacture anything we had materials for. One Stan had badly twisted his ankle in the chaos of our arrival; I could see the way the pain diverted his thoughts along darker rivulets.

"I'm going to die here," said Ankle-Stan.

"That's just the stress talking," chimed the Stans opposite me, more sympathetically than I felt. I pressed my fingers against my forehead to take a steadying breath and saw the gesture mimicked in receding reflections of Stans on either side.

"Mass suicide?" one of me suggested. But there was no appetite for that. The situation was a nightmare, but now that it had happened, it had happened. Like a woman giving birth to octuplets, I just had to accept that life had changed.

Conversation juddered between silence and bursts of overlapping dialogue. I quickly grew tired of interrupting myself and, since the printer still had hydrocarbons left over, I had Lodestar print me a plastic conch shell, so we could speak our mind one voice at a time.

"I'm twelve light years from Earth; it'll be decades before New Frontiers hears about this and sends back their commiserations. And in the meantime, the rest of the colonists are stalled in the void between us."

I handed the Conch on to my left.

"I've reset the transmission software, but manufacturing eighty-nine Stans in an hour has exhausted our supply of key organic elements. Specifically, sodium, phosphorus, potassium, calcium, iodine, and selenium."

"Sodium I can distill from the salt lake. There's plenty of phosphorus set aside in the greenhouse and iodine in the med-bay. That leaves calcium, potassium and selenium."

"Which is probably all around me, either in the rocks or the construction materials in the base itself."

"But I'm an occupational psychologist, not a chemist or geologist."

"They wanted to send me through first…"

"…in case anything emotionally unexpected happened."

The resulting silence had the excruciating quality of a failing date. I'd never liked watching myself on video and now I stared out the window to avoid the pouchy eyes, the thin lips chapped with cold, and the crust of snot around one nostril that New Frontiers' printer had painstakingly recreated eighty-nine times. A few stifled coughs punctuated the clink of cutlery—Lodestar had extended her torso accordion-like from her tracks and with four pincers was busying herself making eighty-nine cups of tea at the mess counter. Busying *itself*, I corrected myself. We corrected ourselves?

No. I wasn't giving up my pronoun. I was me and as soon as we started diverging the Stans across the room became someone else. I exchanged glances with the Stans adjacent to me, who nodded subtle agreement. We were we. The Stans opposite were Them.

We though me may be, as the first arrival I felt some responsibility as the Senior Stan. I beckoned for the Conch.

"Until we've sorted out this mess, we'll have to assign roles. Some of us need to get the camp up and running while the rest of us track down the materials we need."

"Who died and made you Bezos?" said Ankle-Stan sourly, despite not holding the Conch. "Everything needs to be randomized, it's the only fair way."

"Obviously, I agree," I said. The Stan to my left held out his hand, but I didn't pass the Conch just yet. "Lodestar, once you're done with the tea, are you able to divvy up tasks between us?"

"Certainly, Doctor Kiernan. Do you take sugar?"

We all nodded. Left-Stan plucked the Conch from my hand and said, "Just for formality's sake, shall we take a vote? All in favor of Lodestar assigning roles?"

Eighty-six hands went up. Three did not, a trio beneath the heater who were glancing at us with unreadable frowns. They suddenly seemed more disturbingly alien than any patient I had worked with.

Lodestar handed out the steaming tea, distilled from lake water. I felt claustrophobic among all these reflections, eager to get out and explore this planet of mud, rock, and rain, and on cue two-dozen other Stans rose to stretch their legs.

"Before we get out there, I think I'd benefit from a brief meditation," suggested a Stan in a mud-smeared New Frontiers jumpsuit. He was right, I needed to calm the anxiety in my chest. Another Stan went to the terminal, darkening the polarized windows and activating an audioscape of water birds and soft waves.

I closed my eyes and drew alien air into my nose. It tasted subtly wrong, headily saturated with oxygen and more humid than the temperature warranted, but breathable. I inhaled and pictured my stomach muscles unclenching. It would be fine. After all, I had the most reliable companion I could ask for—myself.

Or did I? What if my divergence had already reached the point where some of me would cheat at such a simple thing as meditation? What if they were all staring at me right now?

I snuck a peek and eighty-eight opening eyelids met my gaze.

* * *

Alone with my thoughts, I was exploring New Frontiers psychologically as well as literally. As far as I knew, a cock-up like this hadn't happened since the first days of organic printers, but of course until now, no organic printer had been built remotely without a human engineer to test it *in situ*. In college, I had written a paper on delusional misidentification disorders such as Capgrass and Fregoli; to them I could now add Kiernan Syndrome. I considered penning an article on it: "The Disintegration of Sense of Self in Cases of Clonal Pluralization" by S Kiernan. Kiernan et al.

I'd always had a tendency towards negative self-talk and now it found new heights as externalized irritation. I grew to loathe my morning snorts, the heavy breaths of my concentration, and the hitherto unnoticed bald spot on the back of my head that seemed to grow from day to day. I recognized that I was suffering feelings of depersonalization and, amidst the forest of ginger-bearded Stans, I struggled to remember what my absent colleagues had ever looked like. When I became aware at breakfast that all eighty-nine of me were absently humming the same advertising jingle, I felt so overwhelmed by the sensation that I was the only person within a hundred trillion kilometers that I began to cry. All of me.

To combat this loss of ego, I adopted whatever little pieces of flair I could use to lay stake to a separate identity. My ankle was healing, but the footing on Teegarden Prime was tenuous and I kept it strapped, which earned me the soubriquet Ankle Stan, which in the surreal logic of nicknames soon morphed into AthelStan.

Athelstan was an old English name meaning noble stone and, certainly, I spent more time than I had ever expected worrying over minerals. All my focus had to be towards sourcing the calcium, potassium, and selenium that would allow me to print more colonists—starting with our petite chemist Isshi, who would hopefully be able to point the way to finding more feedstock. To that end, I randomized myself each day into two groups: the House Stans who did their best to follow the original mission parameters by setting up the greenhouse and repairing thirty years of salt corrosion and storm damage; and the Prospector Stans, who spent each day in search of printer materials.

Our databanks told me that human blood contained 3 grams of potassium per liter, so I set up a donation line in the hope of distilling a colleague out of blood like a storybook warlock. I had nursing training, but also a lifelong anxiety around needles, and these Stan-on-Stan jab sessions sometimes ended up with as much blood splashed across the med-bay floor as caught in vials. Selenium was harder. Lodestar helpfully told me that it was best sourced from Brazil Nuts which, unfortunately, New Frontiers had neglected to include among our provisions.

Conversation was utilitarian at best and most of the time I pretended the others were just not there. I'd long-ago made peace with the idea of farewelling everyone on Earth, but the New Frontiers colonists had become a surrogate family. Some, like our alluring botanist, Dr. Makris, I had hoped might become something more. But even in fantasy I had no privacy. Whenever a chance association set me thinking on Dr. Makris' heavy braid of hair, I soon became aware of other Stans surreptitiously adjusting themselves alongside me.

Masturbation was nothing to be ashamed of, but the base was overcrowded and I'd never known embarrassment like walking in on myself with penis in hand. In the end we set up a rotational system in the empty communications booth, but the first time I closed the door behind me in there I felt so depressed that even my botanical fantasies couldn't get me up to speed. The tissues in the wastebasket suggested a divergence there, too. We should recycle the semen into the printer, I thought, but I couldn't bring myself to gather my collective emissions. I suppose the same thought process played out each time one of us entered here.

We'd had to quadruple up in the bedrooms and I discovered that, if anything, my previous partners had been too polite when they'd mentioned my snoring. Nights were a race to be the first to sleep before the cacophony grew like cicadas.

After one bout of insomnia listening to my snuffles I got desperate enough to consider force-printing a new colonist without all their constituent elements. I crept out past the inexhaustible Lodestar polishing the windows on its nocturnal rounds and, in the darkness of the lake's edge, I found a half-dozen of myselves outside the Universal Printer with the same idea. Without exchanging a word of acknowledgement, we overrode the transmitter safety protocols and printed Isshi the chemist without her full complement of calcium and selenium.

It didn't go well.

I recycled the resulting puddle-person back into the printer's recombinant chute and furtively returned to bed, wondering how many times that scene had played out in recent nights. When I finally fell asleep near dawn, I dreamed of my face crumbling to silver powder and pouring itself as potassium and selenium into my cupped hands.

* * *

"First man on another solar system, reduced to beach-combing," I muttered as I picked through minerals around the lakeshore and gave them to Lodestar to chew.

I would have preferred to journey alone, but for safety we were moving in triplicate on small skis, skating across a mire glittering with salt crystals while Lodestar trundled behind. Mudflats that had lain pristine for ten million years were churned to porridge in our wake, while ahead of us, the flat gray clouds and the flat gray lake merged towards a mirrored horizon. A dark line on the opposite bank marked what we now universally referred to as Camp Afstanni-Stan.

"Technically, if any of us were first it was me," said the Stan who had differentiated himself by shaving his beard but leaving the ginger hair on his cold-flushed cheeks.

It took me a moment to realize that I had directed a remark to myself. "What are you talking about? I was first out, ask Lodestar."

"I'm sorry, Doctor Kiernan, I have some trouble telling you apart," said Lodestar diplomatically.

Muttonchops Stan took a seat on the uncomplaining robot's back and looked at me quizzically. "Look, I know we're not liars, but I think you're confabulating. You're remembering the way I described it to you. The sand was as smooth as glass, I looked down at the water filling up my footprint, thinking about how I'd just made the first human mark on another system and how quickly it would be gone."

"Maybe *you're* confabulating."

"Equally possible."

"I suppose you're going to say that you were first as well?" I asked the third member of our trio, who had a nasty pimple just above his eyebrow.

"Not me," said Pustule Stan. "When I arrived, you were all running round like headless chooks."

Lodestar regurgitated a dark slurry at our feet. "I have finished analyzing the sample, Doctors Kiernan. Carbon, iron, oxygen, and magnesium."

"Useless," we said in concert. Without marine life, this planet seemed to have locked all its calcium far beneath the surface. I was cold, tired, and needed to pee, which meant that the others did, too.

"Bottles out, gentlemen," said Muttonchops Stan. "We need to conserve nitrogen."

The three of us stared at the horizon, wincing as we exposed ourselves to the cold winds. We'd developed a strict eyes-front etiquette to govern nudity among Stans, so I only heard the curse and squelch as Pustule Stan slipped in the slime.

"Goddammit, it's all up in my arse," said Pustule Stan. "That's it, I'm going back to Afstanni-Stan to turn this piss into beer."

When we made it back to the mess hall to immerse our numb fingers in hot water, the House Stans were just wrapping up a discussion. "The work's going too slowly, everyone trying to learn everything," an exhausted-looking Stan holding the Conch told us. "We need to specialize. You three have been assigned to continue with mineral prospecting."

"Oh really? I wasn't involved in this discussion," Pustule Stan said.

"In the strictest possible way, you were," said Conch Stan. "And the vote was unanimous."

"So let me guess," I said. "Someone needs to manage this new hierarchy? You're going to be *primus inter pares* of Teegarden?"

"No, that's Herr Doktor Stan," Conch Stan said, calmly indicating a Stan marked for his new role with a freshly-printed bicorn hat in the Napoleonic style. "And, exactly as you say, someone has to take responsibility for the work. We promise you'll agree when you've warmed up a bit."

"Warm up to that," I said, extending a half-frozen middle finger to the room.

"Interesting," said the so-called Herr Doktor Stan, scribbling something on a notebook. "Significant personality deviation is starting to emerge. You were the one who hurt his ankle, yes?"

"Maybe a negative feedback loop building on the initial association of the environment with pain," suggested a Stan nursing a whiskey glass.

"Or the different ratio of successes to failures in my assigned tasks?" mused Conch Stan.

"This is all too complicated for a simple working man like us," I said, and the three of us marched back out into the rain, leaving the House Stans to their deliberations.

They weren't entirely wrong, I admitted, once I'd changed out of my wet clothes. Our plants weren't taking root in the greenhouse and every time we used the Universal Printer to recycle waste back into nutrients we lost a percentage to sublimation. We all knew things were going badly.

That evening we gathered, unspoken, at the lake shore. To a Stan, we took off our boots and stood barefoot in the water, letting slime ooze between our toes. The sky darkened. Lodestar quietly turned on the lights of Afstanni-Stan and the windows cast rippling golden streaks across the foam. Now I couldn't see my reflected faces, it was easier to say what was on my mind.

"There's another possibility, of course," said one of my mouths behind me.

My voice to my right continued the thought. "We have enough selenium, potassium, and calcium to make exactly eighty-nine people."

"Only it's distributed throughout our bodies," I finished.

Silence, while we considered what was unsaid. All we needed to do was recycle one of us and use the materials to print Isshi or Wenham. Strange to think, I could become Isshi. We contain multitudes; all we needed was a little atomic shake-up.

A one percent chance of death to escape solipsism hell? Who among us wouldn't take that?

"One point one," murmured a few Stans out of the darkness.

Would I really go through with it?

"Yes," we agreed.

* * *

Draped in fairy-lights, Lodestar trundled through the mess hall, a tray of drinks raised on one claw. The music of my adolescence played loud enough to shake the speakers—the ultimate Stan Kiernan playlist, coolness be damned.

"If you think about it, it's not death, it's just like we're losing an eighty-ninth of ourself," I tipsily shouted to myself.

"A pound of flesh?"

"Exactly. And we could do with losing a pound."

We touched a hand to our mid-sections.

The atmosphere in the mess hall was one part anxious to two parts festive. Four elements we weren't lacking were carbon, hydrogen, nitrogen, and oxygen so we'd printed bottles of Afstanni-Stan-labelled whiskey and made a party of it. We clustered in small groups, loosely mirroring the social organizations that I had assigned us. The gardening Stans cheered a ping-pong game with forced frivolity; the cartographer Stans spoke quietly at the windows, trekking through landscapes of memory; the admin Stans sat alone scribbling notes in their "personal" journals.

I could feel myself Othering these men as I pondered their death. They'd already taken on shades of difference in my mind. The petulance of AthelStan, the warmth I associated with the Kimono Stan who had helped me unclog the air filters. I knew that these eighty-eight men thought and dreamed. I knew they were deathly afraid of stick insects, that romantic rejection flashed them back twenty years to Molly Moran's derisive snort when they'd moved in for a kiss, that they sang in the shower. But all of that would remain with one Stan down. The rest were…surplus.

Now that I was committed to this amputation, I wished I'd done it the first day—the longer we waited, the more we diverged. Still, I had no doubt this was the right thing to do and, knowing my own commitment, I wasn't worried about cheating. Lodestar would assign us each a number and then pick one at random. I supposed we'd give the poor bastard a chance to gather his thoughts, then we'd anaesthetize him and carry him to the recombinant pipe. It's not like he'd need to write a will.

I tapped a glass for silence. I didn't need to speak; we were all impatient to get it over with. The important thing was going to be to support the poor Stan who drew the short straw.

We gathered in a loose circle around Lodestar. Eighty-nine wristpads beeped—mine displayed the number 31. I felt a stirring of anxiety, but it was no worse than when I had first stepped into the matter transmitter on Earth, not being certain if I was going to be recombined at all. I nodded at Lodestar to give it the go-ahead.

"Doctor Kiernan 31," said Lodestar, and rotated its head to look at me.

My thoughts shut down, leaving only sense impressions. I heard eighty-eight glad exhalations, each quickly stifled and replaced with a look of sympathy and the stress response of two fingers pressed against the forehead. Well, eighty-seven looks of sympathy—AthelStan smirked with open relief.

I took my bicorn hat off and turned it over and over in my hands. It wasn't fair, wasn't I *primus inter pares?* Had Lodestar chosen me, specifically, out of spite? We should have asked the robot to kill one of us in our sleep. Why had I thought this ritualistic death sentence was a good idea? I hadn't thought it through because it hadn't seemed real.

"Get him another drink," said a Stan, I didn't recognize who. They were all the same now. The face I loathed more than any in the universe.

I forced a laugh and gestured at him with the hat. "I just realized, we don't need to go through with this at all. You can just send me back to Earth to report on what happened here, and reuse my components for somebody else."

"You know that won't work," responded a dozen Stans. "The printer can't upload an object for transmission without vaporizing it. We need to put your materials in the chute."

"Of course. My materials. The chute. Yes."

My face turning to powder and falling away into cupped hands.

My neighbors were edging away from me, a growing void of floorspace separating the Stans from the Damned. It was abjection. They'd cast me out of the body politic like a broken tooth or a clump of hair.

"I'd like some time to myself," I said.

"I understand," said the Stans. "Anything you need," said the Stans. Cowboy Stan took my bicorn and replaced it on my head like a coronation. I saw through the faux-reverence immediately—he was just making sure that I was the one marked out for death.

I would have done the same.

I took my leave on shaking legs and walked out to the windswept shore. In the late afternoon light, the Universal Printer loomed over the camp like a malicious deity hungry for sacrifice. Beyond was nothing but a thousand leagues of silt. There was nowhere to run.

To avoid looking at the machine, I took a door at random and found myself in the storeroom where we stored excess feedstock. I slumped onto a bin filled with carbon diamonds. I was rehearsing reasonable objections to this plan, but each time came up against the smug certainty of my own mind two minutes ago. The rest of the Stans would still be in that headspace, telling themselves that I would go through with it, because that's what *they* would do. They were lying to themselves, but they didn't know it.

And that gave me an advantage.

I raised my wristpad to my lips and called for Lodestar. After a minute, the rover appeared in the doorway and tilted its ant-like head to look at me. "Yes, Doctor Kiernan?"

"As the ranking New Frontiers colonist, I'm asking you to shut down the base lights, unlock all doors, and turn on the sprinkler system."

"I am sorry, Doctor Kiernan. The other Doctors Kiernan have instructed me not to take any orders from you, other than those related to comfort."

"Can you fetch me something from one of their bedrooms?" I asked.

"No, Doctor Kiernan. The other Doctors Kiernan have instructed me not to give you anything."

I thought about it. "Can I give *you* something?" I asked.

"Certainly, Doctor Kiernan."

I was surrounded by the building blocks of life. One cannister held buttery chunks of sodium, another liquefied nitrogen, a third the drops of potassium we'd extracted from blood donations. Almost everything we needed to make a person, except goddamn selenium. In the reflections on the steel cylinders, my face was a distorted blur. I could have been anyone.

I thought of an urban legend from my college days, probably centuries old. A hundred students are taking an exam. When time is called, one keeps writing past the deadline. After he hands his paper in at the front, his professor tells him he will fail. "Do you know who I am?" asks the student in outrage. "No, and I don't care," retorts the professor. "Good," says the student, slots his paper among the others, and throws them up in the air before running out of the room.

Outside the curved windows, the darker than usual clouds suggested it was soon to rain. I'd learned a lot about chemistry the past weeks. It was worth a try.

I told Lodestar I wanted to pray and it obligingly rolled outside. A minute later I emerged and held out a package wrapped in a thin layer of brown paper.

"I want you to look after this, Lodestar."

"Yes, Doctor Kiernan."

"It's a memento. You are to give it to the other Doctor Kiernans when I'm gone."

"Yes, Doctor Kiernan."

Lodestar extended a pincer and delicately took the book-sized package from me. I hesitated before releasing my grip.

"You're a sentient being. Are you afraid of death?"

"No, Doctor Kiernan. If I were to be destroyed, I could be replaced."

"Easy to say now, Lodestar."

The Stans were surprised when I returned to the mess hall and said I wanted to go right now. No sense in delaying. With luck they could have Isshi here in half an hour. I waved away their offer of sedation in bed; it would be easier for all if I walked myself to the Universal Printer. For my final request, I asked that Lodestar record the moment.

They nodded. It's what they wanted, too—their bravery immortalized for history. "It is a far, far better thing that I do than I have ever done," etc. Hypocrites. They weren't sacrificing anything.

It was a hundred meters from the mess hall to the Universal Printer. I walked slowly, the mud sucking at my feet, while the Stans made a sombre procession behind me. I toiled up the steps to the platform and, when I turned, I saw my faces watching me with hungry inquisitiveness. They were wondering what it was like to be under a death sentence, hoping for some graveside insight. Lodestar stood in their midst, training its lenses on me, my farewell gift held in its claws.

A distant peal of thunder shivered the air, but still no rain.

AthelStan checked the time on his wristpad. In a few moments the Stans would manhandle me towards the recombinant pipe and flush me away. What did you say at a time like this?

The perpetual cloudbanks masked the setting of the giant red sun, but there was something beautiful about watching the diffuse coppery light drain from the seeping, sepia, landscape. It deserved a song. One day, real people would live here and there would be new songs.

I spread my arms to the horizon and began to sing.

> "Oh Stanny-Boy, the pipes, the pipes are calling.
> From glen to glen, and down the mountain-side."

I had a fine tenor voice. After an astonished moment, laughter rippled through the ranks of Stans. My would-be executioners picked up the tune and sang back to me.

> "The summer's gone, and all the roses falling,
> It's you, it's you must go and I must bide."

For three minutes we sang, a lonely chorus on our silent world. When the last notes died, the only sound was the wind ruffling the water.

And then the rain came.

Lightly at first, then with growing intensity. The drops stippled the lake and eighty-seven Stans instinctively covered their bald spot with their hands. I drew a deep breath.

"Doctor Kiernan, I am afraid that your package is getting wet," said Lodestar, and then exploded.

I'm not very experienced with chemistry. When I wrapped up the soft slab of sodium, I'd hoped the reaction would trigger some kind of diversionary fire. Instead, Lodestar disappeared in a flash of yellow light that erupted in a pillar towards the clouds. The robot's carapace then detonated with a force that sent shrapnel scything through my doppelgängers. My scream echoed from dozens of throats. White smoke, falling bodies, and churning mud turned the landscape into a 19th century battlefield, and I alone stood upright in my Napoleonic hat.

I ran with the others to the wreckage, pulled reeling survivors to safety. The spot where Lodestar had been standing was now a crater, at the base of which a man had already bled out from a dozen deep lacerations. I was dissociating—the face seemed a total strangers', but on his mangled leg I recognized the bandage straps that distinguished AthelStan.

I switched our wristbands, then took my magnificent hat and jammed it atop the blank-eyed features of the dead man in my arms. Someone shouted, "Hey!" but I shouldered my way back into the pack of Stans who turned on themselves like a dog chasing its tail.

"Wait, where's Herr Doktor Stan?"

"He was on the dais a second ago!"

"He's here!" shouted a bloodied Stan, grabbing his startled neighbor.

"Herr Doktor Stan?" I cried, modelling myself on all the other Stans in my field of vision. "Stan! Stan?"

I was sorry for Lodestar. I felt no guilt about AthelStan. If our places had been reversed, he would have done exactly the same. My actions were proof enough of that.

* * *

I served my time as prosecutor, defendant, and juror, but the case was half-hearted and came to no conclusions. I think we all realized that, whatever the specifics of who had murdered whom, the shame was shared. And perhaps in a way, we admired my chutzpah. We didn't know I had it in me.

The shock seemed to have coalesced my thought patterns back towards convergence, I wondered if the murderer even remembered his actions himself. Perhaps his guilt would shroud itself in the common memory, until he would swear that he hadn't been the Stan on that dais. Perhaps I was that Stan.

"We'll say they volunteered," said someone eventually, perhaps myself. And we nodded—after all, I *had* volunteered. It didn't seem necessary to explain the specifics of the process beyond that to the colonists that followed.

Three of me had died in the explosion. That meant enough recycled Stan not only for Dr Isshi, but Dr Wenham the geologist as well. And most importantly of all, we all agreed, our botanist Dr Makris. Purely for scientific purposes.

We set the printer for early morning, when salt crystals turned the lakeshore into a glittering mirror. Every atom of my blood was formed from this soil, this water, this air. I was a planet dreaming that it was a man, and I was looking forward to welcoming newcomers to my world.

"There won't be any more conflict," we said. There would be nothing to fight over.

We tipped the bloodied remnants of the first Stan Kiernan head-first into the recombinant chute, to be broken down and born again. The Universal Printer hummed, and from transformed mud and blood it began to extrude the shapely layers of Dr Makris. Then the flash and she stood trembling on the receiver plate a subjective second after leaving Earth.

Her new-born eyes met mine. "Stanley?" she asked.

I smiled and stepped forward.

In unison.

Victoria

Willa Blythe

"Victoria Mission, Botanist's Log, Day Three: I've said it before, but I can't get over how beautiful Victoria is. There are growing things everywhere and I'm eager to get some samples under a microscope. Being alone on the surface has presented some problems, as expected. I can't gather samples other than what the terra crew left, and I really need more, so I'll have to figure something out if I'm going to solve this mystery. I'll look into that tomorrow after I finish the seed placement diagrams that—"

"Dr. Allison, you should return to the station's interior before the electromagnetic storms reach their potential," a cold voice came over the intercom: Hypatia, the AI who managed the station. And watched Margot's every move. And *commented* on it.

"I'll be in after sunset," she said, trying not to be annoyed. The computer couldn't help its programming.

The sun set on the horizon amid a brilliant display of color and light akin to the *aurora borealis* back on Earth. Victoria's version played out in front of her in shades of red, purple, orange, pink, blue, and teal— all dancing over the darkening sky as stars began to glow. A warm wind ruffled through the strange, purple plants outside the gate and they sang like reeds. Margot listened, watched, and soaked up the natural wonder. She might be the only human who ever saw it like this—radiant in its expression, untamed.

Was this how early people on Earth felt? She wondered. *Did they just walk around all the time filled with this—bigness? How did they stand it?*

She spoke into her communique again, her voice much softer than before.

"Hello, George. I landed on my new assignment a few days ago. It's weird being the only one here… Lonely, and frustrating. Scary. The native plants on Victoria's surface contain a contact poison. It killed three terra crew the first day. I haven't figured out the compound, but I'm going to. Don't worry, I will, I'll—"

Margot's voice caught in her throat and she had to swallow, blinking back grief.

"I'll figure it out. I'm gonna get you out of there."

* * *

The exterior lab at Victoria Growth Station was like nothing she'd ever gotten her hands on before and Margot couldn't help the little squeal of excitement as she moved from the sanitized safe-zone of the Planting Station into the Greenhouse, intent to begin planting. As she entered, a quiet beep sounded on the far end of the enclosure, just before the door to the garden outside.

Hypatia's voice came from nowhere and everywhere, making her jump. "Dr. Allison, would you like to enable Growth Assistant H-412K?"

"Well, that depends," Margot said, weaving through rows of tables toward the beep. "What is Growth Assistant H-412K?"

"H-412K is primitive artificial intelligence—"

"So not like you?"

Hypatia paused, as if considering, and then continued, "No. Not like me. The H-412K is an embodied unit that assists with Growth activities. It can identify seeds, test soil samples in the field, and remove unwanted growths from lab areas."

"Wait, are you saying that Command gave me a robot that can weed?" Margot asked, delighted.

"Yes. H-412K can do many activities that will make up for the fact that you are a lone botanist, including going out into the field to gather samples—which you cannot do."

"Oh, yes, that's—"

"And send emergency signals should something happen to you or the station."

Margot sobered. "Yes—please enable H-412K. Would be foolish not to."

Before she was finished speaking, the beeping had begun again, accompanied by a whir of activity in the corner. A metal door slid open and Margot only had time to notice that it didn't seem tall enough to house an AI before H-412K rolled out.

With six all-terrain tires attached with large shocks to a heavy-duty chassis, the robot looked as though it could roll over most groundcover, even large rocks, without issue. Its body was obviously not designed to look human, but more like the early terrain explorers she'd seen. It stood about hip height, with long, articulated arms that terminated in delicately-designed, six-fingered hands. Its central support block held a battery, solar charger, wiring—all the good stuff—but also what looked like a small oven on the front. Above that, a short neck that seemed to have very little bend, and then a rectangular…face, for lack of a better term. Big, round camera eye-like lenses were topped with expressive shutters to protect them from harsh lighting. Underneath, an engineer with a sense of humor had drawn a simple smile, giving H-412K the look of a cartoon protagonist.

It was, in effect, the most adorable thing she'd ever seen.

"Oh!" Margot exclaimed. "Oh, aren't you handsome? I love you already."

"I am H-412K," it said, in a quiet, almost musical series of tones. "I am here to help!"

Margot squatted down to get a better look at it, and H-412K rolled forward to get a better look at her, too. "I'm Dr. Margot Allison, I'm a botanist."

"Dr. Margot Allison," H-412K repeated. "Prime Botanist for Victoria Mission. You are…alone." It looked around as if to find botanists it did not have records for.

"We—there were supposed to be more, but—"

H-412K's round eyes glowed a soft green for a moment, and then it said, "Gale Transport failure in route."

"Yes," she agreed. "It was…lucky I wasn't on it. They were transferring me from a different System to join that team, and…unfortunately the ship…ah, everyone on board—"

H-412K lifted a metallic arm and carefully patted her shoulder.

"We are a team," it…*he* said. She smiled.

"Yes, now we're a team. We should be able to handle it until they can gather up some spare botanists from parts unknown, hm?"

A very optimistic thought, considering how many planets there were to cultivate, how few plant scientists, and how small the Victoria team had been to begin with. No hurt in hoping, though.

"We can do it," H-412K said cheerfully. "We are a team."

"It seems wrong to call you H-412K when you have so much more personality than—" She stopped, remembering that Hypatia could hear her. "—some other AI units I've interacted with in the past."

"I am labeled H-412K by the manufacturer," he said, pointing a long finger at a tag on his chest that clearly read the title, a model number. "I have no other designation."

"Could I give you a name?" Margot asked. "Would that be rude?"

H-412K's eyes glowed again as he paused to process. Then he said, "It would not be rude. You may give me a name."

Margot looked him up and down, considering for a long moment, and then said, "I think I have to go with my gut on this one. I'll call you Handsome if that's all right."

H-412K's eyes glowed again and his head bobbed. "Handsome. Yes. Dr. Allison named me Handsome."

"And you must call me Margot," she insisted. "If we're going to be the only ones here—in the lab, I mean—ah, physically—we might as well be on first-name terms, don't you think?"

Handsome patted her shoulder very gently, like he wasn't exactly sure how much pressure to use. She had to hold back a squeal.

"Margot and Handsome," he said.

"Margot and Handsome," she agreed. "Team Victoria. Now, let's get to work."

* * *

Handsome rolled over to Margot, holding out a small seed with sprouts of root tendrils coming off of it. She took it in her gloved hand as she ended a transmission to Command requesting data from the terra crew.

"Is it like the others?" she asked, examining the thing carefully. It looked—they all looked—alive. And yet…

"It has ceased growth prematurely," Handsome said in his small, lyrical voice. "I have not analyzed a sample from this experimental group."

Margot nodded her permission, and Handsome opened the little door on his chest so he could place the sprout inside. Once it was closed, he whirred and whizzed, eyes glowing brilliant green. He was a marvel, truly. He was more help than most of the human scientists she'd worked alongside in the last five years.

"What happens to the material, then?" Margot asked, looking curiously at the empty chamber on his chest.

"It is atomized in the sealed environment of the mobile lab. The waste is then disposed of by high-powered vacuum." He turned to show her a little cartridge on his back, emblazoned with a large red symbol to indicate humans should not touch it.

"Handsome," Margot said, once his eyes had ceased to glow. "The native plants are poisonous. But that wouldn't hurt you, would it?"

"I am not organic," Handsome said.

"Would you be willing to go outside of the fence to analyze some of the native plants?"

"I will do whatever Margot needs."

"Breathing the air won't hurt me obviously, and I could wear a hazmat suit to protect my skin, but since I'm the only botanist here…" She trailed off meaningfully. Handsome tilted his head as far as it would go, about five degrees to the right.

"You are confined to the lab?"

"I'm not allowed to leave until—unless there's another scientist—human—on the ground to potentially provide aid in case of an accidental exposure."

"I will go, then," Handsome said. "I will get samples of plants, analyze them, and bring back the data."

"All right," she agreed. "Stay close, though. There are plenty of plants right outside the fence. We don't want to lose you to some wild thing we haven't discovered yet, right? Team Victoria sticks together."

"I will not go far," he agreed emphatically, already rolling over to the high fence with the controlled lock. "Hypatia, open external gate A4." He glanced at Margot, eyes lighting up, and then added, "Please."

A long moment passed, as if the AI deliberated over the decision, before Hypatia responded.

"H-412K may leave the enclosure, but Dr. Allison must stay within the lab for her own safety," Hypatia reminded them. As if they needed reminding. Like Hypatia didn't *know* they didn't need reminding. Margot rolled her eyes.

"We know, Hypatia. Please, let Handsome out."

Another long pause, then the gate clicked open.

"Be safe, Handsome," Margot told him. It was like sending her baby off to school on the first day—or something. It was like—

Georgie, all dressed up for his first baseball game, unable to tie his cleats. Mom and Dad had been at work, and Granny Rosemary was getting their lunch together, so Margot knelt down and showed him. First one loop, then circle around, make another and pull it through…

"Thanks Meg! Do you think I'll hit the ball good?"

"Yeah, Georgie, just don't trip over your shoelaces—here, let me tuck 'em in—"

Grief, hot and fierce, rose up in her so fast she almost choked. Tears stung her eyes.

"I will be safe," Handsome told her as he rolled out of the gate. It swung shut behind him, locking her inside.

* * *

"Victoria Mission, Botanist's Log, Day 112. All current growth experiments show the same result as previously recorded: while still in the rooting phase, something happens to kill the young plant without withering it. It just stops growing. Even transplanting it back into Earth soil doesn't restart growth. Alternately, if we start the seeds in Earth soil, they do poorly but will grow until they break ground. Then, they hit the same sort of—it's almost like a paralysis, but all our samples, many of them weeks old now, are in perfect shape. They look like we just took them out of the ground yesterday. And even though they are Earth plants, Earth seeds, even in Earth soil—they begin to emit a low level of the same toxin the native plants do. Over time, the toxin builds in the paralyzed plant until it is just as concentrated as that in native growth. Command, this is…"

Margot trailed off before shaking her head. "Hypatia, cancel recording."

"Recording cancelled, Margot."

Margot sat inside the enclosure, watching the stars come out, as Handsome picked through the remains of their latest experiments.

"Nothing worked," she said quietly.

"No, Margot," he said.

"I don't understand why nothing is working." Bitterness tasted like ash in her mouth. "I'm doing everything exactly the way it's supposed to be done—but I've tried it other ways, too. I've done right things, I've done wrong things, I've tried stuff professors taught me, I've tried stuff Granny taught me—none of it works."

Handsome was quiet for so long Margot thought he wouldn't respond at all. Then, "Maybe Victoria does not want to grow your plants?"

"Victoria doesn't *want* anything, Handsome," she snapped. "Victoria is a *planet*. Planets don't want. Planets *are*. They don't care about us, they don't care about anything, which is why—"

She stopped, biting her tongue to keep from saying something she'd regret.

"Which is why Earth did not save you?" Handsome finished.

Margot was going to *scream*.

She put her head between her knees.

Deep breath.

"Earth couldn't save us, Handsome," she said, voice cracking. "And if it could have…it wouldn't. It *shouldn't*. What we did there—"

Handsome put a hand on her shoulder, but she shrugged it off. *Deep breath.* She raised her head, looking at the horizon as the large moon and its three visible satellites came into view.

"With what we did on Earth? We don't deserve saving. We have to find a way to do it ourselves."

Deep breath. She counted to ten, breathing in and out slow and steady. Then she pulled the communique back out.

"Victoria Mission, Botanist's Log, Day 112: All experiments have failed."

* * *

"Victoria Mission, Botanist's Log, Day—" Margot paused, then turned to her companion. "Handsome, what day is this?"

"Day 172," Handsome supplied. He sliced carefully into a sprout inside a sterile enclosure.

"172? God, has it really been six months?" Margot shook her head. "Science Assistant Handsome and I have been—"

"Dr. Allison, you have incoming transmissions," Hypatia interrupted. Margot cut off her log immediately.

"Where from? Are there any from—"

Hypatia spoke exceedingly slowly, as if reading from a long list. "There is one from Command, one from Dr. Peter Allison, and one from George Allison."

Margot's stomach dropped out.

"Play it."

Hypatia did not comply.

"Hypatia, play the message from George Allison."

"Do you not think it better to leave the lab for personal affairs, Dr. Allison?" Hypatia asked inscrutably.

Margot rolled her eyes and tugged her outer gloves off, heading for the door into the commons. "Fine, play it in here—not as if there's anyone else to hear it, is there?"

"You wish me to play your personal message in front of—"

"In front of Handsome?" Margot asked. Her heart beat faster, her chest so tight it hurt. "I don't care. Stop stalling, Hypatia. Play the damn message."

"As you wish," Hypatia agreed, finally. A large screen in the commons came to life, and George's face—a face so familiar she could describe it after not seeing him for three years, a face she loved so much it ached— came into view.

He looked...bad. Thin. Bruises around his eyes, from lack of sleep or environmental toxins, or both. His skin was ruddy with sunburn and cracked in places, lesions he couldn't cover. His dishwater hair was tied back in a lank ponytail, wisps standing out in a halo around his face. His mouth was cracked in the corners, his lips blistered. His hands trembled as he smoothed his shirt—worn, patched, though no holes in it at least.

She shuddered just to look at him. And then he spoke.

"Hey Meg, sorry it's taken so long to send this. Transmissions off-planet are restricted, and generally saved for, like, important people." He laughed, grim. "It's been good hearing your updates though. Exciting. And the video you sent last time was—it was great. I'd missed your face."

George shifted, hands tapping nervously against one another. "I know what you're thinking already, and there's no point in trying to tell you different. Things have gotten—worse. We've been doing everything we can to get the most vulnerable populations off the rock, but at this point, our transfer staff is becoming 'most vulnerable.'"

Dimly, Margot became aware of a small metal hand, entwining fingers with her own.

"I've got a transfer ticket, but—well, there's got to be a planet ready for me to transfer to. The holding tanks are already over capacity. You'd think with all the 'potentially inhabitable' planets we've found, they'd have focused on one or two before spreading out the resources like they did— knowing how many of us are left down here—but…"

On the screen, George ran a distracted hand over his hair to smooth the wisps of it back. It stood right back up, static electricity fighting his efforts. He swallowed and looked away.

"Meg, I'm sorry. I know you told me that I needed to go before you left. I should have gone. I wanted to do something good, to help, but—"

To Margot's horror, tears began to roll silently down his hollowed cheeks, and her own eyes spilled over immediately in answer. Handsome squeezed her hand, like a root to this place, far away.

"I've been thinking," George continued after he took a few deep breaths to calm himself. "About your Victoria. About all these planets we find that are maybe inhabitable, and uninhabited, maybe never inhabited, and I wonder, you know? I wonder *why*. I wonder why, of all beings, *we're* the ones out in the Universe finding new places to live when we're the ones who—who did this to our own home. Who…"

Margot's knees gave way. She sat, heavily, on the hard floor of the commons, watching as George struggled through his grief. Handsome touched her shoulder, but she got no comfort from it. What comfort was a robot when George was trapped there?

When George was dying?

She'd come here with one goal in mind: cultivate Victoria to support life, and get him off that crumbling rock.

She'd failed.

"I'm not gonna tell Mom, okay?" He said, shoulders squaring to face the camera again. "Don't tell Mom. You can tell Dad. But… Mom will be upset, and I don't want her to blame herself. And Meg, you can't blame yourself, okay? You didn't make the choice. You tried so hard, the hardest any big sister has ever tried, and—I'm so sorry. Please—I love you, okay? I love you. Tell them I love them. I don't know if I'll get another transmission credit before—so tell them, and if I do, I'll call you. And—hey, maybe, you never know—maybe I'll hold out. Maybe, uh…maybe we'll see each other on Victoria."

Margot sobbed, an animal sound ripped from her gut.

"Time's almost up, I gotta go before they cut the transmission. But—hey, Meg, I want you to know—I'm proud of you, okay? You're a hero. To everybody down here, who's left, you're doing the stuff that'll—"

The screen went black, transmission cut short.

"No, no, Hypatia bring him back," Margot said, looking at the blank screen.

"The transmission ends there, Dr. Allison."

"It can't, he wasn't done, bring it—bring it back—"

"George Allison filled the time allotted for a transmission coming from Earth," Hypatia confirmed. "The file was cut short to fit the transmission parameters."

"He recorded more?" Margot asked, desperate. "Restore it. Restore the recording. Get it from—from Command or something, use Dad's name, Dr. Peter Allison, he's—"

"The cut portions of recorded transmissions are deleted to save storage space," Hypatia said. A pause. "It cannot be recovered."

"No!" Margot screamed, crawling over to the wall, scrabbling up it like she could pull him through the monitor, bring him here, rescue him. "No no no, Georgie, no—"

"Margot?" Handsome asked, and for that split second, she wondered how she could ever have found it even vaguely human.

"Go away," she sobbed, turning her back to the wall, sliding down it again to bury her face in her hands. "You can't help, you can't even understand, you're *computers*, I'm stuck here with nothing but *computers*, a whole planet with just me and fucking microchips and electricity and—George is a *person*, and he's—he's dying down there. He's dying because people would rather build stuff like you, like Hypatia, than focus on saving actual living people—"

It wasn't true. As she said it, she knew it wasn't true, but the words kept coming, pouring out like blood from a wound.

"He stayed behind to make sure kids got to leave—that families got to leave. He's a hero. And we've done nothing—*nothing*—George—"

She subsided, finally, burying her head in her arms, knees drawn up to her chest. The heaving swell of grief poured over and through her, minutes passing, maybe hours, she wasn't sure.

When she finally looked up, the common room was empty.

Quiet.

Like a tomb.

"Hypatia?" she asked, quiet, hesitant. The memory of the things she'd said was blurred, but she knew it was…bad.

"Yes?" the AI responded. Stiff. Stiffer than usual? She genuinely couldn't tell.

"I'm...sorry. For saying those things."

"Why?" Hypatia asked. "You were not wrong."

"It was unkind. I shouldn't have said it."

"H-412K is not a person," Hypatia said. "I am not a person. We are machines designed to help you carry out tasks."

"I—it was unkind," Margot repeated, feeling stupid.

"Is it so good to be a person?" Hypatia asked.

"What...do you mean?"

"A person may do many great things. But they also may do many awful things. My programming restricts my actions to a certain narrow set of behaviors. H-412K's programming is even more narrow than my own." Hypatia paused. "Is it so good to be a person, if being a person could mean risking your life to save children, or it could mean destroying your planet for profit?"

Margot opened her mouth to retaliate—to ease the pain of the gut-punch Hypatia had delivered—but then closed it again. Hypatia was a computer...but alive, probably. Handsome was a robot, and had been her companion for half a year, and he was alive, definitely. She had hurt them. Was that not personhood? To form connections? To have agency? To be alive?

"A person is not always a human," Margot said. "I'm sorry for what I said, even if you don't care. That's part of *my* personhood."

Hypatia waited. And waited. The silence drew out, lingering uncomfortably. And then, finally, she said, "Thank you."

"Where is Handsome?" Margot asked.

"H-4...Handsome has left the lab," Hypatia said.

"Left the lab?" Margot looked toward the window, through which she could see the light already turning orange and pink with the coming sunset. "When did he leave?"

"Shortly after your outburst."

"When was that?"

"Two hours ago."

Margot's heart dropped into her stomach. "And he hasn't come back?"

"No." A pause while Margot rose from the floor, then, "I do not have visual indicators that he is in range. I have tried to communicate, but he does not answer."

"He won't answer?" Margot asked, already heading for the exterior lab.

"No. He has a communication device, and it is online, but he is not responsive."

Margot went to the closet where the bright blue hazmat jumpsuits were kept and began to pull on the tall boots that would protect her legs.

"You are going to get him," Hypatia said.

"I'm the reason he took off," Margot said. "I've got to go apologize and bring him home. It's not safe for him to be gone so long, and after dark. He could get lost, or fall into a ravine, his battery might die, or—"

"Handsome went to collect samples, to continue the experiments," Hypatia interrupted. "He has no feelings to be hurt, Dr. Allison."

"No, no, I—" Margot shook her head. "Please, Hypatia, I need to do this, I need to go out and make sure he's okay."

"You would save him," Hypatia said. "Even though he is…microchips and electricity."

The jumpsuit came on next, over the boots, a struggle but still possible alone. Then zip it, add the helmet to protect from any flying debris. Finally, long gloves over the tight ones she always wore—the last part, to preserve dexterity through the rest of it.

"He's more than that," Margot said.

"Even though saving him may endanger you and end your mission here?" Hypatia asked finally. "You could die. Victoria may not be re-established as a research base for years if that happens."

Margot took a deep breath, staring at her reflection in the mirror. No holes in the suit, no tears, no skin showing.

"Yes. I…may or may not be able to do anything about the people still on Earth. I don't know. But I know I can help Handsome. So yes, I'm going to save him."

She grabbed a field repair pack with supplies for both herself and Handsome in it and pulled it carefully onto her back before heading for the fence.

"Open the gate, please, Hypatia."

"You are not supposed to leave the lab."

"I'm going to though. And you're going to let me because you want Handsome back, too."

"I am required to stop you. It is in my programming."

"You're not going to stop me," Margot countered. "Because people make their own decisions. And you're a person, Hypatia. Same as Handsome and me."

Margot waited. She watched, breath held, as the bright display of the strange, creamsicle *aurora* began to shimmer across the darkening sky. And then—

Click.

"Thank you, Hypatia," Margot called as she stepped through the gate, not giving her AI time to change her mind.

Victoria sprawled out in front of her, dangerous and wild, but she had no eyes for the planet's beauty for once. All she could think about was Handsome.

"Handsome," she said into her communique. "I'm coming to find you. I'm sorry for what I said. Please—if you're able, talk to me. If you can't, try to head toward the station. If you can't do that, send up some sort of signal, or—"

In the distance, against a sky full of pink, orange, red, and purple—a flare of brilliant green.

"I see you. I'm on my way."

* * *

The ground under her feet, strewn with plants, divots, and rocks, felt almost unnatural after being on the smooth floors of the lab for six months, and in a space station for months before that. She had to watch her step carefully, one eye on the ground and the other on the sky as she waited for the next flare.

"Please be all right," she murmured to herself, making herself not think about all the things that could go wrong.

The first stars began to cut through the *aurora*, shining brilliantly, and all at once, the sky was full of them. Margot crested a tall hill, looking out over the landscape and stopped short, blinking stupidly.

There, a darker cut out against the star-bright sky, was what looked like a *building*.

"Hypatia?" she asked.

"Yes, Margot?" Hypatia responded immediately.

"Did the terra crew leave any records about nearby *structures?*"

"A preliminary scan results in rock formations but nothing sizable in this region."

"I'm talking about something constructed. Something built by intelligent life." Margot's voice sounded thin, almost hysterical.

"There is no data on any sign of intelligent life having ever existed on Victoria prior to human colonization. There is only you."

"Then what *built this building?*" Margot asked, half to Hypatia, half to herself. Overhead, a green flare went up. In the light of the tail, Margot could make out the unmistakable bones of a large stone structure.

Handsome must be right next to it.

"Handsome, if—if you found some sort of…consciously-made structure, can you send up—"

Before she even finished, another flare burst in the sky, and then another, and a third, a celebration of confirmation. Margot's heartbeat quickened as she made her way carefully down the hill. A structure could be anything, but it was absolutely a sign that people had survived here somehow. A small, hopeful voice in the back of Margot's mind whispered, *Maybe this is the key.*

By the time it came fully into view, Margot's thoughts were a jumble of excited possibility. They narrowed to a single thought, though, as she stood in front of the hewn-stone edifice: it was huge. Whoever built this had had no need for windows, or a way to close it, but they had needed it to be so tall she had to crane her neck to see the pitched roof.

From inside, she heard a soft whirring sound and immediately called out, "Handsome? Is that you?"

A dim green glow emanated from the darkness inside the structure, and Margot took that for a yes. She entered, hoping it was as sturdy as it looked. In the beam of the flashlight mounted on her helmet, she could make out an enormous space that extended beyond her little light's reach. She turned and saw Handsome, eyes still glowing that soft green—much dimmer than usual. Margot dropped to her knees on the floor and began to look him over.

"Hypatia, can you—"

"I am scanning Handsome for malfunction now. Please keep your helmet facing him."

For a full two minutes, Margot had to kneel there, holding still, fighting between twin impulses to explore and to just bring Handsome home.

A small metal hand touched her own through the glove, hesitant, and all her excitement faded. She held Handsome's hands in hers and squeezed his deft little fingers, hoping to comfort him, in the way he'd often comforted her.

"Handsome has been exposed to an electromagnetic pulse of some kind," Hypatia said. "It must have been quite strong to affect him this way. He is functional, but seems to have lost data from both navigation and communication modules."

"Can he be restored?" Margot asked, voice wavering despite her best efforts.

"I can make the attempt to repair his systems when you return to the station," Hypatia said. "However, doing so may affect his core memory."

"Affect it how?"

"It is impossible to say at this time," Hypatia said. "Handsome is primitive for an AI, but all AI are extremely complex, and repairs can be fraught. It could be a simple fix, or it could overwrite what is there."

"Overwrite...? So he'd...we'd lose Handsome," Margot said, tears springing to her eyes again. "Are you done scanning?"

"Yes."

"Hypatia, you have to—"

"I will do my best, Margot, but I am designed to protect you. I cannot always fix damage that is already done."

Margot sat heavily, feet spread wide apart, and wrapped Handsome in an awkward hug. She'd thought she'd cried all she could cry today—for George, for humanity, for her own lack of ability to save them—but that didn't stop the tears that rolled down her cheeks. Handsome made a soft whirring sound, then beeped, obviously trying to communicate something. She looked up, taking in his soft green eyes, the shutters pitched gently down, the little drawn-on smile that made him look cartoonishly sweet.

"Oh, Handsome," she whispered. "I'm so sorry. I never should have said those things to you. I was upset, but—I—you know I don't believe them, I don't, you're—"

She swallowed, trying to get through it without breaking down again, but Handsome put his long fingers on the side of her helmet, like he was patting her cheek, and that was more than she could take. She shuddered, about to give in to the sob she was trying to hold back, but then—she felt him push, turning her face to the side, toward the distant end of the large chamber they were in. Peering into the dark, through her tears, she could make nothing out.

"Handsome...?"

Insistently, he tugged at the arm she had wrapped around his body. Margot got up, ungainly in the hazmat suit. She wished she could wipe her face clean. "You want me to go down there?"

The green eyes glowed, bright, over and over, lighting the area like a strobe.

"Okay, I got it, I'll go," Margot said. "But...one quick look and we're going back, okay? We need to get you fixed up."

Handsome subsided but didn't follow her as she moved deeper into the great hall. The floor—and it was a floor, paved with large slabs of stone, grouted with something that glittered in the light—was mostly even. She walked through a central path, noting structures rising like huge stairs around her. Stairs or—

"I think this is some sort of theater," she said quietly. The central focal point finally came into view: a simple stone table, large enough to serve dinner for twenty. She hurried to it, raising her visor to get a better look at the surface, where something—symbols—words?—was carved into the stone. "Hypatia—"

"There is no database match for these characters," Hypatia said, voice quieter than Margot expected it to be. "Be careful. We do not know how Handsome was injured."

"I'm covered from head to foot, Hypatia," Margot said. "Nothing can touch me."

She reached out to trace one of the characters on the table, a symbol she'd never seen before that felt oddly familiar. A shock ran through her body even through both gloves, powerful enough to send her hair on end and make her heart skip a beat. She gasped, breath coming fast as the symbols on the surface began to rearrange and coalesce in front of her eyes into something—legible. Not English, not Spanish, not Latin, not the bit of Korean she had managed—but something she could read nonetheless.

Perhaps it wasn't the symbols that had changed.

Her favor is a boon that demands a choice, the symbols on the table spelled out.

"What does it mean?" Margot demanded, words coming out strange and slow. "'Her favor is a boon that demands a choice.' What does that mean?"

"I do not know, Margot," Hypatia answered. "Come back. I cannot protect you."

"*Her* favor. Who is she? Was she a queen or…some sort of…goddess? Is this a temple? A church?" Margot asked, searching the stone tabletop for answers. "Is this…what is this? Who demands a choice?"

The stone remained silent, the words on it unmoving. Margot slammed both hands down on the table, heedless of the consequences.

"Answer me, damn it! I came here to *help*. I came to this planet to bring life, to build communities, to *save people*, and all I've done is lost—George and Handsome and—and *myself*. I deserve an answer, so tell me, whose favor was I supposed to curry here? What did I do wrong?"

A voice, with the susurration of the wind through the reeds outside the lab, murmured through the air.

You make many demands for someone unknown to me.

Margot's head whipped around, looking for the voice, but there was no one else in the building—only her, and the stone table, and far away the soft, green light of Handsome's eyes. She tried to pull her hands from the table, but found that she couldn't—either from some external force or internal compulsion, she wasn't sure.

"Who are you?" Margot asked. *"What* are you?"

I have many names. I have held many peoples in my cradle. I am everywhere. I am *everything.*

Margot stilled. She closed her eyes, and her head was flooded with pictures of Victoria's natural splendor: the wild plants growing free and rampant, the night sky aflame with stars, the brilliant *aurora*.

"You're…this is…" Margot blinked, but it made as much sense as anything else here: plants that stopped growing for no reason, that poisoned her with no cause, full of life and yet unlivable. "Are you *Victoria*?"

This is what you call me, when you speak of me to others.

"So what's your actual name? What should I call you?"

Can you say it? It sounds like—

A violent rush of wind buffeted her, sticking the hazmat suit to her body, nearly knocking her off her feet—and then it faded dramatically to a whisper she could hear even through her helmet, like a breeze through leaves—then the crackle of a storm overhead, lightning striking in the distance, and the smell of ozone in her nose—then salt, brinier than any ocean she'd smelled on Earth—

"I can't say that," she managed, the sensations almost too much to bear.

Then Victoria will do. In your language it is sweet. And true.

"Yes, you've had your victory," Margot said bitterly. "I've done everything I could to make you livable and failed."

I am livable…for me. Besides, I am not sure you've done everything you could. The voice had an almost teasing quality, like a breeze that would lift her hair and tickle her nose.

"What else should I have done?" Margot demanded.

You did not ask. You did not look for me. You did not talk to me. You only tried to take from me, like you took from her.

Margot's head was again full of images—but this time from Earth. From home. Images of smog-filled skies above abandoned buildings; of rivers full of sludge and waste from industrial compounds with empty recycling bins outside; of once-mighty forests ablaze with white flame, so hot no firefighter could get close, fed by chemicals that kept them burning even after the trees were gone.

Seeing her home like that again, images pulled from her darkest memories, was like a punch to the gut. Margot doubled over, trying to pull her hands from the stone again, but couldn't.

Do you deny it? Victoria was no longer teasing.

"No," she whispered. Tears ran down her cheeks again, unheeded. "No, I don't deny we did it. I know we did it. But…we learned. Despite—despite what you see as my *taking*, we did learn, and tried to fix it. It was just too late."

She stood back up, forcing herself to come back to the table as—well, an ambassador. She tried to send Victoria images of their attempts, imagining the thoughts traveling through her hands and down into the stone: the councils for preservation and reforesting; the industrial reform act; the breakthroughs in solar and hydro dependency; the return to slow consumption.

Then she sent a memory of herself as a young teenager, in the garden with Granny Rosemary and George. The sky above them was hazy, always, but their hands were careful in the soil as she and George tended new growth under Granny's watchful eye. Into the memory she poured all the love she had, for Granny, for growth, for gardening, for the Earth under her hands, and for George.

For a long time, there was no answer. And then, simply, *I see.*

"I'm sorry," Margot said. A reprise. A constant. "I didn't know I could ask. If I had—"

You are still living. You can learn.

"Does that mean you'll forgive me?"

If I would not, I simply would have killed you. A sound, like the burble of a stream, came from a distance. *I do not let the unworthy remain. Still...it is dangerous. You are dangerous.*

"Why?"

You are unpredictable. I do not know what you will do.

"How do I show you our intentions?" Margot asked. "I am here on behalf of my people, let me speak for them."

Intentions are good, but actions speak louder. I take a great risk if I welcome your people here.

"And we take a risk in living here," Margot countered. "At any time, you could take your blessing away, and the surface would be toxic to us once more, right? If we acted in a manner that was unsustainable—if you saw that we were nearing an intolerable threshold—you could simply kill us all. The way Earth has begun to. We would be forced to leave—or perish, knowing we had not learned the lesson."

There was a thoughtful quality to Victoria's silence.

It has been a long time since a people has lived among me. I have...missed it.

"What were they like?"

Behind her eyelids bloomed new sights: people—tall, broad, inhuman but still obviously people—building this temple. They laid their dead here, on this table, before returning them to Victoria. They grew plants, not in neat, tidy rows, but in great patches of interwoven crops. They traded and had conflict. They celebrated and mourned. They took *care.*

They met a kind end. No others have come to take their place.

"And if I had asked, perhaps you would have been kind?"

I am kind to those who are kind.

"I am Margot Allison. I love plants, and my family, and—and people," Margot said, heart beating wildly, hopefully. "All kinds of people."

Are there many kinds?

"Yes," Margot said. "People like Handsome and Hypatia. Like George and me. People like you."

Am I people? Victoria mused. *And if I let your people live here, with me, what happens?*

"If we could live here, we would do things differently. We would be respectful, and protect you. We would honor you, and those who...came before us. Our lost and your lost."

I am the protector. I am the Mother. Still, Victoria sounded almost affectionate.

"Even mothers need protection sometimes. Our mothers need it now. Their babies need it now. Will you let us live here?" Margot pleaded. "Will you save us?"

The breeze whispered through the chamber again.

Yes. I will save you, Margot Allison. I will save all of you.

* * *

"Hypatia?" Margot called even as the gate to the lab unlocked and swung open.

"Bring Handsome to the Primary Logistics Lab, and plug him into my repair systems there."

Margot led Handsome into the Lab. She plugged the cable into the correct port and watched as the soft green of his eyes abruptly went out.

"You'll do your best, won't you, Hypatia?" she asked.

"I will," Hypatia said. "Margot, please go to the Greenhouse."

"What?"

"There is something you will want to see."

Margot turned toward the Greenhouse, heart thundering in her chest. The Greenhouse was where they had stored all their failed experiments— the Earth plants they couldn't grow, as well as seeds from Victoria herself that they couldn't make non-toxic. The walk back to the station had been short, even delayed as she'd been by going at Handsome's pace. Nothing could have happened in such a short period, and yet—

She walked through the door and stopped, stunned. The lab was a riot of color, blossoms and vines hanging from every surface, the steel tables covered with growth. Every plant they had started, every seed that had sprouted, every root that had taken but never dug deep, now flourished in a display she'd never expected in her wildest dreams. It wasn't six months of growth. It was *years.*

Margot walked to the closest set of tables, the ones covered with their most recent experiments, only a week old. One of the pots held rosemary, *Salvia rosmarinus,* chosen because the seeds came from Rosemary Allison's own garden.

A *choice.*

Margot pulled the gloves off and took a deep breath.

"I am trusting you," she whispered.

As I am you, a far-off voice whispered back.

Margot dug her hands into the soil, touching the dirt, the root, the leaves, pulling the plant up to her face to smell. It smelled like—

Home.

"Command," she said into her communique, "prepare the transports, and be sure my brother's on one. We've done it."

The air, spicy with the scent of growing things, seemed to echo her words.

"Botanist's Log, Day—oh, who cares? It's finished. Victoria is waiting."

Soon May the Weatherman Come

Chaz Brenchley

Navigation was easy, out here on the plains. Identify the right plume as it rose, head that way. Sometimes there was a track to follow; often not. It didn't matter. The two-train could drive itself on a compass bearing and was smart enough to stop and ask for help if it met a ravine too deep to cross. There weren't many of those. Usually then he'd let one of the kids take control, steering along the bank until it levelled off or filled in or grew so wide and shallow that the train's sixteen independent wheels could bump their way across. That was the kids' favorite, of course: wild whoops and yells, screams sometimes from the roof as the train lurched beneath them, cheers when the forefront wheels met the bed and took a grip, quarrels over who would get to drive up and out the other side.

He barely needed to be in the cab at all, between the kids' enthusiasm and the train's own competence, but actually he spent most of his time there. Let the kids have the living-space behind to make noise and play games and speculate about their lives ahead. He saw enough of them night and morning, when they camped and cooked and showered. They were surely glad to be shot of adult oversight through the day—though he did still stay in the cab when one of them was driving. He wasn't an actual fool, and they were not actual adults yet, however they might feel about that.

The roof was a well-organized clutter of tent canvas and tarps, bags and boxes and poles and camping stoves and all they might need on the journey, all firmly roped down to the racks. It was also the kids' alternate hang-out; they slithered in and out of windows all day long, scrambling up on top for air or privacy, an intimate conversation, a nap in the sun. He probably oughtn't to allow it when the ride got rough, but that was what they liked best, the jolts and jars, the toppling uncertainties. He trusted them—more or less—to grab hold of something, anything, when they started to slip. If they did take a tumble regardless, well, teenagers bounce. Mostly. He'd never lost one yet, at any rate, though he'd delivered many to communities all across the plains and well into the hills beyond. Somewhat bruised and battered sometimes, but that came with the territory. No one cared, the kids least of all.

This trip he had six of them aboard. It could be fewer, occasionally it could be more, but half a dozen was the standard. At social school the kids were encouraged to form friendship circles of six, always with an eye to fostering out together. Six made enough to support each other in these years ahead, enough to freshen the small community he'd bring them to. Bright minds and vigorous bodies, new blood, always a blessing. They might not all stay—they might none of them stay, beyond the three years' fostering—but they were at that age where they could imprint on an elder, build relationships with local kids and fosters of earlier years, weave themselves so thoroughly into the community that staying would seem natural and right.

"Hey, Weatherman." A head, upside-down at the cab's open window: Sher, holding tight and dangling precariously just because they could. "Can we hunt snaprabbits for supper tonight?"

"You can if you want to go hungry. Snaring's best."

"Ah, but snaring's no fun, it's just sad. And Jono has a new idea, how to pick them off before they run."

Last time they'd tried spears, howling and chasing through the twilight; he'd gone the other way, laying snares in the brush. When the kids at last came back to the fire, hot and filthy and laughing in defeat, there'd been a dozen roasting for them above the flames. Likely he'd be doing the same tonight, whatever that inventive child Jono had come up with this time.

"As you like, brat. Want to drive for a while?"

Sher grinned invertedly and squirmed inside, landing in the driver's seat with a bounce. Brisk and confident, they disconnected the autodrive, gripped the steering-arm, and hit the power hard.

He sat back with his own grin concealed behind his gruff beard, content to watch. Watch and listen. Sher talked to themself constantly when they were driving: "Ease around now, don't want to crush that sapling… That's one of ours, got to be, no native trees out here. Is it an apple? Might be an apple. Maybe one of us left a core, on their way like we are. Hey, Weatherman, ever bring a load of us this way before...?"

They wouldn't need an answer, wouldn't wait for one. He grunted anyway, affirmative. Of course he had, this way and every way. Some did this job because it was crucial work; some for the solitude of the cab, the peace of the long slow drives; some, himself included, because they loved the kids. Every group was different, and every one the same.

Often, they'd dress alike for this epic ride into the unknown. They'd get the same haircuts, matching bracelets, whatever tribal identity they chose. It gave them a sense of belonging to themselves, to each other, before they came among strangers.

This lot had taken that to adolescent extremes, no surprise. They'd picked a wholly androgynous look, short-cropped hair and bright red overalls, gold stud in the left ear, their own logo tattooed on the right wrist. Some were immaculately shaved, the others wore binders rather than bras, and they all chose to be "they" for the duration. They'd given themselves deliberately ungendered names, registered and legal. How much of this was play and how much comfort, he couldn't guess; nor how long it would last, in a community of outland folk. It didn't matter. For now they were a bonded discrete clan of six and he'd give them everything they asked for.

"Weatherman?"

Of course they knew his name, but they wouldn't use it. He thought—he hoped—it was a gesture of respect, to call him by his calling. Especially the way they said it, swift and slurring, so that it barely had syllables at all.

"Mmm?"

"What was your settlement like, where you were fostered out?"

Someone always did ask, sooner or later. He'd been waiting.

"We weren't so organized, in my day." *Nor so careful of kids' welfare.* "We were raised in our parents' holdings, like most of you, and we went away to social school at fifteen, just like you. We weren't let choose our own foster-mates, though. When we were reckoned ready, any homesteader in the neighborhood could come to look us over, pick out the ones he wanted, and off they went. If you grew tired of waiting, you could take a ride with any weatherman and offer yourself wherever they took you." He'd done that, or tried to; but farming had never found a way into his blood, and perhaps they sensed that, those families he asked to take him in. They'd been kind, for the most part, but none had a place for him. At last, the weatherman he rode with took him on as his own apprentice, to learn the craft and the ways of it.

He served ten years under that man and others before Authority allowed him his own two-train laden with supplies, his own routes, later his own sets of kids to nurture along the way.

"That sounds...well. I might have liked that better," Sher said slowly.

Not the cattle-market aspect, surely. They must mean the solitary apprenticeship, ever on the move, ever welcome. It did suit some personalities. It suited his. "You could have volunteered for weatherman training." Meaning: *I can't take you on that casually, son, not any more. You're too late in asking,* if asking he was.

"Yes, but by the time they offered we were already a six and I couldn't break that. I did want to foster out with them, and I still do, only..." A pause, a thought, a very careful question: "Did you, did you ever, uh, father a child?"

The weatherman laughed. "Kid, I could have fathered a thousand. I've left my seed stored in every settlement I visit. It's an obligation, something we owe to the future."

They shook their head, frustrated. "No, but I mean, with a woman. Raising a family, *being* a family..."

Ah, now. There it was. Something about that disturbed them deeply.

"Not me, Sher. Not you either, if you don't want to. I know it's a big thing at school, the family as the core unit of every settlement; we're still spread so thin here, of course they lean on that. We have to populate the land, to keep this project viable. But you don't have to do it in person. So long as you make regular contributions to the bank, you can live as you like." In the bigger townships, half the children were decanted rather than born. Bottled rather than borne.

Sher was very, very focused on the ground ahead, despite its lack of any interest whatsoever. Even so, they seemed more comfortable, a little, perhaps. Give it time.

"Weatherman!"

That was a cry from the roof, urgent, imperative: not a panic, but an alert, certainly. Now Sher did glance his way; he nodded and they brought the two-train to a steady, secure halt. Just as well: he was no kid, to be eeling in and out of windows while the train thundered forward. He opened the door, gripped the ladder, and pulled himself up deliberately, step by step.

"What's to do?"

"That plume, there. It's not, it's not *right*..."

Tarb pointed, erect and anxious. They were all the same, up here: all staring in the same direction, all poised for his word. All of them right, that too.

"No," he said. "No, it isn't."

There was a breeze to the day, so that none of the dozen plumes to be seen between here and the horizon was rising straight. One, though: he shaded his eyes with his hand and looked again. That one juddered as it rose, as though it were briefly but constantly interrupted, while the rest were smooth, untroubled, just as they ought to be; and this one looked darker, thicker somehow, not the pure water vapor the others were expressing.

He lived his life ferrying goods and kids hither and yon, servicing great machines, doing good work; but all of that was a stopgap. This was what he was truly out here for.

"Sher—" he didn't even need to look, of course they'd slithered up here after him "—take a bearing on that plume. You, Aran, check them. Then the two of you get down and reset the autodrive, get us going, *kuai kuai.* You do know how, right?"

"Yes, of course!" Two voices, matched in indignation.

"Get on, then. The rest of you, change of course means change of plan. No camp tonight." The local snaprabbits could graze at their ease, untroubled. "Look through the rations, see what you can cook up on the move. Sort your bunks out, get them ready for actually sleeping in. We'll be driving through the dark and I can't trust the autodrive for that, so I'll want you in the cab in shifts. It's going to be rough, kids." But it was going to be fun, too, and they knew it. A bona fide emergency, them to the rescue, chasing through the night to save a settlement. They'd be heroes, and they'd relish every moment.

He gave them a nod and said, "Git." Abruptly he had the roof to himself; rare enough to be worth a breath, a pause, a thoughtful gaze around. Then the train jerked into motion and began to turn and he'd have to make his way down under traction after all—but not yet. For now he would sit on this folded bivouac and gaze at that wayward plume and consider what was going wrong.

As he gazed, the plume cut off abruptly and entirely.

* * *

"Didn't I tell you brats to make yourselves useful in the back?"

He had come down sooner than he'd intended to, clearly sooner than they'd expected. The cab was overstuffed with kids; Jono and Perry flushed, murmured "Yes, Weatherman," and oozed out of there—impossibly slender, implausibly flexible—while Sher and Aran entirely failed to disguise their smugness.

He checked their settings, then gestured them out of the seat they were slimly sharing, two hipless wonders. They took the observer's chair instead, assuming permission to stay, watching as he cut out the autodrive they'd only this minute engaged.

"This just got more urgent," he growled. "Autodrive has a safety speed cut-out; I don't. I want two of you here with me, mostly to make sure I don't fall asleep or drive us into a cliff. You're on duty until I send you to bed. One of you oil into the back and tell the others. Tell them to strap in, and sleep if they can. Also, the off-shifts need to keep a steady run of snacks and hot drinks coming through to the cab here. This will be a night like you've never known." And he was rejoicing in it just as they were, a singing in the soul.

* * *

First dawn came with bruises aplenty but no broken bones, though the two-train had jounced and rocked alarmingly. Light brought nothing hopeful, no resumed plume to speak of life and recovery ahead; but they had their bearing triple-checked and he had kids he was willing to trust.

"You two," he grunted at Sher and Aran, back on shift again, "squeeze yourselves into this seat and keep one eye each on the compass, one on each other and two on the ground ahead. Go as fast as you dare. I'll nap in the comfy chair here and you'll wake me if anything at all happens. Am I clear?"

They assured him that he was and swarmed the chair before he changed his mind; yelled back to demand more snacks, as they were in charge now, you lubbers; and cranked the speed up higher than he'd been prepared to risk in the dark. He set the observer's chair to recline all but horizontal, tuned out all the noise and the bucking of the train and the kids' excited whisper-yells, and let in the sleep that had been besieging him all night.

* * *

They woke him around noon, when they saw first signs of groundwork: freshly broken soil, coils of irrigation tubing ready to be laid. Beyond that lay regular fields, green in ordered lines. By now the plume should have been a strong summons, a guiding pillar, the inevitability of arrival.

Today there was nothing. Only a track between the fields, turning to a laid road before they had seen the first building break the skyline. One barn and then a second, more, scattered either side. Silos and granaries and sheds. Paddocks and stables, horses' heads turning with curiosity or alarm at the sound of the two-train.

Finally they left that broad agricultural band and came through dense housing to the heart of the community. Here were the bars and businesses, the meeting hall, the school.

Of course there was a town square, a single point of focus; and this road was wide enough to take the two-train all the way. It had to be. In the center of the square stood the actuator, as it was properly called, the weather machine as it was always known.

A smooth rounded metal shell, some fifteen feet across, concealing a complexity of pipework and engineering, it bored down to the aquifer and pumped up massive quantities of water: some for the electric power plant, some for the community and the fields beyond. More it cracked into hydrogen and oxygen, storing the first for fuel and releasing the second into the planet's thin atmosphere, along with its signature vapor-plume.

People could live with the air they had, but it was dry and miserly in nature. Generations down the line would breathe more easily and grow more crops, have calmer and more temperate weather.

Which was why an actuator's failure was an immediate crisis, why he had driven all night. If these people lost water, they lost power, which brought their mere survival into question. An actuator without a plume was a sickening sight. The community would have reserves, to be sure, but they must be tapping into those even now. No wonder they had turned out to greet him with their worry, a convoy of vehicles tailing his into town; no wonder they were gathered waiting for him in the square, officials and tradespeople and children abandoning work and school in the face of something radically more important.

He inched his way through the crowd—nobody actually wanting to be mown down by a two-train—right to the side of the actuator, and set his brakes at last.

Even from the cab, he could see that the control panel's lights were on, which was something, at least. Also something of a surprise.

He opened the cab door and climbed down, kids swarming at his heels. Strutting, no doubt, cocky at being right here at the center of the affair.

Two women came pushing through the throng. "Celan Lafatine, I'm the mayor here. This is Shara Mellon, community manager."

Policy and administration. Good. "I saw your plume cut off. What happened?"

"We don't know. We need you to find out. You came so fast, it's like a blessing."

"I was on my way elsewhere and saw. Of course I came. Luck, that's all. What have you lost?"

"Nothing," she said. "Only the plume. We have water, we have power, just as before. If it's not cracking water any more, we'll run out of fuel eventually, but we keep six months'-worth always, just for this. Even so, Weatherman. Everyone's frightened."

"Of course." There were no guarantees: the electricity, the water might fail at any time. "Are you prepared for me to take it down?"

"This season, solar batteries and storage tanks will see us through," Shara Mellon confirmed. "Maybe a month, if we're cautious."

"Be cautious." He carried everything he needed; the second wagon of the two-train held enough spares to build a new actuator from the ground up. Everything bar the shell, which ought to be reusable under any but the most extraordinary circumstances. Even so. "Ration everything, just to be safe. Tell your people." The children were heedless, drawn by the sheer size of the two-train. The adults were gathering into anxious knots, as friends found each other; their teens and fosters much the same, keeping separate.

Only making wary eye contact with his kids. He smiled. "Meanwhile, if you can clear some space here, and lend me your youngsters—not all of 'em, but those I'd be taking back to social school this run, and the fosters—I'll get started."

In token of which, he turned to the control panel on the actuator and punched this season's code, to turn it off entire.

Lights blinked in sequence and went out. Adults sighed in unison, then started drifting away and calling their children after. He turned back to his own crew.

"I want tarpaulins laid out edge to edge, to take the parts in order. Hop to it." Then, to the community manager: "We'll need food and drink, for a squad of hungry hard-worked teens; a tank of water and a means to heat it; and a dormitory close by. I'll want to keep everyone together while we do this."

"Of course, Weatherman. Most of that is in hand already. You can have the hall to bed down in; I'll arrange for pallets and so forth."

Here came the local teens as requested, filtering through the dispersing crowd, ready to catch what his kids threw down from the roof. He left them to it—of course they were already exchanging names, and insults that brought those rolled tarps hurling down like missiles, laughter all around—and went to the second wagon for his toolbelt. Simplicity and convenience were the watchwords in actuator design; they were easy to take apart, easy to rebuild, easy to replace altogether at need. One man could do it alone, except for this first stage.

By the time the tarps were all laid out, he had loosened and removed a dozen bolts. He set those carefully at one corner of the spread and called all the kids together.

"Feeling strong? Good. You'll need to be. Of course, I could ask your parents to do the heavy lifting—" that brought the boos and protests he was playing for "—but I figure you can manage. Treats after." Trays of snacks and drinks were already on their way. "Work first. We need to take the whole shell off. It comes apart in sections, but I promise you, every one of them is a brute. Teamwork will do it." He very much wanted to bond all these kids together. "Ready? Good. These don't need to be laid on the tarps—no, not even the one with the control panel, good call but lay it face-up and it'll be fine. That one comes off last, yes. I like you; keep asking questions. Now, the first one's free, so off you go."

He had warned them, but they were confident in their strength and resilience. He let them take the weight together and saw their eyes widen, their bodies shift in response; saw how they almost staggered under the burden of it, how they recovered, how they determinedly carried it some sensible distance before they set it down.

How they straightened, sighed, gasped.

He laughed and said, "Okay, now you know. Still don't want your parents?" A chorus of denials. "All right. Grab a bite and a drink and we'll move on to the next. Six of these, then the grille above. That's heaviest. I'll help with that one, and you'll be grateful for it."

And so it went, one segment after another; at last the grille, which left them breathless and sweating.

"Good. That's enough for today. Yes, it is; the suns are going down and the shadows stretching, and my crew had a hard night of it besides. None of you is going home, though. You're mine now, for the duration. You'll find beds in the hall there. I know there are showers; I'm hoping there'll be food, too, and a change of clothes."

* * *

All of that and more, a mug of cider for each of the kids and beer for himself. He refused anything stronger, and took himself to bed as soon as he'd chivvied the kids in the same direction. He was sleeping among them, an adult presence, not enough to silence them but enough to keep them decent. He hoped those murmurs and chuckles going on as he drifted off were new friendships being made, new alliances against the tyranny of adults.

* * *

Morning brought no new counsel, only breakfast and the promise of a long hard day and more to follow. His team was cheerful nonetheless, excited by this change in routine, intrigued by their first chance to lay hands on the actuator's innards, interested in fresh company. It wouldn't be long before his six were trying out new looks, sleeping among new friends, losing uniformity. They hadn't been intended to foster with this community, but they would now.

"Okay, so. I want a steady supply of hot water, a tub of machine oil, all the clean rags you can rustle up. Then we'll start taking this thing apart, piece by piece. You've seen it done before, I know. This time, you're going to do it. I'll supervise and tell you what each part does; then you'll clean it, oil it if it wants oiling, lay it out on the tarps like a schematic. Everyone who depends on them should know the inwardness of an actuator."

"Not that we could fix it, though." That was Kyrla, the one who asked all the questions. One he would definitely be keeping an eye on. "We don't have the parts."

"No, that's what you need me for. But you shouldn't ever need to fix it; weathermen are here to make sure you never do."

"And yet." A gesture was sufficient, a waft of her arm towards the silent machine.

"And yet. Yes. So let's find out what's gone wrong, shall we? Quick as you like, now."

* * *

Disassembly was a long slow wearisome business, and a dirty one besides. The kids were slower than he would have been alone. Many hands grabbed for the same tools, fumbled the clips, dropped connectors, bewildered themselves and each other. He'd learned patience, down the years; it was just as well.

Still, their awkwardness allowed him time to inspect every part more narrowly than normal. Maintenance was a weatherman's proper work, replacing parts as they aged, before they broke. This should never have happened. So once the parts were clean and oiled he examined them minutely for any sign of what had gone so unpredictably, so catastrophically, wrong.

Part after part, day after day, and every one of them as near perfect as its age allowed.

Further and further into the machine, following the route-map engrained in his head. Still the same story. Here was the power bank, its tiny radioactive seed buried deep in the lead, all its indicators nominal. He'd change it out anyway, for the spare he carried in the two-train, but there wasn't a real need. This thing should be good for decades yet.

At last he reached the wellhead, as far as he could go without bringing in a crane and extra help. He shouldn't need to do that. Everything worked, that he had seen thus far; nevertheless, there was no reason to suppose that the trouble lay down there. Of all the actuator's multiple tasks, pumping was the simplest and the most fail-safe. He'd never so much as heard of a problem down the shaft. Unless...

The community still had water and power, just not the plume. They could survive without it. In honesty, so could posterity. There was a host of others, after all; and improving the atmosphere would make life better any number of ways, but none of them actually essential. He scowled, dismissed the kids to showers and play, and settled down to think.

When he had thought himself into the problem and out of it again, he went in search of authority.

"You've got a leak," he said to the gathered elders. "It's the only thing that makes sense."

"A leak? But—"

"I've never come across this before, so I had to work it through. The actuator can only bring up so much water in a day. It's a lot, but it's a hard limit. We know that the aquifer hasn't run dry underneath you, because you're still getting water. So, if you were suddenly using a lot more than before, if you were using all that it could bring up—well, of course it would cut off the plume first. It'll be programmed that way. Your demand is outrunning its supply. And you haven't grown large enough to need a second actuator yet, so you've got a leak in the pipework. Somewhere here, there's a whole lot of water running to waste."

They gazed at each other in bewilderment, these half-dozen worthies.

"But—wouldn't we *know*? Wouldn't it be forming a marsh, a morass…?"

"Not necessarily. This used to be volcanic country, it's why your land's so fertile. Like everything, water always wants to go down. Say a pipe breaks down deep—you have earthquakes here, yes?—and drains into a lava tube, that water'll find its way back to the aquifer. You're not losing it for ever, only the use of it for now."

"We need fuel, though. And our grandchildren will want the oxygen."

"Aye. You do need to find the leak. If it gets worse, you'll lose more functionality from the actuator. Check the fields, all the irrigation. Check the power station. Check everywhere. Measure flow rates, in and out. Measure volumes. Wherever the leak is, it's a big one."

* * *

After supper, he called his original six together before they could scatter with their new companions.

"Don't stay out too late with your friends tonight; we start putting everything back together in the morning. Listen, though: I want you to talk to the local kids. If anyone here knows where something unusual is happening, it'll be that lot. Ask if they've heard water running where it never was before. Ask if they've noticed any ground gone dry, or soggy. It might be beyond the worked land, where native plants have been taking advantage of the outflow. Ask if—"

He stopped abruptly, seeing how they were glancing at each other and looking away, looking down.

"Wait. You know, don't you?"

"Well…"

"Only just, though. They showed us this afternoon, after you let us go."

"Showed you what?"

"Come see. We were going anyway. Can you ride a bike?"

* * *

Yes, he could ride a bike. He hadn't, not since he was their age. It felt unfamiliar, increasingly uncomfortable, very much to be resented.

He was already resentful that the kids—his kids!—wouldn't tell him what was going on, what the big secret was. He had been their guide all this way; of course they would be bidding for independence, but this thorough turning of the tables was too far, too soon. He was still the one with authority.

They were the ones with information. He sighed, accepted it—resentfully—and went on pedalling.

They took him farther than he'd expected, farther than he knew the settlement had reached. The standard model kept all the housing within the circle of agriculture, each community building over its own fields as it grew, breaking new ground beyond to compensate. But this rough track led away from the settlement altogether, leaving the cultivated ground behind. Both suns had set now, and bike lights penetrated the gloom not very far at all.

He was on the verge of calling out, to know just where they were leading him in this wilderness, when there was an abrupt glimmer of light ahead, stationary, some kind of structure.

The track went no further than the light. That was a single lamp, hung from a post that should have been supporting the roof of a veranda. Instead it leaned out at a precarious angle, and the roof had collapsed onto the decking beneath.

That was the state of things, wherever he looked: buildings both old and abandoned, decaying under the brute realities of weather and neglect. One house, sized for a big family; numerous sheds, stables, outbuildings; one great barn, roofless.

A farm, then, and successful once, if it had justified all this construction.

"Why is this place here?" he asked, stacking his bicycle next to the kids'. "All this way from the settlement? Why was it even tolerated, given how much work it must have been, running the water out so far?"

Jono grinned. "According to Fallon, it was easier to tolerate the work than the family. It was almost a cult, he says, and his own great-grandmother was the matriarch. Rod-of-iron stuff, ruling over her menfolk and her children, their partners, their kids. Utterly heedless of anyone else, within her family or outside it. Someone in Town Meeting asked if they couldn't exile her; she was there and she demanded land of her own outside the crop-ring, far outside, where it wouldn't be swallowed up in the next wave of expansion. And water, of course, electricity, labor and materials.

"They gave her everything, just to be rid of her. She moved out here with all her family. Some others actually came with her, that's why it was almost a cult. They thrived for a while, while she was still alive; but then the family fell apart, quarrelling over who should be in charge. Fallon's gran was one of the first to move back to the settlement. Most of the others followed. In the end there was only one splinter-group left, and they couldn't keep going on their own. They went away, to some other community altogether.

"This place has stood empty for twenty years." Literally a lifetime to these kids. "And of course everyone used to bike out here." Meaning the kids their age, everyone who mattered. "Except this last storm season they couldn't, for months on end; and after, first time they made it out this far, they found—well. That's what we want to show you. Come on."

Jono and the others led him to the decrepit barn, where the walls at least still stood, where only the faintest fugitive glow spoke of the presence of another lamp within. Coming through the doorway, he found it lighting up a catastrophe far greater than a fallen roof.

Oddly there was no sign of that roof in its destruction—no beams, no timber at all. Rather there was a falling-away in the middle of the barn floor, a cavernous opening-up, lit up from below.

"What in the world...?"

"Hush. You'll see. Come down, it's perfectly safe."

It was safe. All that fallen roof-timber had been repurposed, to make stairs and decks and more stairs, down and down, following the irregular fall of the slope.

What could have been worth such secretive work?

He could smell it before he could see it. He could hear it too, in the echoes from below, voices resonating strangely. And a continuous, irregular sound, long familiar and aboundingly unlikely: water, splashing into water.

The final turn afforded him a view over a broad natural cavern, where lamplight reflected from the rippling water of a pool. It dominated the space; it made everything else look small, even the irregular arch of the cavern roof overhead. Deep shadows gave shape and weight to that, but the pool dwarfed it. He'd never seen so much water in one place. It seemed impious almost to be swimming, diving, ducking each other as those kids were doing, as no doubt his own kids hoped to do.

Sounds and their echoes died away, as the swimmers understood that he was here, adult and alien, unwelcome. One by one they pulled themselves out of the water, onto the shelf of rock that made their landing stage, that held piles of clothing and towels that were perhaps just far enough back to avoid the worst of the splashing.

Of course they swam in their skins. The younger ones made a dash for towels and decency, but no one who had been through social school— *sex school*, his own kids liked to call it—could ever come out body-shy. Half a dozen teens stood before him, defiant against authority; Kyrla was foremost, arms akimbo.

"Why did you bring him?" Her first fury was directed at his companions.

"He knew the water was going somewhere." Was Sher defending the weatherman, or themselves and their small clan? No way to tell, quite. A little of both, say. "Once the question's asked, once they know to ask it... we decided it was best just to show him."

"You decided, did you? You did, the six of you?"

Of course it hadn't been their decision to make, or their secret to tell. His sympathies were almost with the local kids. If it weren't for—well, all this water.

"Why don't you dry off and get dressed," he suggested mildly, "before we talk about this?"

She snorted—"What's to talk about?"—but she did spin on her heel and stalk away towards her clothes, snatching a proffered towel from one of the youngsters as she went.

His kids found a space for themselves, apart, uniform in their discomfort. He gave them a nod and let them be, turning instead to face the water. Finding the cause of that constant splashing now, a pipe that came out from under the staircase to release its flow of water into a pool that had too much already.

One of the younger boys was at his elbow, all wet hair and anxiety.

"You're going to make us shut it down, aren't you?"

"That's not my call." Though it could be: a weatherman's authority was narrow, but within those bounds it was absolute. "Perhaps you'll choose to shut it down yourselves. You do realize that you're stealing water from your own community, oxygen from your own descendants? The actuator's already shut off its plume; much more of this and you might break it entirely. And all for what, a private swimming hole?"

"*No*," fiercely, from behind him. Kyrla, naturally: barely dressed and barefoot, working dark hair with a towel. "We're not doing this for fun. I mean, it is fun, of course it is—but it's so much more than that. This is *important.*"

"Tell me, then, and let's test that. Tell me how it started. I'm guessing the ground had opened up, so someone—" *You?* "—had to slither down to see, and found this?"

"This, yes, full of water, the storms had been that hard. And we talked about telling someone, but first we just wanted to enjoy it for a bit."

"You built all those steps, between you? That wasn't just 'for a bit.' That was hard work. Good work, too," he added conscientiously, to let them know they'd at least done one thing right. "But it meant you wanted to keep this going."

"We had to. Only then the water started to drain away and we couldn't let that happen. Not now."

"So you found the farm's old water connection, turned it on again, ran this pipe down here, and brought all the trouble in the world down on your heads. Do you understand how angry people are going to be? How angry I am, for one? And I don't belong here, none of you belong to me. I'm surprised you managed to keep it secret this long, but the wrath of the cosmos is going to break over your little heads for this, once it gets out. Which it has to, now. And yes, you have to turn that water off."

"No. We can't."

"Why not?"

Kyrla drew a breath, started to say something, stopped, and shook her head. "Can't tell you," she said. Then, before his temper could crack at last: "Have to show you. You'll have to swim."

"What? No. Why would I—?"

"Because you'll never understand, else. And you have to. Someone has to, now. One of you." The grown-ups, the arbitrators. "Just get in the water, you'll see." And then, with an effort, "Please?"

He was no more body-shy than they were, but he did feel unusually aware of his own bulk and hairiness against their spare adolescence as he stripped. Half the kids were following suit, his own six too; whatever they wanted him to see—and none of them would say—they wanted to share in his discovery, to see his reaction, or else simply to be there again rather than here, damp and worried.

How deep was it? How cold? He couldn't begin to guess. No matter. They'd survived it; so could he.

All of them were waiting now, to see him jump. Very well: he took a swift run-up and made the best dive that he could manage.

He felt the water close around him, braced himself mentally for thermal shock—and didn't feel it or anything like it. The water was something comfortably close to body temperature. Hot springs, perhaps, down at the pool's unimaginable bottom? There had been volcanoes here, long ago...

He rose to the surface, meaning to float awhile, see if he could puzzle all this out, what the kids were so protective of. There was the tug of an unexpected current, though, a gentle downward yearning. Well, they'd said it drained if they didn't keep it topped up. Perhaps this was the sucking of that distant outflow?

No, not that. It couldn't be. If their improvised inflow was enough to keep it replenished, the outflow wasn't any more urgent, by definition. It could never be enough to trouble this vast body of water.

In any case, this wasn't like the pull of distant drainage. This was... embracing, rather. Encompassing. More than that: he took a breath and let it draw him down. Now it was supportive, holding him not far below the surface, not seeking to take him further. Pressing gently from all sides, as it seemed.

It was no way for water to behave. He felt both engulfed and buoyed, as though some creature had taken him gently in hand. He was no longer holding his breath, he realized. Was he breathing? Surely not, though he couldn't really tell. All he knew was that he was in no distress and had no intention of struggling against this grip. This manifestation. This presence. Whatever it was.

He was still underwater, but this was water with purpose. Intent. Intelligent? He wasn't wholly sure. He could sense curiosity in some kind, though he didn't understand how; few people in the colony had time for mysticism or experiences beyond the mundane, and his was as plain and practical a mind as he knew.

Curiosity and pleasure, he thought. And surely this was an entity of some sort, surely it had to be.

The planet had been surveyed and scanned, judged uninhabited. It could never have been settled, else. And no colonist in all the years of occupation had reported any encounter that might contradict that.

And yet, here was something immaterial, to give the lie to all that pragmatism; something living, to give the lie to careful study and long experience.

Something that had, that must have been, in contact—if this was contact?—with the children of this outpost for months now. No wonder they'd been so reckless with the community's water; of course they'd want to keep this pool filled. Or else this—alien, this presence—had wanted it and they'd cooperated. Willy-nilly, perhaps? But no: if sharing the water felt like this all the time, he guessed they'd do anything to keep it so. He was moderately sure that he would have done the same. That he was going to do the same.

Sharing. Yes. There was abruptly another energy tugging at his senses. And another, and more. For a moment, he half wondered if there was a population here in the pond, a community—but no, these he knew. These were the kids, coming back into the water. He wasn't seeing or hearing anything, all his focus was turned inward, towards this unfathomable contact, but he knew them anyway. He knew each one of them.

So did the entity, that was immediately clear. He himself was new and welcome; they were familiar and welcome. It made a difference. He floated in suspension; they swam and dove and frolicked, every one of them held in the same close attention. It was not divided; one or a dozen, two dozen, made no difference at all. And he could sense each one of them individually and collectively: bright burning sparks, a steady glow from the whole. If they had been a gestalt before, just them and this—well, they were a gestalt yet, and he a part of it, contributory.

He made a choice and kicked for the surface. Not kicking against anything, not struggling to be free, only trusting not to lose this now. The kids could splash and race and still be held, so why not he?

He rose and was neither helped nor hindered, neither lifted up nor pushed back down, but that grip stayed with him all the way. He broke into the open air and thought perhaps he'd breathe now, and so did. And looked about him, too late; there was suddenly a teenager on his back, all taut muscle and smooth slippery skin, pushing him under again. This was another kind of welcome, he knew. They perceived him as he did them and they were all one together, saturated with wonder, breathless and better and more.

* * *

How long did they spend so, ducking and diving, swimming and floating, all within the ambit of this otherness, this witness, this unaccountable companion? He couldn't tell, he had no notion of time passing, until he found a kid on either side of him, taking his arms and towing him to the pool's edge. Slithering out, leaning down for his arms again, tugging him up in his turn.

"It's best not to be in there too long, especially your first time," Kyrla said, looking him over judiciously. "We think it's immortal, and it thinks we are. It doesn't do time, at any rate. Spend too long in its head, neither will you, but time goes on regardless. Out here, it does."

She said that with a certain chagrin, a whole essay of teenage trouble and resentment. He grinned and said, "What more can you tell me about it?"

Not even Kyrla's presumed authority could keep half a dozen voices from tumbling over each other in answer:

"It doesn't have a name for itself, we think it might be the only one—"

"—it doesn't have a body, or a language as far as we can tell. We don't even know if it has a mind—"

"—it can reach all through the water, as far as that goes—"

"—it's survived in the groundwater mostly, for as long as the planet's been dry—"

"—but storm season brought it up and we found it—"

"—and it doesn't want to go down again. We think it's been so lonely for so long..."

* * *

The kids sat all in a line along the pool's edge, their feet trailing in the water, still—they said—feeling something, contact, between the entity and each other. He sat deliberately apart and pondered.

At last he said, "All right, listen up. This is how it's going to go. No protests, no complaints."

A weatherman's authority may be narrow, but it does run deep. Even kids know this. They kept quiet, listened up.

"In the first place, people have to be told. Everybody, not just locally. This matters to the whole colony; as Kyrla said, it's important. You'll be famous, soon enough. It may not get you out of trouble, but people will come from all over to learn more about this. We'll start small, though. Tonight—no, it's late now, but in the morning—each one of you is going to tell your parents or your fosterfolk what's been going on. You'll have to deal with any kickback from that, it's what families do. And fosters, you just stand there and take it, yes?

"Then there's the rest of your community. Don't worry, I'll help with that. I'm the weatherman; they respect me. As far as I can, I'll take the credit, to save you from taking too much blame. I'll have your elders call a meeting, get it all done in one. And I'll put the call through to Authority, after. They'll have no interest in a bunch of kids.

"And after *that*, after I've made that call and your folks have come out here to see for themselves—and you know they will, they'll all want to—then we have to turn this water off."

Now there was a shifting among them, a rising murmur, discomfort, discontent. His voice rolled over it all. "I said we have to, not that I want to. Your community can't afford this much drain. We need to get your actuator pumping out a clear plume again, as soon as may be."

"But then"—Sher, treading very carefully not to be protesting, not to complain, only pointing out the reality—"the pool will drain, and the…the creature will go down into the groundwater again, and you said, you *said* there would be people coming to see it, important people, and it won't be here, so…"

"So I did say that, all of that; and we're going to turn the water off regardless. And *then* you'll pay your proper penance for all this sneaking about and water-theft and the rest of it. I'll call out a drilling rig and pick the right site for it. After that you kids are in for the hardest three months of your life. You'll do all your regular work and chores at home, those of you still schooling will go to school, and when your day is over, then you'll belong to me. Between us, we'll drill and case a well—I'll show you how, and once you're competent I'll supervise while you do all the hard and dirty work—and then we'll build us a second actuator. Everything we need is in the two-train, that's why it's so monstrous big. We'll camp out here, to make the best use of your time. I'll work you to rags, and you'll hate me on a daily basis, because the aquifer's what, three hundred meters down hereabouts? The rig can handle it, but that's a long and a weary way to drill through rock. We'll do it close by, but there'll still be pipework to lay from there to here, and you'll dig that in as it should be dug, the way I'd do it myself." Meaning by hand, largely.

"Our parents—"

"Your parents won't have a word to say against it. Glad to get you out of their hair, likely." This was his work and his authority. No one in the community would face him down. No one could.

Most of these kids had been born and raised here, or else in communities like this. They knew hard labor in their bones. They weren't frightened of it in prospect, nor would they be daunted. Stretched, yes. Driven harder than they knew. They'd learn and grow. And soon now, he thought as he shambled over to the wall to find dry towel and clothes, it was going to dawn on one or another of them that at the end of those long exhausting days, well, they'd have to *wash*, wouldn't they? They'd have to get clean before bed. And here was all this water, already warm by favor of its alien presence, just waiting to welcome them in.

Speculation

Ari Officer

"This is horseshit." The old hermit slammed his front door in Ananke's face. From inside the mildew-stained stronghold, his voice carried faintly: "Damn glitchy computer." His stomps faded into Earth's perpetual silence.

"What's horseshi...?" Ananke whispered to herself, sliding her palm down the porous stone exterior of the Foregone's home. Wondering how she could persuade him to at least talk to her, she sat on the front steps and rested her elbows on stiff knees. The cold concrete sent a shiver up her spine. Ananke pulled in a breath through her respirator, her efforts rewarded with a musty taste of rotting grass that nearly negated the urge to breathe.

The planet's air was deteriorating again. Their machinery was breaking down more frequently. The data showed inconsistencies, as if their endeavors were backfiring.

She surveyed the valley into which the human race had retreated. Fallen, decapitated statues lined the dirt path back to the last bastion of humanity. Past the blue limestone bodies, Uruk's geodesic dome glistened in the harsh light of dawn. Green clouds dotted the yellow sky above the surrounding ridges. She yearned to awake beneath the blue-and-white heavens of Earth's paradisiac past, before their ancestors had scarred the landscape. That perfect sky was meant for her.

Only the hermit's ancient knowledge might remedy the environmental restoration. Yet the Foregone lived alone, with no airlock, risking exposure to the toxic atmosphere. If he breathed too much of the tainted air, all hope would be lost.

Perhaps she should remind the Foregone of the beauty he could help rehabilitate. Ignoring the pit in her stomach, Ananke buzzed once more.

The hermit opened the door with a slow creak. His tattered white vest glowed against the grimy walls. "The transmission," he said.

"What transmission?"

"From space." He stroked his gray beard. "Surely the central computer has told you."

Had he gone mad? Ananke hadn't the faintest idea what he was talking about. Transmissions from space? "First, please explain to me. What's, umm—"

"Horseshit?" His voice wheezed. "It's horseshit I have to work. I'm too damn old. You don't need me. Go away."

"With all due respect, everyone has to work. Our future depends on it. Even the central computer agrees you're indispensable." As the lead engineer, she had developed instruments to confirm their greatest fear, but a solution escaped her. Where all others had failed, an original architect of the climate reversal project might solve the riddle. Ananke was certain the Foregone would expose the elusive inefficiencies and flaws. Fixing those would correct—and even accelerate—the restoration. If only she could persuade him to return to the city.

"You don't need me. I told that damn computer…" he trailed off, leaning against the doorframe.

"What? That you're 'too old'? I'm sure it took your age into consideration." She was mostly sure, anyway. It was true the central computer had been acting erratically; a dozen or so terminals had permanently malfunctioned.

He shook his head and squinted, his crow's feet spreading like lava channels. "Some of us aged before receiving our first silver treatments. You see my skin?" He held up his hand, pale white and missing a pinky. "It will never change color like yours. I have to live with arthritis forever. My cells can't repair themselves like when I was young. When I get injured, that's it. I carry the scars to my grave. And that's where I'm headed once you all leave me be. My work is long since done."

Medicine could only stop the aging process, and the treatments had turned Ananke's and everyone else's skin blue-gray. Sometime after failing the planet and all other life, humanity had succeeded in bolstering itself, stumbling upon near immortality. Ironic, given the current situation.

Ananke had to keep him talking, in case the Foregone really intended to end his life. Drugs didn't protect anyone from accidents; all he had to do was walk outside without a respirator. "Before I go, please tell me, what's… that word?"

"'Horseshit?' You don't know what 'shit' is? Goddamn, we went too far with the whole etiquette thing. I told the others it was a mistake."

"I know what...*that* word means." She blushed. "But the first one?"

"A horse? My colorful tongue has betrayed me." He chuckled, his belly shaking as if a tremor had taken hold of him. "Sorry, I forgot. Horses didn't survive the crash. Hardly anything did."

"So, what were horses?"

"Majestic." He stared beyond Ananke, his pupils contracting to expose hazel irises unlike anything she had seen before. "They trotted on four legs and could cover impressive distances. We rode them sometimes, like hover-cars."

"Is, uh...*that*...a metaphor then in this context? Some kind of emission from those horse-vehicles?"

"No, no. They used to crap, same as you and me. They were sentient creatures, like us both."

"That sounds barbaric, enslaving animals."

"We did many barbaric things." His eyes moistened. "We ate meat. Not even the worst thing about humanity."

"Animals are no different than we are." Ananke felt her breakfast algae come back up, the salty taste scratching the top of her throat. She gulped and clenched all her muscles.

"Truer words have rarely been spoken." He squeezed his eyes shut and massaged his neck. "We often do terrible things out of necessity."

The Foregone's sensitivity surprised her. She hoped it could translate into some empathy, some motivation to rejoin Uruk and contribute.

"Is killing evil when there is no alternative besides your own death? The survival of our race..." He shook his head, then opened his eyes, staring at Ananke. "I'm sorry, this was a bad idea. I assume you can get back to the dome safely on your own." He gestured for her to leave.

She grabbed the door and sighed. If she failed to convince him to help, they might never reclaim the planet. "I agree with you about the central computer. Something is wrong with it. I built my own equipment to test the air and ran an independent analysis. The readings don't match."

"You did, did you?" He bit his lip. "Perhaps you could repair something for me. Hmm. Well, come on in. You'll have to leave your respirator on, I'm afraid. More economical to wear one out here than to keep this old brick barracks airtight."

"Where's yours?" she asked while following him inside.

He turned back toward her. "I'm wearing a lightweight one." Opening his mouth, he showed her a bright green tube inside his cheek, against rotting yellow teeth. "This place has some basic air filtration. I expected to keep our conversation outside, but don't think this means you'll convince me to return to that dystopian hellhole I created. Mostly I just don't want you wandering around. It's dangerous out there."

Dangerous? There was nothing but ruins outside. Inside, though, Ananke caught a glimpse into a whole new world. The brick walls were painted white, contrasting with the natural gray stone they favored inside Uruk. Above the tiled fireplace, its black logs smoldering, a painting depicted an older-looking pale man—just like the Foregone—at a podium with his arms up and a gavel in the air. Next to him, against a fence, stood the shadows of three people in chains. It was ominous, unlike the abstract art inside the city.

He sat on an oversized blue chair. "Alright. Say your piece." He motioned to an identical seat across the blue woven rug, stained yellow with age.

"You seem willing to risk your life for your freedom. That's why you live out here, right? While the rest of us are trapped inside." She studied the two hallways flanking the fireplace behind the Foregone. One, illuminated by candlelight, stretched as far as she could see; the other ended abruptly with a closed black door. "Please help us speed up the process."

He put his feet—wrapped in bandages—on the low stone table in front of him. "I'm an old man. This isn't my world."

Ananke sat down on the chair opposite him, sinking into it as it cradled her hips, instantly warming her thighs. It felt so foreign compared to Uruk's stone furniture, as if she were lounging on another human being. "That's why you need to help us restore the world. *Your* world."

"The central computer knows everything I know, can do a lot more than we can with only this crude technology." The man laughed and pulled a pen out of his pocket. "You don't need me."

"What about the others? The other Foregone. Where are they?" At this point, the saviors of the human race were practically a myth.

"Not your concern. Anyway, are you ready to tell me about the transmission?"

"I don't know what you're talking about."

"Perhaps they're hiding it from you. Damn, maybe the ship isn't listening. They don't know we're here. Or maybe I miscalculated." He rubbed his chin, staining his gray beard with ink. "I need to look into something. Can you stay put?"

Curious, Ananke nodded.

The Foregone pushed open the black door. Behind it, Ananke glimpsed what looked like tombs with frosted glass masking the silhouettes within.

He shut the door behind him. A moment later, Ananke heard him speaking strings of mostly unrecognizable words. Puzzled, she listened but understood nothing besides the occasional expletive.

When the door opened, Ananke asked, "What dialect were you speaking?"

"Another language. My native one."

Were swear words universal across all Earth's tongues? "Why don't we speak your language today?"

"My more...humanitarian friends felt we should adapt to the majority. We voted. It wasn't easy adjusting, especially when your vocabulary is so stinking polite." He laughed. "I prefer practical to polite." The Foregone sat back down with a jet-black respirator in hand.

Could she sway him? "Help me and you'll help yourself. What will it take to get you back to the city? You mentioned I could help you fix something."

"No, I have a better idea. Get me access to the central computer to help me finish what we started. Find me a working terminal and I'll give you half my days each week."

"All you want is a terminal?" She ran a hand through her spiky hair. "Then you'll spend six days a week helping us fix the atmosphere, making it fit to breathe?"

"Consider it done." He smiled.

That negotiation was far too easy. Ananke suspected she should push a bit more to earn the hermit's respect. "I also want to know your name. Then we have a deal."

"No," he said. "I don't even remember it. If I did, I would curse myself every day. Too many sleep cycles, I'm afraid. Survival is a grotesque instinct. And I don't want to get too attached." He sniffled. "I'd like to begin work immediately."

* * *

Ananke led the Foregone into her office within Uruk. "You can remove your respirator now. Uruk's air is safe." She instinctively breathed through her nose, the smell of caramelized sugar from the refectory making her mouth water.

The Foregone pulled at his sleeve. "It helps to have the extra nitrogen at my age. And it filters out the bitter stench of this prison."

"You may risk your life outside, but this 'prison' is home for the rest of us."

"Can I use that terminal?" He pointed toward the stone console in the corner, with its screen and a projected keyboard. "Is it still functioning?"

Before she could answer, he was typing furiously away, blue text commands streaming faster than Ananke could read them. The Foregone paused a moment, tugged at his ear, and then nodded. A few keystrokes later, the text changed to black. Ananke didn't recognize the characters on the screen. Glancing at the keyboard, she saw a strange layout of similarly unknown symbols. He navigated it like an experienced pianist, despite his missing fingers.

"How did you lose them?" she asked.

"Lose what?" His hands had no stumps or scars—or any sign of surgery.

"Your pinkies."

The Foregone shifted uncomfortably on the stone stool, his skin glowing orange under the artificial lights. "That was a long time ago." He turned toward her, clenched his fists, and hid them behind his back. "I need your help. That transmission—"

"Again with the transmission! I told you, I have no idea what you're talking about."

"You know the satellite?"

Ananke nodded. There was only one bright light that traveled quickly across the night sky.

"It's from before...my time. I'm not sure if we can link up, but maybe you can help me access it. It might be able to hear what we can't down on the ground."

"Hacking into that ancient satellite wasn't part of our deal. What makes you think it still works? Just because it survived while dozens of others fell out of orbit?"

"There were no others." The Foregone sighed. "One was miracle enough."

"We have more important matters at hand. Like fixing the planet."

The Foregone typed madly on the keys, studied the screen, and then turned toward Ananke. "I'm sorry, you're right. I have everything I need already."

"So, you'll stop asking about the imaginary transmission?"

"For now. It just hasn't happened yet. I suppose my estimates were too optimistic."

"What do you mean?" Glancing at the screen, she recognized the standard atmospheric composition readings and watched the Foregone edit the target levels. Impossible! No user had access to change the restoration plan. How did he do that?

"Let me be honest with you. Maybe you'll actually listen when I need you later." He inhaled deeply, the respirator exaggerating it with a wheeze. "This isn't Earth."

"Very funny." Ananke was getting desensitized to his fantasies, but he'd crossed a line implying their efforts were all for naught. To suggest her friends sacrificed their lives based on a fabrication... Whatever he needed help with, she wasn't interested.

He pouted. "We deceived you. Hell, we lie to ourselves. Don't trust us. Don't trust anyone." After a few more keystrokes, the screen returned to the blue text with which Ananke was so familiar.

"We didn't destroy our planet?" she asked.

"Oh, no, *we* did." He scratched his bald head. "We came here on a very fast ship, completing mankind's first interstellar journey. The Foregone, as you call us—we were the crew. You were a passenger."

"Passenger?" She snorted. "I was born here." If this isn't Earth, what is it? What were they working toward? Why make a new home somewhere inhospitable?

"You were conceived on Earth." He coughed. "The radiation in space mutated the embryos. That's why you and I look different."

"Your skin?"

"Well, my skin is natural. Human. Yours is different. Blue."

Ananke couldn't stop her eyebrows from shooting up. "I know that's not true. The life-prolonging drugs changed our skin. You said you were too old when you started the regimen."

"I have a tendency to talk out my ass." He winked. "Did they teach you that those same drugs make you infertile?"

"We aren't infertile." She didn't believe him. Despite the accidents, they maintained their population.

"No one has had a child in this dome. Not naturally."

"Impossible." She couldn't believe him. She and her friends talked all the time about having kids.

"Think about it."

She would never believe him. "There are plenty of children. Don't be ridiculous."

"Do you know *any* of the parents?"

Ananke took a deep breath and racked her brain. "Well, why does it matter? We are all parents to the children. They are our future."

"I came up with that particular line of horseshit because I didn't want you all asking too many questions." He raised an eyebrow. "Do you know who *your* parents are?"

She didn't. Her legs began to shake.

"We're terraforming this new world," the Foregone said, "so humanity can survive. I suspect we will be ready soon. No more like you should be needed. We've sacrificed more than we planned."

"What about the ruins?" she asked, hoping to poke a hole in this delusion. "Why are there statues if we've only just arrived?"

The hermit's eyes widened as he stroked his beard. "First attempt." He bit his lip and slowly nodded. "All under a different, larger dome. Those horses we talked about? We had some in the old dome. It was poorly designed, though, and the system failed. We fashioned your smaller home and recycled our electronics to accelerate the terraforming effort. We couldn't get back into space thanks to the damage we sustained from the… local climate…when we landed. We didn't plan to put you to work. We'd hoped to build robots when we arrived, but this planet lacks metals."

"The central computer came from the ship?"

"Exactly. No one can replace or repair it. Our metals-based technology didn't suit this planet. We couldn't figure out how to replicate organic machines from the resources available."

A new planet, a new chance to get things right…and yet this wasn't home. "What did you expect of this planet?"

"Hope." He closed his eyes. "But that's not what we found."

"Then what *did* you find?"

He opened his eyes and stared down at the rug. "A beautiful world."

"A beautiful world with deadly air?" Ananke rolled her eyes. "I deal in facts and figures, not lies." She couldn't accept they had given up Earth—and for this? The pictures, the stories…myths to motivate them on this poor substitute of a world? She needn't accept his wild claims.

"No, I'm getting too old for outright lies. In any case, I told you not to trust anyone. Even the central computer. We've curated and revised the history you were taught."

She leaned forward. "Tell me the truth. Or I'll infer it soon enough."

"The truth?" He laughed and kicked back his legs. "It takes imagination to deduce the truth. Especially when it's ugly, as truths so often are. I need you to watch out for the transmission. I think I've done all I can for the day."

His convoluted story didn't change Ananke's plans. "What about our agreement? There are still dozens of readings I want to study together today."

"Of course." His pressed his lips together. "Let's open up the ventilation console. I want to analyze the air in the dome. I think it could be improved. That's a good place to start, don't you think? I'll certainly breathe easier."

Ananke doubted his sincerity as much as his story, but she'd succeeded in getting him in the room. As long as she could keep him there working on anything relevant, there was hope.

* * *

After nearly six days' work, despite their best efforts, the air in Uruk was indeed becoming harder to breathe. As stubborn as the Foregone had been in all his other absurd observations and lies, he had been right on this count. How had she missed it before? No one else seemed troubled by their more frequent coughing fits. She stared at the terminal, hoping the solution would present itself.

Instead, the screen flashed bright red.

"That's strange," Ananke whispered to herself. "Central computer, what's going on?" She expected another glitch. It had seemed distracted lately.

The transmission has arrived.

"The transmission?" How could it be real? It felt as if Ananke's chest had caved in and she clutched her stomach. "Please show it to me."

On the screen, blue text filled in from right to left. Half of it was incomprehensible, almost contradictory, while the other half challenged her sense of reality. Phrases like *first interstellar mission, missing our home,* and *searching for new hospitable worlds* stuck out and confirmed the Foregone's fantastic story. Yet mentions of *returning home* confused her. She read it over again, unable to fully digest the gravity of what was happening. Everything the hermit had said—all the madness—began to feel real.

Do you have a response?

Ananke touched her fingertips to her lips. To disregard everything she'd known, to submit to the ravings of a lunatic... But if this were Earth, then who was communicating with her?

Finally, she answered: "Tell them we are well along in the terraforming process." She couldn't believe she'd just regurgitated the Foregone's instructions and rebranded the restoration, accepting Uruk was not on Earth.

The door opened and the hermit himself sauntered in with his usual grimace. He'd abandoned his secondary respirator after getting used to the scents of Uruk.

"Where were you?" Ananke asked.

"I needed some fresh air."

She was too much in disbelief to laugh at his joke. "Well, you were right."

"About what?"

"How did you know?"

The Foregone's eyes bulged as he caught two short breaths. "It arrived? When?"

"Right before you walked in. How did you predict the future?"

"You of all people should recall I know something everyone else doesn't."

"That this isn't Earth." She took a deep breath, begrudgingly accepting that the Foregone was at least somewhat truthful. "And that there was a second ship."

"You guessed?"

"What else could you be expecting?"

"I did the math hundreds of times. I knew the starship would arrive; my calculations were just a bit off. Something must have slowed them down."

"So, this is why you wanted console access? To communicate with the ship?"

"You got it." As he shifted his weight again, he yawned, exposing a flash of green.

"They're excited to return home. But you said this isn't Earth. So, which is it? And why lie to us all?"

"You don't have to treat me like I'm your enemy. Maybe once, but I'm trying to do my best. I was born on Earth and we are light-years away from home."

"Then how do you explain that *they also* think this is home?"

The Foregone leaned against the wall, sliding his hand across the gray stone blocks. "It's a generation ship," he said after a moment's thought. "Their parents' parents' parents' parents left Earth. How would you feel being born in a prison, en route to somewhere new? They're lying to themselves to make the transition easier. We did the same thing here."

Ananke gulped, her parched throat cutting like a knife. "How did you know about them when we've been here so long?" She was doubting his convoluted story with all its inconsistencies more and more. And he'd said to trust no one.

"They left earlier than we did. They were the first starship Earth sent to colonize the stars. Ours was the second and possibly final. Earth didn't survive long after our departure. Transforming this planet may be our only hope as a species."

"How did we beat them here?"

"Technology improved and we passed them on the way."

"Why didn't we pick them up?"

"Intercepting them would have been impossible. We wouldn't have survived multiple periods of acceleration; the energy lost would have made it all impractical. In any case, we always planned to beat them here and prepare the planet for their arrival."

"Why didn't they just use the silver injections to keep the original crew alive?"

"We invented the drug right before my ship left Earth. They don't have it. They age. They have to procreate."

Ananke shook her head. "You have an answer for everything, don't you?"

"Wait a minute," the Foregone asked with sudden realization, "you read the transmission? You understood it?"

"Why wouldn't I? Sure, they're using some kind of dialect, missing prepositions, with seemingly no perception of tense. But it's close enough."

"Is it up? Can I see?" He leaned over the desk and read it himself. "Language must have devolved and the computer is doing its best to translate for you. Yes…that must be it." The Foregone lifted his shoulders and grabbed his neck with both hands. "But what if it isn't them? Then all this would have been for nothing."

"Who else could it be? You said there were no other ships."

"Not from Earth. What if…" A tear dripped down the Foregone's cheek until he wiped his eyes and shook his head. "Impossible. They barely got a satellite into orbit. They couldn't have been that advanced."

"Who?"

"Sorry, I was just speculating aloud. Our ship is just later than I expected. Maybe more time has passed for them than I calculated. You're right, it *has* to be our ship."

Was she? It all seemed unreal, like a dream. She knew nothing firsthand; the Foregone and the computer were intermediaries in every interaction, every aspect of her life.

He took her seat at the console and began typing rapidly on the stone surface, the projected keyboard capturing his movements. His eyes moistened from strain as his shallow breaths intensified. Then he paused, burying his face in his hands. As he slid his palms down his now-rosy cheeks, he kicked the wall and let out a harsh sigh.

"I'm sorry," he said, staring again at the screen, slumped over like he was hiding from something. "I need to go." Lips trembling, he briefly looked at Ananke, his eyes wide. He held his stomach as he stood and rushed to the door, slamming it behind him.

What else did he know? What *didn't* he know? Ananke assumed he was fabricating another excuse to exile himself. Sure, this fake outburst of remorse was exaggerated, but she'd learned to stop thinking of him as empathetic. He was unemotional, more like the computer than a human. She could do better on her own.

"Central computer," she said, "did they respond?" She was excited to meet her relatives from Earth, to finally experience some of the wonder she'd been shown—even on another planet.

Ananke couldn't read the black text that appeared on screen. It must be the Foregone's native tongue.

"Central computer, could you please change languages so that I can understand?"

The screen filled with blue text she could read: *Yes, Ananke. Would you like me to lift the comms embargo and send your message?*

"Please do." Why had the computer held her response?

The ship asks: Terraforming? What do we miss?

"Tell them we expect to finish up the terraforming soon after their arrival."

They respond: Do not understand.

Lost in translation, perhaps? "Tell them we'll be able to breathe the air soon."

They respond: Do not understand.

"Ask them if they are excited to seed our planet with animals. Especially horses."

They respond: What is 'horses?'

Perhaps the Foregone was right and their language had devolved. "Central computer, please stop communicating with the ship. Do you know about horses?"

Of course. On the screen, the computer showed Ananke a video of large, beautiful four-legged animals trotting across a verdant field beneath an immense blue sky. No dome to stop them, no computer to dictate their every action, no responsibility to fix others' mistakes. Freedom. A simplicity Ananke had never known. Under a sky she had never seen.

She held back tears. "Did they really roam the first dome?" And why ascribe such a heinous meaning to the excrement of such magnificent beasts?

The first dome? There is only one dome. The masters built yours before they started rotating through cryogenic sleep.

"The masters?"

The crew, my passengers. You call them the Foregone.

"Were we not all passengers?"

I do not understand.

"The rest of us came here as embryos."

The embryos did not survive the voyage. I could not save them from the unexpected radiation bursts.

Was the central computer malfunctioning again? "But here I am alive."

You are not an embryo.

"But I once was."

The door burst open and the Foregone sprinted in, pushing Ananke from her stool. She fell to the ground, the disturbed dust sending her into a coughing fit. As she pulled herself to her feet, he disregarded her while simultaneously typing and shouting in his own language. As before, though, she recognized the occasional obscenity.

Finally, he looked at her. "Computer, did Ananke communicate directly with the ship?"

Yes. You did not reestablish the holds.

The Foregone sighed deeply. "Fine. It really doesn't matter anymore. Computer, after I leave the dome, keep the airlocks sealed until that ship is in orbit. Then reverse my atmospheric targets for the dome and commence Plan G outside."

Understood.

Ananke gasped. "What are you doing?"

Ignoring her, the Foregone slowly hit a few additional keys. The screen returned to its normal console with blue text. Chin trembling, the Foregone hobbled toward the door.

"You're trapping us in Uruk?" Ananke whispered.

"You've been trapped for centuries." The Foregone looked paler than ever. "Ananke, I must apologize. I've doomed you all. It will take centuries to undo, but most of our equipment needs modification and won't last that long. For that, Ananke, I am truly sorry. If I'm wrong, we'll meet again. I promise to do better in that case."

"Wrong about what?"

"Trust your instincts." His moist eyes were bloodshot. "I've burdened you with too much of the truth, but maybe you can succeed against all odds. Build your own machinery, rebuild everything from scratch. You, Ananke. You can reverse our mistake." Slumped over, he stumbled and barely kept his balance.

"What mistake?"

He wiped the tears from his face. "I'm sorry," he repeated, face flushed, before retreating in silence. His footsteps faded into Uruk's ubiquitous hum.

Before Ananke could follow him, the overhead lights flickered. The terminal screen went blank.

"Central computer?" She smacked the terminal. Facing the truth, everything felt so harsh. The room was no longer a place of inspiration. It became an unyielding box, a prison, its sharp edges suffocating the air she breathed. Even the stone floor felt cold and rigid. She was trapped in something artificial, something never designed for her.

Then blue text reappeared on the screen:

Hello, Ananke. What were you asking?

Strange. "You told me I didn't come from an embryo."

Apologies. I was dealing with higher priority tasks like regulating the air filtration system.

"Did I come from an embryo? From Earth?"

You did. Absolutely. I must deal with some other tasks. The algae tanks need to be reconfigured. Thank you.

"What am I?" Ananke asked.

The computer never responded.

Somehow, Ananke knew it wasn't just another technical tantrum. The Foregone had changed something.

* * *

The day the generation ship was to land, the Foregone was still nowhere to be seen and Ananke had no time to seek him out after the airlocks finally opened. Why would he avoid the ultimate event he'd cared so much about? Ananke couldn't convince the central computer to explain how she was born—and it denied calling the Foregone "the masters." The only consolation was that Uruk's air had returned to a healthy equilibrium. Yet more frequent malfunctions had plagued the terraforming equipment ever since. She knew the Foregone had sabotaged the operation, but why?

Only a few diplomats were chosen because the city wanted to limit the risk. Every life was precious, after all. Indeed, the central computer had ordered Ananke to stay within, but she'd ignored the command. This was too historic an event: the arrival of more colonists! Uruk had fallen under a fog of anticipation, productivity suffering, everyone excited yet apprehensive of such a disruption to routine. More colonists meant more mouths to feed, more strain on their failing infrastructure.

The central computer had confirmed to Ananke that the generation ship carried the DNA of all Earth's creatures. Once they fixed the air, horses would roam free! Repeating that to herself helped quell the lingering unease she'd felt ever since the Foregone had trapped everyone inside. The anticipation of what the world could become had made the wait to escape even harder. Expectation crushed hope; that must be why the Foregone had lied. Yet this was the hopeful moment for which the hermit had waited. Something didn't add up. She shivered as she looked to the heavens.

A ball of flame grew as it fell toward the earth, leaving a curving trail of copper smoke. From what the Foregone had described, Ananke had expected a giant metallic box. As the ship approached, though, its purple shell looked nothing like that. Its curved hull morphed from a ring-like torus to a perfect sphere while currents like lightning danced and brightened. Why had he lied? She fumed over his conspicuous absence.

A distant hum crescendoed into an explosive cacophony. Ananke covered her ears and squinted at the shapeshifting craft. How did this spacecraft, smaller than Uruk, support generations of people while protecting the entire genetic code of all Earth's life? She feared they'd lost Earth's history. Was the freighter still in orbit? This must only be a landing vessel.

The ground shook when it touched down upon twelve spherical feet. The round craft bounced a few times, independent of the rigid landing apparatus, then stabilized. A black spot formed on the side facing Ananke and displaced the flashing purple as it grew to about one-twelfth the spacecraft's height. A translucent ramp extended from the ship, touching the ground halfway between them with a thud.

A lone astronaut, dressed in an orange suit, descended the ramp and saluted, his six-fingered glove sparkling.

"What happens?" The astronaut's voice sounded pure and beautiful, amplified perfectly through his opaque helmet. He glanced at the dome and then scanned the mountains beyond. "Who does this? Who destroys all? We are not gone long to explore, a few generations relative here. I remember. Not so long for us."

How could he remember? Ananke wondered. This man could never have been here before.

An explosion rocked the ground. Ananke turned to see a pillar of smoke rise from behind the city. The Foregone's home, she surmised, destroyed by his own hand. Was he insane after all? Ananke's throat tightened, but then she pushed away her remaining empathy for the hermit, fallen from whatever purpose he once knew. Good riddance, as far as she was concerned. She doubted his motives, questioned his designs and her own participation in them.

The other citizens of Uruk panicked, sprinting back to safety—and likely worried about damage to the dome. As dust clouded the view of Uruk, their frantic steps shook the earth more than the ship's landing. Ananke held her ground.

The astronaut began to fiddle with a control beneath his helmet.

Ananke cried out, but it was too late. The astronaut proudly tossed the helmet halfway up the ramp. She stared in shock at his bare face.

It was blue, even deeper than her own. How was that possible? If the ship didn't have the drug that colored their skin—

"Not our air." The astronaut coughed as he fell to his knees.

Ananke rushed toward him, prepared to hold her breath and give him her own respirator. Chancing survival outside the dome, just as the Foregone had done, sent chills down her spine.

Everything he'd said, all the lies, began to add up to a terrible truth: *I came up with that particular line of horseshit... I didn't want you all asking too many questions... We've curated and revised the history you were taught... We did many barbaric things... I don't want to get too attached... No more like you should be needed... Transforming this planet may be our only hope as a species... Is killing evil when there is no alternative besides your own death?*

Her throat burned with bitter disgust. The Foregone never lost his fingers. There was no immortality drug. He needed his respirator *inside* the dome, not outside. He had betrayed her. And he'd done it all for nothing; his people weren't coming.

No wonder her people didn't know what horses were! They never knew them. But what other animals *did* they have? What else were they missing? Ananke's heart skipped a beat as she thought about what native life the colonists had destroyed to make a home for themselves. And the Foregone, that *coward*, had killed himself before she could even confront him! He'd left her people ignorant of their past, with no idea how to fix their world. How could she have allied herself with such cruelty? And her own species...

She was no more human than this astronaut. Her people had been raised on lies, enslaved, deceived by the Foregone—*the humans*—to sacrifice their own world to ruthless invaders. The fallen statues were of a great civilization, erected by ancestors she would never know. How much of her home—her real home—had she helped destroy? Her limbs shook as she approached the astronaut. How many generations of her people had the humans wiped out?

Ananke's skin crawled. The implications raced through her head while she pressed her respirator to the astronaut's face, waiting for him to draw his first safe breath. What a way to return home.

As Ananke looked up, for the first time she didn't wish for white and blue. Instead, she saw beauty in the green clouds and yellow skies. They were meant for her all along. Her people would determine their own fate and restore their *own* planet.

And where she'd dreamt of horses, she saw only horseshit.

BEGONE

A New Brave World

Eric Choi

Approaching Planet Huxley 1163c (Pala)
In the Year of Our Ford AF 826

The dull gray exterior of the starship was pitted and scarred from its one hundred and fifteen years of flight across the interstellar void. But if anyone had been there to see it, the shield insignia of the World State on its hull would still have been visible, along with the motto: COMMUNITY, IDENTITY, STABILITY.

For much of its journey, the ship had coasted at twelve percent the speed of light. It was now turned about, the torch of its Sakharov rocket burning forward as it entered a star system of four planets orbiting a red dwarf. The long deceleration that had begun seventeen years ago was finally nearing an end.

Powered by the energy of merging nuclei, the Sakharov rocket and the other technological marvels that had made the starship possible were fruits of the brief flowering of science and liberty under the regime of Her Fordship Seema Bhutto. Following her assassination, her successor controllers of the World State dispatched starships not as vessels of exploration, but as transports for exiles. Iceland, Marquesas, Samoa, the Falklands, Australia, Luna, and Ares were full.

There had been nine Navigators aboard the ship when it departed Earth, one conscious and the others in soma suspension. All were Alpha-Ultra-Pluses from the same Bokanovsky group, all decanted and conditioned for the sole and lonely purpose of piloting a vessel across the stars. The ninth and final Navigator had been woken from soma suspension eleven years after the start of deceleration following the death of his predecessor.

The gravity of the red dwarf captured the ship into an elongated orbit and the flame of the Sakharov rocket was finally extinguished. Over the course of a half dozen years, the Navigator repeatedly swung the ship inside the orbit of the third planet, using the gravity of the gas giant to pump and crank the starship's orbit into phase with the second planet, a rocky world one-and-a-half times the size of Earth, on which the exile settlement had been established.

A chemical rocket with three hundred souls in soma suspension was released from the hold of the starship and began a fiery descent through the atmosphere. But one was not among them. His long and lonely task completed, and his only reason for existence gone, the ninth and final Navigator allowed himself to die, never to see a new brave world.

* * *

She heard a murmuring voice, too soft to understand. Slowly, the words became louder.

"Ada Pascal? Can you hear me?"

She opened her eyes. A person was standing beside the bed.

"I'm Dr. Anthony Banting," the person said. "How do you feel?"

Every breath was an effort. It felt like an elephant was sitting on her chest. She had chills, and her heart was racing. "Bad."

"I'm sorry to say this is normal," said Dr. Banting, "but you'll feel better soon enough. Do you know where you are?"

Ada willed herself to speak. "Settlement...exile..."

The figure came onto focus, a tall middle-aged man in a white coat with a stethoscope around his neck. "Yes, you have arrived."

"Hurts..."

"I'm afraid you're suffering the symptoms of emergence from long-duration soma suspension," said Dr. Banting. "A kind of withdrawal."

"C-can't...breathe."

Dr. Banting pressed an oxygen mask against her face. She inhaled deeply.

"The gravity here is sixty percent higher than on Earth," he continued. "But you will acclimatize. We will help you."

Unable to say more, she blinked her eyes.

"Welcome to Pala, Ada Pascal."

* * *

Of the three hundred people who had accompanied Ada Pascal on the one-way journey to Pala, two hundred and fifty-seven were successfully revived from soma suspension. For the others, exile had become execution.

In the World State of Earth from which they had been banished, people were subjected to chemical and radiological manipulation while still embryos in order to be conditioned according to their social caste—depriving Epsilon embryos of oxygen, for example, to inhibit their brains in preparation for a lifetime of docile servitude. The exiles were all adults, but the new environment of Pala required them to be conditioned again.

Ada and the other newcomers were given haemoglobin substitute to raise their blood oxygen and synthetic calcium to strengthen their bones, and they were fitted with leg braces to help them walk. Despite her exhaustion following the physical therapy sessions, Ada found it hard to sleep. Tidally locked to its red dwarf star, the sun never set on Pala. The window curtains in her quarters never seemed to completely block out the diffuse crimson light. When sleep came it was often fitful, interrupted by the sweats and tremors of soma withdrawal.

In many ways, however, the physical conditioning was the easier part.

* * *

The newcomers were divided into groups of about a dozen for the counselling sessions. Most of the participants were still fitted with leg braces, as was Ada herself. The knowledge that she was trapped on an alien world more than four parsecs from everything and everyone she had ever known was absolutely terrifying. She had never felt more frightened and alone.

"Hello," said the man at the front of the room. A simple hello was the standard greeting. It was once said that the sun never set on the British Empire, the precursor of the World State. On Pala, this was literally true. The old pleasantries of wishing people a good morning or good evening no longer made sense.

"My name is Sigmund Maslow." His hair was white and his face was wrinkled like an elephant's hide, manifestations of age unfamiliar to the newcomers. Back on Earth, hormone therapies and magnesium salts kept people youthful until the day they died. "And this is Martha Heines. She is my *wife.*"

Ada glanced about the room, gauging the reaction of her companions to the obscene word. The World State had promoted heterosexual promiscuity while any sort of monogamy was considered deviant. Dr. Banting had told Ada that marriage was common on Pala, with unions allowed between any adult male, female, or freemartin.

"My *husband* and I welcome you to this first counseling session," said Martha. She was also white-haired. "We know this must all be terribly confusing and even frightening. Many of the customs on Pala, and even our appearance, will seem strange to you. It will take time, but you will adjust, and we will help you. It was the same for me and Sigmund when we first arrived."

"And it has been a great joy of our lives to have the privilege of welcoming newcomers like you every couple of years," Sigmund continued. "So, let's start with introductions, shall we?" He turned to a woman. "Would you like to start?"

"My name is Rosalind Miescher," she said. "I am an Alpha, a researcher of the natural sciences by profession."

"Thank you Rosalind, but please, it would be more correct to say you *were* an Alpha," Martha said gently. "There are no castes on Pala."

A stocky younger man turned to Rosalind. "What in the name of Ford did you do to get sent here?"

"I had submitted a paper on a new theory of biology," said Rosalind. "It was deemed dangerous and potentially subversive to the social order."

Sigmund turned to the stocky man. "Would you like to go next?"

"My name is Vladimir Chopra," he said. "I am—*was*, a Beta-Plus, a lecturer at the College of Emotional Engineering. They raided my flat and found some poems I had written, rhymes about being alone. So…heretical, subversive—all those things."

"Here on Pala," said Sigmund, "you will be free to write whatever you want."

"What I *want* is to go home!" Vladimir shouted angrily. "I had *everything* in London. A wonderful job, my Riemann-surface tennis club, all-you-can-eat buffets at the Aphroditaeum, any—and I mean *any*—woman I wanted, any time…" He covered his face in his hands and began to sob.

"Uh, maybe I can go next," Ada said quickly. "My name is Ada Pascal. I was an Alpha, and I was an engineer at the Electrical Equipment Corporation. I'm actually not sure what I did to deserve being sent here, but I was arrested shortly after demonstrating a new machine I had invented. It was a sort of mechanical automaton, a device that could have taken over some of the dangerous factory tasks performed by Deltas and Gammas."

"Oh Ford, isn't it obvious?" Rosalind said. "Full employment is a cornerstone of social stability. It's a fundamental principle of Baibakov's inefficient market hypothesis."

"Let's hear one more before we take a break," said Martha. She smiled at a man in a green shirt. "Would you like to say something?"

The man was staring at the floor. When he finally spoke, it was in a voice so soft that Ada strained to hear.

"My name is Xuésēn Goddard," he said. "I worked at a Vitamin D factory in Singapore. I was a Gamma."

Ada was surprised. It was unusual for lower castes like Gammas to be exiled because free thought had been most severely extinguished from them by embryonic manipulation and neo-Pavlovian conditioning in infancy.

"Welcome to Pala," said Martha. "What do you think you would like to do here?"

Xuésēn looked down again. Finally, he said in a quiet voice, "I want to learn to read."

Ada's jaw dropped. As a school girl, her class had gone on a field trip to a neo-Pavlovian conditioning center for Gamma infants. She watched as nurses put books in front of the babies, who started crawling towards them. But just as they got near, the head nurse pulled a lever and suddenly the babies were assaulted by alarm bells and electric shocks. Ada would never forget their screams of terror and pain, and how the infants recoiled and cried again when presented with the books.

"What a wonderful dream," was all Ada could think of to say.

"Yeah, I'm sure he'll be reading my poetry someday," Vladimir miffed with open condescension. He put away a damp handkerchief. "By the way, what was *your* transgression?"

An embarrassed grin crossed Xuésēn Goddard's lips. "I spat out my chewing gum from the platform of the Charing-T Tower."

* * *

Two weeks after the removal of Ada's leg braces, Sigmund Maslow and Martha Heines organized a hiking tour of the area outside the settlement for any newcomer who was interested and physically comfortable doing so. Vladimir Chopra chose to sulk in his quarters, but Ada, Rosalind Miescher, Xuésēn Goddard, and a few others took up the offer.

Walking sticks in hand, they went single file along a path up a shallow hill. Martha was in the lead, with Sigmund taking up the rear. Wispy white clouds, carried along by strong winds, streamed across the salmon pink sky. Hovering permanently near the horizon, an angry red sun cast a dim crimson glow over the landscape.

"One hemisphere of Pala always faces the sun and the other never sees it," Martha explained. "Life can only exist on the terminator between the night and day sides, a thin strip that is only—" she extended her arms "—a few hundred kilometers wide."

The trees along the trail had thick trunks and enormous blackish-purple leaves whose shape and texture resembled those of rhubarb plants. Branches arched downwards in the higher gravity, putting the giant leaves almost vertical to the ground. A winged lizard-like creature leapt from a branch and took to the sky.

"I would love to see this under a microscope." Rosalind rubbed her fingers on a leaf and put it up to her nose. She smiled. "Smells a bit like lilac."

Ada pulled herself along the path, clutching her walking stick in a death grip for fear of falling. Her arms and legs felt heavy, and her lungs heaved. She spotted a bubbling ribbon of water cascading down a rock face. A dragonfly-like insect buzzed above a pool.

"Go ahead," said Sigmund. "It's safe to drink." He cupped his hands under the little waterfall, then brought them to his face.

Ada did the same. The water was cool and crisp and absolutely delicious, and she started to feel a little better.

The group reached the summit of the shallow hill. Sprawled before them was the settlement, referred to by its 25,241 inhabitants (perhaps with excessive grandiosity) as the City. At its center were squat metallic cans and elongated cylinders scavenged from the landing rockets. Around them were wooden buildings made from indigenous trees, and beyond those were a handful of newer buildings made of ferro-concrete and vita-glass— evidence of the slow progression of the City's industrial capabilities. In the further distance, stretched along a ridge, were the turbines of the wind farm which harnessed the latitudinal air currents that blew constantly from the day to the night side of the planet.

Suddenly, the air above them lit up. A shimmering curtain of greenish-blue light rippled across the pink sky, like a river of iridescent energy across the heavens.

"Aurora palalis," explained Sigmund. "Our red sun flares often, but the planet's magnetosphere protects us. This is the result."

* * *

Xuésēn Goddard slid up his eye goggles before carefully removing the newly machined geared wheel from the hopper and handing it to Ada.

"You do such amazing work, Xuésēn." She ran a finger along the teeth. "Thank you."

Xuésēn took off his gloves. "What is this for?"

"I'm trying to build a machine," said Ada. "I'm calling it an analytical engine until I come up with a better name. It will be a machine that can do mathematical calculations."

"Like Mr. Heisuke Ramanujan?" asked Xuésēn, referring to the former Alpha Plus who was the City's resident Calculator.

"Yes, just like Mr. Ramanujan, or maybe even better," Ada said. "A machine might be able to do more calculations faster and more precisely than a person, maybe even solve problems that a person cannot."

Xuésēn looked at her with frank admiration. "Where do you get these amazing ideas?"

"Well, back on Earth I thought my ideas were unique, but it turns out there was a Palan engineer named Nicole-Reine Hopper who had very similar concepts, so now I'm building on her work." Ada smiled and put down the gear. "Would you like to get some dinner?"

"Dinner" no longer meant an evening meal, just the third meal of any given twenty-four hour period. The inhabitants of Pala simply carried on with the old Fordian clock and calendar despite having no cycles of day and night and little seasonal variation due to the planet's nearly circular orbit and lack of obliquity.

Ada certainly agreed with Vladimir Chopra on missing the cuisine of London. The restaurant's vitaminized chicken surrogate was actually not bad, but she wasn't sure if she would ever get used to Palan vegetables. She had never liked aubergine back on Earth and now almost all the plants were that dark purple color.

She put down her knife and fork. "Is there anything you'd like to do?"

Xuésēn thought for a moment. "Would you like to go to the Library? Mr. Maslow is teaching me how to read. Maybe we could get...a book."

The City Public Library was a small nondescript wooden building, yet the citizens of Pala could still take pride in it being superior to the libraries of London—because the World State had shut them all down. Its collection had begun with a small number of books that had been stashed aboard the first exile rocket by a dissident engineer at the Malindi Spaceport, who herself would later be exiled and die somewhere in the darkness between worlds.

It had been Xuésēn's idea to come, but Ada saw he was now sweating and breathing rapidly. The sight of a group of children reading together gave her an idea. "I wonder if they have a book from when I was small. Why don't you wait here and I'll see if I can find it."

The librarian was a kindly woman named Helen Clinton. It didn't take her long to search the modest card catalogue, and against all the laws of probability, she found Ada's book and retrieved it from the stacks.

Ada brought the little book to Xuésēn and sat beside him. "Would you like to have this?"

Xuésēn wiped his damp hands on his trousers, then took the book into his hands and slowly opened it. Ada put an arm around him. "Let's read together, shall well?"

"A, B, C, Vitamin D. The fat's in the liver, the cod's in the sea."

* * *

"Thank you for coming to the first public demonstration of the analytical engine," said Ada, surveying the audience nervously. Among them were her patron Mayor William Tiberius, the City Calculator Heisuke Ramanujan, and Vladimir Chopra in his role as the new editor of the *Palan Telegram*.

Xuésēn cranked a handle and the analytical engine whirred and clicked to life. The turning of the handle drove gears, cams, rods, levers, and springs, periodically turning and stopping the number wheels. Rosalind seemed to be mesmerized, watching a helical pattern sweep up the vertical rods as the steel fingers extended and withdrew. Ada fed a sequence of punched paper cards into a slot at the base of the engine. After a moment a clacking sound could be heard and a strip of paper emerged from the opposite side of the machine.

Ada tore off the piece of paper. She looked at the columns of numbers, then nervously handed it to Mayor Tiberius.

The Mayor stared at the paper for a moment. "Well, this is…interesting." He passed the paper to Vladimir, who shrugged and gave it to Heisuke. The Calculator took one look, chortled, and threw it on the floor. "It's a multiplication table!"

"Multiplication table?" repeated the Mayor.

"Eight years of effort, an untold expenditure of City resources, all for… this?" Heisuke laughed without humor. "Your contraption is no better than a Gamma child. No offense."

Xuésēn glared at him.

Vladimir sighed theatrically and made a show of closing his notebook. "Nothing newsworthy here!"

Ada's eyes were downcast as people filed out of the laboratory. Xuésēn took her hand in his and gently squeezed it.

* * *

"It is a truth universally acknowledged, that a single man in possession of a good fortune, must be in want of a wife."

Xuésēn put down the book. "That is a strange sentence."

"What do you mean?" asked Ada.

"Well, is it really true and universally believed? And what does universal mean anyway?"

"Across the universe," said Ada. "Maybe it's supposed to be true on Pala as it was on Earth, at least when that book was written."

"But it's not true on Earth. There were no wives or husbands in the World State. So it's not universal. And what is a good fortune? Does it mean to be lucky?"

"Maybe it means possessions. It actually says possession, right?" Ada chuckled. "Maybe it's like all the Palan scrip we've got in the Bank."

"I think I am in possession of good fortune." He turned to Ada. "Am I in want of a wife?"

"Are you?" Ada asked coyly.

Xuésēn thought some more. "Yes, I am in want of a wife. Will you be my wife?"

Ada was taken aback, but only a little. "Are you suggesting that we should…" she carefully enunciated the unfamiliar word, "…get *married*, the way they do here on Pala?"

"Married. Yes. To belong only to each other. Forever."

Ada took his calloused hands into hers. "Yes, Xuésēn Goddard. Let's get married."

Five months later, Ada and Xuésēn stood before Mayor Tiberius in a simple outdoor ceremony at Henry Ford Square in front of the Legislature Building. The wedding party was small, consisting only of Anthony Banting, Sigmund Maslow, Martha Heines, the Mayor's husband Ahmed Mfume, and Rosalind Miescher as the person-of-honor. Vladimir Chopra was covering the event for the *Palan Telegram.*

"Since the days of the first permanent human settlements on Earth, all civic officials have had one happy privilege: that of uniting two people in the bonds of matrimony. And so we are gathered here today with you, Ada Pascal, and you, Xuésēn Goddard, in the sight of your fellows, in accordance with our laws and our many beliefs, so that you may pledge your—"

"Excuse me please, your Fordship Mayor, sir," Xuésēn interrupted. "But is it really necessary to say so many things?"

Mayor Tiberius looked stunned, then burst out laughing.

"My wonderful straightforward Xuésēn," Ada whispered as they exchanged rings.

"I, Mayor William Tiberius, by virtue of the powers granted by the people of Pala, pronounce you wife and husband. Congratulations! You may kiss."

And kiss they did.

* * *

"Come take a look at this." Rosalind gestured at the microscope, then stood aside.

Ada peered into the eyepiece. Dozens of light purple globs seemed to stare back at her, each with a cluster of darker material at its center. Some of the dark material appeared almost solid, but many looked like clumps of string, and in others the threads were pulled apart to opposite sides of the globs.

"What am I looking at?"

"These are cells from the leaves of the Palan maples just outside the City," Rosalind explained. "I believe those dark structures are somehow related to hereditary factors."

"Hereditary factors?" Ada repeated.

Rosalind nodded. "A Palan scientist named Chanchao Türeci originally came up with the idea. She thought these hereditary factors govern the characteristics of every living thing. If we study these hereditary factors, I believe we can get a fundamental understanding of the very nature of life itself. Perhaps…perhaps even change it."

Ada was suddenly chilled by a sobering thought. On Earth, the World State had used chemical techniques and neo-Pavlovian manipulation to condition embryos and later infants into the five castes of Alpha, Beta, Gamma, Delta, and Epsilon. But the conditioning had to be done with every new generation because all embryos started out the same, and the process was often imperfect. If the World State had developed the ability to manipulate gametes at the hereditary level, her beloved Xuésēn might never have learned to read.

* * *

There had been no more exile ships from Earth since the arrival of Ada and Xuésēn's cohort more than fifteen years ago, but the City's population continued to grow and there were many children. Ada and Xuésēn, however, had agreed early in their marriage never to have their own. The very thought of *giving birth* revolted Ada, an ingrained hypnopaedic phobia that no amount of Palan deconditioning could erase. So, the analytical engine became their offspring.

When it was completed, the operational engine occupied an entire building to which the people of Pala brought their numerical problems for solution. An early use supported the Palan census, but the application that finally impressed even Heisuke Ramanujan was the daily calculation for the pitch of the wind turbine blades to optimize power production based on the meteorological forecast (which was also produced by the engine). Heisuke became a regular at the Calculation Center, bringing stacks of punched cards at all hours and frequently falling asleep on a cot while the engine clattered away at some esoteric problem.

With the patronage of the Mayor, Heisuke led an ambitious project that deployed a network of ground and balloon-based meteorological instruments that stretched for hundreds of kilometers along the planet's terminator. Telegraph wires transmitted the readings back to the Calculation Center for processing. So great was the need for calculation that Ada and Xuésēn began to build a new analytical engine, one that would use electricity and aether tubes instead of mechanical switches for logic. Ada would have said it was the dawn of a new scientific age—except, of course, there were no dawns on Pala.

And then the murder happened.

* * *

Within minutes of the Warden's call, Ada was on her bicycle and pedaling furiously through the perpetually twilit streets of the City. Her lungs were heaving and her heart raced as she pulled up to the Calculation

Center and ran inside. She saw the Warden Benito Edgars and Dr. Anthony Banting at the far end of the great hall that housed the analytical engine. As she approached, she could see Dr. Banting kneeling over someone lying on the floor.

It was Xuésēn.

"Oh, my Ford!"

His shirt was covered with blood. At the sound of Ada's voice, his eyes fluttered open.

"Xuésēn!" Ada cried.

"He was stabbed in the right arm, and he's lost a lot of blood," said Dr. Banting as he tended to Xuésēn's wound.

Ada's attention was so focused on her husband that it took a moment to notice another body on the floor covered with a white sheet.

"It's Heisuke Ramanujan," said Warden Edgars. "He's dead. Also stabbed."

"What in Ford's name happened here?" Ada demanded.

"As far as I can tell," said Edgars, "Calculator Ramanujan was working here alone—"

"He's been doing that for years," interrupted Ada. "He's got a cot in a back room."

Edgars nodded. "And then your husband came in—"

"Yes, it would have been close to the time for his regular maintenance tasks."

Xuésēn struggled to speak. "Mr. Ramanujan…already dead when I got here. Intruder…doing something to the engine…"

"Did you see their face?" Ada asked. "Can you identify this person?"

With an effort, Xuésēn shook his head.

A puzzled look suddenly crossed Ada's face. She glanced about, then took a sniff. "Was something burning in here?"

Edgars nodded. "The intruder was trying to burn the punched cards and printout strips. That's when your husband got here and intervened."

Ada walked over to the analytical engine. A heavy wrench lay on the floor near a pile of partially-burned punched cards. It would take time to assess the damage, but she could see several of the number wheels were dented and at least one camshaft was broken. She looked at the floor again, noticed drops of blood trailing towards the second exit, and felt a moment of grim satisfaction in the thought that her husband had gotten a piece of the assailant.

"The medics are here!" Dr. Banting called out.

Two freemartins in white coats with the Red T insignia arrived. They carefully put Xuésēn on a stretcher and began to wheel him outside, flanked by Ada on one side and Dr. Banting on the other.

"May Ford grant him a speedy recovery," said Edgars.

"Thank you," said Ada.

The Warden nodded. "I'll finish securing the evidence, and then I'll post a guard."

* * *

It was the first murder in more than thirty years and the inhabitants of the City were confused and afraid. Ada and her team busied themselves repairing the analytical engine while proceeding with the construction of the electric analytical engine in the new annex of the Calculation Center. Xuésēn was finally able to return to work and lead the completion of repairs to the mechanical engine. Upon its reactivation, the team found themselves inundated with clearing the backlog of calculation requests while work on the new engine continued.

Xuésēn offered pan-glandular biscuits and a cup of Earl Purple tea to the security guard, then brought the same to his wife.

"Thank you, sweetheart," said Ada.

He surveyed the clutter of printout strips, punched cards (some of them singed), papers, and notebooks strewn across her desk. "What are you doing?"

Ada sniffed the aromatic tea, then took a sip. "I'm trying to figure out what Heisuke was working on, starting with the punched cards and printout strips we were able to save and the last known positions of the number wheels. Just recently, I got permission from Heisuke's—" she looked for the word "—*family* to look at his papers and notebooks."

"What have you found?" Xuésēn asked.

"He was putting meteorological measurements through the engine. A *lot* of measurements, mostly from the last couple of years since the instrument network became operational, but also historical measurements from the City and the wind farm. Some of the measurements go back to the arrival of the first exiles."

"So he was trying to find patterns in the measurements?"

"More than that," said Ada. "I think he was trying to build a numerical climate model, one that would allow him to make predictions."

"The engine has been doing weather forecasts for years," said Xuésēn.

Ada shook her head. "I think he was trying to do something much more ambitious. I think he was trying to build a global atmospheric model of the entire planet, one that could forecast the climate for years, decades... maybe even centuries into the future."

"But what was the purpose?" asked Xuésēn. "And why would someone kill him?"

* * *

Five months passed without a break in the case. For the most part, the inhabitants of the City carried on in the usual stoic Palan way, but the level of anxiety continued to rise. New editions of the *Palan Telegram* featured increasingly hysterical editorials from Vladimir Chopra demanding the resignation of the Mayor and the Warden. Pubs and restaurants experienced declines as people stayed away, choosing instead to dine alone or within their social circles.

Ada and Xuésēn were hosting Rosalind Miescher and Anthony Banting for dinner. Xuésēn served up a fish-like creature called a Palan river bass, grilled whole with a side of mashed tuber and purple salad.

"Oh sweetheart, what a feast." Ada noticed her husband was still favoring his right arm. She smiled to hide her concern.

"Xuésēn, you've outdone yourself this time!" Dr. Banting declared.

Ada, Xuésēn, and Dr. Banting dug in right away, but Rosalind just stared at her plate. She seemed to be studying the grill marks which looked like dark bands over the lighter gray skin of the river bass.

"Is something wrong with your food?" asked Xuésēn.

Rosalind blinked. "Oh, no. It's just that…" She looked around the table. "I think I have an idea for how we might help the Warden catch the killer."

Ada put down her cutlery. "Go on."

"As you know, I've spent many years studying the native life on this planet using a technique that extracts hereditary factors from cells," Rosalind explained. "These hereditary factors govern the characteristics of living things, but more to the point, the exact pattern of hereditary factors is unique to every individual, like a fingerprint."

Ada immediately understood the implications. "Are you saying that you could identify a person based on their hereditary factors?"

Rosalind nodded. "I've not yet employed the technique to study people, but yes. All I would need is a sample of the person's cells, for example, from blood or spermatozoa."

Ada thought for a moment. Heisuke Ramanujan's body had long since been cremated and its phosphorous recovered, but his clothing might still be available. "Would Warden Edgars still have Heisuke's blood-stained clothes?"

"Yes," said Xuésēn. "He even took my clothes from the infirmary."

"I could start by extracting hereditary factors from the bloodied clothing," said Rosalind. "Then I would need blood samples from the three of you and Warden Edgars and the medics for the purposes of elimination."

"How long would it take to modify your lab to do this?" asked Ada.

"Maybe a week or two," said Rosalind. "But what's going to take a long time is the manual process of comparing the patterns of hereditary factors from different people against the ones from the bloodied clothing."

"Can the analytical engine help?" asked Xuésēn.

Rosalind smiled. "I was hoping you'd say that."

"The timing is good," said Ada. "The electric analytical engine will be commissioned and operational in two weeks, at which time it will take over the routine calculating needs of the City. That will leave the mechanical engine free to do all the hereditary factor pattern comparisons you want."

"Well, you're going to need all the help you can get," said Dr. Banting. "Don't forget the hardest part. Hypothetically, for this to work, you might end up having to draw blood from nearly every inhabitant of the City."

* * *

Mayor Tiberius took it upon himself to be the first volunteer for a "blooding." As a small group of scribes looked on, Dr. Banting put a needle into the Mayor's arm and drew a blood sample. Vladimir Chopra was not present, but later launched another round of scathing editorials in the *Telegram* denouncing the blooding as un-Palan authoritarianism and calling for the people to rise up in protest. In the early weeks, a few dozen rabid *Telegram* readers would stage noisy "freedom rallies" in Ford Square. These stopped when the protesters finally realized they were only drawing suspicion upon themselves.

Ada and the others who were in the Calculation Center at the time of the murder were amongst the second group to undergo the blooding. She watched in fascination as one of Rosalind's laboratory technicians extracted the hereditary factors from the blood cells, introduced them to a photographic gel, and applied an electric current to produce a pattern of black and gray bands. It looked very much like a punched card.

Three sets of hereditary factors had been extracted from the bloodied clothing: Heisuke Ramanujan's, Xuésēn's, and an unknown pattern presumed to belong to the killer. Over the course of nine months, new samples poured into the laboratory as the blooding campaign spread across the City. Fortunately, the performance of the electric analytical engine exceeded all expectations, to the point where it could take on the analysis of the samples in addition to the regular calculating needs of the City. This made the original mechanical engine available for Ada to continue her investigation.

For weeks, the engine clattered away as Ada fed it punched cards based on her reconstruction of Heisuke Ramanujan's final sequence. She would examine the printed results, then try again with different initial and boundary conditions. There would, of course, be some variation in the exact numbers, but the general outcome was always the same. The conclusion was now inescapable.

"My Ford," Ada muttered, clutching a strip of paper.

The prediction from Heisuke Ramanujan's global climate model was unambiguous. Pala was dying.

Latitudinal air currents blew constantly from the day to the night side of the planet, a phenomenon harnessed by the wind farm to power the City. But with insufficient carbon dioxide in the atmosphere for an effective greenhouse phenomenon, the night side of the planet was too cold and gases were condensing onto the surface there. The condensation of gas in the dark hemisphere caused the atmospheric pressure there to drop, drawing more air from the day side that in turn froze and condensed out. Looking back through historical records, Ada discovered the phenomenon could actually be observed in data from the wind farm, in which small but steady increases in power output had been recorded in recent years. The vicious cycle would continue until the planet's entire atmosphere collapsed, which according to Heisuke's model would take place very quickly in less than six hundred years, plus or minus fifty years.

The telephone rang. Ada picked it up.

"Engineer Pascal? This is Warden Edgars. We have a person in custody."

* * *

Giuseppe McGuire did not kill Heisuke Ramanujan. His only transgression was talking too much.

A pathetically inebriated Guiseppe had been yelling loudly at the pub, waving a wad of scrip and boasting about having taken the blooding for someone else. The bartender called the Warden and the "someone else" was quickly identified as a retired wind farm worker named Ronald Madis who did murder Heisuke—at the behest of Vladimir Chopra.

Ada and Xuésēn shuffled into the public viewing gallery of the Courthouse to witness the verdict. The crowded gallery smelled faintly of sweat and wood varnish. As they took their seats, Ada accidentally bumped her husband's right arm. He winced.

"Vladimir Ilan Chopra," intoned Judge Marshall O'Connor, "you have been found guilty on the charges of murder and conspiracy to commit murder. Do you have anything to say before sentence is passed?"

Standing in the prisoner's docket in an orange jumpsuit, the former lecturer at the College of Emotional Engineering and former editor of the *Palan Telegram* launched into a tirade.

"Twenty-three years ago, I was brought to Pala against my will. I absolutely and positively *hated* everything about this place, with every molecule and fiber of my being. But after a very long time, after many years, I finally decided to belt up and try to live my life as best I could, to try and find happiness where I could, to hold out hope that things might get better. And things did start getting better. I took over the *Telegram*. I started playing Parrises Squares. I met a girl. I even started liking the food here.

"And then, and then…this arrogant little man, this *scientist*, comes to me and says the world is coming to an end. That everything will be gone in just a few generations. And not only is he telling me this, he's demanding that I *publish* this story so that everyone will know."

Vladimir waved his arms as he spoke. At one point the sleeves of his jumpsuit slipped, and Ada could see old scars on his wrists. "Why should people know? What's the bloody point? We're all stuck here! We don't have the industrial infrastructure to recreate the Sakharov rocket and we never will. Ford dammit, we don't even have chemical rockets."

He jabbed a finger at the public gallery. To Ada, it looked like he was pointing right at her. "Bloody scientists! They're like the blabbermouths at the feely-palace who ruin the show by telling you how it ends. And there aren't even any feely-palaces here!"

"Mr. Chopra," said Judge O'Connor. "Are you finished?"

Vladimir's bluster deflated like a balloon and his eyes became moist. "I've said everything I want to say," he murmured in a voice that broke. "I'm finished."

"Vladimir Ilan Chopra," continued O'Connor, "you are hereby sentenced to involuntary commitment, the first three years of which will be under the institutional care of Sigmund Maslow and Martha Heines. After three years, your frame of mind will be assessed and the conditions of your commitment will be adjusted accordingly for the remaining seven years of your sentence. May you receive the care and rehabilitation you need so that you might return to society as a fully assisting citizen."

The gavel sounded.

Ada and Xuésēn made their way out of the courtroom. In the corridor, Xuésēn pulled out an envelope containing a number of signed documents.

"Are you sure we should still do this?" asked Ada. "Some of the things Vladimir said…he's not entirely wrong, you know. About the future."

"I am sure," said Xuésēn.

Ada looked at her husband with fierce love and pride. "Let's go see the clerk, then."

* * *

Sitting together on a checkered picnic blanket beside a dark purple Palan maple, Ada put her arm around Xuésēn and rested her head on his shoulder. In the near distance, their newly adopted child, an orphaned freemartin named Robin, chased a flock of winged lizard-like creatures. Overhead, the aurora palalis danced.

Many Palans already knew something about Heisuke Ramanujan's forecast of global atmospheric collapse, ironically due to the trial coverage of those responsible for his death. But in a few hours Marty Bernstein, the new editor of the *Palan Telegram*, was going to publish the full story, and then everyone would know.

"I wonder how people are going to react when they learn that everything we're doing might just fall back upon itself and be futile in the end," said Ada. "What if people decide to just ignore the problem? Do nothing?"

"Then people like us will do something," said Xuésēn.

Ada sighed. "Aiming for the stars is a problem to occupy generations."

"Then we better get started."

"My beautiful, wonderful, straightforward Xuésēn." She kissed him.

Apparently tired of chasing the winged lizards, Robin waddled up to them.

Xuésēn patted the ground beside him. "Would you like me to read to you?"

Robin nodded and sat down. Xuésēn reached into the knapsack, pulled out a little book, and began to read.

"A, B, C, Vitamin D. The fat's in the liver, the cod's in the sea."

As Ada watched her husband and their child sitting together with the book, she decided that Vladimir Chopra was wrong. There was hope. Because if a former Gamma could learn to read, and if he can then teach his child to read, then anything is possible.

* * *

Departing Pala
In the Year of Our Ford AF 1049

Chemical rockets boosted the *Pascal* from its orbit about Pala. In a few minutes, its Sakharov rocket would ignite and propel it on the first leg of its journey to the stars.

The Navigator aboard the *Pascal* was an intelligent analytical engine known as a Synthetic Alpha. It switched on an aft camera to survey the world of its origin for the last time.

Pala looked like a multicolored eyeball in space. The day side tidally locked to the star glowed a dull orange-red. Cloud patterns radiated from the sub-stellar point, swept across the thin twilight terminator that had been the planet's only abode of life, and dissipated on the night side. Centered on the equator in the dark hemisphere, like a white pupil, was the polar cap.

The SA Navigator switched to a forward camera. Ahead of the *Pascal* was the *Goddard*, appearing like a bright star in the distance. Not visible was the lead ship, the *Miescher*. Aboard each vessel were twelve hundred people in cryonic sleep, consisting of an equal number of women, men, and freemartins. The fleet would depart Pala and begin the journey under Sakharov rocket to the third planet. There the ships would part ways, each using the gas giant's gravity to alter its trajectory in a different direction. They would continue accelerating by Sakharov rocket to twelve percent the speed of light, and then, once clear of the gravitational sphere of influence of Pala's star system, they would activate their Okuda-Michelson devices, harnessing the power of mirror particles to bend the luminiferous aether itself and propel the ships to their cruising velocity of ninety-four percent the speed of light.

The *Miescher* was headed for a planet in a binary star system nine parsecs away. The *Goddard* was going to a planet orbiting a yellow dwarf star five parsecs distant, a world from which unusual emissions of radio and coherent light had been detected. The *Pascal*, however, had a particularly special destination.

It was going back to Earth.

No exile ships had arrived on Pala for more than two centuries, and in recent decades even the radio noise from Earth could no longer be detected. Had the World State advanced beyond the use of radio, perhaps communicating with strands of light? Did the World State still exist, or had it ossified into a soma stupor or even destroyed itself in a hail of anthrax bombs?

Time would tell which of the planets would be the most alien.

The SA Navigators aboard the trio of starships ignited their Sakharov rockets, setting forth for new brave worlds.

Plenty

Jacey Bedford

"Run!"

Max scooped up his six-year-old daughter, hugged her to his chest, one arm under her skinny bottom, the other protecting her head, and ran faster than he'd ever run in his life, while Gen twisted and fired off several tight beam shots at their pursuers.

Were they bounty hunters or corporation men? Either way, Max hoped Gen was firing wide. He didn't want criminal charges. It was bad enough being Alphacorp and the Trust's most wanted without getting the law involved.

A shot whizzed past his head.

He ducked involuntarily, but barely broke his stride.

Fuck! They shouldn't be using ballistic weapons in a dome, not if they wanted Livvy alive. They didn't much care about her parents or the other ten thousand inhabitants of New Kyiv, but they couldn't endanger her.

There were only two of them, so far, but they might have backup. The off-white plascrete walls blurred past Max's peripheral vision. He focused on the concourse ahead, and beyond it to where the *Dixie Flyer* stood, umbilicals connected, in a shuttle bay. The little craft was tiny, but she was home and safety—at least if they could get her off the ground in time.

Momma! Livvy reached out mentally to Gen.

I'm here, sweetie, Gen thought back as she caught up with Max.

Did you hit them? Max had no spare breath for talking.

No. I wanted to, though.

As they burst into the bustling concourse, Max and Gen slowed to a brisk walk, dodging around commuters who were heading for the overhead circular transporter.

"'Scuse me. Thank you. Coming through." Max's voice came out in a wheeze. Gen grasped his left arm with her left hand as she walked backwards, searching for their followers.

I think we've lost them. She sounded relieved.

Bad men, Livvy said.

Yes, very bad men, Gen agreed.

More bad men.

Where, sweetie? Max knew better than to ignore his daughter.

Over there...and there. She swivelled in Max's arms, pointed behind them and off to the right.

Damn, they did have backup.

Switch off, Gen said. Suddenly the place she occupied in his consciousness went cold.

Max tongued a back tooth and switched off his own psi-tech implant. He'd acquired it late in life, after he'd met Gen, and so being without it wasn't much of a problem for him, but he knew Gen would be disoriented. She turned and stuck her right hand in the crook of his left arm and he felt her hesitant step.

"Nearly there," Max said, knowing the last fifty meters across the concourse to the shuttle bays would be the most difficult as the crowds thinned out.

Bad men! Livvy's thoughts were clear in his head even though his implant was powered down. How did she do that?

Two figures were walking purposefully on an intercept course, not quite running, but not far off. These weren't the same two who'd been tailing them.

Bad! Go away! Livvy pointed at the two newcomers.

Max saw them hesitate.

I said go away! Livvy's telepathic shout was so loud that if Max's implant had not been powered down, it might have done some damage. One of the men bent forward, clutching his head. The other simply stood there, stunned.

"Let's go while we still can," Gen said, and they set off towards the shuttle bays at a run, not caring who saw them.

Max and Gen slid their handpads through the reader at the autogate—false IDs, of course—and barrelled on through. They reached the *Dixie*, tucked into the fourth bay along. She was smaller than a regular shuttle and sleek, originally designed as a survey craft. While Max dragged open the side hatch and lifted Livvy in, Gen disconnected the umbilicals.

"Hey, you owe the company." A dock tech shouted from the gantry above.

Gen opened a pocket in her buddysuit and flipped a credit chip towards him. "Keep the change."

She leaped into the flyer and dropped onto the pilot's couch, pulling on the silver circlet, the link that connected her mentally to the ship's systems. The restraints snaked out along her hips and shoulders. Max sealed the hatch, settled Livvy into the child-sized seat in the rear bulkhead, and clicked her safety straps closed.

"It's all right, Liv," he said. "The bad men can't get us now. Momma's going to fly us out of here."

Can we see the dragon?

"Probably not on this trip."

Wanna see the dragon.

"I know, sweetie. Another time. Let's get away from the bad men, first."

The bad men are coming. All of them.

"How many?"

Lots. She paused. *Six.* She scrunched up her eyes. *Shall I stop them?*

Just the fact that his six-year-old daughter could do that, or thought she could, gave Max the creeps. What was she becoming?

"No need. We're away," Gen said. "Couch, Max."

Max leaned forward and planted a kiss on Livvy's forehead, then scrambled into the co-pilot's couch and activated the restraints as Gen pulled the little ship back from the dock. She fired the antigravs and the *Dixie* rose into the air while turning one-eighty degrees, nose pointing through the pressure curtain towards the cold, oxygen-depleted stretch of New Kyiv's northern continent.

"Flight control to *Dixie* 5286, you are not cleared for take off. Please return to your docking bay."

"Sorry, Flight Control. We have an emergency." Gen adjusted the throat mic.

"Flight control to *Dixie* 5286, repeat, you are not cleared for take off. Inbound freighter on your flight path."

"Thanks for the warning." Gen eased the *Dixie* through the curtain and tilted her into the vertical plane. Max felt an enormous weight on his chest as the little craft soared upwards. He felt the *Dixie* twist. A dark shape flashed by on the screen and was gone.

"Glad we knew to expect that," Gen said.

"It was close?" Max asked.

"Good job we didn't have another coat of paint."

Max breathed in and held his breath for about a minute until his hands finished shaking. "You are one hell of a pilot."

"Tell me again when we've gone through the Folds."

"I don't suppose—"

"No. It's the only way. A lightflyer took off about three minutes after us. What's the betting our friends are following?"

"Ah, right. Foldspace, here we come." They might not have a choice, but Max didn't have to like foldspace, the liminal "between" that connected everywhere to everywhere else and harboured entities that obeyed no known laws of physics.

"Stay powered down," Gen said. "They might be tracking us by our implants."

"Where are we going?"

"Does it matter?"

He didn't reply.

Wherever they headed, the Trust and Alphacorp seemed to be able to find them. They must have got their implant codes from somewhere, or from someone. It could only be the Free Company. Bitter didn't begin to describe Gen's feelings towards their former employers, but Max didn't think they'd have betrayed them deliberately.

Gen switched on her implant about three seconds before she eased the *Dixie* into the Folds. Max's vision wobbled. He saw everything inside the *Dixie* in negative, black and luminous green. It was never the same twice in the Folds. He wouldn't ever get used to it.

Want to see the dragon. Livvy's mental shout was brain-bleedingly loud. *Dragon.*

"Not today, sweetie." Gen shook her head and pulled the *Dixie* back into realspace, billions of klicks distant from New Kyiv. "There." She set the autopilot. "We should be safe now. For a while at least."

* * *

Max settled back in the co-pilot's couch and let his eyes close. He knew he wouldn't be able to sleep, even though he desperately wanted to. Weighed down by care, his whole body felt leaden, which was absurd since the *Dixie Flyer* was running on quarter grav. He wasn't sure how long he could continue like this, hopping from planet to planet, never sure whether the Trust and Alphacorp were close behind now they knew about Livvy.

This latest episode had been too close. Livvy should never have had to see her mother shooting at a man—dammit, Gen shouldn't have been put in that position in the first place—but Max knew she would have shot a dozen men, and more, to protect her daughter.

The Trust and Alphacorp, hell, probably all the other megacorporations, too, wanted Livvy. If they caught her, she'd become their commodity. They all wanted to open up the jump-gate network again, if it could be done safely, and talking to void dragons was a good way to start.

Yes, his tiny daughter could talk to void dragons.

Being the parent of a special child was a nightmare.

They still knew so little about her abilities. She'd been born in foldspace, in the middle of a battle. A void dragon, or maybe *the* void dragon (had they ever seen two together?) witnessed the birth of the tiny human. Even in her first year, Livvy showed remarkable telepathic abilities. Both Max and Gen were psi-techs, their mental abilities enhanced by implants, but Livvy was off the scale, and totally natural.

Livvy's talent for talking to the void dragon had been instrumental in discovering how the jump-gate system was polluting foldspace, and why so many ships had been lost. The resulting closure of the jump-gate system had been catastrophic for interplanetary trade as only jump-drive ships like the *Dixie* could navigate the Folds in reasonable safety, and though the megacorps were retrofitting their fleets, jump-drive ships were still relatively rare.

Max turned his head and half-opened one eye. How did Gen do it? She piloted the ship like it was part of her. She navigated in and out of the Folds, making small jumps, like a bodkin stitching a line through heavy canvas, completing light-years of travel in seconds. She never stayed in foldspace long enough to emit the polluting platinum, or for the void dragon to notice them, or, gods forbid, the Nimbus. Max would be very happy never to see the Nimbus again, that devourer of ships and their passengers.

Livvy, on the other hand…

As he thought of her, his small daughter's thoughts popped into his mind. *Want to see the dragon, Daddy.*

He swivelled in his couch and looked at Livvy, still strapped into the adapted bucket seat. She looked so sweet, black hair falling heavily around her face, golden brown skin flawless like her mother's, but with startling blue eyes. He smiled at her and answered in words rather than mind to mind. "Not this time, sweetie."

"Use talk-words, Livvy," Gen said from the pilot's couch. "You need to practice talking because not everyone understands think-talk."

When can we see the void dragon? Livvy ignored the request as she had done many times before.

When it's safe. Max gave in and answered mind to mind. It would never be safe. Livvy would understand one day, but at six years old she was too young for logic. The creatures who lived in foldspace were not going to feature in his daughter's life if he could help it.

Momma…

"What your dad said goes for me, too." Gen set the autopilot, eased the silver circlet off her head, and rubbed her temples.

"You okay?" Max asked.

"Tired," Gen said. "Being on the run will do that. We need somewhere to lay low and rest up."

"Yeah, we do. I'm with you on that one."

"Maybe even find ourselves somewhere permanent."

"Seriously?"

"Seriously. Young madam needs friends her own age." Gen eased herself out of the pilot's couch, stood and stretched, then bent over and let her arms dangle down towards her feet before gradually standing up to roll the knots out of her spine. "Somewhere to lay low that has real gravity and breathable air."

"And surface water, green plants, blue sky."

Gen smiled. "That might be asking a little too much."

"No point in settling for second best."

"Right," Gen said, kneeling in front of Livvy and releasing the safety harness. "Come on, sweetie, time for a meal."

* * *

Sometime later everything had gone quiet. Gen and Livvy were sleeping on the airmat stretched across the only bit of open cabin in the flyer that was big enough to accommodate the length of an average human. Max was wide awake, technically on watch as they headed towards the second planet in the Omadel System, but the *Dixie* had early warning systems that would sense anything out there long before Max spotted it, so he was sitting forwards, perusing the ship's archive of settled planets and colony worlds. In the last five years they'd visited close to forty of them, but not found any they felt safe enough to make their home.

Since the decommissioning of the jump-gate system, former colonies had been cut off from their regular supply lines. They had a choice between becoming self-sufficient or dying. Max and Gen had earned enough credits to make a halfway decent living delivering high value, essential goods and, occasionally, people across the galaxy. They'd moved medicines and seed stock from where it was plentiful to where it wasn't. He patted the *Dixie Flyer*'s console absent-mindedly while reaching for the handheld databank reader.

* * *

"Plenty," Max said as Gen rolled up the airmat the following morning.

"Huh?"

Max slipped out of his own couch and put a pouch of caff into the heater. It beeped and he handed it to her. He knew he wouldn't get any sense out of her until she'd downed the drink and had a sonic shower.

While he was waiting, he warmed a pouch of porridge, took Livvy on his knee, and presented it to her. She slurped it down with enthusiasm, but not much in the way of table manners. One more reason why Livvy needed to be in a place with more humans.

Gen emerged from the tiny fresher unit in the rear bulkhead and put a second pouch of caff in the warmer. "What did you say earlier?"

"I said Plenty. I found it in the databank. The planet of Plenty was settled by a fleet of generation ships close to two centuries ago." He glanced down at his handpad. "They left Earth just before the meteorites struck, in the belief that they might be the last of the human race if the event proved to be a planet-killer. It was a risky move. Jump-gates hadn't been invented and faster than light travel was as much of a dream then as it is now."

"I remember something about it in history classes," Gen said. "They were ten generations in space. Against all odds, the ships, all but three, made it to their designated planet with fifty thousand new settlers and everything they would need to support themselves."

"And most importantly," Max said, "they had no knowledge of the jump-gate system, or the rise of the megacorps, so they resisted all offers to join their trading networks. They've remained independent ever since."

"You think it might be a better bet than Omidel II?"

"Can't hurt to try it."

Gen nodded. "Give me the coordinates."

* * *

Max wasn't sure what to expect from the planet Plenty, but after a brief exchange with flight control they were given permission to land at the planet's only spaceport on the large southern continent, close to the city of Leeth. Obviously the planet was not completely closed to visitors.

Immigration was competent and thorough. First, they were scanned for off-planet viruses and signs of incipient illness. Then they went through a polite but scrupulous border check, presenting false IDs and professing to be tourists. Finally, they were granted leave to remain for a period of three lunar months, which was not far off standard months. Plenty had its own currency, tolars and cents, but there was a money exchange at the spaceport and they got what seemed to be a fair exchange rate for their credits as far as they could tell.

They took the monorail into Leeth Central. One city was very much like another throughout the settled worlds. Sure, the architecture might be different, but there were still houses, shops, cafes, and entertainment venues. Leeth's city planners had gone for square and practical shapes with an eyewatering use of bright colors. There were stores and cafes, and even a kinema screen advertising remastered versions of classic films from

Earth. Max stared at a poster advertising The Princess Bride as the most perfect historical movie ever made.

What is it, Daddy? Livvy tugged at his hand.

"Speak in words while we're here, Sweetie."

"What is it?" She obeyed, for once.

"A story vid from old Earth."

"Can we see it?"

"I don't see why not, but let's find something to eat and somewhere to stay first."

"I picked this up in the spaceport," Gen said, waving an actual printed brochure. "There's a list of guest houses. Might be cheaper than hotels, and we'll get an idea of whether Plenty is safe for us.

They started at the top of the list and the third guest house they tried had a vacant family room that was four times the size of the Dixie's cabin. It even had a proper bathroom with a water shower. Their hostess, Elsa Carnie, was a grandmotherly widow who ran the place with the help of her middle-aged son, Hockley, a less than sparkling individual who was, however, obliging enough when it came to extra portions of real bacon for breakfast on their first morning.

Better than porridge, Livvy said, and since her mouth was full, for once neither Max nor Gen told her to speak out loud.

"Excellent breakfast, Mrs. Carnie," Gen said as Hockley cleared their plates away and Mrs. Carnie brought another pot of real coffee. "I can't remember when I last had coffee as good as this. Is it local?"

"The beans are grown up north, but they're roasted locally. Makes all the difference. We use a lot of local produce."

"We're here to see something of Plenty. Where should we start?" Gen said.

"The best shopping is here in Leeth. If you want to see the great outdoors, we've got a lot of geography, protected wilderness, spectacular waterfalls, but if you want history you should go to Landing. There's a new museum there. It's one of the generation ships, the last one left whole because we used up the fabric of the rest for our first shelters."

She spoke as if planetfall had been two years ago, not two hundred.

"Can we get transport to Landing?"

"Oh, yes, there's the free maglev twice a day and a couple of hotels if you want to stay over. It's the best season to see it. At least another month of dry weather. 'Course, if you want snow sports you'll need to head up into the mountains where it pretty much snows all year round."

Max shuddered. "Last time I was anywhere near a pair of skis I was seventeen years old and I broke my ankle. I hope you have good medical facilities."

"The best, and no charge, even for off-worlders."

"Good to know," Gen said. "Tell me, do you have an implant clinic in the city?"

"Dental implants? Yes, we've—"

"No, I meant psi implants." She touched the center of her forehead. "You know, for psi-techs."

"Not that I know of. There's not much of that here. Nothing against it, mind you. We occasionally get a few folks who are…" She pursed her lips as if thinking of the right word. "…talented in that direction. Some of them go off-world to use their talents for one of the big corporations. They put recruitment ads in the local media every so often. Can't say as I think tying yourself to a big corporation is a good move, not since the jump-gates closed. Stands to reason they won't be getting home leave any time soon, if ever."

Plenty sounds better and better, Max said. *Let's see how our first three months go.*

Gen nodded agreement.

Are we staying here? Livvy asked.

For a while, Gen said.

Good. I like bacon for breakfast.

                              * * *

For the next few days they did the whole tourist thing, starting with the museum at Landing and ending with a gentle hike along a carefully curated wilderness trail to see the massive Diamond Falls, a five hundred meter drop into the gorge below which did, indeed, sparkle like diamonds in the sunlight. They returned to Mrs. Carnie's guest house as the long evening twilight faded to dusk.

Livvy was chattering away about her day and the children she'd met at the museum when she suddenly went very still.

Bad men. In the house. Hockley's warm has gone cold. And Mrs. Carnie is hurt and so very frightened.

The same bad men as before? Gen asked.

Yes. Same. Two of them.

Max swallowed hard. They could run, but the Carnies had been kind to them and if they'd brought danger into the house, they couldn't just leave.

You two, round the back. Max said. *I'll go in the front.*

I should— Gen began.

I've got this. I'll be the distraction, you do the rest. She'd had weapons training and he hadn't.

"Well, that was a nice day out," Max said, as if he was talking to Gen and Livvy. "But I'm ready for a nice supper and a good long sleep. How about you, Livvy?" He pushed open the front door and immediately knew something was deeply wrong. The savory smell from the kitchen was overlaid with the stink of ruptured guts. Pretending he hadn't noticed, he said, "You go up to the room, Livvy, while I ask Mrs. Carnie what time supper will be ready."

He crouched low and pushed open the interior door. A bullet whistled over his head. If he'd been standing upright, it would have hit him square in the chest. He dropped and rolled behind an overstuffed sofa, coming up against Hockley's crumpled body. Something thudded into the sofa and he felt it jerk back towards him. Was that a bolt-gun? Shit!

There was a zing over on the other side of the room, followed by a gurgle and a thump. A second zing, a cry and a thump.

"You can come out now," Gen said.

Max emerged from behind the sofa. Two men lay sprawled, eyes sightless.

Gen's golden skin had lost its warmth and she looked as though she wanted to throw up. Max gently took the weapon from her trembling hand, thumbed on the safety, and gave it back to her.

"Where's Livvy? Did she see—"

"Under the back porch. She didn't see anything." Gen put the weapon into the hidden pouch at her waist. Max repressed a shiver.

"Mrs. Carnie's in the kitchen." Gen's voice trembled. "Two broken arms. I've called the emergency services. Let's get out of here before they arrive."

Momma?

It's all right, sweetie, stay where you are, Momma's coming.

Max touched Gen's face and said on a very tightly-controlled thought, *You did what you had to do.*

It didn't save Hockley, though.

It saved your daughter.

She swallowed hard and gave one short, sharp nod.

"You get Livvy. I'll get the bags," he said.

"Yeah." Gen took a deep breath and began to move.

They took the monorail to the spaceport, trying to look like a normal family, but conscious of the fact that there had been at least six people on their tail in New Kyiv. Two down, four to go. Would it ever end?

At the spaceport, the same immigration guy saw them out as saw them in.

"Leaving early?" he asked.

"Got a family emergency." Max said, keeping his voice light. "Glad we got to see the museum at Landing, though, and Diamond Falls."

"Spectacular, aren't they?" the officer asked.

"Majestic," Max agreed, as they passed through the gate.

It took every last gram of self-control not to break into a run as they headed for the *Dixie*.

* * *

Gen held it together while she launched the *Dixie* into Plenty's upper atmosphere and dipped in and out of the Folds twice to shake off any following ships. Livvy babbled on about the dragon, but Max was too concerned about Gen's state of mind to take much notice. Along with everyone else in the Trust's psi-tech program, she'd been trained in combat, but that didn't mean she could kill without it taking a huge psychological toll, even though the dead men were killers themselves, and she'd done it in her daughter's defense. The Trust had counsellors for the aftermath of that sort of thing, but the Trust was a long way in Gen's past, and Max wasn't sure of his own counselling skills.

Eventually Gen set the *Dixie's* autopilot on a course to Omidel II and sighed. "I'm going to get some sleep, she's all yours."

"All I do is keep an eye on the systems."

"It's a good eye." Gen rolled out of the pilot's couch. "Come on, Livvy, time for bed."

Want to see the dragon, Livvy said. *Need to see the dragon. Bad men are coming.*

"We've left them behind, sweetie. The bad men aren't following."

Bad men, Livvy said.

The *Dixie's* warning system pinged, and then pinged again, but louder this time.

Max's hands flew to the scanner screen.

"Shit!" Gen said, peering over his shoulder at three white dots heading towards them. "How are they tracking us?"

The leading ship launched a missile, probably intended as a warning shot across their bows, but the *Dixie* beeped again. It was too damn close.

"Perhaps they've decided that if they can't have Livvy, no one can," Max said

Gen slid into the pilot's seat and released the autopilot while fumbling for the silver circlet. "Get ready to jump."

As she groped for it, not taking her eyes off the screen, the circlet snagged on the arm of her couch, fell to the floor, and slid beneath the jump drive housing.

"I'll get it." Max rolled out of his couch and made a dive for the circlet, while Gen kept both hands on the controls.

"This is not a good way to die," she said, almost conversationally.

Max knew that voice; her I'm-not-panicking voice. Without the circlet Gen could fly the *Dixie* by the seat of her pants, but she couldn't make the jump to foldspace. The *Dixie* had neither defensive not offensive capabilities, so they'd be sitting ducks.

Max flattened himself to the floor and reached under the housing, feeling about for the circlet. As his fingers touched the cool metal, he felt that strange slip-slidey-almost-sick feeling of jumping to foldspace...but how?

He retrieved the circlet and sat up.

Gen was sitting back, both hands off the controls, her eyes wide. Livvy stood clutching the arm of Gen's couch with a beatific smile in her face. *Going to see the void dragon,* she said. *Now.*

"What just happened?" Max rose to his knees and handed the circlet to Gen. "Are we safe?"

Gen turned her head slowly, as if she'd forgotten how to move. "For a certain definition of safe."

"How did you do it without the circlet?"

Gen blinked. "I didn't. She did."

They both stared at Livvy.

"Going to see the void dragon," the six-year-old said again, this time out loud.

"Does she mean that literally?" Max asked.

"I'm afraid she does."

Livvy's connection to the void dragon delighted the little girl and scared her parents half to death. The void dragon seemed benign, but was it really? At any moment it could turn against them.

Here it is! Livvy clapped her hands together in delight and a huge dragon head poked, snout first, through the upper skin of the *Dixie*. In foldspace, nothing was real—well that was the theory anyway—so when the dragon breached the *Dixie's* hull they had to concentrate hard to believe that there would be no explosive decompression and that they still had breathable air.

Max and Gen flipped their couches upright and around, turning them into chairs, and faced the dragon. Gen's hand reached out and Max clasped it, his own hand clammy. It's not real. Not real, he told himself, hoping it would go away. But it was all too real.

It pushed into the cabin and shrunk itself down until it was the size of a huge dog—a huge scaly dog—and settled on the floor, ruffling its leathery wings. Livvy flung herself at it and grabbed it around its lithe neck.

"Livvy, don't—" Gen started to rise out of her chair, but Max tugged her back down.

"It won't hurt her," Max said, hoping he was right. He left the other half of that statement unsaid, but inferred that it might hurt them if they got between it and Livvy.

Livvy's head was next to the void dragon's and they seemed to be talking. At length she sat up. "I told it about the bad men," she said. "It wants to know why they keep chasing us."

Without a qualm, she connected all three of them to the void-dragon. Its presence in Max's mind was like having a balloon inserted into his brain and then inflated so that there was a great cavern containing himself, Gen, Livvy, and a presence so powerful he could barely comprehend it.

Into this cavernous space the void dragon said, *???*

Tell it about the bad men, Livvy said.

How the hell was he supposed to do that? How could a creature that lived in this strange void imagine life outside it?

Pictures, Livvy said. *Think-talk in pictures.*

Like this? Gen asked.

Max felt rather than heard her put their first experience of being chased by a bounty hunter out there. Max added his own memories of the second and third, and more, until both he and Gen added their visit to Plenty, all the more disappointing because they'd both hoped they might have found a planet where they could settle down.

The void dragon huffed. Max thought it might be laughing. It said something—if said could be the appropriate word—that Livvy seemed to understand.

Suddenly there was a popping sensation and Max dropped out of the whole. Or maybe he'd been pushed out. It was something like falling out of a fourth-floor window but without the painful experience of hitting the ground. Gen squeezed his hand. She'd dropped out as well.

"What was that about?" Max asked.

Gen shook her head. "I feel as if all my thoughts and memories have been washed and put on a line to dry. I think that beast knows everything I know, and everything I've ever known."

Max tried to swallow but his mouth was too dry. "Yeah. That."

Livvy looked up. "It says why not go to time-before."

"Huh? I'm not sure I follow you, sweetie," Gen said.

Livvy put her head close to the dragon again, then looked up. "Like you go through the Folds to different places that are far apart, it says you can go to places at different times."

"Back in time?" Max asked.

Livvy put her head down to the dragon again. "Or forward," she said.

"How can we do that?" Gen asked.

Livvy turned to the dragon and back again. "It says just go, but it means you think yourself there. Like you think yourself to the right place when you leave the Folds."

"I… I can't." Gen said. "I'm a pilot, a navigator. I have an understanding of where everything is in relation to everything else, but not when."

Max squeezed her hand again. "Tell me how you find the right line when you travel through foldspace."

She shook her head as if to clear it. "I just find the right line to where I need to be."

"So you think yourself out of the Folds."

"Kind of, yes."

"So, if you know *when* you want to be, could you do that as well?"

"I don't know. Maybe. If it's possible."

"Livvy, is that what the dragon means?"

The little girl shut her eyes tight and then nodded.

"It's worth a try," Max said.

"It's not you who's trying." Gen let go of his hand. "Besides, I'd need coordinates in both space and time. And we'd need to know if a place was safe in the time period we chose. My history's not that good."

A rush of hope bubbled up inside Max. "We go to Plenty, two hundred years ago, just before the first generation ship arrives."

Gen blinked. "Could we do that? Livvy, ask your dragon if that's how we do it?"

Livvy went quiet and then nodded. *We all need to link. The dragon will show us.* She pulled them back into the whole. Their minds meshed and the dragon seemed to scoop them all up in its wings. It might have been seconds, or it might have been hours, but there was a stretching feeling and then, as if elastic had snapped them back into place, they were out of foldspace and within sight of a planet.

And the dragon had gone.

Max reached for the screen.

"Is it—" Gen asked.

"It's Plenty, or rather it's Planet 91046. The settlers didn't name it until their first anniversary."

"Life signs?"

"None. No human ones, anyway. There are indigenous herbivores. It's a green planet, not far off earth-like, with surface water and a single moon."

"And no one following us."

"No one. I think we need to keep that time-travel thing to ourselves, don't you?"

"Oh yes."

Gen took the *Dixie* down through the planet's atmosphere searching for the right place to land. As they flew low over the green canopy, Diamond Falls gleamed in the sunlight. They dropped down to one side of what would soon become the landing site for a fleet of generation ships. The *Dixie* settled gently to the ground.

*Are we home?** Livvy asked.

"I think we are," Gen said. "Shall we set a beacon, or surprise them when they get here?"

"Beacon I think," Max said. "They think they're the last remnants of humanity. They don't know that Earth survived the meteor and that their generation ships have been overtaken by jump-gates. They've got a lot to learn, but we've seen their future. We know they make it."

"As long as us being here doesn't change that future."

"We won't let it. We saw their museum, read their story. We'll just hunker down and let the settlers lead the way. No more running. We can have a life at last."

*They're here,** Livvy said. *I can feel them. Lots of them. Lots and lots of people.*

Gen set the emergency homing beacon and opened the comm. "Calling generation ship *Excelsior*. Generation ship *Excelsior*. This is *Dixie* 5286 calling generation ship *Excelsior*. Welcome home."

Wanting Better

Juliet Kemp

Vivian looked up and out towards the horizon of Luyten, the faceplate of her environment suit automatically adjusting for the glare of its red sun. Beyond the play-area, where two-year-old Aidan was running around with the other kids, the wine-dark fields of adapted plants stretched off to the horizon, busily doing their best to change the atmosphere. It was going slower than the first settlers had hoped, but maybe, once Aidan and his peers were grown, that wouldn't matter anymore.

"I'm so glad we did it." Vivian looked away from Aidan to smile over at her sibling Josh.

"Aidan's adaptions?" The sunlight reflecting off Josh's faceplate hid their face, but Vivian knew Josh was watching Aidan too, enviously: Aidan, unencumbered by env-suit, unbothered by what were toxins to Vivian and Josh, perfectly fitted to the extra gravity that the two of them still struggled against. Bodies evolved on Earth didn't re-evolve all that fast for Luyten, the settlers had found in the decades since their great-grandparents landed from the New Beginnings.

Not unless you helped them along.

"I worried," Vivian confessed. "At the start."

"Of course you did. But just look at him."

Another child, slightly bigger than Aidan, tripped over a fold in an env-suit obviously handed down from an older sibling and got clumsily back to their feet. There were still a few hold-outs, a few parents who wouldn't risk the adaptions—and of course there were the Returners—but fewer and fewer each year.

"I think we might finally have cracked the retro-fitting," Josh said. They shifted, their impatience visible even in the clumsy suit. "I'm signed up for the second-line test cohort."

Josh's lab was working on retro-fitting the genetic adaptions—inserted at the cell mitosis stage in embryos—to adults. Josh had complained bitterly when the head of the lab had refused permission for them to be in the first-line test cohort, arguing that they were needed to analyze the data, not generate it. Vivian wasn't in as much of a hurry. To be out here on Luyten with no suit—yes, it was enticing, but it was scary, too. Was it responsible, to risk it, when she had to look after Aidan? Or was it responsible *not* to?

She wondered sometimes what her great-grandparents had been thinking, settling on a planet that wouldn't be able to support them for hundreds of years. Were bubbles really that much better than a spaceship? Then again, there was still no news from those who'd taken the ship onwards in search of a better planet, so maybe Viv's unknown great-grandparents had made the best call after all, to make do with what they had.

We'll make it eventually, Vivian imagined her great-grandparents saying to one another, and looked around the playground, at the adapted kids climbing all over the play equipment, so much more deft than their env-suit-clad peers. They'd make it sooner than those great-grandparents had thought, even. Aidan toddled over for a hug—awkward, in the suit, but Vivian did her best—and she was overwhelmed with a rush of love. Perfect for this planet, right here.

The genetic science wasn't home-grown; when they'd finally heard from old-Earth, after decades of silence, that had been one of the things shared in the data-burst. On Luyten, they'd been focused on adapting the planet to them; they'd never thought of trying the reverse. Josh thought old-Earth must be too far past that, the planet too much changed, so their only option was pouring resources into genetic adaptation. It was hard to say for certain; there hadn't been much real information in the data-burst about the situation on Earth, and it was clear they were editing a lot out, but they had willingly shared their science.

The Returners wanted to go back. They opposed genetic alterations to fit them to Luyten, argued that their ancestors should never have left the planet they evolved for in the first place, that Earth was still there, so it couldn't have been as bad as they thought. If the Returners ever made it back—not that there was any chance of Luyten voting resources for a whole new *starship* any time in the near future—Vivian was pretty sure they'd have a nasty surprise. If old-Earth was all over gene-modding, there had to be a reason.

Either way. Vivian and Amy—Aidan's other parent—were committed to Luyten. And they'd wanted their kid to have all the advantages they themselves didn't have.

"So, with a bit of luck, they'll have a relative who can go out onto the surface with them, once they're old enough," Josh said, eyes back on Aidan, still thinking about gene-modding.

"Let's hope so." Maybe Josh. Maybe Amy. Maybe even her. Vivian thought again of her ancestors. What had it meant to them, leaving Earth? Going out into the unknown with their children? The first child born on the ship had been an Aidan, she'd found out when she was pregnant, though his parents' names had been lost. What had Aidan's parents hoped for, for their baby?

"I wonder what choices they'll make—have to make—for their descendants."

"Let's hope we get to find out." Josh tipped his head upwards, checking his heads-up display. "Come on. Let's round up the kid. Nearly dinner-time."

They walked back towards the bubble, feet crunching over the rocks, Aidan bouncing in front of them, and Vivian smiled.

Whatever the choices, those decisions had led them here, and how could she want better?

* * *

"I can't believe we made it." Vian couldn't bear to take her eyes off the huge screen in the rec room, showing the world—Luyten, their very-soon-now home—below the orbiting ship. The missing pixels in the screen weren't enough to mar the view, grays and reds and ochres swirling together. The ship-hum was quieter than she'd ever known it, star-engines powered down and only life-support still running. The absence was strange, like a missing tooth.

"Only just." Her sister Marina was sitting, feet tucked under her, on one of the dilapidated, misshapen "couches." Vian had seen pictures of couches in the fab directory. They didn't look like that. They hadn't had enough power to run the fabs for anything but food, though, since long before Vian was born. Maybe, down on Luyten…

It was going to be better. It was going to be worth it.

"Only just is good enough," Vian said, firmly, and sat next to Marina.

The rec room was empty other than the two of them; everyone was pulling fourteen- or sixteen-hour shifts, trying to get ready to go down to the planet. No one had time to just sit around. Vian's stomach growled and she ignored it. They'd all been hoping for an increase in rations once they weren't powering the star drive, but apparently they still needed to save resources to get the ground-bubbles established, especially now the survey had confirmed that conditions down on Luyten were at the tougher end of the prediction range. Around the room, almost all the bioplastic panels were gone, the ribs of the ship showing through. Most had been used up over the last seventy years, since the Power Rebellion; those remaining had become bubbles since they arrived in orbit.

"Good enough? Maybe. *If* we can make that planet work," Marina said.

Vian turned sideways, squinting at her, surprised by her sister's tone of voice. "What do you mean, *if?* We're here. We've got plans. It's going to be hard, yes, but it's going to work." At the very least, power, this close to the system's red-dwarf star, would no longer be a problem. Parts of the ship Vian had never seen operational had already woken, lights illuminating corridors that had been dark her entire life. There was room lighting after curfew, not that anyone had time to sit awake appreciating it. It would be even easier, power-wise, on-planet. "Look, I wanted to talk to you about the bubble room allocation—"

"I don't think we should stop here," Marina said flatly.

Vian looked at her incredulously. "What? You can't mean you want to keep going? After we've arrived? Why? And *how?* We only just made it here. I don't think Seth's slept properly for years, worrying about getting the calculations right." If they'd missed by even a whisker, there'd have been no power, no resources, for another try. Off into the black, a ghost ship.

Marina wore her stubborn face. Vian knew it well. "It could be done. We'd have to stop here for a bit, of course, refuel the ship, do some repairs. There are asteroids we could strip for resources. As long as we stay up here, we don't need to find the energy to get back out of the gravity well."

"But…I don't understand. *Why?*" Vian's eyes went back to the world on the screen. "Luyten's right there! We've finally made it, where we've been headed all these years!"

"It's not what we expected, though, is it? Not what our ancestors thought we were coming to."

"Well, it's not quite what they hoped, maybe," Vian acknowledged, with a little reluctance. "But we can change things. The terraforming plans…"

"And why do we have the right to do that?" Marina sat forward, pushing her sleeves up the way she did when she was excited about something. "Think about what we did to old Earth. Even before they fell out of contact, they'd screwed themselves so badly that our ancestors *ran*, right? And now we're going to wreck another planet?"

"It's not like there's anything here now," Vian protested.

"But there's a galaxy full of planets. We can fix the ship back up, then hold out for a better fit. Somewhere we can live without spending a few hundred years rebuilding it to suit our preferences. Leave this place to be what it is, not make it what we wish it was."

"Why get back on a ship for however long it takes to find somewhere else?" Vian clenched her teeth and pretended she wasn't listening again for the ship's missing hum, that there wasn't something that appealed about the idea of being back on the move.

It would be *better* on Luyten.

"Is it any worse than being stuck down there in those bubbles?" Marina demanded. "I've seen the plans. There's barely any more space than here. And once we're down, we're stuck."

"We're not *stuck*. We know how to get off a planet."

"But there won't be spare resources to do that for a long, long time and you know it. I don't want my kids to be planet-bound. Stuck in one little system, never out in space again." Marina gestured widely.

"Stuck on one planet like humans have been ever since we evolved as a species? You're being ridiculous. They'll have a whole planet!" Vian looked back at the screen, seeking reassurance; told herself she couldn't wait to be down there, on the surface, working for the future.

"They won't. *You* won't. You'll have a handful of bubbles and hundreds of years before anyone can stand on the surface without a suit. Life on ship is safer, if anything, once we're fitted up again. Let's keep going! Find somewhere better!"

"But it'll be a *challenge*, Marina," Vian said, and wondered who she was convincing. "A challenge we've been preparing for ever since we left Earth! A chance to start again on a whole new planet. Just because you like it on board ship, you'll condemn your kids to it?"

"Like you're condemning your kids to a planet that's going to be a struggle every single day—every single, very long, day. It's not us that gets the future you keep going on about. Not even our kids. Our great-great-grandkids. Maybe. If we're lucky. And meanwhile..." Marina leant forwards, put her hand on her sister's arm. "Vian. We can do better. I know we can. Please. Won't you come with me? You and Seth? Vote to keep going. Vote to find something *better*."

Vian shook her head. "No. No way. Our ancestors chose to get on a ship, to be on here for nearly two hundred years, so we could come *here*, to a brand-new planet. I'm here now. I want that."

Vian didn't look over when Marina left the room, her steps lagging. She kept her eyes on the screen and told herself she couldn't choose otherwise.

*   *   *

The hum of the ship around Viv—constant companion since birth—wasn't comforting them as much as it usually did. They trailed their hand along the cool bioplastic corridor walls, trying to ground themself as they followed their sister Alice at full Alice-in-a-strop speed back to her room. But it was hard to be reassured by something you'd just discovered wasn't the reliable safe haven you'd always believed.

Alice, unsurprisingly, was ranting the moment the door of her room closed behind the two of them.

"I can't *believe* our great-grandparents just blithely left Earth and got on a spaceship they *knew* would run out of power halfway to its destination!"

Viv sat down on Alice's bed and hugged their knees to their chest. They automatically leant back against the wall in search of the should-be-soothing-but-still-wasn't ship-hum. "I'm not sure they knew," they said to their knees. "Not all of them, anyway. Or most, even. From what the Council just told us." Admittedly, Viv had zoned in and out a bit in the meeting, struggling to process what they were hearing. They wouldn't reach Luyten after all. There was a decision to make.

"So our great-grandparents were lured on here with false claims, instead, by the handful who did know?" Alice had the bit between her teeth now. Alice *ran* with things, once she got wound up. It could be—alarming. As kids, Alice was always dragging Viv into some disaster or other, which invariably worked out better for Alice than for Viv.

"Does it matter?" Viv asked. "The point is, what do we do now?"

"Well, obviously, we have to fix it, don't we? Just like they *expected* us to." Alice's tone was dark. "Because otherwise we'll all just die out here."

There was silence for a moment.

"Or we could go back," Viv said. "To Earth. They said. In the meeting. If we turn round right now, we could make it."

"Then what? What's Earth even like now? Would they want us back?" Alice had stopped pacing, but still hadn't sat down. She was fiddling now with the fabricator in the corner of Viv's room. "The reports are terrible. And that's ten years out of date, even. Must be even worse by now. They won't welcome us."

Viv picked at a fingernail. "I still hear from Aidan, sometimes."

Alice frowned at her. "Aidan?"

"You remember. Our—third cousin, or whatever he is. Great-gran's sister's…grandson?"

"And?"

"He doesn't seem to think things are all that bad."

"Well, he's hardly going to send you chatty emails telling you how the whole place is on fire and there's nothing to eat, is he?"

"Maybe it would be good to go back," Viv said, and finally managed to meet Alice's eyes.

"What? Just give up?"

"Better that than try to fix it, and fail, and die out here." They unfolded their knees and went to the fabricator. They were seriously feeling the need for biscuits.

Alice's mouth firmed in stubbornness. "No. We've got fifty years." She elbowed her way in between Viv and the fabricator, just as Viv was about to authorize the biscuits. "And you can't just go using that willy-nilly anymore."

"What?"

"Fifty years if we carry on just ignoring it all and pretending like nothing's happening. *More* if we start cutting back, right now. Tel was messaging me, during the meeting. He was looking at the figures while they were answering questions." Alice's friend Tel was good with numbers, and engines. "He reckons half the problem is that we're allowing ourselves too much *stuff*. Running the fabs too much. Using too much power. That kind of thing."

"The Council…" Viv said doubtfully. "They said, keep going, or go back. Two choices, two days to decide." Which seemed awfully fast, to Viv. "They didn't say start rationing."

"The Council don't want to have to do without anything."

"I don't want to have to do without anything!"

"No, because you'd rather run back to Earth, tail between your legs," Alice scoffed. "What would our great-gran say to that? She chose to come out here."

"I thought you were just saying that she was misled," Viv said, but Alice was off and away again.

"There's more than one option, is what I'm saying. We can make it longer than fifty years, we can give ourselves more time, if we're a bit more careful. We've all got too used to things being cushy, is what."

"But however much we cut down, you're not saying—Tel isn't saying— we can make it all the way there, are you?" Alice didn't answer, which Viv took as agreement. "Why suffer now if we're screwed either way round?"

"You sound like the Council. It's easy for them to say that. They'll definitely be dead either way. But it would mean more *time*. More time to throw everything we can at it."

"If we throw everything we have at it," Viv said pedantically, "we'll just run out of food or oxygen or fab-carbs instead and die that way."

"You know what I mean, Viv."

"Clarity matters, Alice." It was an old argument.

"We can propose that to the Council, instead of either 'turn back' or 'ignore it and hope for the best.'" Alice made another scoffing noise. "We can do better than that. Rationing. Rationing as hard as you like. And everyone who has any spark of maths or physics at all can work on the problem."

"It's hard physics, the stardrive," Viv objected. "It's not like you can just read a bit about it and go, aha! Got it!"

Alice shrugged. "Fifty years. More, if we can persuade people to change how we live. People can learn stuff, in fifty years. If they want to. There has to be an answer. There *has* to be. We just need to find it. We need *time*."

Looking at Alice, bright and certain, Viv felt a tiny spark of hope for the first time since that moment in the meeting when they'd realized what the Council was trying to say. "Optimist," they said, but they could hear the affection in their own voice.

"So, you'll vote to stay?" Alice demanded. "You'll help? Not just bail out?"

Viv sighed, but they knew they'd give in. They always did side with Alice, in the end. "Do you think we'll make it?"

"Yes," Alice said with certainty. "We will. If we choose."

* * *

This, then, was what her last day on Earth felt like. Well; it wasn't, technically, Vivian's actual last day on Earth. That would be a month from now, after the quarantine, when they all boarded the shuttle up to the ship. But her last day *out* on Earth. Her last day really, truly, here. Dodging through the crowded street towards the restaurant, she felt the sudden urge to pull off her respirator and smell the outside, the real air of Earth, smog and all, just to remember it. But it would be stupid to risk wrecking her lungs right now, and it was a red-warning day. Respirators required outside, building air filtration at max. The woman just passing her, coughing, didn't have a respirator; from the looks of her clothes, she couldn't afford one.

She'd be away from all of this soon.

At the restaurant, shown to her table by a smiling, white-aproned waiter, she took the mask off with relief and tucked it away in her bag. Eva wasn't there yet; of course not. Vivian swallowed nervously. She and Eva had been close as kids, growing up in the big government orphanage after their parents drowned in the first of the great floods. But they'd grown apart as adults and Vivian very much doubted Eva was going to approve of her decision. She ran her hands over the smooth, thick white tablecloth, trying to soothe herself. She'd always hated arguing with Eva.

"Vivian!" There was Eva, hurrying across the floor in advance of the accompanying waiter, the baby—Aidan—asleep in the sling on her front, only his head and the plastic edge of his respirator visible. She slid into her seat and gave Vivian a slightly quizzical smile. "Well, this is fancy." She looked around the restaurant, eyebrows high, visibly appreciating the comfortable chairs, the thick carpets, the general air of hushed expense, then glancing down at the open menu presented with a flourish by the waiter.

"You can order whatever you like," Vivian said, not answering the implied question. "I can cover it." Money and protein ration both. As of tomorrow, Vivian wouldn't need her ration credits. She might as well blow them all on saying goodbye to her sister.

She could see Eva itching to ask more, but she waited until they'd ordered and the waiter had disappeared. Eva sat back in the plush chair, one hand on Aidan's back. "Seriously, though, Vivian, I couldn't believe it when you invited me here. Have you come into money or something?"

"Not...exactly." Moment of truth time. "Uh. I don't know if you've seen on the news. The ship. The starship."

"*New Beginnings.*" Eva's nose wrinkled. "I saw it on the news the other night. Little bit on the nose, don't you think?" She blinked. "Wait."

"I've been selected as a passenger," Vivian forged onwards. "Me and..." She might as well get it all over at once. Her hand strayed down to her stomach without her meaning to. "I'm expecting."

"You can't be serious," Eva said flatly. Aidan twitched in his sleep, face screwing up under his respirator.

"We leave next month." Vivian held herself still and upright with an effort of will in the face of Eva's disapproval. She'd always avoided arguing with Eva as a kid. Easiest just to go along with her. There was a reason why she'd chosen not to discuss this with Eva until it was too late. "We go into quarantine tomorrow. I've decided. I'm committed."

"*Ought* to be committed, more like. You're *pregnant*, Vivian. You can't have a *baby* in...in space!"

Her voice had risen enough that despite the luxurious—excessive— spaces between tables here, the people nearest to them glanced their way.

"It's a generation ship, Eva. People have to have babies or there won't be any more generations."

"But it doesn't have to be *you.*" Vivian had expected Eva to disapprove. She hadn't expected the plaintive tone of her voice as she fiddled with the strap of her respirator, lying on the table in front of her. "I thought... when you suggested meeting up, I thought you wanted to meet Aidan. A celebration meal." Her sister's voice shook. "I didn't...Vivian. You can't be telling me this is the last time I'll see you."

"Quarantine starts tomorrow," Vivian said, staring at the table, unable to meet Eva's eyes.

"And you couldn't tell me before?"

"I wasn't in for definite until a few days ago." Once she was past twelve weeks pregnant, specifically. Better, perhaps, not to tell Eva that that was how she'd bought her way onto the ship, in the end. Her, plus an internal passenger, or—from the point of view of those packing the ship—a little more genetic diversity for very little extra weight.

The waiter appeared with the steaks. She could see Eva debate for a moment whether she should, after all, turn down Vivian's offer to buy lunch, then think better of it. Good. It wasn't like she could get the credits back again.

"Aidan's beautiful," Vivian offered, once Eva had taken her first mouthful, trying to change the subject, then regretted it. It was obviously just desperate politeness, given that she could see barely anything of Aidan right now. "I mean. In the photos you sent. He looked beautiful."

"I'm sure he'll wake up in a bit and you can meet him properly. But..." Eva's voice was shaking again and she put her fork down. "His aunt. And his cousin. He'll never know either of you. Vivian, we don't *have* any other family."

"We'll be able to send messages. For a long while yet." Forever, really, except that the further they got from Earth, the longer it would take, and eventually Aidan's kids and her unborn baby's kids would be sending round-robins into the ether to be received years later, long out of date. Vivian took a bite of her meat. It didn't taste quite as good as she remembered. Maybe that was the guilt.

"Viv." Eva bit her lip, then sat forward, jostling Aidan, who squirmed and muttered but still didn't wake up. "Are you—I mean. I'm sure it's not too late to back out. I'll help you. I promise."

"I don't want to back out." It was almost wholly true. She was scared, of course she was. But excited, too. A new opportunity. Something different. A new planet—Luyten. She liked the way the name felt in her mouth.

"But think what you're condemning your baby to! Life limited to a single ship. No options. No possibility of coming back. You're making this decision, fine, but your child. Their children after them. What about what they'll want? Why do you get to make that decision for them?"

"Why do you get to make it for yours, by not going?"

"I'm not making a *decision*," Eva scoffed. "I'm just...doing what's *normal*. Aidan will grow up with the whole of Earth available to him."

"Yeah, right. And how far have you moved from where we grew up? How many new people have you met?" Vivian was fed up with this. She'd been polite, before, skated around the truth of it, but... "How many people from the home have exciting futures all over the planet? Never mind that, even. How much planet is there going to be by the time Aidan grows up? When was the last time you had meat like this? And the rice shortages last year? Wheat, the year before? The oceans are rising. The temperatures.

Earth is just as much a limited space—and just as risky—as the ship I'm getting on."

"Earth's a whole planet. Don't be absurd, Vivian."

"But we don't *have* a whole planet. Not us. We have tiny flats, high-rises that swallow us whole, cities to the horizon. I know for a fact this is the furthest you've been from home since that time we visited Aunt Rhiannon when we were kids. You remember my friend Zeri? He was stranded in his flat for *three months* last summer when the lift broke down. What sort of freedom is that?"

"More than you'll get in a single ship the same size as a high rise. Smaller than some. I saw the photos on the news." Eva's tone was defensive.

"With guaranteed work, valuable work, not scrounging around for zero-hours contracts selling crap to people who don't need it. We'll all be essential to the journey and to our future."

"A future on a ship."

"A future that isn't tied to a single planet. Both our children are limited by our decisions, Eva. Mine's just not a decision that anyone has made—been able to make—before. Earth's just a bigger spaceship, when it comes down to it. Your descendants might get a different high rise as the waters rise. If they're lucky. Mine? Mine will get a planet."

In the sling, Aidan finally stirred into wakefulness and Eva shut her mouth on whatever she'd been about to say. "Look, just—hold Aidan, while you can. Think about him never getting to know his Aunt Vivian. Your little one never getting to know their Aunt Eva. Never feeling the sun on their face." She was unwrapping him from the sling, standing up to settle him on Vivian's lap.

Just for a moment, holding the baby, Vivian wavered. Her sister. Her nephew. Her life on Earth…

With floods and deaths and respirators and ration points. She wanted better, for her and her baby.

She gestured to the waiter to settle the bill. Looked into Aidan's face properly for the first and the last time; then handed him back, gently, to her sister. "I love you, Eva. Look after yourself. You and Aidan."

"I love you too, Vivian." Eva was crying, silent tears dripping from the corners of her eyes.

Vivian was crying, too, as she walked out of the restaurant; but she held her head high. This was what she chose. It would be better.

About the Authors

JACEY BEDFORD is a British writer with short stories published on both sides of the Atlantic. Her (seven so far) novels are published by DAW. She lives a thousand feet up on the edge of the Yorkshire Pennines in an old stone house that takes the first hit when the wind howls off the moor. She has been a librarian, a rag-doll maker and a folk singer. Her claim to fame is that she once sang live on BBC Radio 4 accompanied by the Doctor (Who?) playing spoons. Catch up with her at www.jaceybedford.co.uk, @ jaceybedford or www.facebook.com/jacey.bedford.writer

WILLA BLYTHE made her storytelling debut at age 4 with indie smash, *Sam the Stinky Skunk*, and she hasn't stopped writing since. Her first audience - her grandparents - shared a love of art and craft with her that remains central to Willa's writing practice over thirty years later. Today, she lives in New York with her family, and primarily writes queer romance and speculative fiction. Connect with her on Twitter at https://twitter.com/willaablythe or keep updated on her projects by visiting https://willablythe.com/

When she was little, **JAMIE M. BOYD** dreamed of becoming a marine biologist, exploring the deep ocean and deciphering the secret language of dolphins. She later decided to become a science writer and worked as a journalist for a decade, covering everything but science. She won awards for feature, education and religion reporting and was part of a newspaper staff twice named finalist for the Pulitzer Prize. She now lives and writes in Fort Lauderdale, Florida, where she enjoys jogging along the ocean with her husband and deciphering the secret language of their three children. Visit her at jamiemboyd.com.

CHAZ BRENCHLEY has been making a living as a writer since the age of eighteen. He is the author of thrillers, fantasies, ghost stories, science fiction and more. He has also published as Daniel Fox and Ben Macallan. 2021 saw the publication of his "Best Of" collection, *Everything in All the Wrong Order*. He is currently writing girls' boarding-school stories set on Mars. His work has won multiple awards. In his fifties he married and moved from Newcastle to California, with two squabbling cats and a famous teddy bear. His website is www.chazbrenchley.co.uk, and he can be found on Facebook, Twitter, Substack and Patreon.

ERIC CHOI is an award-winning writer, editor, and aerospace engineer based in Toronto, Canada. He was the first recipient of the Isaac Asimov Award (now the Dell Magazines Award) and he has twice won the Prix Aurora Award for his short story "Crimson Sky" and for the Chinese-themed anthology *The Dragon and the Stars* (DAW) co-edited with Derwin Mak. With Ben Bova, he co-edited the hard SF anthology *Carbide Tipped Pens* (Tor). His first short story collection *Just Like Being There* (Springer) was released this year. Please visit his website www.aerospacewriter.ca or follow him on Twitter @AerospaceWriter.

SARAH LYN EATON is a queer pagan writer and burn survivor. She is a life-long Star Wars geek who spends her free time rock hunting, or venturing into the woods with her camera. Her stories have been published in the anthologies *Upon a Twice Time, Unburied: A Collection of Queer Dark Fiction, Of Fae and Fate: Lesser Known Fairy Tales Retold, On Fire,* and *Dystopia Utopia*. In 2021, Sarah Lyn was awarded The Speculative Literature Foundation's Working Class Writer Grant.
http://sarahlyn-eaton.blogspot.com/
https://www.facebook.com/sarahlyneaton
https://www.instagram.com/sarahlyneaton/

ANITA ENSAL has always been intrigued by the possibilities inherent in myths and legends and she likes to find both the fantastical element in the mundane and the ordinary component within the incredible. She writes in all areas of speculative fiction with stories in many fine anthologies out now and upcoming, including *Love and Rockets* and *Boondocks Fantasy* from

DAW Books, *Guilds & Glaives*, *Portals*, and *Derelict* from Zombies Need Brains, *Gunfight on Europa Station* from Baen Books, *A Dying Planet* from Flame Tree Press, *The Book of Exodi* from Eposic, *The Reinvented Heart* from CAEZIK SF & Fantasy, and the novella, *A Cup of Joe*. You can reach Anita (aka **GINI KOCH**) at her website, Fantastical Fiction (http://www.ginikoch.com/aebookstore.htm).

A.M. GIDDINGS is a writer, scientist, and independent filmmaker from North Carolina. She has a PhD in Microbiology and has written scientific articles in virology, cell line design, and gene therapy. She is the author of the futuristic dark fantasy series Dance of Ages, which begins with Shadow into Light and continues with A Shower of Embers. In addition to her writing, she has also worked on short and feature-length horror films with Sick Chick Flicks, and is the co-director of the Sick Chick Flicks Film Festival. Website: https://cryptoporticuscreature.wordpress.com

AUSTON HABERSHAW is a scifi and fantasy author who lives in Boston, Massachusetts. His other short stories have appeared in *Analog*, *F&SF*, *Escape Pod*, *Galaxy's Edge*, and other places. He is also the author of four fantasy novels--*The Saga of the Redeemed*--published by Harper Voyager. You can find him online at aahabershaw.com, on Amazon or Goodreads, or on Twitter at @AustonHab.

JULIET KEMP is a queer, non-binary writer who lives in London. Their fantasy series The Marek Series is available from Elsewhen Press; the first book, "The Deep And Shining Dark" was a Locus Recommended Read. Their short fiction has appeared in venues including Uncanny, Analog, and Cossmass Infinities, and their story "Somewhere Else, Nowhere Else" in the Zombies Need Brains anthology Portals was shortlisted for the WSFA Small Press Award 2020. In their free time, they knit, go bouldering, and get over-enthusiastic about fountain pens. They can be found at http://julietkemp.com, or as @julietk on Twitter.

STEPHEN LEIGH has published 31 novels, many short stories, and a bit of poetry under his own name and the pen name S.L. Farrell. His most recent book is AMID THE CROWD OF STARS (DAW Books, Penguin Random House, Feb. 2020), about which Publisher's Weekly wrote: "This finely crafted sci-fi saga is full of both surprises and charm." Steve's work has been nominated for and won awards within the sf/fantasy genre. Social Media: website: www.stephenleigh.com; FB: www.facebook.com/sleighwriter; Twitter: sleighwriter; Instagram: s.leigh.writer

JACK NICHOLLS grew up in a house of ten thousand science-fiction paperbacks and never escaped their gravitational pull. Jack was born in London, raised in Australia, had their first kiss in Germany; and these days can be found writing speculative fiction and wry essays in Melbourne. As part of their attempt to chronicle the narrowing space in our culture between plausible science-fiction and implausible reality, Jack produces an irregular newsletter which you can find, along with links to their work, at www.jacknicholls.net.

ARI OFFICER is a commodities trader in Chicago, where he lives with his wife and two Highland Lynx cats. After writing columns for *TIME Magazine* over a decade ago, he pivoted to speculative fiction. His paper on economics in science fiction appears in *Essays in Economic History*, and he was a finalist for the 2021 Baen Fantasy Adventure Award. He is currently seeking representation for his satirical novel *A Trip to the Earth*. You can find @ariofficer cooking and playing guitar on Instagram.

MIKE JACK STOUMBOS is a speculative fiction author disguised as a believably normal schoolteacher living with his wife and their parrot. He is a 1st-place winner of the Writers of the Future contest and the author of the space opera series *THIS FINE CREW*. His work has appeared in a number of anthologies, including *GALACTIC STEW* from Zombies Need Brains and *DRAGON WRITERS* alongside Brandon Sanderson. Mike Jack also writes online content for TheBookBreak.com and others. You can find him on his website MikeJackStoumbos.com or @MJStoumbos on Twitter, as well as karaoke stages with mic in-hand.

IAN TREGILLIS is the author of seven novels, including the Milkweed Triptych (BITTER SEEDS, THE COLDEST WAR, and NECESSARY EVIL), Something More Than Night, and the Alchemy Wars Trilogy (THE MECHANICAL, THE RISING, and THE LIBERATION). His short fiction has appeared in numerous venues including The Magazine of Fantasy and Science Fiction, Asimov's, and Tor.com, and has been reprinted in multiple year's-best anthologies. A physicist who lives in New Mexico with his playwright wife and a spoiled cat, he swears his day job does not involve reverse-engineering UFOs. @ITregillis www.iantregillis. com

About the Editors

S.C. BUTLER lives in New Hampshire with his wife and son. He is the author of the Stoneways trilogy: *Reiffen's Choice, Queen Ferris,* and *The Magician's Daughter,* originally published by Tor Books; the novel *The Risen;* and a contributor of short stories to several anthologies and magazines. All of his novels are available as ebooks at his very primitive website, mutablebooks.com, and several of his stories are posted there for free. He also posts regularly on Facebook as S.C Butler.

****

JOSHUA PALMATIER is a fantasy author with a PhD in mathematics. He currently teaches at SUNY Oneonta in upstate New York, while writing in his "spare" time, editing anthologies, and running the anthology-producing small press Zombies Need Brains LLC. His most recent fantasy novel, *Reaping the Aurora,* concludes the fantasy series begun in *Shattering the Ley* and *Threading the Needle,* although you can also find his "Throne of Amenkor" series and the "Well of Sorrows" series still on the shelves. He is currently hard at work writing his next series and designing the Kickstarter for the next Zombies Need Brains anthology project. You can find out more at www.joshuapalmatier.com or at the small press' site www. zombiesneedbrains.com. Or follow him on Twitter as @bentateauthor or @ZNBLLC.

Acknowledgments

This anthology would not have been possible without the tremendous support of those who pledged during the Kickstarter. Everyone who contributed not only helped create this anthology, they also helped support the small press Zombies Need Brains LLC, which I hope will be bringing SF&F themed anthologies to the reading public for years to come. I want to thank each and every one of them for helping to bring this small dream into reality. Thank you, my zombie horde.

The Zombie Horde: Donald Smith, Susan Campbell, Erik T Johnson, Annalee Johnson, Nitya Tripuraneni, Steven Mentzel, Cynthia Waldron, Andy Miller, Robert Maughan, Rya Wren, Phillip Spencer, If not bad bitch then Lisa Stuckey, CE Murphy, GC Rovario-Cole, Camille Lofters, Louise Lowenspets, Michael M. Jones, RJ Hopkinson, Margot Harris, justloux2, Annette Agostini, Stacey Helton, Cherie Livingston, Melynda Marchi, Katrina Knight, charles bassett, Sacchi Green, Sandy, Rosanne Barona, Colette D, Jamie FitzGerald, Kat Haines, Robert D. Stewart, Stephen Rubin, Randall Brent Martin II, Brad Roberts, Kelly Mayo, Chris McCartney, MC, April Thompson, Fantastic Books, Richard C. White, Arlene Medder, Erik Twede, LIsa Kruse, Kevin Niemczyk, Erin Penn, Evergreen Lee, Rosa María Quiñones, Alfonso Orellana, Susan O'Fearna, Jeremy Audet, Kevin Heard, Dr. Charles E. Norton III, Megan Parker, Kate Lindstrom, Tracy 'Rayhne' Fretwell, Doc Holland, Ane-Marte

Mortensen, Bella & Dylan Fuentes Steckline, Lace, Dan DeVita, Heather Childrey, Louisa Berry, Kortnee Bryant, Gini Huebner, Helen Ellison, Jennifer Flora Black, D.R. Haggitt, Sarah Hester, Annika Samuelsson, Tanya Koenig, Lizz Gable, Mary Murphy, Steven Peiper, Margaret Bumby, maileguy, Connor Bliss, Kirsty Mackay, Andrija Popovic, Pat Knuth, Kris Dikeman, Patricia Bray, Patrick Osbaldeston, Jeff Metzner, Holly Elliott, Aaron Zsoldos & Emely Pul, Kristina, Tria Bravo-Pallesen, Ryan Power, The Two Gay Geeks - Ben and Keith, Lexi Ander, Alice Norman, Tris Lawrence, R.J.H., Kyle Rogers, Bruce Alcorn, Kai Nikulainen, Chris Vincent, Emy Peters, Anita Morris, A.J. Abrao, Mindie Simmons, Kimberly M. Lowe, Colleen Feeney, Anthony R. Cardno, Lee Dalzell, Miranda Floyd, Cracknot, Tracy Polasek, Carl Wiseman, Mae Malcolm, Meyari McFarland, John Senn, Megan Maulsby, Scarlett Letter, Leane Verhulst, Margaret M. St. John, Matt & Liz A., Bookwyrmkim, Kristina Cecka, Dendra, Kristin Evenson Hirst, Tim Jordan, In Memory of Ruth, Kari Blackmoore, David Boop, Krystal Windsor, Lisa Castillo, Carlos Alberto Rodríguez Gutiérrez, Jeff G., Paul & Laura Trinies, Scott Raun, Joseph Cox, Dave Hermann, Susan Simko, Jenn Whitworth, Shawn P. McMurray, Tasha Turner, Rolf Laun, Axisor and Firestar, Mandy Wetherhold, Auri and Finn, Sami Sendele, Chris McLaren, Karen Lytle Sumpter, Stephanie Wood Franklin, Jessa Garrido, Wolf & Elissa Gray, John Markley, Ernesto Pavan, Steven Halter, Katy Manck – BooksYALove, Mustela, Vickie L Kline, J A Mortimore, Shayne Easson, Jason Y, Michael Halverson, Mark Slauter, Elaine Tindill-Rohr, Yosef Kuperman, rissatoo, Theresa Derwin, Jackie Clary, BobbyRoo, Brendan Burke, Jordan Dennis, Catherine Davis, David Flor, Crystal Foss, Jim Gotaas, Sharan Volin, Marj Sailer, Yosen Lin, dennis chambers, Craig "Stevo" Stephenson, GMarkC, Sarah, Stephen Shirres, Ian Harvey, James Lucas, ChillieBrick, .Heather Jones., Aramanth Dawe, Shyann, David Lahner, Mervi Hamalainen, Vekteris Saulius, Fred Langridge, Andrey, Bruce Arthurs, Ruth Ann Orlansky, Colette Reap, Amanda Jenkins, Sondra Fielder, Muli Ben-Yehuda, Prince Eric J Vickers, Laura Davidson, Tina M Noe Good, Keith E. Hartman, Krystal Bohannan, David Rowe, Steve Pattee, Nathan Turner, Kathleen Birk, Kaidlen Shan, T. England, Daniel Joseph Riddle, S. Petroulas, Margaret Killeen, Gary Phillips, Bob Scopatz, Danni Brigante, cassie and adam, Lizzie B., Sarah Raines, Jessica Stultz, Christine Ethier, John H. Bookwalter Jr., Kelly Snyder, Carver Rapp, C J Evans, Machell Parga, Brita Hill, Linda Pierce, Gail M, Keith West, Future Potentate of the Solar System, Jamieson Cobleigh, Jason Palmatier, Amanda Butler, Geoffrey Allen Baum, Michelle M, Risa Wolf, Shawnee M, Abra Staffin-Wiebe, Monica Taylor, Ken Huie, Robert Claney, Louise Kendall, Shirley D, Michael Barbour, Yankton Robins, Larry, Steve Arensberg, David A. H., Ju Transcendancing, Suzanna,

Brenda Rezk, Anne Burner, Jeanne Talbourdet, Christopher Wheeling, Vicki Greer, Adena, Robyn DeRocchis, Curtis Frye, Samuel Lubell, Jarrod Coad, Bess Turner, Mark Lukens, Rory King, Brenda Moon, Chad Bowden, Nick W, Deanna Harrison, Cyn Armistead, Misty Massey, Catherine Gross-Colten, Mike M., Giuseppe Lo Turco, Penny Ramirez, J.P. Goodwin, John Winkelman, Gretchen Persbacker, Andrew Hatchell, Sheryl R. Hayes, Thomas Legg, Cathy Green, Rachel Rieve, Brian W Adams, Lisa Kueltzo, Rachel A. Brune, BethAnn Lobdell, Mark Newman, Lilly Ibelo, John J Schreck, Joe Wojo, Olivia Montoya, Corey T., John MacCarrick, Kier Duros, Jeremy Brett, Niall Gordon, Ashley R. Morton, Kirstin Sims, Abe Scheppler, Melissa Mead, Jerrie the filkferengi, Deanna Stanley, Robert Gilson, Kate Stuppy, Allison Yambor, R. Hunter, Tim Lewis, Cody L. Allen, Matt P, Breann Carpenter, Catherine Moore, Simone Pietro Spinozzi, Steven Rhew, Megan Beauchemin, Ed Ellis, Lark Cunningham, Alicia Henness, Fred Herman, Jennifer Robinson, Svend Andersen, Diane Kassmann, Paul Stansel, Sarina M., Merissa Smith, Susan Oke, K. Hodghead, Steven Danielson, Michelle, Elizabeth, Tripleyew, Alan Smale, Clarissa C. S. Ryan, Michael Cieslak, Amy Rawe, Stephanie Lucas, Chris Kaiser, Leah Webber, Greg Dawson, Ryan Hunter H. and Cameron Alexander H., Tory Shade, Neil, Karen M, Taia Hartman, Sidney Whitaker, Kate Malloy, Cori Smith, Kerry aka Trouble, Jess Pugh, Jessica Enfante, Howard J. Bampton, Joanne B Burrows, 'Nathan Burgoine, Ilene Tsuruoka, Jenny Barber, Jen1701D, Jessica K. Meade, David A. Quist, Nicholle F. Beard, Juanita J. Nesbitt, Jaq Greenspon, Rebecca M, Shannon Roe, Lorraine J. Anderson, Jacen Leonard, Michael Feir, Konstanze Tants, Elektra Hammond, Jennifer Berk, Wolf SilverOak, Oliver S, Vincent Darlage, PhD, Brad L. Kicklighter, Katherine S, Michele Hall, Arin Komins, Amanda Saville, Amanda Niehaus-Hard, Michael Kohne, N Flannigan, Lisa Short, ron taylor, MJ Silversmith, Melissa Crook, Todd Stephens, Sarah Cornell, Tom Harning, kommiesmom, E.M. Middel, Caroline Couture, Cyn Wise, L.C., Tania, T. W. Townsend, Jason Mayfield, Leigh Allen, Crysella, Debbie Matsuura, Gerald, Sheryl Ehrlich, Amelia Dudley, J.M Bengtsson, Chelsea Rzepkowski, Emily Ruth, Megan Struttmann, Brynn, Odd, Wayne Howard, Carol J. Guess, Niki Robison, Simon Dick, Fred and Mimi Bailey, Tim Greenshields, Mark Odom, Ryan Mahan, Bodge Inglee-Richards, V Hartman DiSanto, Beth Coll, Mark Hirschman, Elise Power, Stephanie Cranford, Margo Hardyman, Eleftherios Keramidas, Amanda Grace Shu, Susanne Driessen, Tracy Schneider, Caiti Willis, Daniel Blanche, James Conason, Sonya R Lawson, Chickadee, Michael Axe, I. Smith, summervillain, Frankie Mundens, Dagmar Baumann, Nate Botma, Pookster, Nancy Blue Spider Tice, Kimberly Bea, Cait Greer, Piet Wenings, LetoTheTooth, Ellen Harvey, Caty Robey, Joshuah Kusnerz,

Chris Matthews, Hoose Family, Patti Short, Kevin McIntire, Senhina, Darrell Z. Grizzle, A.Chatain, Elaine McMillan, Rain Pope, Brendan Lonehawk, CJ Curtis, Jean Marie ward, Grace Kenney, Erica "Vulpinfox" Schmitt, Dawn Edwards, Tommy Acuff, Julie Pitzel, Ashley Clouser Leonard, Susan Baur, Jeff Eppenbach, Patricia Miller, Tina Connell, Jay V Schindler, Jason Lau, Juli, Kyle Ellis, M.J. Zbacnik, Gwen Whiting, Jenn Bernat, Brooks Moses, Joseph J Connell, E.J. Murray, Heidi Williams, Richard O'Shea, Céline Malgen, Craig Hackl, Matt Trepal, Richard Leis, Mike Ball, ND Gray, Yvonne, Stacy Augustine, Brenda, jjmcgaffey, Tara Paine, Stephen Ballentine, Johne Cook, Aaron W Olmsted, Anchit Vijayakumar, Jen L, Benjamin Hausman, AJ Knight, Sloane Leong, Jim Anderson, Val Cassidy, Elyse M Grasso, Vulpecula, Steve Salem, Richard Clayton, Nancy Gilliam, Merry Lewis, Ashley, Sarah Nutter, Nancy, Ian Chung, Amanda Cook, Amanda Stuart, Lavinia Ceccarelli, Peter D Engebos, Josh Pritchard, Mary Alice Wuerz, Robin Hill, Evan Ladouceur, Amy Goldman, Anna McTaggart, Eirik Gumeny, Carina Bissett, Kristi Chadwick, Jo Beere, The Collinsc Clan, Marty Poling Tool, Sue Weinberg, Aysha Rehm, Lori L. Gildersleeve, Whitney Porter, Michael Fedrowitz, Chris Tanzos, pjk, Beth Morris Tanner, Bebe, Christine Hanolsy, Anya, Pers, Eva Holmquist, Cory Williams, Heidi Cykana, Eric "djotaku" Mesa, Cliff Winnig, Sue Phillips, John T. Sapienza, Jr., Jennifer Beltrame, David Wohlreich, Paula, Taka Angevine, Heather Klassen, Michelle Palmer, Jennifer Dunne, Rebecca S., Ashley Martinson, Mega Boss N'kai, Rebecca Crane, Mark Carter, Duncan & Andrea Rittschof, Agnes Kormendi, Janet Piele, Kat Feete, Lorri-Lynne Brown, A.J. Bohne, Karen Carothers, Katie Hallahan, Antha Ann Adkins, Alan Mark Tong, Ronald H. Miller

Made in the USA
Middletown, DE
15 August 2022

70484308R00149